RESCUING ZOE

The Guardians: Hostage Rescue Specialists

ELLIE MASTERS

JEM Publishing

Copyright

Editor: Erin Toland

Proofreader: Rox LaBlanc

Interior Design/Formatting: Ellie Masters

Published in the United States of America

JEM Publishing, LLC

ISBN-13: 978-1-952625-09-1

Dedication

This book is dedicated to my one and only—my amazing and wonderful husband.

Thank you, my dearest love, my heart and soul, for putting up with me, for believing in me, and for loving me.

If it weren't for you, this book never would have come to life.

Books by Ellie Masters

The LIGHTER SIDE

Ellie Masters is the lighter side of the Jet & Ellie Masters writing duo! You will find Contemporary Romance, Military Romance, Romantic Suspense, Billionaire Romance, and Rock Star Romance in Ellie's Works.

Sign up to Ellie's Newsletter and get a free gift. https://elliemasters.com/RescuingMelissa

YOU CAN FIND ELLIE'S BOOKS HERE: ELLIEMASTERS.COM/BOOKS

Military Romance

Guardian Hostage Rescue

Rescuing Melissa

(Get a FREE copy when you join Ellie's Newsletter)

Rescuing Zoe

Rescuing Moira

The One I Want Series

(Small Town, Military Heroes)

By Jet & Ellie Masters

EACH BOOK IN THIS SERIES CAN BE READ AS A STANDALONE AND IS ABOUT A DIFFERENT COUPLE WITH AN HEA.

Aiden

Brent

Caleb

Dax

Rockstar Romance

The Angel Fire Rock Romance Series

EACH BOOK IN THIS SERIES CAN BE READ AS A STANDALONE AND IS ABOUT A DIFFERENT COUPLE WITH AN HEA. IT IS RECOMMENDED THEY ARE READ IN ORDER.

Ashes to New (prequel)

Heart's Insanity (book 1)

Heart's Desire (book 2)

Heart's Collide (book 3)

Hearts Divided (book 4)

Hearts Entwined (book5)

Forest's FALL (book 6)

Hearts The Last Beat (book7)

Contemporary Romance

Firestorm

(KRISTY BROMBERG'S EVERYDAY HEROES WORLD)

Billionaire Romance

Billionaire Boys Club

Hawke: Billionaire in Paradise

H.R.H. Richard: Nondisclosure

Brody

Contemporary Romance

Cocky Captain

(Vɪ Kᴇᴇʟᴀɴᴅ & Pᴇɴᴇʟᴏᴘᴇ Wᴀʀᴅ's Cᴏᴄᴋʏ Hᴇʀᴏ Wᴏʀʟᴅ)

Sweet Contemporary Romance

Finding Peace

Romantic Suspense

ᴇᴀᴄʜ ʙᴏᴏᴋ ɪs ᴀ sᴛᴀɴᴅᴀʟᴏɴᴇ ɴᴏᴠᴇʟ.

The Starling

Redemption

~AND~

Science Fiction

Ellie Masters writing as L.A. Warren

Vendel Rising: a Science Fiction Serialized Novel

Contents

ONE

Zoe

Once upon a time, there was a girl.
Who didn't believe nightmares were real.

But the girl woke up
Trapped in a nightmare.

That girl is me.

IT'S BEEN TWO DAYS SINCE THEY ADDED THE LAST GIRL. EVE ARRIVED
much as we all did, struggling, snarling, and full of fight. Like me,
she survived her first beating. She's quiet now. Recovering from her
injuries. Now, she whimpers and cries, just like the rest of us.

Like Eve, I fought when they took me, and like her, I suffered. I
cried.

I'm smarter now.

We all are.

While nobody knows where we are, or where we're going, we are headed somewhere.

We're fed, watered, and they remove the foul-smelling bucket of waste once a day. I think. Measuring time is difficult, but we know one thing. They want us alive when we get to wherever it is they're taking us.

To monsters who wait...for us.

To the beginning of a living hell.

After Eve's arrival, the metal floor of our prison vibrated. A low, persistent drone shook the shipping container. Sometime later, hours maybe—it's hard to tell how much time passes in here—a soft up and down, side to side, rolling motion confirms our fears. We're being shipped to the next destination in our descent into hell.

The days pass with the relentless march of time. We can't stop it, slow it, or reverse it. Minutes last hours, hours last days, and the world no longer makes sense. With only suffocating darkness to pass the time, I lose more and more of my sanity with each passing day.

My fingers plait a tiny braid. I make one for each day, or at least I think the time between one opening of the shipping container and the next is one day. It's when they feed us and water us like the animals we've become.

There are ten braids now.

A loud *bang* sounds, and I nearly jump out of my skin.

Men's voices rumble outside.

I scurry back, not wanting *them* to touch me, to hurt me. Three girls got too close. They were dragged out. None returned. Thirteen of us remain, shadows of our former selves.

When the doors open, all we see is darkness. What little light there is from the moon filters down through stacked shipping containers, to cast shadows upon shadows. I prefer the formless blackness to the

2

shifting shadows. They don't open the door during the daytime. It's always night.

Always dark.

A hand reaches in and removes the waste bucket. Footsteps recede while someone else places a large bowl of water just inside. We wait for the man with the bucket to return and toss it back inside. Covered in filth and grime, the bucket no longer bothers me.

When water comes, no one touches it. We fear what might be in it more than we fear dying of thirst.

We wait.

We wait until the doors close. Until the metallic *thunk* of the locking lugs tells us we're once again locked inside our stifling prison.

Safe.

Only then do we move.

One girl.

One girl finds the bowl in the blinding darkness.

One girl takes a sip.

And we wait.

If she doesn't pass out from whatever drug they may have laced it with, we share the water. Small sips that do nothing to quench our thirst.

But it keeps us alive.

We survive together, thirteen girls bonded by a nightmare.

Each girl takes her turn to test the water.

Today, it's my turn.

I lift my head from my knees and reach for the bowl. Dipping my finger into its contents, I croak out a scratchy, "W-water." There is no food. Gnawing hunger claws at my belly, but it's thirst that drives me.

Sighs sound all around me in the dismal darkness. It's been too long without water. The only thing carrying me through, the only reason I hold onto hope, is that I believe we're more valuable alive than dead. I know what fate awaits us. We all *know*. But it's still better than death.

I take a long pull, swallowing water down a scratchy throat, which still hurts from all the screaming during my abduction. It feels as if I *broke* something inside because my voice is nothing but a breathy whisper now.

As the first girl, I'll drink more than the rest. That way, the drug, if it's there, will be more likely to take effect on me, thus saving the others. I scoot back against the wall and slide the bowl to Bree. She came the day after I arrived. Our fingers interlock as I tip my head back to wait.

If nothing happens, Bree will take a sip and pass it to Dawn. Dawn will pass it to Anna, and Anna will pass it to Freya. On down the line, we'll share until the last drop is gone.

Then we'll wait for the door to open again.

We don't have the strength to fight. Not that I'll waste my energy on these men. I'm saving mine for the real monsters to come.

Not sure if my eyes are open or closed, fetid darkness folds around me. My thoughts wander, like they do every hour of every day, to the last moment I was happy.

I don't focus on the men who snatched me off the street.

Instead, my thoughts go to the brilliant-blue skies and white sand beaches of Cancun. Crystal-clear, tropical waters sparkle beneath a bright sun. The festive spring break party atmosphere lets a smart girl lower her guard.

I lost my freedom in the span of a heartbeat, on my very first night in paradise.

I thought I could walk from the beach to our hotel by myself. I gave no thought to the vulnerability of a pretty, young girl walking alone. I didn't *think* I was alone. People were all around me, partying, with far too much liquor flowing in their veins.

I felt *safe*.

But I was separated from the crowd. They yanked me into a filthy van. Took me to a filthy house on a filthy street. There I was stripped, examined, and left to huddle on a filthy floor with a filthy flea-infested blanket. Then they shoved me inside a filthy shipping container twenty feet long with ten other girls.

Has it really been ten days? The braids in my hair don't lie.

What are my friends doing now? Did they call the police? Do Mexican police care about American girls who disappear? Or do they think I got drunk and passed out in some foreign bed with some nameless boy?

I'll never know. Austin must be going ballistic, worrying about me. My overly protective brother will not stop until I'm found. And my father? He'll do whatever it takes to bring me home. I cling to hope, even knowing how desperate that makes me.

"How do you feel?" Bree keeps her breathy voice soft. We aren't allowed to speak to one another. That freedom, among many things, was violently taken from us.

"Good so fa…" I struggle to complete my thought as darkness overtakes me. My eyes droop. My muscles relax.

"It's drugged." Bree's voice sounds far away and defeated.

Hands reach for me and drag me over a rough metal floor as I dream of a happy, vibrant girl who doesn't believe in nightmares.

TWO

Axel

"ALPHA-ONE TO ALPHA-THREE." MAX'S VOICE CRACKLES THROUGH the radio. "Axel, you gotta see this." His tone makes my skin crawl.

"Copy that." I hold my position, weapon leveled on four men lying face down on a dirty floor. Zip Ties bind their wrists at the small of their backs and join their ankles together.

Legs bent. Backs painfully arched. Shoulders straining. They're furious with my handiwork. Took less than thirty seconds to truss them up, but I've been hog-tying cattle all my life. For the record, humans are much easier to subdue than calves.

"You got this?" My attention shifts to my buddy, and teammate, Griff.

"Go ahead. I got this." He spits into the eye of one of our prisoners. Bastard curses in Spanish. "Sorry, bud, a little spit in your eye is the least of your worries." Griff gives the prisoner a love tap to the kidneys with the tip of his steel-toed boot.

Our angry friend's thick muscles bunch. Fury darkens his face. He, and his buddies, aren't going anywhere, and I think they're finally figuring that out.

7

I don't move until Griff gives the okay.

We're a six-man team. Knox and Liam stand outside, guarding our retreat. Griff's with me. Max and Wolfe moved through, looking for the target.

"Alpha-three to Alpha-one, headed to you." My radio squawks as I relay my intention to move my position and join up with our team leader, Max.

"Copy that." Max sounds frustrated; his irritation vibrates in his clipped reply.

We've been on assignment a week while our target suffered at the hands of these men.

Our target? I grind my molars until my teeth throb and the muscles of my jaw ache.

Our target is my best friend's little sister, an annoying little scrap of a girl who made my life miserable with her hopeless crush. Only, she's not a girl anymore. A sophomore in college, she's more woman than girl. Which is a big problem. Last year, I had to do something about her hopeless crush and finally set her straight.

I was an asshole and broke her heart, but there was no other way. She needed to move on.

And now she's been taken.

"Status." That voice belongs to CJ, our mission commander.

CJ's been at this game twice as long as any of us. Famous for bringing the Fairy-tale serial killer down, along with his copycat wannabe, Prince Charming, he freed half a dozen women while on vacation. In our community, CJ is a legend. Now he leads all the Guardian teams.

I work my way deeper into the building, knowing CJ follows our progress via the helmet and body cams streaming our every move. Our success and failure broadcasts in real time to command.

It's dark. We cut the electricity to the entire block. The flashlight mounted on my helmet provides all the light I need as it pierces through the dimly lit hall.

"Do you have the package?" CJ's voice crackles with impatience, locking my molars tight together. We can't afford to be late and this feels all kinds of *too fucking late*.

Cancun is famous for kidnappings of rich Americans and pretty American girls. Spring break is their fucking hunting season. They pluck innocent college coeds off the street like it's nothing. Unfortunately, Zoe is what they look for, a willowy blonde knockout with bright bottle-green eyes. It's her most striking feature.

I pass down a hall. Weapon up. Scanning left to right. Finger on the trigger guard.

Max and Griff cleared these rooms on their way in, but I never assume. Those who do don't last long in our line of work.

Methodically, I scan the long hall, clear each room as I go, and make my way to the last room at the end. I meet Wolfe there with a lift of my chin. He responds in kind.

The room's empty.

"Fucking hell." My nose wrinkles at the smell of blood, sweat, and human excrement. The stench is enough to make me gag. Breathing through my mouth only makes it worse. Foulness floods my senses.

Zoe was in this room.

Past tense.

Mission failure.

Ratty blankets form amorphous lumps on the dirty floor.

Lumps.

Pleural.

Not unexpected. We know the men who took Zoe are part of a human trafficking ring. That's why we're here. We're the hostage rescue specialists paid handsomely to bring stolen girls home, preferably safe and sound. Although we're only hired to recover Zoe, we'll save them all. Forest won't have it any other way.

There's easily a dozen or more blankets strewn about. A dozen lives taken. The bitter tang of failure coats my tongue. I'm not used to that sour taste.

Guardians never fail.

Tell that to Zoe. Tell her how this isn't a colossal fucked up failure.

If she's still alive.

My helmet light pierces the gloom, revealing dried blood and fetid urine stains. They kept the girls in here like animals. The blood comes in various forms: dried pools on the floor, stains on the blankets, and splatter marks on the wall. Urine stains are everywhere.

These men are sloppy. Damaging their merchandise cuts into their bottom line. By the looks of this place, all the girls suffered. Some more than others.

My Zoe suffered. I suppress the angry growl rumbling in the back of my throat.

In my six years as a team guy, I've seen a lot of fucked-up shit. When I left the Navy, I thought the worst of human depravity was behind me. How wrong I was. This is some fucked-up shit.

I used to hunt dangerous men, relieving them of the burden of their pathetic lives, or returning them to whichever prevailing authority waited to extract their pound of flesh.

Now, I retrieve the fallen, the broken; those who've been taken. I'm a Guardian, a hostage rescue specialist dealing with a catastrophic mission failure. The girls are gone. From the looks of it, we're hours late, maybe even a whole day late.

This job isn't any easier than my team days. In many ways, it's far worse. Revulsion coils in my gut, thinking about what these girls endured.

Girls. Young women. Innocent victims.

That's not an emotion I ever felt for the targets I disposed of during my time in the Navy. I dispatched lives without a bit of compassion or lick of guilt cluttering my conscience.

"What did you want me to see?" I turn my attention to our team leader. Max could've told me about this shit instead of dragging me from my position.

"You tell me." Max gestures to another room. The door sits off its hinges and is propped haphazardly against the wall. The low beam of his flashlight barely lights up the doorway. I push past and look inside.

"Christ!" My heart rate quickens before I can force it back to its slow, plodding pace. The veins in my temples bulge as fury fills me. "Fucking pigs."

Max follows me into the room. He orders me to tell him what I see.

"It's a procedure room." My nose wrinkles at the stench. There's more blood here than in the other rooms. Layers of dried blood pool on the floor beneath an examination table. It tells the tales of multiple victims enduring unspeakable acts.

"Well? What do you think?" Max watches me closely. Like the rest of the team, he's aware of my personal connection to this mission. They all know Zoe's mine.

"It's a gynecologic exam table."

"No shit, Sherlock." He spits on the ground. "Expound on that."

As team medic, my medical skillset comes in handy in the rare instances when one of us needs a little patching up in the field, but there's no reason for my medical skills here.

The back of the exam table is set at an incline. Two metal poles with heel cups extend from the end. Unlike a normal GYN exam table, this one comes with shackles. Shackles bolted at the high end for the chest. Shackles to secure wrists a little lower down. Another runs across the hips to hold an unwilling patient as they thrash. Finally, there are two more straps at the feet.

"What were they doing? Rape?" Max growls.

"Could be." I echo his rage. "The table definitely places a woman in a vulnerable position, but I doubt their customers would pay for damaged goods." I glance around the filthy room, looking for anything that might explain what they did in here. "Check the trash can."

Max heads over to a waste container. Instead of checking, he picks it up and brings it back to me. I'm smart enough not to reach inside. Who knows what might stick me and transfer disease.

Disease?

My eyes narrow and I pull out my knife. Using that, I dig through the contents.

"You seeing this?" My question isn't for Max, but for Doc Summers watching from command.

"Yes." Her crisp voice tightens. A tough cookie, nothing phases our indomitable lead physician.

"See what?" Max peers into the trash can.

"Those are STD kits. Tests for gonorrhea, chlamydia, and…" I sift through the contents. "IUDs? Doc, am I correct?"

Static over the coms crackles then clears. "Looks like they tested the girls for sexually transmitted diseases and inserted IUDs." Her voice softens. "At least that answers one question."

"What's that?" Max turns the can over and dumps the contents on the floor, spreading them out. He does this to send better pictures back to base.

I glance at the trash and count IUD wrappers. "Looks like thirteen."

"Sixteen chlamydia swabs. Thirteen IUDs." Doc Summers confirms. "I'd mark that at sixteen victims."

"Not thirteen?"

"If some of the girls already had IUDs, they wouldn't place a new one."

"How fucking considerate." My stomach twists. They want the pleasure of raping their victims without the unwanted side effects pregnancy brings.

"Search the place." A new voice rumbles through our comm channels. Forest Summers' deep baritone is unmistakable and elicits an ass-puckering gluteal clench.

What the fuck is CJ's boss' boss doing on Overwatch?

My team worked with Forest Summers on an operation in the Philippines that went to hell in the blink of an eye. We're a bit sensitive about that particular failure.

That had definitely been a FUBAR moment. We lost the head of our organization. I'm surprised we weren't all fired on the spot. A couple months later, we redeemed ourselves and rescued him in a brilliantly executed raid, but still, that's not something a person ever forgets.

Forest continues, "There must be something that says where they took the girls. See what the prisoners have to say."

"With pleasure." Not a fan of torture, per se, I love a good interrogation.

"We're on it, boss." Max gives a nod. All final orders come from him. I tap the button for the team only comm channel. "Alpha-four, we *need* to know where they took the girls."

With Forest Summers' interest in the mission, *need* means necessity.

"Copy that." Griff loves getting his hands dirty.

If we can get the intel we need, we might be able to salvage this operation.

THREE

Zoe

I WAKE TO VIOLENT JOSTLING FOLLOWED BY THE SENSATION OF THE floor rising beneath me. The upward climb stops with a sudden jerk. Then we free-fall. Our screams end in a heart-wrenching, bone-jarring lurch moments later when the shipping container jerks.

My mouth feels funny, dry like cotton. My tongue sticks to the roof of my mouth. My throat hurts. My lips sting and crack when I move them. When I open my eyes, they peel apart a gritty crust. This doesn't feel right.

My eyes are open. I think. There's nothing but darkness. I wave my hand in front of my face and blink. Yes, my eyes are open, but why can't I—memories return, tumbling one upon the other, each worse than the one before. An anguished moan escapes me.

No. No. No.

I remember being taken. A dirty room. I was strapped down. Touched. Pain. Sharp, brutal, cramping pain followed.

I remember the other girls like me, stolen from our pretty little lives. We huddled on a grimy floor, wrapping threadbare, flea-infested

15

blankets around our nakedness as they stole our dignity and shattered it into a million pieces.

Panicked breathing huffs in my ears. I don't know if it's me or someone else. I think all this bone-jarring jostling means we've completed another step toward our destination and the monsters who wait at the end.

The shipping container tilts. We slide uncontrollably, crying out as we tumble over each other. A leg jabs me in the side. A foot clocks my jaw. My teeth slam together. A hand slaps my face.

I do the same to the others. My arms and legs flail wildly as I tumble. My toes dig into something soft. My elbow hits something hard. My nose presses against someone's belly.

This is different from the slow, barely perceptible movement of the open sea. Which means—I hate to think it—but we've arrived.

My mind fills in with details of an industrial port. Massive cranes off-load cargo containers stacked high on the decks of container ships. They lift. We wobble, then pitch and drop. Then they lower us until we come to a rest. The entire container shudders as we slam down on something hard.

My imagination is scary accurate.

Men's voices carry through the metal walls of our prison. Shouting orders.

A hissing vibration follows. Something slithers across the roof and falls down the other side. I imagine we're being tied down, on a rail car or a truck.

And where will they take us?

Fear pounds through my veins, running away from an unknown, but highly imaginable threat. A hand reaches out in the darkness. Fingers grabbing, seeking. I take it and we clasp tight, holding hands, sharing strength.

"What do you think is going to happen?" It's Anna. She was here before I arrived. I only saw her face once, but I know every intimate tremor of her voice.

What's going to happen? Depraved men noticed us. Weighed our worth. They took us. Now, we belong to them.

We're to be sold into sexual slavery. We're all young, between seventeen and twenty-two. I'm right in the middle at nineteen. What the final condition of our enslavement will be is anyone's guess.

There are far too many possibilities.

I don't want to think about any of them.

That's what hurts the most. The unknown.

The complete uncertainty of our future hurts the most. Will we stay together? Serving in a brothel, handcuffed to a sweat-soaked, stain-filled cot? Or will we be separated and forced to face our future truly alone?

That terrifies me the most. It's what will break me. I'm sure of it.

I can't face this alone. I'm not strong enough. As much as I hate to admit it, I'd rather die than face any of this alone.

Anger rises within me. How dare they take my future without my permission? I hold on to the rage for as long as I can, because hopelessness is my greatest enemy.

The men who grabbed us never touched us *in that way*. Their sinister smiles and lusty leers did tell the truth about our future. Not that they didn't hurt us. Not that they won't hurt us again.

They beat us into submission until we became compliant and accepting of our circumstance. I have the bruises to prove it, but none *violated* me. Or any of the others.

There was that exam, and excruciating pain, when the man with the mask did something *down there*. I spotted and cramped for days, but nothing since the terrible cramping stopped.

17

We all have that nasty experience in common.

I swallow down my fear and answer Anna as best I can.

"I don't know." I don't have the strength to offer any relief from the terrible future awaiting us.

How can someone do this to another human being? What gives them the right to steal our futures? To trap us in the darkness where our worst fears take root?

"I want to go home." Anna's soft sob makes me angry.

We all want to go home, but then I realize what I'm doing. She doesn't deserve my anger. *Save it. Save it for the monster to come.*

"I do too." I miss my family. My father with his warm brown eyes. I miss my protective older brother, Austin, who always watches over me and keeps me safe.

Do they know men with cold hearts, and without conscience, snatched me off the street?

Are they looking for me? I bet Austin is. He'll move heaven and earth to find me. Daddy too, and he has the resources to hire people to *find* me.

But what about the other girls? Do they have anyone looking for them? Anyone with the financial resources to hire someone to rescue their stolen daughters?

I think not.

"Are you okay?" Anna sniffs with pain.

"Just bruised. Are you?" I check myself for injuries after that tumble.

"I'm alive." She doesn't say it as if it's a good thing.

"As long as we're alive, there's hope." I give her hand a squeeze and try to believe my words. The problem is—I don't. Death is preferable to what waits for us out there.

We call out to each other, going down the list of names we shared with one another. Fear vibrates in everyone's voice. I gather all that fear inside of me and smother it as best I can.

I don't accept this is how my life will end.

There must be something I can do—some way to stop this madness.

I refuse to give up, and I'll fight. I'll fight until I take my last breath.

My father will find me. Austin has friends, one in particular with the skillset needed to rescue me. Not that Axel gives one shit about me. He made that perfectly clear, but he'll do it for Austin.

I just need to hang on until a rescue happens. Giving up isn't an option.

A sigh escapes me, filled more with despair than the anger I need to sustain me.

Despair is the true enemy. Hopelessness and discouragement are its allies.

These are the internal monsters I fight.

Indignation rises within me. I want to shout *You can't do this to me! To us.*

But they can.

They already did.

They took me, and they'll sell me. I can scream and curse all I want, but in the end, the only one that hurts is me. There's no way out of this nightmare.

Be patient. Hope for a miracle.

I need a knight on a white horse, a savior who will rescue me and be utterly ruthless to them. If not, then my future holds nothing but misery and most likely death.

My future no longer belongs to me.

It's theirs.

Property.

I'm to be sold.

To be used.

And finally—to be discarded when they no longer have use of me.

This isn't the kind of life a person grows old in. I can rebel all I want, use up vital energy resisting, but in the end, only one fate awaits me. This is something I accept, but I'll drag it out as long as possible.

There are thirteen of us in this living hell. Those who survive will be the ones who wait. Who discover the monsters' secrets and use them to fight.

I tuck my knees beneath my chin and curl in on myself. Here, in the dark, I'll bide my time, shore up my defenses, and dig in to survive whatever comes next.

Some interminable time later, the motion of the shipping container stops. We scoot as far from the door as possible. Men's voices are heard again, all around us. A hissing/rasping sound makes my skin crawl. Then we're moving again, lifting in the air, swaying back and forth, careening toward our fate.

We land with enough force to smash my molars together. A clunking at the front has me gritting my teeth. Then a sliver of light breaks through the oppressive darkness. It widens into a blinding wedge spilling through the open door.

Two men barge through. Big men with barrel chests and pockmarked scars. A jagged scar puckers one of their faces, dragging down from his eye to the corner of his mouth. Three round, coin-sized scars pepper the other man's bare chest. Bullet wounds if I have to guess.

During our stay inside the cargo container, we made a mistake. We forgot about our state of dress, or complete lack thereof. In the light, with the men's eyes on us, we're reminded of our nakedness. We remember to shield our bodies from their hungry stares, but they're not interested in us like that. Which forces a hard swallow down my throat. We aren't people to these men. We're nothing more than product to be moved from point A to point B.

I'm not sure what scares me the most. That they aren't interested in our naked flesh. Or that I care.

They march straight toward us.

Scarface yanks Eve by the arm, hauling her to her feet. She kicks and screams as he drags her out. Bullet-chest pulls Anna up by her hair. Her hands subconsciously fly to his, trying to save herself. He yanks her to her feet and pushes her toward the light. Anna screeches as she's dragged away.

The rest of us stare at each other, huffing against fear.

The men return. Bree and Dawn are taken next with as much compassion as Eve and Anna. These men don't care if they hurt us. We're a job, nothing more.

The rest of us scurry back as if huddling in a corner can save us.

They return, and Freya and Cloe are taken next.

I refuse to be dragged out like an animal.

When the men return, I struggle to my feet. I barely have enough strength to wobble. I dare not look them in the eye. I won't survive their lack of compassion. Before they can grab me, I stumble toward them, bracing myself on the wall to keep from falling down.

It doesn't keep them from putting their hands on me, but the one who takes me, the one with the scar on his face, treats me with far more gentleness than he did the others.

I practically feel like a queen as I stagger into the light.

Two flatbed trucks wait outside with cages built into the beds. The first one holds Eve, Anna, Bree, Dawn, Freya, and Cloe. Tears stream down their cheeks as they huddle naked inside the cage.

The other is empty.

Scarface grips my arm, but it's more for show. There's nothing like the bruising hold he used on the others. He walks me to the truck, where he helps me up and inside. There's no struggle in me as I allow his assistance. Unlike those in the other cage, I slump with defeat and make no effort to cover my nakedness.

Why bother?

None of it belongs to me anymore.

The men bring the others out of the shipping container where they join me.

I scan my surroundings, looking for anything that will tell me where the hell we are. Other than the heat and stifling humidity, we're surrounded by lush vegetation.

The men are a mixed bag. In addition to the two who dragged us out, there's a mixture of races. We're somewhere tropical, but that's as far as I get. My hope is the drive will reveal something, but like everything else, hope is snatched from me.

The men cover our cages with thick canvas tarps, tying them down and closing us in.

The Diesel engines crank over and chug along as we bump over unpaved roads to our next destination.

Frankly, I'm too exhausted to be scared.

I want to know what lies at the end.

Who dares to claim my fate?

FOUR

Axel

GETTING INTELLIGENCE OUT OF RELUCTANT PRISONERS REQUIRES A certain amount of finesse. Nearly every Guardian comes to Guardian HRS after serving in the military. Most of us are team guys. There are a few specialty-trained special ops, like our medical team. Then there's Delta team. It's a mixed bag. The only team led by a woman, it boasts two females among its ranks. They work in a more official capacity, often teaming up with the FBI on domestic hostage situations.

Regardless of where we come from, we're proficient in enhanced interrogation techniques, a euphemism for *how-to-fuck-with-people-so-they-tell-you-shit*.

Perfected by the Central Intelligence and Defense Intelligence Agencies, we know how to get information out of people. Unlike the CIA, DIA, or US Military, there are no governing agencies watching over our shoulders. That means we get to be a little more creative.

And some of us are a little more skilled in systematic torture than others. Griff is Alpha Team's go-to torture guy, and by the low chuckle over the comm, he's excited to begin.

Max, Wolfe, and I return to where our prisoners patiently wait for interrogation.

Liam and Knox will remain outside, guarding us, while we roll up our sleeves and get a little upfront and personal with our new best friends.

With four prisoners, we have a few options. Griff's eager to begin. I'm not one of our torture experts. Frankly, I don't have the particular mindset required for fucking people over.

The moment I enter the room, I raise my weapon on the prisoners. I am, however, an excellent shot. In addition to team medic, I'm the best sniper on our team—the best of all the Guardians. It's not false bravado.

I'm that good.

Griff walks in a slow circle around the four men hog-tied on the floor, telling them in a very calm voice what's going to happen over the next little bit. The men's bodies are already fatigued. I tenderized them for Griff, placing them in an enhanced stress position.

The hog-tie contorts their bodies and draws their arms and legs behind their backs where they're secured together. It places tremendous strain on shoulders, knees, thighs, and hips. They've been in the position for the better part of an hour. No doubt, they're eager to be free.

"Who wants to go first?" Griff continues pacing in a slow circle around the men. When no one answers, he lightly taps each of them with the toe of his boot. "Eeny, meeny, miny, moe."

Their muscles clench, and their scowls deepen. They're determined to fight, but we're only beginning this game. One of them will crack.

"Catch a tiger by the toe." The taps of Griff's boot get progressively harder as he moves along, selecting his first victim. "If he hollers, let him go." The taps are now solid

24

kicks to their unprotected midsections. "Eeny meeny, miny, MOE!"

Max and Wolfe move to the man selected. Wolfe cuts the tie securing his feet to his hands. They don't remove the ties binding his hands and feet. With his hands behind his back, he's vulnerable. His balance compromised due to his feet being tied together.

Nothing is accidental.

Expecting the man to lash out, Max punches him in the stomach, a solar plexus hit, which leaves the man breathless and huffing in pain.

We all endured torture during our training. Survive, evade, resist, and escape; SERE is the quintessential survival training program of the CIA, military, and military defense contractors. SERE provides challenging training in evading capture, surviving in austere environments, and escape. The goal is to strip a person down to their breaking point.

There's one question that remains in all our heads after SERE.

What happens when it's real? When that last bit snaps? Simulation can't prepare a person for that moment when they're stripped of their humanity. When the only thing holding you together is your force of will when faced with death, or something worse than death —whatever that may be for each individual—what happens next?

I've been trained in all of that, as well as the most challenging bit, resisting interrogation, but even I know nothing can prepare for the real thing. Nothing simulates real fear. In training, there's always that bit of knowledge that it's all fake. There's an end to the torment, therefore, it's possible to endure.

Griff's going by the playbook. Why deviate when it's such a damn effective process?

The beating phase already began with the kick to their guts. Now he separates one from his fellows. All attention will go to him while his friends watch, knowing they'll be next. It's a wonderful beginning to the psychological phase that happens later.

Some things we can't do.

Subjecting them to temperature extremes and deafening noise are simply not practical. We really aren't interested in drawing the attention of the local police. Which means, Griff will focus on physical torture, beatings, and binding them in contorted positions. Sleep disruption and deprivation are also in the toolkit, but take time. Not preferred, but may be unavoidable.

The longer this takes, the further our quarry can travel. More time means we're less likely to turn this whole shit show around.

"Put him on his knees." Griff looks around the room for props to aid in his impromptu interrogation. He'll place this man in another stress position, then beat on him a bit.

I settle in to wait and take bets on which of the four will crack first. I only hope they have something worthwhile to share.

"We can take this slow and easy..." Griff runs his hands over his first victim's shoulders, touching him with forced intimacy, rubbing the sore muscles of his neck and shoulders. He moves his hands over the man's chest, his touch bordering on being sexual, soft like a lover.

It's uncomfortable to watch, but I know what Griff's doing. He's playing on the man's homophobia, letting his revulsion build.

"Or..." Griff removes his hands from the man's chest. "Hard. And. Fast." He lands three blows in quick succession, doubling our man over.

A big man, larger than me, Griff is a solid wall of muscle. He looks like he'd be slow with all that bulk, but I've wrestled with the fucker on the mat. Griff's reflexes are lightning quick.

Even after expecting it, I miss when he goes on the attack. But that's Griff. The man is death walking.

Griff doesn't let the man recover. He rears back, exaggerating his motions. He wants the man to see what's coming this time. He slams his fist into the prisoner's gut. It's so fast, so sudden and unexpected, the prisoner doesn't have time to tighten his abs and guard against the punishing blow. Or the one that follows.

Huffing with each breath, Griff pants as he demands answers.

Max and Wolfe stand to either side. They grip the man by his arms, holding him in place.

Stage one has begun.

Griff softens up the first man for a bit, using him as a living punching bag. Griff's grin is an eerie sight because he becomes something altogether different at times like these. The bastard is a scary motherfucker.

After roughing up the first man, Griff points to the next one, and we go through round two. I'm expecting a long night. The first, most crucial phase of torture, establishes one vital thing.

We're in control.

We control their pain.

We control whether they live or die.

There's not a damn thing they can do about it.

Once we establish those facts, despair sets in, and that's when they become malleable to the psychological aspects of torture.

Chances are, they'll all die, but we'll give them a little hope they might survive. That way, they'll spill their secrets. One of the things we have going in our favor is our employer has no issue with ridding human traffickers of their lives.

"I will break you." Griff moves on to the third man.

He stares long and hard into the man's eyes, most likely assessing where this prisoner falls in the rank and file of the organization. He doesn't necessarily need the weakest to break. He only needs to find the one with the most to lose.

Without warning, Griff's in motion again. A fury of fists rains down on the man, then Griff adds in a roundhouse kick striking the man's jaw. That brings a howl of agony. From the way the man's jaw sits a little askew, I'm guessing Griff dislocated it. That might make it harder for the man to spill his secrets.

In between Griff's punches and kicks, Max interrogates. His questions will help us discover where they took the girls. A glance at my watch reveals two hours have passed. Funny, it feels much longer.

Wolfe unceremoniously drops the man beside his fellows and grabs at the yet untouched final member of their little quartet. This man's eyes show white all around. The others crumple on the floor and curl into fetal positions as they nurse their wounds.

So far, none have cracked.

Before Wolfe can drag the fourth man fully to his feet, I sense victory. He points to the door and stammers something unintelligible in Spanish. Griff leans close and forces the man to slow down.

Griff's eyes widen, then he looks at me. "He says he took photos. Wasn't supposed to and tossed the phone outside in the bushes."

"On it." We checked the men for cell phones after we tied them up. We checked for weapons as well and retrieved quite an arsenal. But we didn't find any cell phones on them. That's not surprising given an operation such as this. Cell phones can be more of a liability than anything else, as will soon be the case.

"Alpha-five, Alpha-three headed out." Last thing I need is Liam or Knox blowing my head off thinking I'm a prisoner escaping.

"Copy that," Liam responds, letting me know he received my message.

I lower my weapon and head outside. Griff can finish his grizzly job while I search for a phone.

"What's up?" Liam meets me at the door.

"Somewhere in the bushes is a phone." I glance around the building taking note of the low scrub. Where would our pretty boy have tossed his phone? It had to be somewhere convenient, close to where we subdued them. Unless it wasn't us he was hiding it from?

The first place I look, right outside where we're holding the men, is a bust. I make a quick circuit around the building. There are very few bushes and a complete lack of cigarette butts. Men like these tend to chain smoke, and human behavior being what it is, they probably had smoke breaks built into their day.

Where did these assholes hang out to shoot the shit and smoke?

Across the way, I spy a rusty shed. All around, thick bushes crowd the dilapidated building.

Bingo.

After ten minutes of crawling in the dirt, I find it.

The battery is nearly dead. The first thing I check is the camera roll. My gut knots with fury. Sixteen terrified faces stare out at me. All have been stripped. Bruises mar most of them. Their expressions filled with fear and something much more concerning. They've given up hope.

Except for one. One girl looks at the camera with fury simmering in her eyes. Zoe Lancaster is a feisty girl, not yet broken at the time this picture was taken. I call it in.

"Alpha-one, package found. Identity confirmed."

"Alpha-three, get your ass back in here." Max pops on the line.

"Copy that." I check the power input of the phone. Surprisingly it's not that out of date. As I trot back to the building, I pull out a cord from my mobile charging pack and plug the phone in. The last thing we need is the battery to die.

Step one, confirm Zoe Lancaster is one of the girls held for processing.

Step two, locate where they took them. Hopefully, one of the contacts on this phone will answer that question.

Keep the fire in your eyes, Zoe. Stay alive. I'm coming for you.

Shit, we've wasted so much time.

FIVE

Zoe

THE RIDE LASTS FOREVER. I'M NOT SURE HOW LONG WE BUMP ALONG the bone-jarring road. At some point, we blissfully transition to pavement. The flapping of the tarp around our steel cage beats at us, deafening in intensity and drains what remains of our strength. That, combined with the tires droning over the road surface, keeps me on edge.

We huddle together. Moving to this new mode of transportation brings all our fears screaming to the surface. Odd how the impenetrable darkness and oppressive silence of the shipping container felt safe compared to this.

Crazy what the mind does to protect itself.

Eventually, our ride ends. The truck squeals to a stop. Men's voices surround us.

Again.

They untie the tarp and draw it back, leaving us to blink against the harsh sunlight. It's hot, humid. The air is thick and sticky. We're soon drenched in sweat and nearing heat exhaustion

The door to the cage creaks open, and the men shout for us to get out. I don't hesitate. My energy will serve me best if I save it for later. This isn't the place to make my stand.

The first of us to get up, I move to the opening. Rough hands grab my arms. I'm half carried, half lifted, out of the cage and set down with far more care than I expect.

The other girls do not and suffer as a result.

The expressions on the men's faces darken at their refusal. One of them hops into the cage. He yanks Iris to her feet and shoves her toward the opening. There, two men grab her and practically throw her to the ground. She falls on her knees and cries out.

The other girls should take their lead from me. Resistance really is futile and only leads to further harm. Half a dozen men swarm the truck.

I school my features into those of a beaten, subdued woman, but beneath the façade, pure fury surges in my veins. Our fight hasn't really started yet. Until it does, I'll bide my time and play the game. I'll be the meek, defeated, defenseless girl they expect.

"Let go of me, you bastard!" Katie lashes out as the man in the cage grabs at her arm. She screeches and claws at him. Her foot kicks out, barely missing his groin.

Wrong move.

I cringe as he punches her in the gut. She doubles over, crumpling at his feet. He moves as if to stomp on her head or kick it. One of the men shouts something in a language I don't understand. It has the flavor of Spanish, but I recognize none of the words.

The man in the cage holds his kick, sparing Katie from head trauma. Instead, he hauls her to her feet and shoves her through the opening into the waiting hands of two more men. They practically fling her to where Iris and I wait.

Joy shouts at the men, snarling and spitting as her turn comes. The man in the truck doesn't waste any time. He buries his fist in her belly. Joy crashes to the floor and curls in the fetal position.

Grace and Hope, smarter girls, scramble to their feet. They clutch at the bars and stare wide-eyed at Joy sobbing on the floor. Grace makes her way to the back of the truck, needing no encouragement to leave the cage.

Like they had with me, the men help her out and lower her to the ground. Hope stumbles to the opening. She reaches down as the men reach up. Soon, she huddles with the rest of us. The man in the cage hauls Joy to her feet and pushes her out.

We're naked, afraid, and surrounded by six males, all in the prime of their life. One man for each of us.

We hold hands. Our voices remain silent while our eyes connect. Fear joins us together. I hope the other girls learned a valuable lesson.

This is not our time.

Which means, I need to bury the fury inside of me somewhere deep and hidden. Honestly, I don't know if I'm that strong.

It's much easier to give in to the wildness inside of me, that animal instinct that calls to fight or flee. But surrendering to that urge only welcomes more pain. Katie and Joy learned that just now.

The men bark orders at us, telling us to follow them. They surround us, forming a cage around us. Joy refuses to stand. One of the men grabs her arm and violently yanks her to her feet. He cuffs her in the head, making her stumble, then bodily pushes her forward.

Hatred swarms in my veins, and I dig in my heels at the injustice.

What if I'm wrong and this is our last chance to fight?

When one of the men raises his hand to strike me, I duck and take a step forward.

Now is not the time.

I keep my eyes on the ground. I don't want these men to touch me any more than absolutely necessary. I don't look at them. I don't acknowledge them. I certainly won't goad any of them into hitting me, touching me, or hurting me.

Tears spill from my eyes, tiny drops of weakness that I hate.

We march where the men command. Our destination isn't a ship or a truck, but rather a large steel building.

They walk us right up to the door and shove us through into a room that looks like it's transplanted from a high school locker room. It's a group shower with two center poles holding multiple showerheads.

No privacy.

The intricate tile work comes as a surprise. White and blue scrollwork lines the floor. And it's clean. Remarkably clean. The tile squeaks beneath my dirty feet.

The men separate us into two groups, pushing me, Joy, and Hope to the set of showerheads on the left and Grace, Katie, Iris to the one on the right. As we're already naked, there's no reason to strip.

Oddly, I wonder what are the chances we might be treated to the luxury of warm water?

I consider that to be quite low.

The men head to a container by the wall where they pull out boxes. These they take to a row of benches beyond the showers. Each box is opened. I glance quickly to the unguarded door leading out the way we came. The men are being very lax in leaving an avenue of escape open.

By their unhurried movements, I understand. Even if I make it to the door, what next? I can't outrun them. I have no idea where to go. Talk about being naked and afraid. My chances out there are much worse than my chances in here.

The men return to each of us holding a fresh bar of soap along with a razor and shampoo and conditioner for our hair. The one tending to me puts the soap in my hand. He sets the razor, shampoo, and conditioner on the floor, then gives a jerk of his chin toward the shower. This is repeated all around me.

No reason to ask what he wants.

I'm sure we all stink. Over the days traveling inside the shipping container, my nose accommodated to our combined stench.

We were taken, caged, and now we're being cleaned up for presentation.

I've read enough books to know what comes next.

Beside me, Joy refuses another order. She's cuffed around the ears and dragged back to her feet by her hair again. An animalistic noise rumbles in my chest. It's the sound of hatred, not fear.

I don't let it out. Instead, I nurse my rage, collecting it within me to be used when I need it the most. With my guard giving me the eye, I reach for the faucet and turn it on. Cranking it all the way around, if there's heat, that's where I'll find it.

Joy keeps up the fight, spitting in her guard's face. She falls to the ground again, sucker punched in the gut. As she huddles in the fetal position, her guard gets in a few kicks with his boot before hauling her to her feet again.

I smother a groan of despair and cover my belly in sympathy. Wincing as she's hauled up, I cup my jaw in sympathy when the man plows his fist into her cheekbone. All the other girls look away. Not me. I want to remember every cruel act.

He turns on the faucet, cranking it until the water barely spills out, then he shoves her beneath the cold stream. She screeches and dodges out of the spray, only to be bodily placed back under the water. Her cheek swells to twice its normal size, and her eye turns red, then deepens to purple.

The control I have over my anger slips. I want to bolt forward and kill the man who struck her, unleash my fury in a blinding rage and enact supreme justice on them all, but as I shift, the guard watching me shifts too.

My gut tightens. I may want to slaughter them all, but that won't be today.

If there's any killing going on, it will be us. We're like lambs, compliant little things marching toward the executioner.

Only instead of death, we face something far worse.

There's a reason they're cleaning us.

We're naked, completely stripped of anything that connects us to our past. It's a wonder none of them have taken what's not been offered. There's nothing we can do if they tried.

Which means, we're not meant for them.

It's too fucking obvious.

I don't know whether to cheer that thought or cower from it.

If we're destined for a brothel, it doesn't matter if these men avail themselves of a free sample. Which tells me we're not meant for the common man. Not a single one samples the weight of a breast, or places his hand to feel the heat between our legs.

Beside me, the cool spray of the shower warms. It turns hot and steam fills the room. All of us, with the exception of Joy, enjoy the treat.

With my spine set straight, I walk under the falling water. Chin high, I wash. I ignore my nakedness and avoid looking at all the dirt and grime swirling down the drain. All that filth is being washed away.

My long, blonde hair grows heavy. The wet curls kiss my ass. I lather my entire body until I'm covered in suds. They cascade between my firm breasts and slide down the flat plane of my belly. I refuse to look at any of the men as I wash between my legs, but my heart races with the indignity of it all.

For now, my body is mine. I'll take care of it as best I can. A few bruises are scattered here and there, all healing and sporting various shades of putrid yellow and green.

After sudsing up, I still feel dirty and start all over again, beginning with my long tresses. I could pull my hair forward to cover my breasts, but a quick glance at my guard shows he's not interested. In fact, he's bored by the whole show. What man in his right mind yawns in a room where half a dozen girls shower in the nude?

Half a dozen.

Our numbers have been cut in half.

Where did the first truck go? What happened to Eve, Bree, Dawn, and the rest?

SIX

Axel

———

TOO LATE TO RESCUE THE GIRLS AT THE INITIAL HOLDING SITE, WE race against time to discover where they were taken. That's the tricky part and isn't our wheelhouse. We're the pointy tip of the spear, sharpened for one purpose. Guardians are men who do whatever it takes to save the innocent.

The four men we interrogated are no longer among the living.

The Guardian's motto repeats in my head. *Whatever it takes.* We see a lot of fucked-up shit in this job. Our team leader, CJ, meets us at the closest airstrip, and we pile into a private jet.

Fortunately, the phone I obtained is an older model. We only need a thumbprint to access the device. I carry that grisly bit of fun in a plastic baggy.

"Got something for you." I toss the phone at CJ, then lob the thumb at his face.

"Nice." He snatches it out of the air with a shake of his head. "Grab your seats, buckle up, and put your tray tables in their full and upright positions. Time to get the hell out of here, buttercups."

I stow my weapon and gear in a box in the far back. With a rip of Velcro, I divest myself of the body armor we wear and take in a steadying breath.

Where are you, Zoe Lancaster?

The rest of my team follows suit, then we all drop into the plush, overstuffed, first-class seats. What a far cry from the back of the C-5s and C-130s from my military days. Those planes are cold, noisy, and lacking in any creature comforts. In this respect, Guardian HRS is a massive step up in the world from my team days in the Navy. We're well funded, courtesy of one Forest Summers, our billionaire investor who sees to it that we never lack for anything we need.

Two other people accompany CJ. They're not Guardians, but rather a part of our impressive technical team. One is a young woman named Mitzy. She's a micro-sized ball of OCD energy. Super smart, at least with computers, every shade of the rainbow is well represented in her spiky, pixie-dust hair. Makes my eyes cross every time I look at her. A tech genius, she plucks the phone and thumb out of CJ's hands before he has a chance to hand them over.

She and a new recruit, a nerdy-looking guy barely old enough to grow facial hair, sit at the front of the plane where several computer screens are mounted along the bulkhead. I'm not sure how Guardian HRS finds its employees, but if that dweeb is here, he must be something special.

Funny, because he's the kind of kid who probably got bullied in high school. Some might look at me, high school jock, good looking (if I do say so myself), the guy who slept my way through the high school girls. It's all true. Some would say I'm also one of those bullies who would torment a guy like him.

I check all the boxes. Cocky. Arrogant. Popular. An early developer. While my classmates' voices were still cracking, I packed on muscles, bulked up, and shot up in height. I've always been the biggest, strongest kid, and with the exception of my fellow Guardians, that remains the same today. Around the Guardians, I'm ordinary and average.

But I was never a bully.

As far as the dweeb goes, I didn't punk the geeks at my school. A protector of those weaker than myself, I guarded them in and out of school, making sure those who would bully them didn't. As for those who did? Well, they found themselves at the wrong end of my fists. I tended to get into a lot of trouble growing up.

"You think they'll find anything worthwhile?" Knox takes the seat facing me and buckles in. His long, lanky legs stretch out as he settles in.

"I don't know." I give a jerk of my chin toward the front of the plane. "Who's that with Mitzy? I haven't seen him before."

Knox looks over his shoulder. "That's the new kid, Jeremy Spratt. Supposed to be a coding whiz or something like that."

"All of the tech team are computer gods." Whiz seems superfluous.

Knox thumps his chest. "We're all godly in our own way."

"You forgot to leave your modesty behind."

"Just speaking the truth." He glances over his shoulder again. "I'm not hopeful they'll find anything useful. We blew this mission."

"They moved them hours before we got there." Maybe only minutes. We could've missed them by that much, not that we'll ever know. As for us blowing the mission, I disagree. We acted on the best intelligence we had at the time. Alpha team shouldn't take the brunt of this heat. We will. It's the way of things, but it's not all our fault.

"Right—hours." He pinches the bridge of his nose and squeezes his eyes shut. "If we'd only gotten to them on time. Who knows where the hell they are? By the time they find anything useful, the girls could be anywhere in the world."

"They'll find something." I can't help it. Knox is probably right. What are the chances an underling has anything on his phone that can help us? Those girls are lost in the wind, and all because we were a moment too late.

The plane starts rolling. The rest of our team settles into their seats. I lean back and close my eyes. We've been up for nearly twenty-four hours straight. Time for a nap.

Sleep when you can.

My BUDS instructors hammered that into me. A program designed to push the body and mind to exhaustion, sleep deprivation is a part of the game. You learn to catch zzz's whenever, and wherever, possible.

When my eyes open next, we're cruising above the clouds. A blanket of fluffy white rolls beneath us.

"Damn." I wipe the sleep from my eyes. "I missed the whole takeoff."

It's the best part of flying. During my team days, we didn't get to look out the window and watch the world fall away as we climbed into the skies. Military transport planes don't have tiny Plexiglass windows for passengers to grab a view. Everything is utilitarian and functional to a fault.

Knox's large frame looks very comfortable in the oversized chair opposite me. He's got a tablet out and earbuds in. With his legs crossed, he bounces his ankle over his knee.

I'd ask what he's watching, but movement at the front of the plane draws my attention. I unbuckle and stretch out the kinks in my body. Knox gives me a passing look, then turns his attention back to whatever he's watching.

Behind me, Max and Wolfe are passed out. Liam and Griff play cards, passing the time. I head back to the lavatory to take a piss, then move up to the front of the plane, itching to find out how badly we've fucked up.

Mitzy and Jeremy sit shoulder to shoulder. CJ stands behind them, arms crossed, a scowl fixed on his face.

"What's up, boss? Anything helpful?" I stand beside him and try to make sense of the computer screens.

"Maybe." The muscles of his jaw tic.

A quick scan of Mitzy's screen brings bile clogging the back of my throat. Sixteen faces stare out of tiny boxes.

"What's that?" I lean close, hovering over Mitzy's shoulder.

"Trophies." She leans back with a sigh.

"What do you mean by that?"

"Whoever you lifted this from, his boss is going to be pissed." A full-body shudder works its way from the top of her neck all the way down to the base of her spine.

"Why's that?" I lean closer, needing to see.

"He obviously wasn't supposed to take them." CJ shifts beside me.

"Is there anything worthwhile?"

"We've got enough to identify the girls." He rubs at his jaw. "Begin the notifications."

Notifications in our line of work generally means all hope is lost.

There's no way a man like me will ever know what those girls endured. I've never been on that side of the power game in my life. I've always been the biggest, the strongest, the one other people fear. I'm the one they come to for protection. It's how I wound up as a Guardian.

I can't imagine what it must feel like to be female: small, fragile, weak, and afraid.

43

The pictures are not authorized. This much is true. They're taken without thought. Quick snaps of the camera taken as discreetly as possible.

My eyes hone in on Zoe Lancaster. Suddenly, there isn't enough oxygen in the cabin. Jesus, she's been stripped down to her bra and panties. Her hands are tied over a beam. Bruises cover her flesh. A man holds her head back, forcing her to look at a photographer charged with taking the photos that will consign her to a fate worse than death.

The bruises surprise me. She fought the men who took her. She was always a scrappy little kid. Pride swells within me. She's a fighter, and that'll serve her well in her trials to come.

Pride will also be her downfall.

Women taken into sexual slavery are punished for their strength. Men see it as a challenge to break women like Zoe. Once they do, they generally dispose of them. Killing them outright or giving them to the men who serve them.

"Is that it?" I glance down at Mitzy. "Stolen photographs? That's all we got?"

"That's not all, but it helps." She points to her screen. "We're processing facial recognition and should have their identities in a few hours."

Hours. Right.

Hours during which those girls are subjected to the cravings of monsters.

"Easy, Axel, they're selling the girls." CJ thumps my arm. "That much is confirmed. There's no reason to take the photos if they're sending them to a brothel. Those are for an auction."

"How is that good?"

"Because it means we have time."

"Time?"

Mitzy spins around and looks up at me. "Yes, dickhead. Time. Time to crack this phone wide open if you'd stop breathing down my neck."

"I'm not breathing down your neck." Except I am. I hover behind her, leaning forward to get a better view of her screen. Her spiky hair moves each time I breathe out.

"Yes, you are. Now take your Neanderthal self and go do—" she flaps her hand, "whatever it is you brutes do when you're not saving the world."

"I'd love to be doing exactly that, but I kind of need you to do your job first."

"I can do my job a whole lot better, and more efficiently, if you'd leave me to it." Mitzy rolls her eyes and gives a dismissive snort.

"So, the phone's a total bust?" I'm not leaving. Mostly because I don't want to give her the satisfaction of bossing me around.

"Not a total bust. There have to be communications, instructions, orders sent to the twat-waffle who had this phone. If we're lucky, there'll be emails to track, or something else."

Looks like a goddamn needle in the haystack. But, I don't say that out loud.

"What now? Where are we headed?"

"Resupply and regrouping. We're headed to HQ. Forest wants a detailed recap of the mission."

Forest? She says his name with the casual ease of a close friend. To me and the rest of the guys, he's anything but a friend. He's a force to be reckoned with and a boss who demands excellence, not dismal failure.

"Glad I'm not Max." I swallow thickly. As Alpha-one, Max gets to take that bullet for the team. Yet again, I'm surprised at Forest

45

Summers' interest in this operation. He doesn't usually get this involved. "What a cluster fuck this mission has been."

"Not really." Jeremy Spratt speaks for the first time. His barely out of puberty voice cracks and is pitched entirely too high for a man. Shit, he's just a kid. A kid who's six-four like me, but he's skinny as a rail, weighing in at easily half my weight. A stiff breeze would be able to blow him over.

"Looks like it to me." I make a sweeping gesture. "Do you see any girls on this plane?"

"Excuse me!" Mitzy huffs with indignation. "Last I looked, I've got boobs."

"You know what I mean." I give a shake of my head. "You don't count."

Mitzy jabs Jeremy in the ribs. "And that right there is what I'm talking about. We're invisible to the *Guardians*." She emphasizes her point with air quotes.

Jeremy smiles back, exchanging a smug expression with Mitzy.

"That's not true." I shouldn't dive any deeper into this conversation. Mitzy is whipcord smart and never backs down. "Everyone's a vital part of the team."

"Right." She gives a dramatic roll of her eyes.

"You know what I meant. I was talking about the girls."

"Your precise words were '*Do you see any girls on this plane?*' You said it while staring at me." She pulls at the neck of her shirt and makes a show of looking down. "Yup, I've got boobs." She looks left, then right. "Two, right there." Mitzy turns toward Jeremy with the collar of her shirt gaping. "Don't you agree, Jeremy?"

Jeremy's face turns fifty shades of red. He tries not to look, but Mitzy cups his chin and forces him to look down her shirt.

"Stop teasing the new recruit." CJ yanks on Mitzy's arm. "Jeremy, ignore Mitzy. She's failing to make a point."

Jeremy's eyes, which were about to pop out of his head, suddenly shift away. Yeah, he was taking an eyeful down Mitzy's shirt.

"Us tech guys *are* invisible to you." Mitzy twists in her seat and hits me with her fiercest stare. Combined with her cute, upturned, button nose and pert little mouth, in trying to be fierce, she inadvertently looks like an agitated pixie. I'm reminded of a Tinkerbell tantrum, full of spunk with the bite of a gnat. And glitter. Tons of glitter. I'd swat her, except CJ would take my head off.

"Without us, you thick-headed Guardians would be stuck twiddling your thumbs." Don't know how the fuck she does it, but Mitzy manages to look down her nose at me from a goddamn sitting position.

"You just said *guys*." I lift my hands in defeat, but I'm not against making my point.

Her eyes narrow. "You know what I meant."

"As did you. Now, as for the mission, work some of your famous Mitzy magic. Find where they took those girls." We're wasting time. I don't like that one bit.

Jeremy turns back to the computer. Indecipherable code fills the screen. I can't make sense of it, but he leans forward studying it.

"We will, just as soon as you leave us to it." She blows out a breath. "Look, I know what this means to you. We'll find her. I promise."

I certainly hope so.

I may not have been a bully growing up, but I was certainly an asshole. Especially when it came to Zoe Lancaster. She was the little girl who never got the hint, following me around with sad puppy dog eyes until I had no choice but to irreparably break her heart.

Now, it looks like I've lost her forever.

SEVEN

Zoe

IT'S FUNNY HOW THE MIND WORKS. IT DOESN'T MATTER THEY'VE taken my clothes, my freedom, or my dignity. The hot water sluicing down my body feels like heaven; invigorating even. The water washes away the terror of the past however many days. It's a moment of bliss I allow myself to fully embrace.

Lord knows there will be very little of that in the future.

My spine straightens. I stand tall and hold my chin high.

It's only a moment, but in *this* moment, I'm free. I refuse to follow the malignant path my mind wants to travel. Whatever comes next, it's not something I can stop.

Not that I won't fight. As long as breath exists in my lungs and blood pumps in my veins, I *will* fight, even if that only means I'm barely surviving.

As long as I'm the one who controls my emotions, I win. I won't let them turn me into someone festering with hatred or cowering with weakness.

I won't lose who I am at my core.

I will survive.

However long it takes before I find my way free of this living nightmare, I'll submit. I won't resist. I'll do nothing that might cause me greater harm.

My father should know by now that I've been taken. He won't leave me to die. Whatever it takes, he'll go the distance to bring me home. I trust him, and I know Austin. My brother's calling in every favor in the book.

My job is to keep myself in one piece for as long as humanly possible.

My guard clears his throat, bringing an end to my moment of solitude.

I open my eyes and turn my attention to him. He taps the face of his watch and gestures toward the benches. The point is made.

Time for the next step.

I give a sharp nod of my head, letting him know I understand. He's yet to speak a word of English. I don't know if it's because I'm beneath the courtesy of his words, or if he doesn't speak my language. Not that it matters.

With one gesture, I know what he wants me to do.

Quickly, I finish my shower. My moment of tranquility, and the relief it gives me, is at an end.

The other girls finish up their showers as well. One by one, we turn off the water. Even Joy follows the command.

Slowly, I pad over to the bench. My arms curl around my chest. Not in a futile attempt to hide my nakedness, but because a chill overcomes me. My guard follows behind me, guiding me to my place at the benches.

He points to a thick, fluffy towel. I could wonder at the change in the towel from the ratty, flea-infested towels in that awful house, but

I don't allow my mind to wander down that path. After I dry myself, my silent shadow points to a thin shift made of soft gauzy fabric. There's no bra. No panties.

Not that I should expect such luxuries.

Considering what we're being prepared for, it makes sense.

Funny how detached I've become.

How accepting I am of my fate?

Nobody speaks.

It's eerily quiet, like the calm before the storm.

We each seem to have our own guard. Other than helping us out of the truck, none have touched us. Well, with the exception of Joy. The bruise on her face has doubled in size.

The boiling hatred I have for these men remains alive and well. I don't give that up. Instead, I feed my anger slowly, keeping it banked for when I need it the most.

Once the light shift settles around me, my guard points to a basket with a hairbrush and a wide assortment of beauty products inside. I look at him, not sure what he wants me to do with it. The brush I understand and reach for that. The rest, I leave behind. There's no way I'm putting on makeup for a monster.

My guard gives a sharp shake of his head. He points again to the basket and then gestures to the far door. My eyes pinch in confusion, but then I understand when Grace carries her basket and heads to the door with her silent shadow half a step behind.

Slowly, I return the brush to the basket. I'll give my guard no reason to strike me for failing to obey.

Through the door lies a long hallway with six doors. Grace goes left, I'm guided to the right. At the end of the hall, my guard opens a door and gestures for me to enter. I take a step in and balk a little at the makeup desk with its rows of lights. He points to the chair and I sigh in resignation.

Patience is not only a virtue but a precious gift.

Patience will lead me to freedom.

Things could be worse. Instead of a warm shower, we could've been tossed under icy rain falling from grimy showerheads. We could've not been given the gift of a shower at all. As I sit in front of the mirrors, a quick glance at my reflection has me biting at my lip. It's a bit chilly. My nipples, reacting to the cold, are embarrassingly peaked beneath the thin fabric. My cheeks heat in shame as a shiver rushes down my spine.

My bottle-green eyes, one of my best attributes, reveal the despair I'm trying to ignore. They know the truth. I'm not as strong as I think. Whatever happens next will break me. But it's not like I can rewind time. I can't go back and make different choices.

I must play the cards in my hand. As shitty as it looks, sometimes the underdog wins.

Let's just hope that's me.

A throat clears behind me. My gaze flicks to the mirror, where I see my guard's reflection. He casually leans against the wall behind me. Arms crossed, one leg kicked back, a bored expression fills his face. He studies me, eyes constantly searching for any sign of resistance.

But I think we understand one another.

If I don't fight, he won't strike me.

He doesn't seem to be in a rush, so I take my time combing out the tangles from my hair. The fresh citrusy scent of the shampoo lingers and the coconut essence of the conditioner layers on top. I smell like a fruity drink. Clean and fresh, I'm perfect for defiling.

Jesus, my thoughts are morbid.

After finishing my hair, I twist my lips and stare into the mirror. My silent guard stares right back. Another chin lift and he gestures to the basket with the makeup inside.

Never big on makeup, I hope his expectations are pretty low. The liquid foundations are a complete mystery to me. I never figured out how to use those. The powder foundation, on the other hand, is the exact same brand I use at home. Another chill worms its way down my spine. I don't think it's anything more than a coincidence until the brushes catch my eye. They're the same. As is the eye shadow pallet and the colored lip balm. Like liquid foundation, me and lipstick never get along.

My stomach twists as dread creeps through my veins, turning them to ice. I can get past the powder foundation, but the rest?

I'm quick with the makeup. It's not something I normally fuss with. In less than ten minutes, my eyes are lined and the lids dusted in neutral shades. The spray of freckles across my nose disappears beneath a light covering of tinted mineral powder. My pale lips pop with a light-rose lip balm. When I look in the mirror, my reflection almost seems normal. I'm not caked in makeup, but this is more than what I put on for daily wear. If not for the barely-there shift, I look like I'm headed out for a nice dinner with my father.

My chest squeezes with pain. What is my dad going through right now? He must be sick with worry. I know my father. Slow to anger, once it takes hold, he's is a force to be reckoned with. But who can he get to help?

I'm sick of staring at my face in the mirror. It seems silly to force me to put on makeup when any moment I'll probably break down and burst into tears. My guard tells me to get up with a sweep of his arm and gestures toward another door. Each step brings me closer to the monster who waits for me.

Monster or monsters?

I don't know why I keep thinking there will only be one depraved man at the end of this. Keeping to our silent bargain, I don't resist

53

and he doesn't hit me. I stand and press out the wrinkles of the revealing shift. It's more of a mannerism than anything else, something my hands do without thought.

My hand trembles as I reach for the doorknob. Anything could be waiting for me on the other side. Out of everything I think it might be, I pull up short at what looks to be a photoshoot. Bright lights are everywhere, mounted on poles and tripods. Circles of lights are everywhere. Spotlights flood the room with harsh white light. Bright canvas drapes fall from the walls, forming a neutral backdrop.

I pull up short, gawking. A broad hand pushes against the small of my back, a not so gentle reminder from my guard. Guess he doesn't like me coming to a sudden stop.

The other girls are here. Eyes wide. Shocked expressions. Two men hold fancy cameras in their hands. Cameras with short lenses, longer lenses, and they each have an assistant with a ring of cameras draped around their necks.

I glance at the other girls and share in their shock.

The thing about this is that it looks expensive. We've come a long way from the filthy floor and flea-ridden rags of our first stop on this insane journey.

My emotions range all over the place. Shock and fear remain ever-present. Revulsion for these men. Hatred that they so easily steal our freedom. I shiver involuntarily, then forcibly make myself stop. I refuse to show weakness and remind myself what I've given away out of necessity, and what I will never surrender under any circumstance.

My eyes focus on the canvas backdrops and I retreat inside my mind to a place these men can't ruin. They stole my future, but I can live in my past where happier times linger.

I took my sophomore year in college to spread my wings, daring a trip to Cancun with my friends to spend a week having fun in the sun. What a mistake this turned out to be.

Freshman year, I went home. That had been a horrible mistake. My brother's best friend, Axel, was there visiting. The boy I crushed on pretty much from the moment I understood boys and girls could like each other, broke my heart. I'm still desperately in love with him. I can't imagine a day in my life when I won't feel something for the boy who was my everything until he broke my heart.

Boy, do I have it bad for Axel. He didn't let me down gently either. When he finally told me to stop *embarrassing* myself, that he never liked me and would never like me, he set off a nuclear bomb, incinerating my heart and destroying any self-confidence I may have had.

I probably deserved it.

I've been in love with him only my entire life. To him, I've been nothing more than an irritating nuisance.

Axel destroyed me. As I sift through my memories, I can't find one without him in it.

When I was six, he was everything to me. He walked me to and from school every day, showering me with smiles and promises of a future together. Of course, I was a little girl, and he was an older boy, twelve years old, but that didn't matter to me. I was deeply and profoundly in love, or at least as madly in love as a six-year-old could be.

He was my first crush, but that's the problem. He was my first and only crush. No boy could ever compete with Axel.

I never looked at another boy. Didn't care about any of them because my six-year-old heart simply believed. As the years wore on, I became more and more obsessed, while he became more and more aloof.

I didn't know the only reason Axel walked me to school was because my father demanded Austin walk with me every day. Where Austin went, Axel followed. He was never there for me. He couldn't care less if I existed. He and Austin were best friends. They still are,

55

which is why going home for spring break freshman year was such a disaster.

I got it in my mind to make a play for Axel. After all, I was finally a woman, and moderately pretty by my estimation. It was finally time to show him how perfect we were for each other. He could no longer call me a little girl. I was a woman and ready to show him precisely what that meant.

Cue mega-disaster.

I threw myself at him. He cut me off at the knees.

Funny how the worst memory of my life brings a smile to my face.

A bright light flashes making me blink.

The photographer takes a picture while my mind drifts to another time and place. My fingers curl in anger, pissed the man steals that moment of bittersweet happiness. Before I know it, I'm pushed forward to the canvas.

"What a pretty thing." The photographer speaks the first English I've heard all day. "What were you thinking about just now? Your serenity was beautiful."

My lips thin, refusing to answer. My memories are not among the things these men can take from me. And I refuse to give them anything of Axel. Good or bad, as horrible as his final words to me were, they're all I have left.

"Too proud to spare a word for me?"

He smiles as he speaks, but danger lurks in his tone. The hairs on my arms lift, warning me not to be the girl who sticks out.

"No, sir." I cross my hands in front of me and glance down, looking as meek as possible. "I wasn't really thinking of anything." Hopefully, the use of 'sir' will massage his male ego and he'll leave me alone. I flutter my lashes and peek up at him. My shoulders hunch forward and I pray he finds my words sufficient.

"Now, that's better." He glances at a man I didn't notice before. A man with a clipboard. "This one will fetch a good price."

There's nothing practiced about my gasp. I take a step backward, the urge to flee overwhelming, but where would I go?

"You've got amazing eyes, very unusual, and your coloring is unique. Is that your natural skin tone?"

Bastard is determined to drag me into conversation.

"It's a tan."

"You have freckles, but they're light. Do you cover them with makeup, or is it natural?" He peers at me, eyes narrowing. Before I can answer, his camera goes up and presses against his eye. He takes several pictures before lowering the camera. "You would've done well as a model. You've got the bone structure for it, but not the height. A classic beauty, your eyes are the most stunning shade of green I've ever seen. Bright, electric green. A man can lose himself in those eyes." He glances over at the man with a clipboard again. "What do you think?"

"My client will be pleased."

My hands press against my belly with that bit of news. *His client.*

One man.

One monster.

Have I already been sold?

EIGHT

Axel

FRUSTRATION BUILDS WITHIN ME. WITHOUT AN OUTLET, I'M READY to fucking explode. There's a problem with luxury jets. I'll say that right now. Everything is bolted to the floor. There's nothing to pick up and throw.

Forest would fire my ass if I lifted one of the seats and smashed it against the bulkhead. But that's what I want to do. I need to throw shit around for a bit. Some good ol' senseless destruction is what I need to cool off.

I jab my fingers through my hair and tug at the roots. Images of Zoe flash in my mind. An annoying six-year-old in pigtails obnoxiously following my every step. The awkward sixth-grader with her hopeless crush. How fucking embarrassing that had been for me, a senior in high school with a swoony sixth-grader crashing my dates.

Other images superimpose on those; things I can't get out of my head. Zoe stripped and tied as she huddles on the dirty floor. Tears streaming down her face as they load her up in a car, or a truck, or God knows what.

Zoe making a pass at me last year when I went to visit Austin. She blossomed into a fucking beauty, but I'll always see the annoying six-year-old version of herself. The little girl who trailed behind me as I pretended she didn't exist.

"Fuck!" The urge to slam my fist into the bulkhead nearly overwhelms me.

Where are you, Zoe?

"You okay?" Knox looks up from his tablet.

"Do I look okay?"

"You look like shit."

I pace up and down the aisle, alternately digging my fingers into my hair and trying to yank it out by the roots. *Come on.* I silently urge Mitzy and Jeremy to find something on that phone that will help. They certainly look busy as I march toward the front of the plane for the tenth time.

Mitzy shoots me a dirty look. Jeremy's spine is practically bent double as he hunches over the computer. I don't know what the hell he's doing, but his fingers fly lightning fast over the keys.

"Go sit down." CJ kicks out his leg, stopping me in my tracks. "You're wearing on everyone's nerves."

Only because following orders has been ingrained in me through intensive training do I shuffle back to my seat and collapse in a heap of exhaustion. My nerves are shot. My mind spins with all kinds of horrible thoughts about what's happening to Zoe while we cruise blissfully along at thirty-five thousand feet.

My fists curl and I close my eyes. *I'm going to find you, lost girl. I'll bring you home, one way or another. Whatever it takes.* And that's the worst rub of them all. As the hours pass, the likelihood of our mission ending in body retrieval escalates.

I sink into my thoughts and the pace of my breathing eases. At some point, I must've fallen asleep because I'm brutally awakened when the plane banks hard to the left.

"What's going on?" I rub at my eyes again. "How long have I been out?" I blink sleep encrusted eyes, trying to clear the foggy veil of sleep from my mind.

"Well, if it ain't Sleeping Beauty." Knox stares at me. A smirk fills his face and he regards me with a smug expression. "Enjoy your nap?"

A glance out the window and I bolt out of my seat. Those aren't the rolling hills of California, home base of the Guardians. We're soaring over water, not land.

"Where the fuck are we?"

"Over the Gulf. Why?"

"You know why."

"We're headed to Columbia." His smirk intensifies.

Max and Wolfe crowd around Mitzy and Jeremy. I push out of my overly stuffed, overly comfortable chair, and slide determinedly to the front of the plane.

"Did we just make a hard turn?" My demand comes out as a growl.

"It's called banking, not turning." Mitzy returns my growl with a smug snort. "Planes bank. Cars and trucks turn."

"I'll take that as a yes." Not in a mood to verbally spar with the pixie, I punctuate my words with a grunt. "And we're *banking* why?"

"We found them." The grin on CJ's face stretches ear to ear.

It takes a minute before I respond. My heart just about stops.

"Where?"

"Barranquilla." CJ crosses his arms and stares down at me.

"Fuck." Known for its thriving drug trade, Colombia is nearly as well known for being the kidnapping capital of the world. It's an up and coming powerhouse in the world of human trafficking. Of course, it would be fucking Colombia. Nothing like a rotten paradise. "How the fuck did she get there?"

"Cargo container." CJ crosses his arms. "We traced the ship to Barranquilla. It docked not too long ago and is still in port, off-loading."

"Are we hitting the port then?" I'm ready to storm in like thunder and save the day. "Or are we too late again?"

We have a chance, but we're still in the air.

"How long until we land?"

"Half an hour." CJ pulls at his chin. "Half an hour to land. The port is about an hour away from the airport. The team's greasing our way as we speak."

I understand that. Bribes to the right officials will have them turning a blind eye to our team on the ground. My attention shifts to Max. "What does port security look like?"

His expression is troubled.

"What's the problem?"

Max points to the computer screen. "The ship's been in port for almost a day. It's halfway through off-loading its containers. Mitzy and Jeremy are tracking the one the package is in."

The package. We use that word for a purpose. It's a part of our lingo but it rubs me the wrong way. In this case, *the package*, is someone I know well—a scrappy little girl who annoyed me for years.

"What's the problem then?"

Jeremy glances over his shoulder. His attention lands on me, then slides over to Max. "That container has been off-loaded."

"Shit." I scrub at my hair. Every time we seem to get close, we're one step behind. "What now?"

The only reason I'm not freaking out is because Jeremy doesn't look bothered by this small, inconvenient detail. His attention swivels back to the screen.

"We're pulling up surveillance tapes to find out when it was off-loaded and where it went." He points to a fuzzy image on the screen. "So far we've combed through the first two hours the ship's been in port. The container the girls were in is a smaller, twenty-foot container. Those are generally stacked at the end and off-loaded first. It's slower going than we'd like, but we're tracking each of the containers as they come off. Some are easier than others."

Mitzy glances up at me. "We're going to find her. It's just a matter of time."

"Doesn't feel that way."

She presses her finger to the screen. "One of the marvels of modern-day technology is we don't have to look at all the footage to find the container. I'm hacking into their monitoring and control systems as we speak. Every container is logged."

I shift a step closer to Max. "What's our game plan?" If we'd been a day or two earlier, we could've assaulted the cargo container while it was at sea. While massive structures, they typically run on a skeleton crew. It would've been nothing to subdue the crew, locate the container with the girls, and take them off the ship. Now, we risk losing them to the wilds of Colombia.

"I'm in." Mitzy sits back, beaming with pride. She threads her fingers together and cracks them all at once. Then she leans forward and digs into the data. Meanwhile, the plane noses down, shedding altitude in preparation to land.

At some point, we'll all need to take our seats, but we're too

63

engrossed in what Mitzy and Jeremy are doing. Remarkably, Mitzy says nothing about the four of us breathing down her neck. I've seen this laser-tight intensity in the little pixie too many times not to hold my breath.

Like a dog with a bone, she's found something, and she's determined to locate her quarry. Not more than five minutes later, five minutes that feels like five hours, Mitzy gives a little *whoop* of excitement.

"Found her!" Mitzy beams with pride.

CJ leans in while I crane my neck to make sense of what's on her screen.

She taps Jeremy's hand. "Scroll to time oh-five-thirty. You should see the container off-loading."

Jeremy fiddles with the security feed he tapped into and rewinds. There, dangling in the air, a twenty-foot cargo container sways in the grip of the off-loading crane. My gut tightens and my scowl deepens with the knowledge Zoe is inside that beat up shipping container.

"How long?" I grind out the words.

"Three days." CJ places his hand on my shoulder. "But I'm sure they took care of them."

"I bet they did." I'm going to murder the assholes who subjected Zoe, and the other girls, to such barbaric conditions.

We all watch the crane move the container off the ship. It sways back and forth, drops with a gut-wrenching lurch. For a moment, it's as if the container free falls through the air, but the cables grab hold and it jerks to a stop. Backing away from the ship, we follow the crane as it moves the container down toward the ground.

Instead of stacking it with the scores of containers waiting for placement on railcars, the container comes to rest on the back of a semi-truck. I glance at the timestamp on the video and curse.

"We're three hours behind them."

"We'll find them."

"How?" Maybe if that truck was in the States, there would be plenty of traffic cams to follow its progress, but this is Colombia. We'll be lucky to track it a mile.

Mitzy flashes me a grin. "You'd better buckle up, Guardian. We're landing soon."

"And then what? We don't know where that truck went."

"Oh, you have such little faith in us. Remember, we use our brains, not our brawn, to figure shit out."

"And you're going to be able to track a semi that left the port over three hours ago?"

"Not me personally, but you'd be surprised at what a satellite can do."

"A satellite?" I look between Mitzy and CJ. "Is she shitting me? We don't have access to that kind of tech."

"*You* don't." Mitzy flashes a smile. "But I do." She spins back around and elbows Jeremy in the ribs. "Come on, newbie, let's show him what we can do."

CJ crosses his arms and turns to Max. "Get your team settled. We leave as soon as the plane lands. Ground assets are already in play. Check your gear and get your shit ready. We're not wasting a minute once we touch down."

Max gestures for me and Wolfe to follow him. He thumps Knox on the shoulder as he heads to the back of the plane. "Come on, we don't have much time."

Liam and Griff, who've been watching from their seats, put up their card game and join us at our lockers in the back of the plane.

"I want everyone suited up. We'll be met on the ground by a van. As soon as the doors open, we leave." He opens his locker and begins pulling out his gear. Wolfe joins him and straps on his tactical vest. Griff and I step around them, then we're on our knees getting ourselves kitted out for a rescue.

NINE

Zoe

To keep panic from overwhelming me, I breathe. In and out, I focus only on the even rise and fall of my chest. It's supposed to calm me.

My muscles lock. My eyes unfocus. Everything blurs around me. I try to escape the nightmare, but I'm tied to the constraints of my body. There is no calm.

"She's not like the others." The photographer walks in a circle around me. "I wonder if we can keep her?"

The man with the clipboard lowers it. "You know the rules. Payment has already been taken and bids are underway."

What rules? I shiver involuntarily. What bids?

The photographer lifts his camera. "She doesn't fight or cry. I say we take her last. Maybe then..."

"Get the shots of the others and let's get started." He seems to be the one in charge. No one questions him. "We have a good showing."

I suddenly realize the clipboard isn't a clipboard, but a tablet instead. He keeps checking it, nodding as if pleased with what he sees.

The photographer moves around to each of us, taking pictures of our faces, not our bodies.

"She'll fetch the highest price." The man with the clipboard assesses me with a cruel, merciless gaze.

I stare deep into his black eyes. His dispassionate gaze does something to me. It takes away my hope. In his eyes, I sense a finality to my plight.

I see death.

I say goodbye to everyone I know. I say farewell to my brother, my father, my friends, and finally to the man who broke my heart.

There's no escape from what's going to happen.

He leans toward me. The fetid stench of his breath makes my nostrils flare. "You think you can hide from this. Disappear inside your head? They all do. You have no idea why you're here, or what your fate might be." He pinches my chin between his thumb and forefinger. I wince as he forcibly tilts my face to meet his stony glare. "I bet you think you're to be sold. That happens for some. But not you."

My stomach clenches at the chill in his voice. That's absolutely what I thought. If not that, then what? If not sold, what else is there?

"We start with her." He snaps his fingers and points to Joy.

Joy struggles when two men grab her arms. She kicks and screams as they drag her toward one of the canvas sheets. They place shackles around her wrists, then toss ropes up and over a steel bar. The rest of us crowd together, clasping hands, and fighting tears.

Terror fills Joy's face as they tie the free ends of the ropes to the shackles at her wrists. My brows pinch together as the men step away. At a signal from the man with the clipboard, they yank on the ropes. Joy's arms rise over her head and keep going until she's lifted off her toes. She dangles in the air as the man with the clipboard gives a nod.

"Let's begin."

The photographer takes several pictures. Joy twists in front of me, flailing and kicking. Then I notice the cameras on tripods. I missed those. They're mounted all around. Not cameras, but video cameras. They're videotaping this, or streaming it live?

A quick glance at the man with the clipboard/tablet thing and I know that's what this is. That video feed is streaming to his device. And where else?

Joy cries out and my attention shifts back to her. The terror in her eyes, her strangled screams, and the way they're brutally cut off are things I'll never forget.

All the while, the photographer documents her murder with the click of the lens.

Tears fall, blinding me. I squeeze my eyes shut and fall to my knees with a long, low moan.

What hell is this?

Katie screams. She bolts for a door, but she's caught at the waist. The man holding her returns her to where the rest of us huddle as a group, but the man with a clipboard shakes his head.

"She's next."

Katie struggles harder, kicking and hitting the man holding her. How do I stop this? What can I do? Reasoning with these monsters will do nothing.

But what are they doing?

Why are they doing it?

Monstrous men sit on the other side of a computer screen with how many others? How many men *bid* to watch this? The man with the tablet used that word.

Bid.

Lily and Grace cling to each other. Hope holds my hand. Iris rocks on the floor, knees drawn up, head pressed against them. Her low moans are indecipherable. The need to go to her, to comfort her is powerful, but what comfort can I provide when we share the same fate?

Katie's small frame is nothing to these brutes. They put her in the chair and fasten shackles to her feet. Her arms are bound behind her as she struggles and bucks against the men to get free. All the while, the video cameras record.

All I can think about is that I wish I had run. When the men cornered me in the alley, I wish I'd been smarter, faster, stronger. I wish I never set off alone.

I was wrong not to resist. I missed an opportunity to make a break for freedom. Now, it's too late. It's too late for Joy. It's too late for Katie. It's too late for us all.

"Please. Please don't do this." Katie cries out. "Whatever you want. I'll do whatever you want." Her wide eyes flit around the room. "Please…" Whatever she says is cut off when the man behind her places the plastic bag over her head.

Hope's grip tightens in mine, then she empties the contents of her stomach on the floor.

Katie's body is eerily still.

Tears stream down my cheeks.

There's no waking from this nightmare.

When they take away Katie's body, I release Hope's hand.

"Take me next." I puff out my chest and square off my shoulders. This is the bravest thing I've ever done, and the most cowardly. It's not like my action saves anyone. I simply don't want to watch another girl die. I hate myself for it, but it's the truth.

The man with the clipboard cocks his head and takes me in. "Is that so?" His eyes narrow.

"Yes, take me." I'm asking him to kill me. To let me be next. Nothing about this makes sense.

"And you think this saves any of them? That we immortalize your sacrifice and stop there?"

Immortalize my what?

My sacrifice?

He's crazy as a loon. This is no sacrifice. It's brutal, inhumane, and insane. They're all insane.

"Why? Why are you doing this to us?" I might be dead in the next little bit, but dammit, I need to know why this is happening to me. What did I do to deserve this—this senseless end?

"Ah, finally, she says something intelligent."

He does it again, that slow sweeping gaze of his takes me in, assessing, weighing, and measuring my worth. The tablet buzzes and he snaps his gaze to it, presumably to read an incoming text. Then his eyes are back on me and he shakes his head.

"The boss has spoken. *You* are to be last." He snaps his fingers and one of the men trots over. "Grab a camera and turn it on this one. Marcos wants a feed on her as she watches the others." His attention returns to me. "You are going to make us millions, little puta."

My mouth opens and closes, trying to form words that make sense, but there is no making sense of insanity.

71

"Put her in the chair." He sneers at me. "We want you to be comfortable."

My stomach drops. It plunges to my feet and keeps on going. A shakiness works its way down my limbs. I need a fucking chair, because there's no way I'm staying upright. Blackness crowds my vision. Dread coils in my belly and fear races through me. I waiver on my feet, and then I fall.

I slump right into his arms. The tablet clatters to the floor as he catches me. Through the low buzzing in my ears, he shouts commands as my foggy brain focuses on the tablet and what it contains.

My body jerks as I'm manhandled into position. Just like Katie, I'm bound to the chair. A scream erupts beside me and I blink away the floaty feeling clotting my mind.

Lily hangs over a man's shoulder, kicking and screaming, as he carries her to the center of the room. Another man brings forward a plexiglass box and sets it on the floor. I'm confused what they're going to do with it until another brings a bucket and fills it with water.

Lily dies only a few feet away from me. I shouldn't have watched. I should've looked away, but I couldn't. I couldn't leave her to die alone as these men cheered and paid for the privilege of watching her die. She suffered greatly and I was helpless to stop it. All I can offer, the only thing I have, are the tears streaming down my cheeks.

The horror of our circumstance is indescribable. My lungs burn with frantic gasps. My jaw clenches as I think of a million ways to make these men pay.

But I can do nothing.

I can't remove this pain in my chest. I can only endure.

They take Hope and her ending is far worse than the others. Iris is dragged to her death, kicking and screaming. Grace and I exchange a glance as they drag Iris's lifeless body away. Grace is next and there's nothing we can do. She reaches out. Her fingers brush against my arm. It's a farewell of sorts, an acceptance of death.

I know evil exists in the world, but knowing about it, and living through it, are two different things. To take the lives of defenseless women without reason? I can't comprehend the level of depravity. My mind isn't capable of processing it. I can't bear to watch it, but I do. I exist in a state of traumatic shock while they take Grace.

I stay with her for as long as I can, refusing to let her die alone, but my mind fades out. My eyes are open. Her screams pierce the air. I see and hear none of it as I reach a breaking point. My mind snaps and shatters, until I'm no more.

Hands are on me, loosening the shackles confining me to the chair. I move under my own power, listless and alone. Trapped in this godforsaken nightmare, there is no escape.

Every inch of me trembles. My heart screams with an agonized cry for the life I'll never know. The love I'll never have. For my family. My friends. For the future taken from me. My hopes and dreams are at an end. All I have to do is endure whatever torture they have in mind for me and find the sweet blissful release of death at the other end.

Cuffs are placed on my wrists. Cuffs wrap around my ankles. My arms lift up and out to the side as they pull on the rope. They return to kick my feet out where they fit a steel bar between my ankles, ensuring I can't move. A man steps in front of me and uncoils a bullwhip.

Unable to move, there's no place to go. No way to hide. No escape from the pain.

They rip screams from my throat. Pull ear-piercing shrieks from my lungs as they cut through the thin shift covering my body. Once that falls away, they flay my skin.

I cry. I sob for my stolen freedom. I mourn the loss of innocence.

My mind drifts in desolate blackness punctuated by the sharp crack of a whip as it bites into my skin. These heartless, barbarous men cheer me toward death, but they don't rush to finish me.

I will make them millions.

That's what he said.

I say my goodbyes to my father, my brother, and my friends. No one will ever know what happened to me, or the evil that caused my suffering in the end. I say a final farewell to Axel, the man I loved even after he threw me away.

I'm happy to have known love, even though it was one-sided, and I'm grateful my family will never know how much pain I endured at the end. My goodbyes are said in the tears rolling down my cheeks as hope abandons me. My thoughts grow murkier. Time slows, then stops altogether as I slip away and let go.

TEN

Axel

"Do you think she's in there?" Griff looks up from peering through his scope.

My gaze swings from the flatbed truck with the cage on it to a steel building. My insides twist with the knowledge Zoe had been crammed inside that thing and brought here.

Whether she's in there or not doesn't matter.

She either is, or she isn't.

Either way, the next few minutes will decide whether Zoe lives or dies. If she's not in there, we've lost her forever. If she is, then we have a chance to save her.

The spot between my shoulder blades itches like a motherfucker. I hope she's in there. If not, I'll never be able to look Austin in the eye again. How am I going to tell him I lost his baby sister?

"She needs to be in there. That's all there is to it." Power of positive thinking, right?

Our team split into three groups. Griff and I watch one of two entrances. It's the one closest to the flatbed. Liam and Wolfe watch the other entrance on the side of the building.

How Mitzy was able to find this place is an act of brilliance. She located the container holding the girls. Watched as it was placed on the back of a semi-truck. Following what limited traffic cameras that are operational in this godforsaken country, she tracked that truck to a construction site. There, we watched, mouths agape, as thirteen girls were bodily yanked out of the container and split among two trucks.

She did her best to follow them both, but we lost one. The other is parked within spitting distance of where Griff and I wait.

Max and Wolfe complete a circuit around the building, placing tiny boxes of Mitzy magic. We could cut the security feeds, but that risks alerting whoever's watching to our presence.

Mitzy, or Jeremy—I'm not sure which one I'll have to kiss—produced tiny wireless devices that supposedly interfere with the cameras. I think she mentioned hijacking their feeds. Regardless, the tiny black boxes will loop the last five minutes of what they record, while we sit and wait. That's the only sucky part. We have to locate all the cameras and wait for Mitzy to break into the software to get that damn loop going. It's agonizing, all this waiting.

But the waiting is over.

"Alpha-one to Alpha-three, ready for breach."

"Copy that." It's too easy to focus all my attention on that door. All I can think about is rushing in. Shooting assholes who think to kidnap young women and steal their freedom. Fortunately, my training is solid. Head on a swivel, I scan and rescan, looking for possible threats.

Liam and Wolfe take out what little security exists outside the building. Whoever these people are, they're overly confident. Their security is too light.

Max and Knox make their way to our position.

"Cameras are looping. We can waltz right in." Wolfe taps my shoulder in encouragement.

"Feels all kinds of wrong." My molars clamp tight. Something definitely feels off, but it's not the lack of security. That itching sensation between my shoulder blades is something I trust. "We need to hurry." Not sure why I blurt that out, the feeling bursts from my gut. Every instinct tells me we need to charge that door.

But we won't. That's how people get shot.

Max gives a nod and activates his comlink. "Alpha-five status."

"All clear." Liam's voice is crisp through the comms. "Back to you."

"Copy that." Max grabs my arm. "You feel anything?"

It's killing me laying here in the dirt. After far too many days of hunting, we're close. I feel it deep within me. Max gives me the side-eyes. I don't believe in all that psychic crap, but he does, and let's face it, my instincts are uncanny. Realizing I didn't answer him, I respond.

"We need to go—now." My voice is urgent. My gut insistent. "We need to fucking move." I'm restless, but I won't move until Max gives the order.

She's in there. I know it, sixth-sense or not, a visceral connection ties me to Zoe. Responsibility or guilt, I grew up with her doting on me, and enjoyed it more than I should. I feel her presence inside that building, her fear, then a sudden silence. I feel it down to my core.

Griff holds up an infrared detector. "Nothing outside. Movement inside the building, far side. Nothing behind that door."

"Check." Max rises to a crouch. Wolfe follows. I continue my scan while Griff moves beside me. Movement off our six catches my eye. My weapon lifts, tracking the movement.

"Liam and Knox," I say with a whisper.

77

"Roger." Max holds up his hand and gives the signal.

We move in formation, bringing the lethal force of years of combat special ops training with us.

"Hold up." Liam's voice comes over the radio. "We've got one leaving the house. We go in hot or we wait. Alpha-one, your call."

My gut seizes. The need to breach that building overwhelms me. Max looks to me. He sees the urgency on my face and calls it.

"On three," Max calls it.

We're going in hot.

"In three, two…"

The four of us move together as Knox's shot rings out. With our presence formally announced, my thoughts laser in on the mission and my singular need to get to Zoe.

Max, Knox, Griff, and I move together, weapons out, scanning as we approach the door. That shot brings men spilling outside. They're wild, haphazard in their actions. Untrained. It's total chaos, which is where we excel.

They don't stand a chance as we pick them off. I begin with the first man, placing a bullet in his brains. Griff takes down the second. Max and Knox grab the next two. It's like a day at the fucking arcade.

They rush out, night blinded, which means they can't see shit. Knox fires off a few more shots, sending each man to the grave with lethal accuracy.

We barely stop in our tracks to take aim. Our formation remains tight as we pick them off, never missing a shot. We cross the grass from our hiding position and head toward the open door, slowing only to step over bodies, double-tapping them in the chest as we go.

One bullet to the head. Another to the chest.

No man rises after that.

It feels fucking fabulous.

Angry voices shout from inside. We make it to the door and press up against the steel of the building. Gunfire rings out. Random shots meant to scare us. We don't even flinch.

Three more men run out, blindly shooting into the dark. Liam picks them off.

One. Two. Three.

They're down on the ground.

Max signals to Knox. It's time. We hear no other activity inside.

Knox moves in. Max is right behind him, hand to his shoulder. They crouch just inside the doorway, weapons drawn as Griff and I follow them in. Wolfe and Liam come next. We clear the room and move forward.

Showers?

The silence is startling as we move through. The next door opens into a hallway with several doors. Nothing to do but clear each one. Fuckers. This is going to slow us down.

Wolfe and Liam move to the left while Griff and I head right. Max and Knox hold steady, guarding our rear. Griff and I burst through the first door and pause.

A makeup counter? Fucking weird.

Clean the girls. Make them pretty. Put them up on an auction block to be sold? We'd better not be too fucking late this time.

A door leads out, but we've got more rooms to clear. Griff glances around and finds something to wedge the door shut. No one will get around us through that door. We back out and head to the next door.

"Clear," Griff calls out to the team.

"Clear." Wolfe and Liam clear their first room.

I signal Max, using a combination of signs to tell him what we found. The room is clear and blocked. Liam and Wolfe join us. Liam nods, confirming the same thing. Like us, they wedged the door closed.

We repeat this, until we're inside the last two rooms. Max stands outside the first room with Liam and Wolfe, while Knox watches out for Griff and me.

Sixth-sense or not, a tingling sensation hits my spine. It's too strong to ignore. My hand goes to the doorknob. The only thing keeping me from barging through is the operational conditioning beaten into me over years of training.

I feel it deep in my gut. I need to get inside.

Now.

"On three, two…" Max counts us down.

I turn the knob.

We barrel through. An angry voice on my six goes down with the squeeze of my finger. I adjust my aim to the next target and take the shot. Two men down. Griff takes down another three before I scan back to twelve o'clock and practically burst a lung when I see Zoe.

She's restrained and immobile. Arms lift out to her sides. A bar forces her legs apart. She hangs limp, trussed up like an animal. Welts mar the perfection of her flesh. Strikes from a bullwhip cut deep. Blood weeps down her body and drips onto the canvas at her feet. Her head hangs listlessly, lolling to the side. There's no movement.

None at all.

Pops of gunfire sound out as my team clears the room. All that operational conditioning goes to hell as I rush to Zoe without any care for my safety. All I know is I need to get to her.

Hold her.

Save her.

Ignoring unfriendlies in a room is never a good thing. A man charges in my periphery. A pop sounds. He goes down, courtesy of Griff, who always has my back. I reach for my knife and cut through the ropes binding Zoe's battered body in place.

There's no sign of life.

Her body crumples, but I catch her mid-fall, draping her over my shoulders. I free her ankles but can't figure out the damn bar wedged between her feet.

Gently, I lower her to the ground and go to my knees. I use my teeth to rip off my tactical gloves. Pressing the pads of my fingers to her neck, I close my eyes and feel for a pulse.

Please be alive.

I feel nothing. Nothing.

"Unresponsive," I call out to no one in particular. *No pulse.* I lower my face to hers and turn my cheek waiting for breath to ease out of her lungs. "No breath. No pulse."

Max walks up behind me. His radio crackles as he reports in. "Hostiles subdued. Eyes on the package. No signs of life."

Her battered body tells a tale I can't comprehend. I've seen the face of evil in the world. I've seen worse done to men, but on a woman, it's different. What Zoe endured is gruesome.

My medic training kicks in. I tilt her head back and give two rescue breaths while I watch her chest rise and fall. Then I move beside her and begin chest compressions.

Griff and Knox work to release the cuffs at her feet while I pump on her chest. They teach us to push to the beat of 'Stayin Alive.' I thought it was funny as shit at the time. Now, it just fucking pisses me off. There's nothing funny about this.

Staying-alive-Staying-alive-ah-ha-ha-ha-Staying-alive...

My breaths sound like a damn Choo Choo train. *I think I can I think I can.*

"Come on!" I growl at her, willing Zoe to take a damn breath, twitch, or ... I don't know?

Show some goddamn sign of life?

Tell me I'm not too fucking late.

Knox frees her of the damn bar and gently closes her legs. He pulls out a shammy from his pack and covers her private parts, providing what little modesty he can. Don't know why that matters so damn much, but it does.

Her tits bounce up and down each time I pump on her chest. I'm fucking pissed at the degradation she endured. The torture they put her through. It's a good thing everyone is dead. I'd tear them limb from limb if they were alive.

"We need to move," Max barks the order I know is coming.

"We can't move her," I huff in-between compressions.

"You have five minutes, then we're out. The rest of you—you know the drill. Tag and bag."

Tag and bag.

The team goes around the room taking headshots of the dead and bagging anything electronic they may have on them. Pockets are emptied. Everything that remotely looks like possible intel is gathered in Ziplock bags.

Our mission is over, but that doesn't mean Guardian HRS is finished with this nasty little group of human traffickers.

I don't understand the murderous look on Max's face, not that I have the time to focus on anything other than bringing Zoe back. And I will bring her back.

Breathe, Zoe. Goddammit, breathe!

Cardiopulmonary resuscitation has come a long way over the years. It's all about compressions. Breaths are no longer a part of it, but I can't help but fall back on the algorithm I was taught way back in basic. Thirty rounds of compressions. Two breaths. I pause my compressions and move to her mouth. I don't care about her cracked lips or the blood crusting them. I pull in a lungful of air then breathe it into her still form.

Her chest rises.

I take another breath and blow life into this fragile woman; the little girl I couldn't stand always hanging around me. I take back every nasty thought I ever had and pray, *Please don't take the girl.* I don't understand why, but I'm not ready to lose Zoe. She's too much a part of who I am.

My gaze trips on the marks littering her skin, cutting deep into her breasts. Whip marks wrap around her neck, slicing deep furrows. Nothing nicked her artery or the vein.

The cameras.

It doesn't take a genius to put two and two together.

Fucking animals were making snuff films.

Where are the other girls?

Headed back for another round of compressions, I scan the room. It's only then that I learn what placed that murderous look on Max's face. Liam and Knox are busy in the corner, but they're not tagging and bagging men.

My hands go to Zoe's breastbone. I locate my position and put the heel of my palm on her chest.

Then I freeze. Did she just?

I lean down and her chest lifts the tiniest bit. It's not much, but she's fucking alive.

A barely audible inhale makes my heart sing with joy. I take her hand in mine and pat the back of it. "Come on, Zoe. You can do it."

She takes another breath, then follows that with a sputtering, weak-as-fuck cough, but she's alive.

"We gotta move out." Max stands over me.

I reach down to take her in my arms, then pause at her ravaged body. Beneath Max's glare, I pull on the Velcro fastening on my vest and remove it. Then I yank off my tee-shirt. He glares at me but gives a nod. He'll give me this. I place my shirt over Zoe's head, lift her to a sitting position, and tug it down while she groans and winces in pain. My tactical vest goes back on.

They've done a number to her with that whip.

"This is going to hurt, honey," I warn her as much as I'm able, then lift her into my arms.

Her low, painful moans are a sound of beauty to my ears. It means we weren't too fucking late. I cradle her in my arms, then look to my teammates. Knox, Liam, and Griff drape two bodies a piece over their shoulders. We didn't save them, but we will bring them home to families who will have the peace of mind knowing what happened and can bury their loved ones with closure.

That could've been Zoe in Griff's arms.

I clamp my molars together and focus on what's important.

Max takes point and leads us back the way we came. Wolfe takes the rear, covering us. The rest of us are useless with the burdens we carry.

"No..." Zoe's whisper-faint voice breaks the silence. Her body twitches, but in her weakened state, she falls still again.

Max leads us out of the building and a mile down the road where our van is hidden in the brush. We pile in. All of us.

My team.

Zoe, who fades in and out of consciousness.

And the bodies of six young women taken too soon from this world by monsters.

We speed down the road, heading for the airstrip where a luxury jet will take us home. The ride to the airfield fills me with unspeakable emotion.

We saved Zoe, which means she'll be heading back home where her family will take care of her and tend to her wounds. My guts twist in knots knowing that won't be me. But why? Why do I care about that at all? It's not like she's mine. Her recovery is not my business, but fuck if I don't want it to be.

"We need a hospital." I urge Max to divert. "She's in shock."

"We're headed to the airfield."

"Fuck that."

"Alpha-three, zip it. You're out of line." Max switching to my callsign is the only thing that keeps my mouth shut.

I keep my arms wrapped around Zoe, growling when Griff tries to help settle her on the floor of the van. No way in hell is she lying beside the dead girls. It's a goddamn horror show back here.

Max and Knox stay up front. There's no sign of pursuit. Liam and Wolfe sift through the cell phones we collected and match up fingers to phones. Facial recognition hasn't hit this part of the world yet.

I don't know what we'll be doing when it does. Lopping off heads and carrying them in a basket?

That's some sick shit right there.

My attention shifts from Liam and Wolfe to Griff. He hovers beside me, wanting to help, but keeps his distance. My protectiveness is no shock to my team. Zoe's connection to me is well known, but I sense Griff knows it's more than that. I hate to think he's right.

I feel his stare and the judgment that comes with it. Operational conditioning means we keep our emotions out of the mission. Our rescues are *packages* and our job is to deliver them to safety, not to become emotionally attached.

Zoe shifts fitfully. I rock her in my arms. Frail and small, she weighs practically nothing. She's always been small, petite, but toned, tight with muscle. Her body is a wasted mess, and that's not just from the whip marks that crisscross her entire body.

She looks nothing like the kid I remember, a fierce little thing. Scrappy and full of spitfire. After high school, I lost track of her when I enlisted in the Navy. Then there was BUDS and I entered a different world.

Truthfully, I didn't think twice about Austin's annoying little sister. Life went on, and I moved with it, until last year when I took leave and spent it with Austin. His little kid sister wasn't so little anymore. She was still fierce and determined to get what she wanted. It just so happened she wanted me, and that was a major no-go on my part.

"What the fuck did they do to these girls?"

Griff's brow lifts. "You want the fucking play-by-play?"

"No." There's no need for that. I really just want him to stop staring at me and passing judgment on my actions. I should've settled Zoe in a seat beside me instead of holding her in my arms. Her tiny body curls in my lap. She sleeps fitfully, dozing in and out of consciousness. I hold her because it won't be long before she's taken from me.

She'll eventually go home to Austin and her dad while I move on to the next mission. Damn if I don't want to leave her side, though. I want to be there for her as she works through this tragedy, and that's a problem.

It's a huge fucking problem.

Griff and I don't speak about the other truck and the girls we lost to the slave trade. Did they suffer the same fate as these girls? Or are they, even now, being auctioned and sold to the highest bidder?

Honestly, I don't know which fate would be worse.

Zoe's eyelids flutter, and she struggles in my arms, pushing against me until she faints with exhaustion. So fucking weak.

If we'd been a minute later, we'd be hauling back seven corpses instead of six.

"Shh." I lean down and whisper in her ear. "You're safe, honey. You're going to be okay."

"Five minutes out." Max twists in his seat. "How's she doing?"

"She's alive. Comes and goes. I don't think she knows what's happening." As I speak, a whimper escapes her cracked and bloodied lips.

"Here." Max hands me his water. His gaze cuts to my hand, the one that holds Zoe's. I brush the pad of my thumb across the back of her hand while he arches his brow.

Well shit. First Griff? Now Max? I remind myself they know about my personal connection to Zoe. I'm not that far out of bounds providing a little tenderness.

Except, I know it's shit.

This isn't tenderness.

It's a whole lot of something else. My professional detachment doesn't exist, at least not where Zoe's concerned.

"Thanks." I reach for the water bottle and ignore Max's intuitive gaze.

"We've got good news." Max ignores the scowl on my face.

"Yeah?" Griff asks as I try to wet Zoe's lips. "What's that?"

"She needs an IV and medical attention." I practically growl in frustration. "We need to get her to a hospital."

"The medical team just landed. Doc Summers is on the ground. Your girl will get the care she needs on the way home. No need for a hospital, not that we'd take her to one here."

My girl.

Damn straight she's mine.

"Copy that." I get it. I really do.

Zoe's in urgent need of medical attention, but the way things work here, she's likely to die in a local hospital. Our medical team is top-notch. Recruited from the Air Force's special operations surgical teams, they perform life-saving surgery in the field. I trust Doc Summers. I trust her with my life, and right now, my life is all about Zoe.

ELEVEN

Axel

MY ARMS TIGHTEN AROUND ZOE WHEN WE PULL UP OUTSIDE THE JET. The back doors to the van open. Doc Summers is there. She glances at the bodies placed gently on the floor. It's the best we could do given the circumstances. Horror floods her features before she turns her attention to the woman cradled in my arms.

In the blink of an eye, she's all business.

My medic training kicks in. Words spill out of my mouth relaying the CPR I performed and Zoe's most recent set of vital signs. I'm nothing more than the medic giving a report to the doc, at least until they try to pry Zoe out of my arms.

Doc Summers jumps back at my growl. Her head tilts to the side, regarding me, then she gives a nod and steps aside. A stretcher waits behind her, propped up on the tarmac, and her team surrounds it.

I do an awkward crab crawl out of the back of the van, nearly tripping on my way out. My arms tighten around Zoe and she gives a low groan of pain.

"Sorry." I wince knowing I'm any part of her pain. "You're going to be all right. I promise."

I can't help but look down at Zoe as my boots hit solid ground. Her body is a mess of bruised flesh, angry welts, and hundreds of cuts oozing blood. But that's not what catches my breath. Her eyelids flutter, then snap open. It takes a moment before her eyes focus. She scans my face and pinches her brows as if confused. I don't know if she recognizes me, but hope she does.

I *want* her to know I rescued her. Something shifts inside of me, needing her to know I'll do whatever it takes to keep her safe. I'd walk through hell if I thought it would lessen her pain. I'd trade places with her in an instant if I knew it would spare her from dealing with the trauma of her abduction, torture, and the attempt on her life.

Those fucking men, killing girls for pleasure, will meet up with the business end of my weapon. We killed everyone at the building, but I want to know who was giving the orders.

"It's me. I've got you. You're going to be all right." Up close, her bottle-green eyes steal my breath. They're spellbinding. Uniquely beautiful.

A man could lose himself in their soulful depths and be happy forever. Funny how I never thought that before.

I can't help but stare. Does she know it's me? There's no recognition in her eyes, only pain and torment. As if to echo my inner thoughts, her eyes widen with alarm, flood with fear, and then drift off in despair.

Not sure what kind of reaction I expect, her limp acceptance concerns me. It's like she's not fighting anymore. There's no relief in her rescue. Zoe simply seems to fade away behind those mesmerizing eyes.

"She's in shock, lost a lot of blood." My arms curl as I bring her in closer, pulling her toward my chest. The need to hug her, and comfort her, overwhelms me. If I could, I'd take all her pain and bear it for her. I hate to see her suffer.

"I see." Doc Summers stands to the side while I carry Zoe to the stretcher. I don't want to let her go. As soon as I do, they'll kick me to the side and do what they do best.

Save lives.

"You did a great job." Doc Summers places her tiny hand on my shoulder after I lay Zoe on the stretcher. "It's Axel, right?"

"Yeah." Her team crowds around me, but my feet don't move. I won't leave Zoe's side.

"She's going to live, but I need you to step aside." The doc's voice is sweet as shit, soft, compassionate, but determined.

I'm in her way.

No fucking way will I move. A low rumble sounds in my chest.

"Alpha-three..." Max's voice snaps through the air. He comes behind me and grabs my arm. "Let them do their job." Yet again, Max reverts to my call sign, reminding me of our mission, one that's not finished until we deliver those poor girls back to their families. "Help the others—"

"If you don't mind..." Doc Summers steps forward. "We could use another set of hands."

Her team doesn't need another set of hands. They're completely self-sufficient. They work as a unit, moving in synchrony, much like Alpha team does.

I will get in their way.

I know what she's doing and if I didn't need to be by Zoe's side, I'd be on my knees in gratitude for what she offers. I am thankful. I'm just too preoccupied to say it.

"By all means." Max releases me and turns about to help with the grisly task of off-loading the bodies.

"Thanks, Doc." I don't care about the funny looks her team gives me and rush back to Zoe's side.

"Please, call me Skye. Doc sounds too military-ish. I'm pretty informal, but you do as I say. Just so we understand each other."

"Copy that, Doc." I won't argue with that.

When she gives me a hard stare, I see her true strength. She may be small, slight, and female, but this is her territory. I'm the interloper and she's in charge. I swallow my pride and give in.

"What can I do, Doc?"

"Start by calling me Skye." She glances at one of her teammates. "Ryker, why don't you let Axel place the IV while you get a cannula going. Tia give her something for the pain. Watch her respiratory status."

"On it." Ryker steps aside and hands me the IV kit. He keeps his eye on me while my hand shakes.

Well aware I'm inserting a needle into Zoe's arm, I buck up and settle my nerves. It's been a bit since I've done this. I'm sure Ryker can slip in an IV in his sleep. Doc Summers—Skye—shows great kindness in letting me stay.

Fortunately, I don't embarrass myself in front of Skye's top-notch medical team. I get the IV in on the first try. Ryker is right there with a bag of fluids. He helps me secure the IV, taping it in place.

"Hold it high and let it run in. Tell me when it's getting low." He leaves me with the liter of fluid and goes to set up a nasal cannula for Zoe.

Skye's team consists of an emergency doc and trauma surgeon, a respiratory technician, Ryker, and a nurse anesthetist, Tia. Skye's the ER doc and team leader. Everyone knows that. She's also Forest's sister, which means I'd better not fuck anything up. I know Tia and Ryker from before. They were with us during the catastrophe in the Philippines, but the other doc is new to me.

Right now, he and Skye complete a head-to-toe examination, looking for any life-threatening injuries requiring immediate attention.

"Increasing oxygen. Her pulse ox is low," Ryker reports his actions to Skye.

"Is she okay?" I glance at Zoe's chest. Her breaths labor as she struggles to breathe.

"Nothing to worry about." Skye listens to Zoe's chest with her stethoscope. "We won't know for sure, but you said you did compressions. She probably has some fractured ribs, maybe or maybe not a pulmonary contusion."

Skye's words drop the bottom out of my world. I have to hold on to the stretcher for a second. To think I caused Zoe any additional harm guts me.

"It's okay." Skye puts a hand on my shoulder. "It happens with CPR."

Yeah, but I'm the one that cracked her ribs and maybe bruised up her lungs. After everything else, that just sucks big-assed monkey balls. Too choked up to speak, I give a hasty nod and squeeze the IV bag. That's my one job, and I'm not fucking it up.

Two jets sit on the tarmac. The one my team flew in and the one that brought Skye's team.

Behind us, my teammates take care of the girls' bodies. We haven't been too kind to the poor things. Not nearly as respectful as they deserve. Necessity required a hasty retreat. I can't be prouder of my team for taking a moment to pay their respects to the unfortunate girls.

CJ stands over the bodies, head bowed, with his hand to his heart. Mitzy and Jeremy stand beside him. As my team removes one body at a time from the van, and take the required photos for identification, they pause and bow their heads in prayer. Then they wrap each girl solemnly for transport.

93

To my surprise, Jeremy kneels by the side of each girl. His lips move. His right hand touches his forehead, the middle of his chest, then his left and right shoulder forming a cross. He kisses his fingers and presses them to the forehead of each girl. His actions shock the hell out of me. Not what I expected from the nerd, but I'm damn proud of him.

"Let's get her on the plane." Skye's soft voice sounds behind me and my teeth clench.

I'm not ready to step aside, but I know I must. I hold the IV bag up high, letting the fluid run into Zoe's body. She lost a shit ton of blood.

If I say nothing, will they forget I'm here? I'm not sure I can bear being separated from Zoe. It feels wrong leaving her in the hands of strangers. What if she wakes up? What if she needs me?

My mug may not be the one she wants to see, especially after the way I handled her obsessive crush, but after the trauma she endured, she'll need something familiar to hold onto.

I want that something to be me.

But it's time. My guys finish loading the jet. CJ and Max take Skye aside, probably getting an update on Zoe's condition, or they're figuring out which of them will report in to Forest. It should be CJ, but Skye is his sister. They talk for a moment, heads bowed together, then separate with a unified nod.

That's it.

It's time for me to leave.

I take Zoe's hand in mine. Whatever pain medicine Tia gave her seems to be working. Zoe sleeps peacefully, oblivious to the injuries she endured.

"Take care. You're stronger than you think." Before anyone pulls me away, I lean down and gently place my lips on her forehead with a reverent kiss. "Get better, sweetie." Her eyelids flutter beneath my kiss, but she otherwise doesn't react.

I doubt she knows I'm here.

The IV bag is nearly empty. "Ryker..." I hold up the bag showing him the contents are nearly gone.

"Gotcha. Thanks." He digs inside his bag and pulls out another liter of saline. In an economy of movement, he swaps out the empty bag for the full one.

I step back and head over to my team. They gather at the base of the airstairs leading up into the jet. CJ and Max complete a mini debrief, standard for all our operations. As much as I want to stay with Zoe, I belong with them.

They say nothing as I approach. The only acknowledgment of my arrival is how they open up the circle to let me crowd in. Shoulder to shoulder, Max recaps the mission. Each of us contributes some little bit.

Despite what we found inside, our execution couldn't have been better. CJ asks a few questions. He and Max will work on a mission debrief during the flight home. I assume Mitzy and Jeremy will be hard at work cracking cell phones and that tablet we found. I'll probably get saddled with matching fingers and thumbs to their corresponding phones.

They don't put that kind of shit on the brochure, but these are the joys of the job, and why we get paid top-notch.

There's more to that operation than what we found. Guardian HRS will be hard at work to bring the rest of it down, probably for years to come. It bothers me that there are still six young women out there. I say a silent prayer to whomever cares to listen that those girls don't meet the same fate as the ones we found tonight.

My gut squeezes for the nth time, thinking about what Zoe endured. She watched those other girls die. What lasting trauma does that kind of shit leave on a young woman's mind?

"I need to call Austin." I blurt the words out in a rush.

I can call him on the plane, but it feels wrong to wait another second before telling him we found his sister. Technically, notifying our client is CJ's job as mission commander, but Austin is my best friend. I don't have to make the official call, but I'll let him know we found Zoe and are bringing her home.

I step away from everyone and dial Austin's number. He picks up on the first ring.

"Fucking please tell me you have good news?" Austin's voice is tight with worry.

"We found her." I don't waste a second giving him the news. Normally, I'd fuck with him a bit, just to be a prick about it, but not now.

Not about this.

"And is she..." His voice cracks.

Something deep within me shifts, like the flicking of a switch, a feeling rushes through me. It's primal and raw, possessive as shit. She's no longer Austin's little sister. This feeling grows within me until I finally accept what it means.

Zoe's mine.

And just like that, it's settled.

"She's alive. Beat up, but alive." I rush to tell him what he needs to hear, although I'm overwhelmed by what just happened.

Zoe's more than a little beat up. The trauma of her kidnapping will leave scars for life, both physical and mental. Austin won't be the one to put her back together. That responsibility is no longer his, but rather mine.

"It's bad, Austin." I won't mince words with him. He needs to know what to expect. "Is your dad with you?"

Technically, Mr. Lancaster is our client, not Austin. I'm not sure when CJ will be making the official call, but I owe it to the man who has been such a prominent figure in my life to tell him myself. I give a little grin knowing he'll continue to be so but in a much different fashion.

Austin and I spent all our time together growing up. If we weren't cutting it up at my house, we were getting into trouble at his. Mr. Lancaster raised me as much as my father did. Whipped my ass a few times more than my father, too. Austin and I had a lot of fun growing up, which meant we got into our fair share of trouble.

"Are you with her?" Austin's voice shakes. "Can I speak with her?"

"I am, but she's sedated." He knows what that means. I'm not getting into the gory details with him over the phone, but I'm not sugarcoating it either.

"Good." His voice tightens. "She needs you. Don't fucking leave her side."

"I don't know if I can do that. She's with our medical team. They flew down to meet us and will take her back to the States. I have to stick with Alpha team."

"Shit. Yeah." I can practically see him tugging on the roots of his hair. "I guess so. I wish you could. She needs someone she knows."

"I'm not so sure she'll agree, not after how I handled things."

That's something she and I will deal with later. I don't see it as a problem.

Austin never seemed to mind his sister following us around. He never really cared about the crush she had on me. It was always something he accepted as a fact of life.

"That doesn't matter. She knows you. You're familiar. I hate the idea of her waking up surrounded by strangers."

97

I understand. I feel the same damn way. I want to tell him I'll stay by her side, but that's not my call. Max lifts his finger in the air and twirls it in a circle. It's the sign to move. It's time to load up and go.

Behind me, Skye's team pushes Zoe on the stretcher toward their plane. My stomach knots and my throat tightens as I turn away. When I get to the foot of the airstairs, CJ and Max stand with Skye. I keep my head down, not wanting them to see the anguish on my face.

"Axel, hold up." CJ catches me off guard.

"What's up?" With a foot half raised to take the first step, I kind of wobble.

"Change in plans." CJ gives Max a look.

Max gives one of his silent chin bumps, which says he's cool with whatever CJ is going to say.

"We talked with the Doc, and she feels, considering the trauma Zoe endured, that it would be best if you flew back with them."

My heart lodges in my throat and just about bursts. Speechless, I'm reduced to gaping like a goddamn idiot.

Skye Summers places a hand on my arm. "But only if it's okay with you. I know how you guys don't like being separated from your team. She's sedated and unlikely to wake during the flight, but I think it'll help if someone she knows is with her, at least until her family can be there. I hope it's not too much to ask?"

Too much to ask? I'm fucking ecstatic.

TWELVE

Zoe

I EXIST IN A FOG OF NOTHINGNESS.

This isn't what I thought death would be like. Darkness surrounds me, consumes me, but it feels too tangible.

I'm too aware of my body.

A light flow of air dances across my body, prickling my skin, and drawing it tight as goose bumps pebble my skin. The air tastes funny, dry with a hint of metal. A low, drone buzzes in my ears and vibrates in my bones. Sensation is everywhere, more prominent beneath me where my shoulders and back press against a hard surface.

Am I supposed to feel things in death?

If so, my cracked lips hurt. The crust covering my eyes makes it impossible to pry my lids apart. Not that it matters if I'm dead, but I kind of want to see the afterlife.

I try to move, but my body's unresponsive and limp. It won't let me shift positions, but something tells me I probably don't want to do that. A low throbbing sensation pulses head-to-toe.

Everything hurts.

I think.

Since I can't open my eyes, I do the opposite and pinch them tight together. The crust digs in, but some tears flow outward softening it. Cotton fills my mouth and sharp pain exists in every breath. Agony envelops me, leaving nothing spared.

Every breath?

I shouldn't need to breathe if I'm dead.

Where am I?

Fear floods me. Adrenaline kicks into my system, hijacking veins and arteries as it surges through my body. Memories return. Horrific images that make me cry out.

Something warm and solid presses against my shoulder. I buck and thrash with images of death flooding my mind.

"Shh, Zoe, you're safe." A low, rumbly sound rolls through the air, landing on my senses with an odd familiarity.

"Where..." Cuts in my lips crack and bleed when I try to form words. If I'm breathing and speaking, I can't be dead. My muddy mind picks through my thoughts, trying to parse them into something I can understand.

"You're safe." A hand grips my shoulder. Fingers dig into my skin. They're gentle but firm.

Solid.

Protective.

I try peeling my lids apart, but they're too gummed up and don't cooperate. My tongue pushes past the dryness of my mouth to trace along cracked and bleeding lips.

"Where am I?"

Who am I with?

Something tells me not to ask that out loud. Adrenaline races around my body, igniting fight or flight instincts. Unfortunately, my body doesn't want to listen, let alone cooperate. When I try to lift my arm, nothing happens.

"Doc, she's coming around." That low, raspy voice once again stirs memories, familiar moments locked in my past.

"Keep talking. Say her name. She'll respond to that." A soft, feminine voice responds to the man.

I piece that together. One man. One woman.

There's no malice in either tone. Which is weird. My body is primed to flee, telling me I'm in mortal danger.

They feel—safe.

I'm really confused, because I thought I was dead, but I don't think that's the case anymore. So, if I'm not dead… Sudden dread coils in my gut and a tiny mewling sound fills the air as memories flicker and flash.

Death.

All I see is death.

That's me making that noise.

I sound so pitiful.

"Zoe, you're going to be okay. Just relax and keep your eyes closed. You're safe, and you need your rest. Try to go back to sleep."

Warm, melodious, and seductive, I latch onto each word and follow it as it washes over me. My thoughts tumble and spill about, fragmenting and dissolving as I try to catch and hold them. A heaviness floods my body. The adrenaline is spent. While I try to cling to the voice, comforting blackness folds around me. I drift into it and float in nothingness.

He says I'm safe, and I believe him. Whoever *he* might be.

It's instinctual, my knowledge I can trust this man. Like he's a part of me, something missing and found again. I embrace the warmth of that thought and let sleep overcome me.

He'll keep me safe.

I drift away. The low droning noise continues, lulling me deeper and deeper into sleep. Only I drift too far. Nightmares overtake me. They fill me with fear, cutting and slicing, smothering and drowning, gutting and beating me until I gasp for breath.

A strangled sound escapes my throat, clawing its way up and out into the light. My body fights an overwhelming need to flee, but the heaviness in my limbs traps me. I feel like I'm thrashing and fighting, but only the tiniest flicker moves my fingers and curls my toes.

I refuse to be trapped and focus all my strength into forming three tiny words.

"Where. Am. I?" The words come out slurred and feathery light.

A hand presses on my brow and strokes backward through my hair. The oppressiveness of the fear fades as fingers tangle in my hair. The voice is back, murmuring words telling me not to be afraid.

My eyes feel different, no longer glued closed by that gooey crust. I squeeze my eyelids tight together, then slowly peel them apart.

I see a chiseled jaw peppered with stubble. Warm, arresting sky-blue eyes flicker back and forth. He stares down at me with tenderness and concern. There's strength in his face, a sense of overwhelming confidence, as if he knows all the secrets held by the world. I feel small and vulnerable beneath his troubled gaze, but oddly comforted. It's almost as if this is where I'm supposed to be.

"Hey there, welcome back." His lips curve into a smile that stretches up to caress the corners of his eyes.

"Back?" Back from where? I try lifting my arm, but terrible weakness weighs it down. "What's wrong with my body?"

"Skye, she's awake." He glances away briefly and I almost cry out. I need the strength in his eyes to keep the fear at bay. Somehow, I need to siphon some of it out of him and inject it into my useless body.

A presence moves in my peripheral vision and a light shines down on me. I squint against the blinding intrusion. Something cold presses against my chest. It's there and gone before I can blink.

"Keep talking. Her sedation is wearing off. A comforting face will ease some of the shock."

What shock?

A flutter of fear remains, teasing at my memories. Something happened.

"I don't know what to say." His rumbly voice is a light caress against my senses.

That voice is magical and does something to me; it soothes my senses and lulls me into a peaceful trance. I want to bask in the warm familiarity of it and pretend I'm not wherever *here* might be. Or maybe, wherever I was before I got here.

"Say whatever comes to mind," the woman says in a soft, soothing tone. "Keep it light—simple."

A low, throaty rumble vibrates the air. A soft sigh follows. The hand returns to my forehead and fingers run through my hair. They catch on tangles and gently work their way through.

I brace for a harsh tug, but he works the tangle until his fingers slide through without pulling. Over and over, he combs through my hair, teasing out tangles until his fingers glide effortlessly from root to end. It's easily the most comforting thing I've felt in my entire life, and it doesn't hurt.

"Austin is going to be there when we land."

"Land?" I'm confused. Austin?

"Yes. I'm taking you home." The protective tone in his voice touches my heart. I believe him. I may not understand what's happening, where I am, why I'm here, or why I'm not dead, but I believe this man.

I wish I could remember why I thought I was dead.

Clearly, I'm not.

So, what happened?

My brows scrunch as I try to make sense of things. Meanwhile, I enjoy the rhythmic draw of my hair as he runs his fingers through it. The light tugging on my scalp eases me. I could stay like this forever.

Except for the pain.

Wait.

Pain?

I take stock of my body and realize every single part of it is in agony. Except my toes. A quick wiggle and yes. I confirm it. They don't hurt.

Concerned about this new fact, there isn't an inch of me that doesn't sting, burn, ache, or throb. The fog hanging over my thoughts thins.

Somehow, for some reason, I thought I was dead, which I'm not. This amount of pain belongs only to the living.

"What happened?" My lips crack with the words and grate against a soreness in my throat.

I'm sore inside and out? How weird. Why would my throat hurt? My voice is raspy, and my throat is raw.

"How about you try to rest and we'll talk in a bit." This voice is familiar, but deeper than I remember, more defined, more male, more—everything.

My lids flutter and my vision clears. I take in the cut of his jaw and eyes I recognize.

"Axel?"

"Yes, brat, it's me." The skin around his eyes crinkles as a smile fills his face.

Brat.

That's the name he gave me years ago. It was well-earned. Axel was my everything. I remember now. As the fogginess in my head lifts, I remember him. He's the one I idolized growing up. The boy I followed like a lost puppy without understanding why. He's the man I lusted over as I grew into my teenage years while he became a man. He was always a part of my life until he wasn't.

Until he wasn't...

My brow furrows with memories I don't want.

I'll never love you, you little brat. Get that through your thick skull. You and I never were, and never will be, a thing. You're a goddamn, fucking kid with a silly schoolgirl crush. Find someone else to bother and stay the fuck away from me.

His words cut deep, gouging my heart and leaving permanent scars. I'll never forget those words or the pain he caused.

But why is Axel here? Why is he being nice to me? Why does concern and worry fill his expression like I'm some fragile, broken thing ready to fall apart at any moment?

Why does he care?

I shouldn't be, but I'm glad he's here. He may not believe like I do, but something bigger than us binds us together. It's a truth I've always known, even when he pushed me away.

He takes a wet washcloth and wipes my brow. He dabs my dry and cracked lips, wiping the corners of my mouth. His movements, incredibly tender, confuse me. Axel isn't a tender man. He's a fierce warrior, a trained killer, not this caring man.

I wince as the wet cloth rubs across my chapped lips. A coppery tang coats my tongue and spills down the back of my throat.

Why is there that much blood from chapped lips? Why does my voice sound hoarse? Like I've spent all night at a concert screaming my head off with my friends?

My skin burns. Maybe I sat on the beach too long and got a sunburn?

I think about it, but that doesn't seem right.

Axel wasn't with me in Cancun.

"W-why are you here?" I croak like a toad.

I can't think straight and it bugs me. I can't talk right and don't understand what's wrong with my throat. Gaping holes fill my memory, and that doesn't feel right either. I struggle to fit all the pieces together.

I take in a deep breath, hoping that'll help. My senses are immediately flooded with Axel's unique scent; dark, yummy chocolate mixed with the fresh loamy smell of a forest after a spring rain. My eyes close as I breathe him in. It's been far too long since I've seen him.

Voices whisper behind me. One is soft and feminine, the other deep and rumbly. Only bits and pieces reach my ears.

How's she doing? The deep baritone is loud, but the volume of his voice drops while he's speaking.

Her skin is torn to shit.

How bad?

I strain to focus on the man's voice. The woman is close, a few feet away, but I can't locate the male voice.

There'll be scars, Forest.

Anything broken?

Thankfully no.

Sexual assault?

We haven't examined for that.

Skye, you have to—

We're not equipped for that on a plane. When we land, we'll do a thorough exam and take care of everything.

Plane?

My mind completely skips over the casual mention of rape.

The pieces fall into place.

I'm not in Cancun.

My body involuntarily stiffens as a flood of memories returns, drowning me in a tidal wave of horror.

"Hey there..." Axel's deep voice tries to soothe me, but I'm overwhelmed and begin to panic.

I close my eyes in a futile effort to block out his concern. I can't stand having him look at me with pity filling his expressive face. His thumb gently strokes along my cheek. The contact barely registers until it's all I can think about. He's being kind when he'd been so cruel to me the last time we spoke.

"What happened to me?" My thoughts and emotions are out of reach. I feel something lingering at the edges, pushing its way to the surface. Something bad happened, and I need Axel to tell me.

Now.

"We'll talk in a bit. Right now, how about you rest?" He takes my hand and gives it a light pat.

A light, patronizing *pat!*

Rest? I don't want to rest. I want to know what the fuck is going on. What happened? And why does it feel as if my entire body has been worked over?

Why am I so goddamn weak?

Overwhelming anger coils inside of me, tightening in my gut. It slithers through me, seeping into my bones.

"Tell me." I grit my teeth. I don't know what Axel thinks he's protecting me from, but I'm not a little kid anymore.

His Adam's apple bobs as he swallows. His gaze sweeps down my body, beginning at my face and moving all the way to my toes. My skin burns beneath his gaze, tightening each time his eyes pinch as if he sees something revolting.

I know I made a mistake. I acted the colossal fool when I threw myself at him, but the disgust in his face is not warranted. I never asked him to save me.

Save me?

"Breathe, Zoe."

Fuck him.

"Settle down." He places his hands on my shoulders as I buck.

"Don't tell me to settle down." I gasp, desperate to breathe.

"Zoe!" The sharp snap of his voice cuts through to me.

Cuts.

The cracking of a whip.

Pain.

Delirious insufferable pain.

"Fuck, what's happening?" Desperation sounds in his voice.

"She's hyperventilating." That's a new voice, another male who probably wants to tell me what to do. "A panic attack."

I can't catch my breath. Sucking in air, my chest labors to fill my lungs. But it's not working. My lungs burn. Dark spots dance in my vision. Blackness crowds in from the edges. Darkness reaches for me...

No, no, no.

A metal door closes, locking me inside a box. Other girls are with me. We're terrified and scared. Their dead eyes condemn me for being the one who lived.

No!

I don't want the darkness, but it doesn't care what a defenseless female wants. It crowds around me.

Smothers me.

It draws me in and drowns me.

THIRTEEN

Axel

"WHAT THE FUCK?" I'M LOOKING FOR SOMEONE TO BLAME AND Skye's the closest person to unload on. "What did you do?"

Her head cocks to the side and her lips press together, but she says nothing. She *ignores* me, but Tia doesn't. She gives a sharp shake of her head, telling me to cool off and back down.

I'm too prideful to apologize, so I don't.

"I've seen shock before, but that came out of nowhere." Tia presses a stethoscope to Zoe's chest. "What were you talking to her about?" She's pissed that I yelled at Skye and turns the tables on me. The woman is ballsy and I respect that.

I won't apologize for my outburst, however. I really want to know what happened.

Skye and Doc Martin check Zoe and go over her vitals. They put their heads together then give Tia orders for administering more sedation.

"You can't keep her sedated forever." My eyes narrow as Tia pulls up more medication and injects it into the IV tubing. The second liter of saline pours into Zoe's veins. She's severely dehydrated, that combined with her blood loss, almost put her into cardiovascular shock. Now, we're dealing with psychological trauma on top of the physical kind.

Zoe's completely unresponsive, trapped somewhere inside her head. I shake her gently but can't get her to rouse.

The fear in her eyes reached right inside me and grabbed my heart. I've seen my fair share of combat. Tia's right. We've all witnessed what traumatic stress can do to a person's mind. When the scars run deep, psychotic breaks are not unheard of, but I hate to think Zoe suffers from that on top of everything else.

"The sedation is just to keep her calm." Skye places her hand on my shoulder, forgiveness shimmers in her eyes. "I don't want her thrashing and ripping out the stitches we placed."

I get that and can't help but sweep my gaze up and down Zoe's body. They removed my shirt from her once we got on the plane. While she was unconscious, Tia sedated her while Skye and Doc Martin sutured the deepest cuts closed. Her skin looks like hamburger, shredded to pieces, many of the cuts deep into the muscles. It's going to take a long time for her to heal.

Only a thin sheet covers her nakedness. If I had another shirt, I'd cover her in it. Zoe's always been a modest girl. I can't fathom how shocked she'll be when she comes back around and realizes she's naked in front of strangers.

I'm still amazed how much the Guardian HRS medical team is able to do with their limited gear, but this is what they train for. In fact, they can put someone under general anesthesia, salvage limbs, and muck around a man's insides like it's a walk in the park. Stitching up a young woman is child's play to them.

Skye lifts the thin sheet to check on the stitches across Zoe's abdomen. A horrific gash cuts across her midsection, where it sliced through skin and muscle. Not to mention over a hundred more welts and cuts crisscross her flesh. Zoe will heal, but her body will carry the scars for life.

Her reaction, the fear and thrashing, scare the fuck out of me. It came on so quickly, I didn't recognize it for what it was, and I don't know how to help her deal with it.

A post-traumatic flashback.

My eyes close as I take in a breath. She suffered horribly at the hands of those men.

Men who my team killed, but I only need to know one thing.

Who hired them?

Once Mitzy and her tech wizards figure that out, I'm headed on a killing spree.

Skye purses her lips and holds out a hand. "Get me the suture kit. She pulled some of her stitches apart."

Zoe's shaking was so violent it looked like a grand mal seizure. The blood drained out of her face. Her jaws locked. Her eyes rolled into the back of her head where they fluttered violently. Then her entire body jerked while she gasped for air. I thought it was simple hyperventilation, but it was more than that.

I'm forced to give up my position by Zoe's side while Skye bends to the task of suturing Zoe's skin. Skye's movements are methodical. Her hands steady. Zoe's being taken care of by the best of the best, but I can't help it. I need to be by her side.

"You should sleep." Ryker kicks at the chair facing him. He's one row up from where Zoe's stretcher is locked in for the flight.

This jet, like the one my team flew in on, boasts nothing but the best. All the chairs recline into beds. We're used to traveling around the world in style.

"I don't think I can sleep. If she wakes up..."

"I'll wake you. You're not going to be any good to her if you're strung out and exhausted with no sleep."

Ryker's got that right. It's been far too long since I got any real sleep. I've been catching micro-naps here and there since this mission began well over twenty-four hours ago. Hell, I think I'm close to forty-eight.

"Don't know if I can sleep." My body may be exhausted, but my mind buzzes something fierce.

"Then just kick back for bit. Tia loaded your girl up with Ativan. She'll be out for a couple hours."

"Not sure I'd call her *my girl.*"

"Really? I just assumed from the way you've been hovering, not to mention Skye never lets people get between her and her patients unless they're family, or in a relationship."

"I know Zoe, but we're not like that."

"You sure about that?" He flashes me a smirk as he pushes out of his chair, leaving me to gape.

There is no romantic relationship, but that doesn't mean I don't care about Zoe. I've known her practically my entire life, and I promised Austin I wouldn't leave her side.

"Here." Ryker returns and throws a shirt at me. "Get out of your tactical vest. You can borrow my shirt while you chill out and relax. If she stirs at all, I'll grab you."

"Thanks." All I've thought about is Zoe.

I forget I'm still wearing the bulky tactical vest. I shrug out of it and slip on Ryker's shirt, then fall into the seat with a heavy sigh. I'm tired. Physically tired. Mentally spent. Worried beyond measure for Zoe. I'm pissed this happened to her.

Bending over, I unlace my boots, then lean back and pinch the bridge of my nose. It's the last thing I remember before someone shakes me awake.

I blink to clear my eyes and see Ryker standing over me.

"Hey, bud, we're about half an hour out and getting ready to land."

"Is Zoe..."

"Still sleeping. But I thought you might want to switch seats. You know, in case she wakes up as we land?"

"Ah, great. Thanks." I rub the sleep out of my eyes and stretch. A quick trip to the lavatory and I'm back by Zoe's side.

"How're you feeling?" Tia vacates her seat beside Zoe.

"Like I've been run over by a Mac truck. How's Zoe?"

"She's been sleeping since I gave her the sedative. It's starting to wear off." Her brows tug together and I can imagine what she wants to say, but won't. For any man to see his woman brutalized, mutilated, and barely surviving an attempt on her life, is unfathomable.

"She's my best friend's little sister." It's impossible not to cringe when I look at Zoe. She looks so goddamn fragile lying on the stretcher.

The thin sheet's been replaced with one not soaked through with blood. Tia gives an understanding smile. I barely contain my fury as I stare down at Austin's sister.

My fists curl as the impulse to kill rolls through me. The bastards who did this will pay. That knowledge thrums through my veins. Due punishment is a certainty, and I'll do it real slow, enjoying their screams as they die.

Tia leaves me and joins her husband, Ryker. The two of them glance at me, troubled expressions furrowing their brows. When they see me staring back, they turn away. I'm getting looks like that from Skye's entire team.

If I were Zoe's boyfriend, I'd be a raving lunatic on a killing spree. As it is, I'll still be going on that murderous rampage, only I'll do it with the intelligence provided by Guardian HRS intel team and the combat skills of my team.

I won't go in hotheaded.

When I kill, I'm deliberate about it.

This is far from over. The boss man won't let a trafficking cell like this stand for long, especially since they're killing defenseless women for sport.

Fucking snuff.

The idea of what we walked in on turns my stomach.

The call bell flashes overhead and we're told to prepare for landing. Zoe sleeps fitfully on the stretcher, battling demons that will stay with her for the rest of her life. If I can do one thing, it will be to bring the monsters who did this to justice.

Guardian justice.

It won't ease her pain, but maybe it'll bring her some degree of relief from the memories.

I take her hand in mine and hold it all the way through descent and landing. Her lids flutter open when the wheels bounce and the engine roars. She curls her fingers in mine, giving them a good, hard squeeze. It's good to see her strength returning.

"Where are we?" I barely hear her soft voice. When I don't immediately answer, she repeats herself. "Axel? Where are we?"

"Hey, welcome back to the land of the living, brat. How do you feel?"

What a fucked-up thing to ask.

"What's going on?" She lifts a hand, then stares at the IV in her arm with confusion.

"How much do you remember?"

"More than I want to, but how did I get here?" Her eyes pinch and she presses her lips into a thin line. "Where am I? Please, tell me."

I try giving her a reassuring smile, but the pain in her eyes tells me none of that is helpful. The plane rolls to a stop. Soon, we'll be outside. "I'll answer all your questions once we're off the plane."

"I thought it was a dream." Her voice is so soft, I lean forward to catch what she's trying to say.

"What?"

"You rescuing me." The corners of her mouth tilt up on the end of her breathy sigh. "I'm sorry to always be such a *pain in your ass*."

Those are pretty much the exact words I threw in her face last year.

"It's nothing, just doing my job." The words spill out of my mouth like a reflex before I have a chance to consider how they may sound.

"I can still be thankful, can't I? Or is that not allowed?" A shadow falls over her features, a sense of profound sadness and loss. "It's not like I asked you to save me. I didn't arrange for this to happen."

Holy shit. Talk about inserting my foot in my mouth.

"Hey, I never said you did. What happened is unconscionable and I'm happy to do my part. I'm really glad you're still here."

After everything she's been through, she's allowed to be a bit off, but that's an odd comment. Best to switch topics because I'm not really sure what we're talking about, and there's no way in hell I'm responding to what she said.

"Austin and your dad should be there when we land. They're worried about you." I hope to God they're outside waiting for us. The sooner I can dispense my duty and hand her into the waiting arms of her family, the better.

She's mine.

The thought comes unbidden, full of possessiveness and something I can't explain.

Seeing Zoe in such a helpless state stirs emotions I'm not prepared to handle. I tell myself this overprotectiveness is just me standing in for Austin. He'd feel what I'm feeling, which makes the odd stirring in my heart less scary.

"Were you?" The rasp in her voice stirs my anger. We saw no signs of choking, which means the hoarseness came from her screams.

"Was I what?" I cradle her hand in mine and lower my head. I nearly kiss the back of her hand but shift to place my forehead there instead.

"Were you worried about me? Or am I just a job?"

Well, shit. Her spunk, while not appreciated, is returning fast. If she's willing to pick a fight, she must be feeling tons better. I'm taking this as a good sign and not rising to the bait. The last thing she needs is the two of us arguing, especially considering the last time we saw each other she was climbing into my bed naked and trying to seduce me. I threw her out on her ass with a string of expletives.

I regret that now. She didn't deserve that. Not from me.

"You know the answer to that."

She flicks her eyes dismissively and tries to roll away from me. A low groan escapes her when her body refuses to cooperate. She gives up and stares at the bulkhead, frustration evident in the tiny lines of her face. It's the one thing they spared when they whipped her. Not a single cut mars the perfection of her angelic face.

"Everything hurts." Tears well in her eyes, but when her gaze returns to me, she stiffens her upper lip and curls in her lower lip to stop the trembling there. Poor Zoe, she tries to be so brave, but I see through her tough exterior. "I must look horrible."

She's unraveling.

"Doc Summers and Doc Martin stitched up the worst of the cuts. There were quite a few, um—lacerations." My tongue trips over itself explaining her injuries. "And you don't look that bad, considering..." I try to keep things light. Positive.

"Is that what we're calling it? A *few* lacerations? I don't feel *good*." Her eyes close and she pulls her hand out of my grip. "I feel like death warmed over. I thought I was dead, but I guess I'm not that lucky."

"You're here. Nothing's broken. You need a bath..." I make a show of fanning my hand in front of my face. She doesn't pick up on my humor. Her words chill me, although I recognize them for what they are. Survivor guilt is a real thing and difficult to overcome.

"Sorry, they let me shower before trying to whip me to death. If I smell funky, it's not my fault. I was scared to death."

More words about death. We need to move off that train of thought.

"I was just trying to lighten the mood. You're pretty when you smile."

"But not pretty enough for you. How about *you* stop following me around like a lost puppy. I'm alive and evidently stitched up. You can walk away knowing you did your duty. I don't need you hovering over me. Go away." She rips her hand out of mine and sniffles a sob.

Ouch.

Why is she lashing out at me? When I try to take her hand back, to provide some reassurance, she flicks at me and draws away.

"Hey, how're you doing?" Skye interrupts and presses the back of her hand to Zoe's temple. "I'm Dr. Summers, but you can call me Skye." Skye's attention shifts to me for half a second before returning to Zoe. "You lost a lot of blood and are severely dehydrated. We have an IV running along with antibiotics and pain medicine. You've been kept sedated during most of the flight. If you want, we can give you a little more sedation while we shift you to the ambulance and take you to the hospital."

"Do I have to go to a hospital?" Zoe's voice cracks. Her chapped lips break open and bleed anew.

"Yes. I'd like to get some x-rays, do a few more tests, and a more thorough exam." I remember what Skye said to Forest through the video feed. She wants to look for evidence of sexual trauma and what comes with that.

Fury coils within me as I think about everything those men took from Zoe.

"I don't like hospitals." Zoe's tone is soft, resigned, and helpless.

"You'll like this one. Private room. Private floor. Private medical staff. I assure you, we'll take excellent care of you. I need to ask a few questions about what they may have done." Skye gets straight to the point. "And we'll need to do a GYN exam."

Zoe's eyes close tight. "No need. They already did one. Shoved something up inside of me. Made me cramp and bleed, although I don't really feel it anymore."

"They placed an IUD." Skye doesn't pull punches. "We saw what they did at the house, but did anyone assault you?"

"I'd say they did, but you mean sexually." Zoe's snarky reply doesn't faze Skye. She takes it in stride and powers through.

"I do."

"Evidently, they didn't need me for *that*." Zoe's words come hard and fast.

Her anger is brewing. I see it as a good sign. She needs to work through her emotions if she's going to heal. Anger is simply the outermost layer.

Disgust and anger swirl inside of me. The depravity of those men— they need to be put in the ground.

120

"As far as you know, you weren't sexually assaulted?" Skye is persistent and there's no sugarcoating anything.

"As far as I know. It would've been preferable to what they did." Zoe's eyes latch onto mine. I'm not sure what look she sees on my face, except her expression screws up into distaste. She hurls her next comment at me. "What are you looking at? I'm not some broken doll."

"Never said you were." I hold up my hands and back away. "I think you're amazing and tough as shit. You're fucking incredible." I'm doing a shit job expressing myself.

"Then stop looking at me like that."

"Like what?" I feel nothing but profound respect. To survive what she did takes a mountain of strength.

"Never mind." With a huff, she turns away, dismissing me.

It's an odd feeling knowing one of our rescues. On our missions, there are no introductions. We keep our identities masked, use call signs, refrain from small talk. Our job involves one directive, secure the package and deliver them back to their families, or into the rehabilitation home Forest created to help rebuild lives, as safely as we possibly can.

Frankly, everything about this *is* different. Everything inside of me says Zoe is more than a simple mission, more than my best friend's little sister.

She's mine.

The air around us pops as the front door to the jet opens. The warm, dry air of Northern California rolls in. I don't want to walk away from Zoe, but Skye edges me out, and Zoe doesn't look like she cares to talk to me anymore.

Skye asks questions about that exam. I grab my gear and exit the plane. If Austin is here, I need to prepare him for the damage his sister endured.

The bright California sky is cloud-free. I hold a hand over my eyes and squint against the glare. Three vehicles wait for us: an ambulance with its back doors open is ready to receive its patient, and two dark SUVs. The back door of the lead car opens and Austin climbs out. His steely gaze latches on to me and I give a tiny nod.

In that small gesture, we communicate several things. I have his sister. She's safe, but damaged.

The other door of the SUV opens, and Mr. Lancaster gets out. Dressed in his signature dark suit, he's one of San Francisco's leading personal injury lawyers. He makes money hand over fist, millions a year, but his net worth means nothing compared to the massive man who exits the other car.

I suck in a breath and stand a little taller. I know Forest Summers, probably better than I'd like. We, Alpha and Bravo teams, failed to keep him safe during that disaster in Manila. We rescued over a score of young women who'd been pressed into sexual slavery but lost him to a monster. It took two months before we freed him.

Forest strides toward me, long legs devouring the ground. He extends his massive hand and swallows mine in his grip. I'm a big guy, well over six feet tall, but Forest is massive. He towers over me.

"How is she?" His deep rumble is felt more than heard.

"Alive. Traumatized." That about sums it up. She's angry at me, which pisses me off. Let's be real here; I should be her fucking hero. But it's not about me. Her anger is a good thing. If she's lashing out at me, she's working through things.

I'm more than happy to be her verbal punching bag.

While we exchange hellos, Austin and his dad approach. Forest shoves out his hand, shaking with Austin and then Mr. Lancaster.

"We can't thank you enough, Forest. Bringing my baby girl back to us safe and sound is more than I ever hoped for."

Maybe not as sound as he'd hope, but I keep my thoughts to myself. My job finished the moment we pulled Zoe out of that building and put her on the plane. I'm surplus muscle now.

"Mr. Lancaster, are you prepared for the state she'll be in?" Forest broadens his stance and clasps his hands behind his back. His expression turns serious. "In these kinds of situations, I generally advise clients to say as little as possible. The most innocuous comment can set a victim off. Hold her hand. Give her a kiss, but don't crowd her. Try not to touch her too much. Physical touch may be a trigger. Don't comment on her physical state. We know it's bad. Victims are often very sensitive about how others perceive them after the fact. There are many triggers we don't yet know about."

Well shit if that's not true. I set one off during the flight and I'm pretty sure Zoe and I were dancing around another trigger during that landing.

"How's she doing, son?" Mr. Lancaster acknowledges what Forest says, then turns to me.

"She's awake and talking to the doctor. They want to take her to the hospital, where they can do more thorough exams."

"Did they..." Austin's face turns beet red as fury runs through him.

I get it. I totally get it.

"They forced all the girls to undergo a gynecologic exam, but we're fairly certain there was no sexual assault. Skye, um, Dr. Summers, is talking to Zoe about it now."

Actually, none of it makes sense to me. Why perform a GYN exam, check for STDs, insert an IUD, if they were only going to use the girls to make snuff films? Seems like a lot of bother for no reason. Although...

Austin takes a deep breath. "That should make me feel better, but is it true? Did they try to kill her?"

123

No doubt, Forest briefed Austin and his dad while we were in the air.

"They nearly succeeded." I tell Austin and his dad what we found, about the dead girls and the CPR I performed on Zoe. Their expressions darken and I'm glad I went with the short version. Austin will get me alone later. He won't be able to rest until he knows everything I do.

Our conversation ends when Ryker exits the aircraft carrying one end of a stretcher. The ambulance crew moves into action, coming to stand at the base of the stairs with their stretcher on wheels. Ryker moves deliberately, trying not to jar Zoe. Tia holds the other end of the stretcher.

Although it looks ungainly, it's clear they've done this dozens of times.

Rather than move Zoe off the folding stretcher, they simply place her on top of the one from the ambulance.

Forest Summers clears his throat. "You should go to her. It'll make it easier knowing she's supported."

Austin and his dad leave us to reunite with Zoe. I give them space, knowing this is a family moment.

"How long have you known her?" I jump at Forest's deep voice.

"Since she was four or five."

"That's a long time."

"I suppose. It feels as if I've known her my entire life."

He rocks back on his heels. "Your team landed half an hour ago. They're back at base unpacking their gear. You'll join me for the debrief." I take note of how he doesn't ask. I'm being *told* what I'm to do. Forest rarely involves himself on a personal level.

Something's brewing.

"Yes, sir." I should leave it at that, but curiosity gets the better of me. "Is this the first snuff operation you've brought down?"

"Sadly no, but the other one wasn't like this. It was a fight ring operation with boys. Give me your impressions with this one. Anything stand out?"

I'm used to debriefing CJ, and very rarely his boss, Sam, who runs the Guardian HRS program. I've never had a conversation with the boss of it all. Forest Summers is quite the legend among the teams and he's talking to me as if it's an everyday thing. It's hard not to let that get to me.

"Actually, something is bothering me."

"What's that?"

"I don't understand the snuff operation, especially since they never raped any of the girls."

"Do we know they didn't?"

"Zoe says she wasn't raped. I assume that goes for the other girls."

"Of course, and I think you're right. We'll need it confirmed though." His icy gaze doesn't leave Zoe from the moment Ryker and Tia unload her from the plane, to the reunion with her family on the tarmac, and through loading her into the ambulance. "Unfortunately, she's the only one who can answer that, and those questions will be—delicate."

I don't envy the poor fucker who debriefs Zoe. What a tough job. Hopefully, Mitzy will recover something of it from the phones and tablet we recovered. I'm certain at least one of those assholes took a few pictures they shouldn't have.

FOURTEEN

Zoe

I HURT.

Everywhere.

From my hair to my toes, every cell in my body screams in agony. My skin's been sliced and diced. My body used as a punching bag. Everything stings, burns, or throbs, and there's an odd pulling and tugging thing going on every time I move.

The doc says it's the stitches.

My muscles ache, but not in a good way. They've been pulverized. The fibers of my tendons and ligaments are torn from being stretched too far. I'm surprised my shoulders aren't dislocated from the way they strung me up like a sack of meat.

On a plus note—no broken bones.

It's a goddamn miracle.

My attitude is in the shitter. It's coming out in my language.

Focus on the positive, Zoe.

Those are words my father says when I let defeat overwhelm me.

He's big on the power of positive thinking. I'm big on the fact I'm alive. Not that I feel good about it. How can I when I'm the only one who survived?

Not *everything* hurts. My hair doesn't hurt.

In fact, when Axel ran his hands through it, the constant throbbing of cut skin, sore muscles, and torn ligaments receded. His hands felt good; tender, sweet, and soothing. When he touched me, all my pain melted away.

I think that's because I'm a silly girl who's still foolishly in love with a man who can't stand the sight of me.

The pain returns a thousand-fold, leaving me to grit my teeth and brace against each agonizing breath. My ribs hurt. Tiny knives stab into my lungs with each excruciating breath.

My father may be on to something about that positive thought thing. The moment I stop thinking about Axel, my pain increases.

My silly schoolgirl crush on him is stupid. I thought I was over him. Evidently, I'm not.

To my dismay, my feelings regarding him are now magnified to inhuman proportions due to the fact he rescued me.

Hello hero-worship.

He saved me and a part of me will always think he did so for reasons that have nothing to do with his job. My deepest desire is for him to see me as a woman rather than the little brat he grew up with. I'm not a kid anymore, and I wish he would take a moment to really look at me. If he did, he'd see what I already know.

We belong together.

But that's something only a total nut-job would believe. Especially after I tried to seduce him last year. I thought if I crawled into bed with him, gave him my body, that he would see we were right for each other. If we had sex, he would see me as the woman I am rather than the annoying pest who bothered him.

The sobering truth is I mean nothing to him, and after what he saw, I'll forever be soiled in his eyes with no hope for anything more.

He rescued me, not because he's my hero coming in to save the day, but because my rescue had been assigned to him and his team. That's all I am to him.

A job.

This is a truth I need to accept. In addition to that, he'll only ever see me as damaged goods. Life sucks.

As if to prove my point, and contribute further to my sense of self-loathing, he doesn't come over to see if I'm okay. Instead, he disappears inside a black SUV without a backward glance as I'm wheeled to the waiting ambulance.

Well, good, fucking riddance, Axel. I hope I never see you again too.

I may be emotionally infatuated—he's been the love of my life since the very first day he walked me to kindergarten—but that doesn't mean I can't move on. I must, and I will.

We'll call it a temporary setback. All these thoughts mean nothing. His was the first friendly face I saw after nearly dying. It's no wonder I'm fantasizing about him again.

What a way to unravel a year's worth of trying to hate him? It took the better half of last year to bury my feelings. He unraveled all my good work in seconds.

The universe is definitely playing one hell of a sick joke. The one man who couldn't care less if I exist is the one who saved me. It's fucking hilarious, and I would laugh, if I didn't think it would hurt so much.

It's not fair.

Fat, weak, tears leak from my eyes. I want to walk, preserve some measure of my nonexistent dignity, but Skye says I'll only pull out the stitches again. I didn't realize there had been a first time.

I don't like being this weak and helpless.

"Zoe…" My brother's soft tenor floats to my ears.

"Austin?" I blink to clear the tears. I'm trying so hard to be strong, but seeing Austin releases the floodgates. I fall apart and turn into a blubbering mess, but I've never had to be strong for Austin. I never had to prove anything to him.

When he takes my hand in his, it becomes too much. Tears blind me and my sobbing makes everything hurt even more.

"Hey, baby girl." My father moves to the other side of the stretcher.

"Dad?" I can't believe they're both here.

"It's good to see you." My stoic father chokes up. It's the first time I've seen him cry.

"I'm okay, Dad. Or, I will be." He needs to know I'll be okay. I'm not, and I won't ever be *okay*, but he doesn't need to know that. "It's so good to see you."

"It's good to see you. I thought we lost you."

I thought I was dead, so we're on the same page about that.

He takes my hand in his and presses it to his cheek. It's wet. His tears are real, and all I can think about is how frightening that is for me.

If I'd died, that would've been the end for me.

I wouldn't be in any more pain, but Austin and Dad would live with their loss for the rest of their lives. Unlike Axel, I know they would miss me terribly. Axel would probably breathe a sigh of relief.

"Are you okay?"

I give a slight nod.

"I was so scared. When your friends called and said… Well, it's been a living nightmare not knowing where you were, if you were okay, if you were…"

"Dad, I'm happy to be home." I'm so not okay and I'm still far from home.

Anger wells up inside of me and I bite my tongue. He's been living a nightmare? I'm the one who was kidnapped, stripped, and locked in a dark shipping container for days on end. I'm the one who was forced to watch the other girls die as they were murdered for sport in front of me. I endured all of that.

Me.

All the while knowing it was only a matter of time before my turn came.

I lived the nightmare. I was treated like an animal, my life debased to nothing more than a bid on a computer screen.

I lived that. Not him.

He may have worried about me. He may have hired the Guardians to find me. But he slept in his comfortable bed while I struggled to survive.

Skye mentioned something about a hospital and that's where I want to go. I love my father, but right now it's really hard to look at him. I don't want to say something I'll regret, but I'm a hair's breadth away from losing my ever-loving mind.

"You're indestructible." He smiles down on me, but there's a quiver in his lower lip I don't think he means for me to see. "You've always been my *little fighter*."

It's the first time he's ever called me that. I've been his *little girl* but never a fighter. I don't deserve it, but why not?

Why can't I be a fighter?

If I knew how to fight, I could've fought off the men who dragged me into the van. I could have escaped the men who imprisoned me in that house. Who locked me inside a shipping container for what felt like years but was probably just a few days.

I could have fought, if I'd known how.

If I knew how to defend myself, I wouldn't have been a helpless idiot. I wouldn't have walked blindly into what should have been my death.

Maybe I could've saved the others. It's a sobering thought. I wriggle on the stretcher. It's too damn hot and I'm forced to stare right at the sun. It's directly overhead in a sky of washed-out blue. I'd cup my hand over my eyes, but the thought of putting in the energy to lift my arm escapes me. I'm too fucking weak.

I hate that.

If my dad doesn't stop, I'm going to really lose it. A string. That's what's holding me together. A very frayed string that's unraveling as we speak.

"I'm going to be okay." He needs to know I'll get through this, even if I know I won't.

"Mr. Lancaster, we need to get her loaded into the ambulance. One of you can join us, the other can meet us there."

Yes, the hospital where I'll undergo more degrading tests and exams. I pinch my eyes shut, knowing it's necessary.

"Do you want to go?" Austin asks Dad if he wants to join me.

Honestly, if I can't have Axel by my side, I want Austin. He'll see beyond the damage. My father only sees his baby girl broken beyond repair.

"You go, Son. I'll meet you there."

Thank fuck for that.

Skye joins us in the ambulance. The rest of her team stays behind.

"You must be Zoe's brother?"

"Name's Austin." My brother gives her a cheeky grin. He's a huge flirt, but I saw a ring on her finger. Austin won't be getting anywhere with Skye anytime soon.

"Well, I'm Skye. It's nice to meet you. It's helpful to have someone she knows with her. I'm glad you're here instead of her father."

"Why is that?" Austin sounds surprised. "What hospital are we going to?"

"Well, it's more a private facility. Forest set it up for those we're able to bring home. Once we're certain her injuries are taken care of, she'll be free to go home, but I want to offer an alternative."

"An alternative?" Austin's face screws up in confusion.

"Yes." Skye shifts in her seat and places her hand on my shoulder. "Zoe's been through a traumatic experience. No reason to mince words. It doesn't help to talk around this. She survived kidnapping and torture."

Well fuck, there's no mincing of words there.

I barely react, but Austin cringes. I was brutalized and nearly killed. Honestly, I'm glad she doesn't dance around the subject. It feels better to hit it straight on. It's not like we're trying to hide it like it's some dirty secret. I'm more grateful for that than I think I should be.

"We've found transitioning back into a person's old life, resuming normal activities too soon, often causes more problems. Most family members feel the opposite. They want to shelter and protect their loved ones. This makes sense on the surface, but we have years of experience and hundreds of success stories under our belts. I hope you'll believe me when I say we know what's best for your sister, and that may not be to take her home."

"Problems?" Austin grabs my hand again. "What kind of problems?"

"Zoe..." Her attention shifts back to me. "We offer everyone who comes to us the same thing, and I hope you'll accept."

"And what's that?" I hate how weak my voice sounds.

"A chance to rebuild and work through your trauma. Think of it as a temporary pause in life. We won't hide what you've endured. There are no euphemisms. You were kidnapped, tortured, and meant to die. They tried to murder you and nearly succeeded. We're here to help you to face what all of that means and to find healthy ways to heal, physically, mentally, and spiritually."

"You want Zoe to go where?" Austin doesn't sound convinced. "Won't she be better at home, surrounded by family?"

"Like I said. Most family feels the need to protect and shelter their loved ones. The problem is they only remind our rescues of the trauma they endured and turn them into lifelong victims."

"She is a victim, and she needs time to heal."

"Do that and she'll always be a victim. It'll scar her for life. Is that what you want for your sister?" Skye crosses her arms.

"That's not—"

"You won't intend for that to happen, but it will. I hope you don't mind me being blunt. We have a lot of experience with this kind of trauma and several intensive programs that will allow Zoe to work through her experiences in a healthy and positive way."

It's weird. I listen to them talk about me, as if I'm not here, and there's a sobering difference in the words they use. For Austin, I'm a victim. To Skye, the things I endured are *experiences*. I don't know why, but those sound more manageable. Like something I can deal with.

"How long are you talking about?" Austin lifts my hand and gently kisses the back of my knuckles.

"Six months up to a year. Sometimes longer. It really depends on the individual."

"You think I need this?" I've remained silent, soaking in her words. The idea of *going away* and *working through my shit* is unappealing. I want to get right back into the swing of things, but there's something about how she says it that makes me think I need to listen.

"What you've experienced changed everything about you. We're going to help you put all the pieces together. Heal your body, heal your mind, and give you the tools you need to feel safe again. You'll leave as a survivor, not as a helpless victim. You'll once again be in control of your life, rather than subject to the whims of the forces around you."

Helpless victim.

Shit, is she a fucking mind reader?

"Considering what happened, it would be helpful if you stayed at the Facility and work through our program."

Austin bows his head. His shoulders slump and his body shakes. I see the proof of everything Skye mentioned in the words he doesn't say. She's right. In his eyes, I'm a victim.

I always will be.

Unless I take control.

My dad wants me to be his *little fighter?* I don't know about little but I will take back my life. Whether I have to fight to do so is irrelevant. I won't let anyone look at me like I'm something less because of what happened to me.

"I don't want to be a victim. I want to be a survivor."

135

"And what about us? What about Dad?" Austin asks the questions, but not to dissuade me. He's always been smart about things, and protective of me. I think he knows I need this.

"You tell him I'm strong, that I'm a survivor." I sniff as tears fill my eyes. I'm so fucking weepy. The words I'm telling him are lies. Given the option of working Skye's program or living with the look in Austin's eyes every time he sees me, I'd rather fall apart amongst strangers.

"Our program is open for family visitation." Skye's tone is low and soothing. She really believes what she's saying. "We're not taking her from you. We're simply giving her an environment where she can heal. When she's ready, reentering her life will be seamless. There is support for you as well. It's an inclusive program."

"And what about my classes?" I can't flunk out of my sophomore year. That's a failure I can't bear. If I can't complete the year, it means my kidnappers win. I can't let them take that from me.

"We'll make necessary arrangements with your professors for online completion of your last semester. Of course, you're free to decline."

"Do I have to make up my mind now?"

"Of course not. First order of business is to make sure you recover physically. Some of the cuts are quite deep. The risk of infection is very high, given the condition we found you in. There will be physical therapy…"

Austin smiles at me. "Whatever you want, little Z. We'll back you up. I guess just send the bill to our father. He'll pay whatever it takes." His attention shifts to Skye.

"Actually, there's no fee. We offer this to everyone we rescue free of charge. We'll talk more about it later and I'll tell you our story."

"Our story?" My brows pinch together. "What does that mean?"

"Only that you're not the only person to survive tragedy. Remember, there is always light in darkness. It's up to you to find it, but it's there. My brother and I are survivors. We know what you're going through. We'll be there to guide you, but the work will be yours. I think you'll discover you're much stronger than you ever realized."

"I don't feel strong right now. I feel like it's my fault this happened to me."

"And that is one of the first things we'll work on."

"What's that?"

"The voice inside your head that tells you lies. You never asked for this to happen to you. None of it is your fault."

"I wish I believed you."

"In time you will, but you can decide later. We'll tell you more about it when you're feeling better."

"I don't think I'll ever feel better."

"We'll work on that as well."

"You keep saying 'we.' Who are you talking about?"

"Me and Forest." She leans back and uncrosses her arms. "He's an interesting character. I think you'll enjoy working with him. It might be a few days before he checks in on you. He's a little busy right now."

"If you say so. All I want is to sleep forever."

"No, you don't. There's too much living to do. Trust me, Miss Zoe Lancaster, your life is just beginning, and it's going to be amazing. I promise."

"I wish I felt as confident about that as you."

"Well, that's why you have me, and Forest—and the others."

I want to believe Skye, but the moment I close my eyes, suffocating darkness pulls me under, and the screams of dying girls fill my ears.

FIFTEEN

Zoe

It takes more than five weeks before I leave the hospital. Skye wants to keep me longer. There are complications with the long gash across my belly. Infection set in and, evidently, I spent a few days out of my mind while they pumped me full of antibiotics and powerful sedatives.

My dreams were fevered dreams. Dreams of Axel standing over me. His lips press into a grim line, but love and devotion shine in his eyes. In one of my dreams, he leans down to brush the hair off my forehead and plant a kiss there. Sometimes, I feel the imprint of his lips. I find myself touching my forehead more often than I want to admit.

It was probably Austin rather than Axel, or my dad. That makes much more sense, but my fevered brain creates the fantasies it wants, and I selfishly keep them. Even knowing they can't possibly be real.

When I stop to sit and think about it, my mind needs the escape, a vacation as it is from the real world. It manufactures dreams of a hopeless love to protect me from the darker things lurking in the fringes of my mind. They're terrible, monstrous things. Things that trigger me if I let them.

I have triggers now.

That's new.

It's one of the things I work to control. I'm—*mostly* successful, but sometimes the darkness isn't something I can push away. It consumes me and drowns me in screams and pain and flashes of memory so real it feels as if I'm there, reliving everything over again.

The fear and stink of unwashed flesh overwhelms me. The lethargy that comes with severe dehydration fills my limbs and makes it impossible to get out of bed.

I hallucinate about drowning in a bucket and of being suffocated in a plastic bag. Knives slash and cut, disemboweling me as my life bleeds onto the floor. All the while, cameras record everything, sending my suffering to nameless men who cheer me toward death.

Each and every time, Axel swoops in and saves me. Then he turns his back and walks away.

Frankly, the hallucinations about Axel are tiresome.

I'm so over him.

As for my mind? Maybe it needs to go a little crazy before coming to terms with what happened.

I don't regret the fantasies about Axel.

It takes another two weeks before Skye stops fussing over me. My nightmares relent a little bit. The flashbacks become more removed. I learn to breathe easier and stop being so jumpy.

Three more weeks pass before Skye releases me from physical therapy.

I don't go home. Dad's not happy about it, but Austin understands.

I enter the Facility as a new resident. The place has no name, or rather that is its name, the Facility. It's rather generic and uninspiring, which is funny.

Although after several weeks, I kind of get it.

No longer a newcomer, the Facility is my refuge. Its residents are my new friends. Sometimes, I have to stop and pinch myself. My kidnapping doesn't seem real. It feels like it happened to another person.

Other times, it's entirely too real. Too close.

We're all survivors of the unimaginable. Each one of us comes with a story, but none of us are defined by it.

That's what they teach us.

It's not about coping but taking control. Control the memories. Control our obsessive thoughts. Control the present. Control our future. We're empowered to take back power over our lives. Rather than being defined by why happened, we control how we want to proceed.

We're in *transition*—that's what they call it—a place between one life and the next.

The Facility is not a home, not quite a place to heal. There's much more going on. It's a tool to help us rebuild.

"You coming, Z?" Moira gestures for me to join her and the others. We finished Group and are supposed to head to the mats for a little physical therapy.

That's another euphemism around here.

Physical therapy.

We're not talking about the kind of physical therapy with rubber bands and exercise machines. PT here lasts hours and has only one goal in mind. Complete and utter physical exhaustion.

As for 'Z,' I left my name behind at the hospital. We all get to pick new names on our first day. I chose to shorten mine rather than get rid of it entirely.

I like Z. It reminds me of the warrior princess, Zena. I think it's actually spelled Xena, but I prefer Z. Since I get to choose, Z it is. I like my real name. Someday, I might feel comfortable wearing it again.

"I'll be with you in a second," I call out to Moira as she rushes to gather her things. "Austin's visiting today."

"Oh, Austin…" Moira places the back of her hand to her forehead, tips her head back, and swoons. "Mr. McYummy."

"Ugh gross. That's *my brother* you're talking about."

"Yes, tall, dark, and oh so yummy." Her smile brightens. "He's lickable."

"Eww! There's nothing lickable about Austin. That's disgusting."

"Only to you." She laughs hard, robustly, and full of life.

It's something I'll never get used to. Frankly, I don't get what the other girls see in Austin. To me, he's simply Austin. There's nothing special about him. According to Moira and the other girls—heck even some of the boys—he's swoon-worthy. I want to gag.

Moira makes a crude gesture to show what she wants to lick.

"Ick, I'm never getting that visual out of my head." I shudder.

"And yet it's firmly stuck in mine. Tell your brother, I say hi." With that, Moira trots out of the room.

The Facility sprawls across a couple hundred acres along the Pacific Coast Highway. Most of the buildings cluster at the north entrance. Our dining facilities and classrooms are located there, as well as the visiting area. It's amazing, like *more* than amazing. It's a great place to heal.

Visitors aren't allowed inside the Facility proper. As for the rest of the grounds?

They're unique.

Perched near the edge of hundred-foot cliffs that plunge down to a rocky beach, the Facility overlooks the Pacific Ocean. The land provides ample opportunities for us to practice our growing skillset.

When Skye told me I would learn how to move past my trauma, I didn't understand. I didn't believe.

Technically, we're not moving on. We're doing quite the opposite. My program is nothing like Moira's, or Peter's, or even little Zara's. Some things are the same, like Group, which just ended, and sparring practice, which I love. Talk about confidence building. I might come out of this a warrior princess. I'm learning all kinds of kick-ass moves.

Moira heads to the courtyard now. The weather is mild enough that most of our training takes place outside. I hate to miss the opening stretches and feel a little guilty because I'll be rushing Austin through his visit.

With that thought in mind, I race to the visitor entrance. Austin kicks back in a chaise lounge while my father anxiously paces back and forth. He stops the moment I enter, although his back is to me. It's almost like he senses me, which is weird.

Dad spins around and turns his gray eyes on me. Austin has the same slate-gray eyes. They're striking and maybe I see a little of what Moira's talking about. Austin is hot, and my father is what I'd call an attractive, older man. That's as far as I take it, however.

Unlike the two of them, I have mother's eyes, a brilliant green that practically glows. My dad says she was outrageously beautiful. He's a little biased, but from the few pictures we have of her, I'm inclined to agree.

"Zoe!" My father holds out his arms, spreading them wide as I race into his embrace.

"I didn't know you were coming." It's the first time I've seen him in months.

I knew he *would* come eventually, but not this quickly. I bury myself in his arms and take a long, hard sniff of coming home. He smells of coffee and chocolate, two of the most amazing scents in all the world. "I've missed you."

The rehabilitation program at the Facility consists of two parts of a whole, at least for those who will be returning to lives with their loved ones. Not all the residents here have that luxury, which is why visitation is restricted to the visitor center.

Moira has nobody who will visit her. She's a runaway and alone in the world. About a third of the residents are preteens, or teens, who've been rescued out of abusive foster homes. The rest are, like me, abductees freed by the Guardians. Our stories are as varied as they are the same. Some tragedy resulted in an abduction, repeated rape generally followed for most, and some degree of physical torture and mental degradation was added into the mix.

We're the land of misfit kids, fucked-up children and young adults. We range in age from Zara, at the tender age of eight, to Moira, who's a few years older than me. I guess sex traffickers prefer young blood because there's no one over the age of twenty-two.

As for Moira, she lived on the streets from twelve until she was trafficked at sixteen. She spent five years in sexual servitude before one of Forest's Guardians rescued her.

We're all traumatized misfits finding a new way in life.

However, unlike most of my new friends, I have a loving family waiting for me on the outside—which is where the other half of the Facility's work comes in. As much as I'm involved in rehabilitating my life, Austin and my father receive intensive therapy as well. I haven't seen my father since the hospital.

"It's so good to see you." I cling to my dad, unwilling to let him go.

Austin coughs into his fist behind us. "Don't forget about me. It's been a couple weeks since you've seen me."

"Has it?" Funny, it feels like he visited yesterday.

"Tell me everything." As much as I'd like to say that's my line, it's not.

I repeat back the carefully scripted lines we're allowed to share. I ask about their lives first. We do an obligatory amount of small talk. Then they ask me not *how* I'm doing, but rather to share some small part of my day.

We sit together in a corner, our visit overseen by the ever-vigilant staff looking for activation of my triggers, and share as much as we can. I learn about my father's latest client and the Porsche he bought. Austin tells me about studying for the California Bar Exam. He's following in Dad's footsteps.

When it's my turn, I share the most interesting part of my day.

"Hey, Austin, do you remember Moira?"

"Who?" His brows pinch together, but he can't hide his interest.

"You know, blonde, bubbly, and gorgeous."

"Um, not really."

"Oh please, she practically jumped your bones when you were here last."

Visitors aren't technically allowed inside, but that doesn't mean curious friends don't sneak around and spy. Moira crashed our last visit, flustering the staff. I thought it was hilarious.

"Okay, why do I care about Moira?"

"Because she says you're *lickable.*"

Dad coughs, but he can't hide his grin. Austin gives away his embarrassment as a flush rises in his cheeks. His fair skin makes him fun to tease. My complexion is more like Mom's with an olive glow.

We spend the next half hour following our scripted lines, sharing as much as we can while dancing around the things we're not supposed to discuss.

Eventually, my father's gaze lifts to the single clock in the room. It measures down our allotted time, which we ignore. I'm actually having fun, and almost feel *normal* around them.

At least until my father's eyes pinch with pain. It changes everything. Our *minder*, the invisible person monitoring our interactions, notices, but before she, or he, can come out and end our meeting, I stand and glance back at the door.

I don't want my dad to know I saw his pain, or the way he looked at me as if I was some broken doll slowly getting patched together again. My fingers curl as I fiddle with the seams of my loose-fitting pants.

"It's been great seeing you, but I'm late for my next session." I don't tell them what my next session is. It would traumatize my father.

Austin gets it. He noticed the change about a breath or two behind me. Movement at the door and our *minder* is there to gently end our session.

"I love you both so much." I kiss my dad and hug Austin.

"When do you think we can see you again?" Austin gives me a ten-second hug. He misses me.

"Soon."

We say our goodbyes as the *minder* ushers them out. I spin around, ready to race to practice, when Austin calls out. "Hey, Z! I wanted to tell you—"

Whatever it is he wants to say will have to wait. The door slams shut behind me as I head to my favorite part of the day.

It's time to get the shit kicked out of me.

When I approach the training center, class is already in full swing. We spend our afternoons here, where we learn how to become survivors instead of victims. Today is Wednesday, which means my favorite instructor is here.

Towering above the common man, Forest Summers is nothing short of massive. More than massive actually, he's tree-trunk huge and fierce. God, the man can make my blood run cold with his icy glare. But at the flick of a switch, his gaze softens, the corners of his mouth turn up, and we all laugh hysterically at nothing. Glacial cold one minute, and a gooey mess the next, he's a paradox that inspires me.

We know his story and we know his success.

We know how he was once small like us, powerless against the monsters who tried to ruin his life. We learned how he and his sister, Skye, my doctor, overcame adversity and built a safe place for victims to shed that terrible label and become powerful, confident survivors.

I aspire to be like them.

One day, I will be.

For now, I'm learning.

Moira stands with Forest. Looks like it's review day. Since I missed warmup and stretching, I stay to the back and stretch while focusing on Forest's instruction. There are twelve of us total in this group; ten girls and two boys. Some days, Skye comes along to prove to us that we can do this no matter our size.

My first day, she and Forest provided a demonstration. I still hear Skye's crystal clear voice ringing out across the mats. *"We all need to know self-defense."* Forest stood behind her, hands clasped behind his back. *"It brings a sense of safety, confidence, and achievement."* I didn't believe her, but then I was new. This demonstration was my first insight into how the Facility would help me.

"Do you think a woman my size stands a chance against a man like Forest?" I

147

shook my head, vigorously, while everyone else grinned. I thought they were smoking something, or were brainwashed, at least until Forest attacked Skye.

I don't know what she did, although I'm learning some of the moves, but she's a tiny thing, shorter than me, and she brought Forest to his knees.

After Forest could breathe again, he explained how we were all going to become proficient in Krav Maga, a tactical defense system, and the most effective form of self-defense in the world. I thought they faked the whole thing. Their little demonstration irritated me, at least until Forest called me onto the mat. Over the next two hours, he taught me the basics. Simple moves he made me repeat over and over until I was sick of it. Then he came at me, surprising me. I reacted instinctually, using the moves he drilled into me over the past two hours.

I didn't take him down.

I've yet to really take him out, but I got in one hammer strike. For the rest of the day, I floated on cloud nine because if Skye could do it, I could too. For the first time, in a very long time, I saw a future I controlled. That's the real power of the Facility. They're teaching us how to stay in control.

Which is why this remains my favorite time of day. I throw myself into practice with all my heart, scraping the last dregs of my strength until I collapse into dreamless sleep afterward.

I have a pretty good feeling they're well aware of the dreamless sleep byproduct of the intense physical training. I had nightmares when I first arrived. Now, I'm too tired to dream.

SIXTEEN

Axel

THE TWO MONTHS SINCE I LAST LAID EYES ON ZOE LANCASTER FEEL
like an eternity. My thoughts constantly turn to her and linger.

Does she remember my visits to the hospital? Would she even care?

All the long nights I stood beside her, held her hand, and prayed the
infection didn't take her life, are precious to me. If I lost her to
something like that, after rescuing her from hell, I wouldn't
survive it.

She's on my mind, obsessively so.

I find myself thinking about her at the oddest times. Most of those
thoughts are simple things. But my dreams?

Fuck if my dreams don't turn more X-rated by the day, and my
mornings are filled with unfulfilling orgasms as I rub one out in the
shower with thoughts of her swirling in my mind.

This is new, but not unwelcome. I never thought of her like this, but
she's become all consuming. The need to make her mine keeps me
hard most of the day.

Left to myself, I never would have left her side, but I don't get to make those choices. Forest took me away from Zoe, sending Alpha team on one mission after the next in search of those missing girls.

We scoured cesspit after cesspit of sex and drug traffickers. Infiltrated what cartels we could and came home empty-handed every damn time. Unfazed, and fiercely determined, Mitzy would find some other lead and we'd head out again.

And again—fruitlessly so.

She's frustrated, as we all are, and practically pulled every rainbow-colored hair out of her head. In fact, the last time I saw her, half of her pixie colored hair had been shaved off. It looks cute on her. I don't think I'd say that about any other woman, and I'll never mention it to Mitzy, but it's the truth.

As for hair?

Zoe's long mane practically glows beneath the California sunshine. It bounces with each of her delicate steps, free and full. I watch from the shadows, growing harder with each passing moment as she stands at the back of her group and stretches.

Her face is a mask of concentration as she watches the mat. Mine is more one of discomfort as I make a slight adjustment of the athletic cup, which grows more uncomfortable by the second.

I've never been aroused by her before. Now, she's all I can think about. Specifically, fucking her and making her mine.

Mine.

It's on a nonstop loop in my head.

"You okay?" Griff glances over at me where I shift from foot to foot. No matter my stance, there's no escaping the raging hard-on trapped behind the plastic athletic cup.

"I'm fine."

"You don't look fine. You look like you want to bite someone's head off."

"I'm good." I'm frustrated, which is making me more and more irritated. The thoughts in my head are very inappropriate.

"If you say so." He doesn't look convinced.

Our entire team is here. It's a part of our job. Once a month, we put pressure on the residents—those who are ready—testing what they've learned. Showing them their success when appropriate. Honing in on their weaknesses as needed. Everything guides the next month's training, personalized to each individual's progress.

This is the first time Zoe will be subjected to Alpha team's unique form of testing, and she's been assigned to me. Or rather, I let my team know, in no uncertain terms, that she is mine.

With the rampant sexual thoughts swirling in my head, I'm regretting that choice. If all I can think about is fucking her, what's going to happen when I have to put my hands on her?

You'll fucking explode.

Damn straight, I'll explode. I reach to my crotch for another fruitless adjustment.

I thought my possessiveness was nothing other than a byproduct of Zoe's rescue, but the intervening months prove otherwise. I'm completely, and utterly, devoted to her. I think about her daily. How is she progressing? Is she healing? Does she think about me?

I need to know she's going to be okay. Until I'm confident of that, I'll stay by her side. Or at least as much as my job allows.

Frankly, I'm worried.

Forest doesn't believe in coddling people. He tests his little rescues daily and puts pressure on them to determine when they're ready to move to the next phase. I would argue against his methods, but his success rate is unprecedented.

Trust in the system. That's what he says when questioned.

This is where Alpha team comes in. We're a part of that system, a rather nasty part.

Griff stands beside me, bouncing on the balls of his feet. He stretches his neck side to side, limbering up and shaking out his hands.

"God, I hate this." The man who excels in brutal interrogation techniques is squeamish when it comes to hitting a woman. Frankly, it's funny as shit. The man has a tender spot.

"You know it's for the best." I try to reassure him, but all it does is remind me that soon enough, I'll not only be hitting Zoe, but doing far worse.

Maybe.

We have to see how she handles herself before moving on to the attack phase.

"A day of getting kicked in the nuts? There's nothing good about that," Griff grumbles beside me.

"Just make sure your cup is on straight." I give a huge grin. Last time, Griff forgot his athletic cup and spent the night icing his balls.

We hold nothing back. Forest says their attackers won't hold back, so why should we? I just hope Zoe's been paying attention in class, and reach down to make sure the boys are covered.

Decked out in full body armor and tactical gear, our job is singular in purpose. We're going to attack, and then abduct, whoever we can over the next week. We'll take them out as a group, and pick them off one by one, constantly testing their situational awareness and ability to escape.

Normally, I look forward to the week we spend at the Facility, but I'm itching to get out into the field and finish our mission.

Bravo team is out there now, chasing down yet another lead. I'm not sure why, but I feel like I owe it to Zoe to find those missing girls. If I can do that, maybe it'll help her heal. Right now, I'm worried. All our leads are dried up.

"You ready?" Griff gets the signal from one of the staff.

He pulls the tight black mask over his face. It's yet another tactic to make this both more realistic and yet not. We're nameless, faceless attackers meant to inspire fear and test the foundations of the tactical self-defense the residents are learning.

Zoe won't know it's me when I take her out. She's not supposed to know anything about me. Which sucks. I want her to know I'm here. That I'm thinking about her.

I want to sit with her and talk about how she's doing. Hell, I'd settle for taking her down to the rocky beach below for an afternoon of picnicking and soaking in the California sun.

"I'm ready." I pull down my mask. This is the worst part of our job, but necessary, and beneficial. If they can evade capture in a realistic abduction, they'll build the confidence to survive anything. I flick on the switch to the box at my larynx, which will disguise my voice.

Don't know what the fuck I was thinking when I asked to be assigned to Zoe, but she's mine for the week. My job is to stalk, abduct, and train. I hope she's far enough along, because I won't be gentle. If I set off one of her triggers, I'll hate myself forever. But this is essential to her recovery. I can't fail.

"There's our cue." Griff activates his vocal modulator. Even our distorted voices are a part of the process.

Forest finishes demonstrating the Hammer Fist strike, one of several key defensive moves, and gestures for us to move in. Griff and I set out, two towering men who inspire fear. We're big men, stacked with muscle, and in the best condition of our lives.

Dressed all in black, the students cringe as we march right through their ranks. We split apart and come to stand to either side of Forest.

On cue, Griff and I do an about-face, snapping our heels together at the end. Several of the girls flinch. There're twelve of them total; ten girls ranging in age from fourteen to twenty-two, and two scrawny preteen boys.

Each member of Alpha team is assigned to two targets. I'm not sure which one of the boys is mine, but I'll find out soon enough. Max, Knox, Liam, and Wolfe move in silently from the edges.

It's the very first test.

We direct the student's attention forward, while presenting a threat from behind. Max creeps in behind Zoe. I told the fucker to leave her to me, but he slowly moves in. I'd give a sharp jerk of my chin, but that would alert our students, and I won't do that.

Awareness of their surroundings, at all times, is lesson number one and the first test they'll all fail.

Forest stands tall, dwarfing both Griff and myself. We stand over six-foot, but look small next to the gentle giant.

"Listen up, class." Forest waits until all eyes are on him. "Today you'll be tested. My Guardians have offered their services to see how well you're learning your tactical defense moves. You've each been assigned to one of the men. They'll test you over the course of this week. They'll work with you, refine your skills, and test your ability to escape, evade, and survive. The kid gloves are off. You may pass on this if you need more time, but I wouldn't have you here now if I didn't believe in you. You're ready, whether you feel it or not. Our monitors will be watching, as always. You *are* safe, but this will be uncomfortable. It's meant to be as realistic as possible. Your triggers may activate. You may uncover new triggers you're not yet aware of, but this is why you're here." He raises his voice at the end, booming across the open courtyard. "What are you?"

"Survivors?" His class mumbles a weak response.

"Say it again. What are you?" The air vibrates with each powerful roar.

"Survivors." They sound more confident, but still unsure.

"What are you?" Forest shouts as he riles them up.

"Survivors!" One of the girls jumps to her feet. Her expression is wild and unhinged.

"What are you?" Forest continues the chant.

"Survivors!" All the kids jump to their feet, screaming out their fury.

These are helpless victims, traumatized beyond what any human should ever bear, but they're taking back their lives. It's so fucking profound the corners of my eyes might be a little moist, not that I'll ever admit that to anyone.

I scan them, taking each of them in. I take bets on who will crack first. Then my gaze lands on Zoe and her eyes, which widen with fear but shimmer with excitement. It's an odd dichotomy. I sense she's looking forward to this.

Despite what Forest says, and her enthusiasm, I feel he's moving too fast with her in particular.

Forest calls off two names. The girl who was the first to jump to her feet makes her way toward Griff. She's a pretty blonde. Most of the residents are attractive, young males and females. Unfortunately, that seems to be one of the requirements for abduction into the slave trade. Another girl rises. She's pretty too, with long, straight brown hair, and wide, innocent doe-eyes.

As for the rest of them, all their attention focuses forward waiting for Forest to call the next set of names.

Max gives the signal.

Max, Knox, Liam, and Wolfe rush in. They grab three girls and one of the boys. Before they have time to scream, my team has them face down, hands tied behind their backs. Two more breaths and they tackle four other kids and take them down amongst their screams. The blonde and brunette who were walking to the front cling to each other, shaking. Zoe stands stock-still, arms wrapped around her body. The last remaining kid is on his ass, trembling.

Forest blows an air horn. The men of Alpha team immediately release their hostages and bend down to cut the ties they placed on the first set.

"Your first lesson..." When Forest shouts, the air thunders. "Maintain situational awareness at all times. Those men have been here since I started talking, slowly moving in. They've been standing in full sunlight for three minutes and not one of you noticed them."

My teammates join us up front, forming a semicircle behind Forest.

"I said you would be tested. You failed the first test. Does anyone know what that test was?" His expression softens as he looks out at the dozen terrified survivors. "No one?" He rocks back on his feet. "Then I'll tell you. You thought you were safe. That nothing bad would happen to you here. You are complacent." He lifts a finger and points at them. "Today, you'll work on your tactical defense. Tomorrow, and over the next week, you'll be stalked and attacked as your situational awareness is tested. You'll either fight off your attacker and evade capture, or you'll fail. And what do we do with failure?"

I feel bad for them. Shock and awe tactics would not be my choice, but Forest says to trust his methods.

The blonde he called out first raises her hand.

"Yes, Moira?"

"If we fail, we learn what we did wrong, we correct, and practice so we can do better the next time."

"Correct." His gaze once again sweeps the kids. "Over the next week, each of you *will* fail. If you didn't, then we have nothing to teach you. Behind me are six of the most elite fighting men in the world. They're bigger than you. Stronger than you. Faster and smarter than you. They're highly trained in physical combat. You will lose, but failure here, in the Facility, means you'll learn and you won't make the same mistakes out there." He points vaguely outward. "Do you understand?"

The kids gulp. Their wide-eyes take my team in. We're a formidable force. Decked out all in black, with our faces covered, we epitomize their worst nightmare. Forest is either bat shit crazy or a fucking genius.

"Now." He pauses until their attention returns to him. "Who's willing to accept this challenge?"

I expect all of them to run. To my utter amazement, twelve hands raise high in the air.

Well, shit. I've never seen more courage in one place. It's daunting.

"Moira and Stacy, you're with Number Four. Z and Andrew, this man here, Number Three." They approach cautiously. While I watch Andrew and Zoe, Forest calls out the rest of the names. As for us, we are nameless, designated only by our team number.

Andrew is a kid about twelve, underdeveloped and scrawny. Zoe locks eyes with me and steps forward with her chin raised and shoulders rolled back. I extend my hand to Andrew, taking it lightly so as not to squeeze too hard.

His expression fills with awe and the tiny bump of his developing Adam's apple bounces as he gulps down a swallow. I guide him to the side and extend my hand for Zoe to shake.

Will she make her first fatal mistake?

Like Andrew, her hand lifts to take mine. I grab her and use her momentum to spin her around until she faces away from me. My left arm grips her waist holding her immobile against my chest. My right hand places a knife to her throat.

Andrew gasps.

Zoe reaches for my hand holding the blade and tries to get free. Only she's too weak and I'm far too strong for her to break my lock.

"First lesson." I keep my voice deep, not that I need to disguise it since we're all fitted with voice modulators. Some of these kids, like Zoe, are ones we've rescued. Forest needs us to be faceless strangers, not the heroes who saved them from something far worse than death. "I am not your friend." I take time to enunciate my words. This needs to sink in.

I release her and sheath my knife.

She clutches her throat and stumbles forward, breathing heavily.

I'm breathing a bit fast too, but not out of fear. Holding her against my body heats my blood and turns me on. My dick is not going to survive, not pinned beneath an athletic cup. I grit my teeth and try to ignore the raging hunger stirring in my loins.

Focus Axel!

Right. It looks like I'll be rubbing another one out later tonight.

Or two.

Probably three.

My arm's getting a workout with all the filthy fantasies running through my mind and Zoe stars as the leading role in all of them.

"Now, try again." My command cuts through the air, and she stares at me with spitfire blazing in her eyes.

"You, fucking bastard."

What a filthy mouth, little Zoe.

My erection grows and I resist the urge to adjust myself in front of her.

"Exactly. That's what I'd be doing if this were real. You'd be on your back while your attacker fucked you then slit your neck. So, try again." I snap the command and watch her stiffen in response.

My girl doesn't like anyone telling her what to do. I get it, but her stubbornness is her worst enemy right now. I need her to follow my lead and obey my commands. It's the only way to ensure her safety beyond these walls.

We're told to be rough on them, but goddamn, this is going to be hard. I don't let her answer. I'm not interested in what she has to say.

"Andrew, approach me again." I snap my fingers and point to Andrew. "Z, pay attention."

Andrew takes a few steps back. His brows draw tight in thought, but he doesn't move. I urge him on.

"I'm a stranger drawing you in with a handshake. I can either shake your hand and let you go, or I can trap you in like I did Z. What can you do to prevent that from happening?"

His mouth twists and his eyes tighten, but he's thinking it through. Today is a day of exercises. Repetition is the key, establishing patterns of movement and behavior until it becomes second nature to them.

"If your attacker is in close range…" I take his hand and draw him against my body like I did Zoe, spinning him around to face outward. "You don't have the momentum to throw a punch or to kick, but you do have your elbows." I hold him tight and look at Zoe to make sure she's watching. "Stabilize yourself. Firm up your core and your legs. Shift your weight forward and strike with your elbows." I show him what I mean, grabbing his arm to demonstrate where to dig in. "Your goal is to surprise me and get me to loosen my grip. As soon as I do, you run."

I release Andrew. His eyes widen and he nods as he sucks in his lower lip.

"Try again." I take a step back and extend my hand.

Andrew shakes my hand, knowing what'll come next, but I still surprise him with the speed with which I spin him around and pin him against me. He hesitates for a second, but then lashes out with

159

his elbow. He hits me weakly in the ribs. My grip tightens around his throat.

"Not hard enough. You have to fight like your life depends on it. Now, if your elbow doesn't work, what can you do?"

"Bend forward and jab again, but go for your face?" He's hesitant, but correct.

"Exactly." I'm proud of him. "Do that now."

He surprises me, bending sharply at the waist and jabs his elbow into my cheek. My hold relaxes and he spins out of my grip. Without any further coaching, he knees me in the groin. Hard. When I huff in pain—cup or no cup that shit hurts—he pushes me, takes two steps back, then turns on his feet and runs.

I take in a deep breath and turn to Zoe. My hand extends and I give a little flick of my fingers.

"Your turn."

SEVENTEEN

Zoe

MY HEART BEATS SO FAST IT'S READY TO EXPLODE. FROM THE moment Number Three, or whatever his name is, attacks me and puts a knife to my throat, my body doesn't stop trembling. I'm terrified, but I'm also a little pissed off. Enough anger stirs inside of me to keep me from flipping the fuck out.

He messed with my mind, shaking hands all normal-like with Andrew, then turning the tables on me. Of course, I fell for it. I'm too damn trusting, too naïve. Which is how I got kidnapped in the first place.

It's my fault I didn't take things seriously.

I *thought* I was safe walking alone until they grabbed me. I *thought* I could escape until they caged me. I *thought* I would be sold to some monster until they tried to kill me. Always, in the back of my head, I *thought* I would find a way out.

I never understood I lost control. I never fought back.

I'm so fucking stupid.

Number Three cocks his fingers, egging me on. The distortion of his voice weirds me out. Not being able to see his face terrifies me. There's no compassion, no humanity in him. Doesn't he know what we've all been through? Would it be that hard to give us a little bit of a break?

To be honest, I can use a little bit of handling with kid gloves.

"Come on, you can do it." His damn fingers bend again.

I wrap my arms around myself and hunch inward. With a shake of my head, I tell him I'm not ready.

"How's it going?" The deep rumble of Forest's voice sounds behind me. For as big as he is, how does he sneak up on people like that?

"I can't do this." I back up toward Forest, knowing he'll protect me.

"Nonsense. You're ready." He believes in me and broadcasts his faith with each word he says. If he believes in me, why can't I believe in myself? "There are only two reasons not to do something. Either you can't, or you won't. One's a limitation beyond your ability. The other is a choice you make. You can do this. Are you saying you won't? That you won't take control of your life?"

Fucking hell.

All I want is to crawl under a rock and go back to my previous life. I want to return to a time when I was oblivious to the existence of evil in the world. Back to when I felt safe like nothing bad could ever touch me.

"You're stronger than you know." The man in black takes a step back. The voice thing messes with my mind because it's at once familiar and entirely foreign. "Fear is your enemy. Conquer your fear and you can do anything. Now, take my hand."

He extends his hand and a sense of overwhelming familiarity washes through me. I'm not sure what it is, whether it's my faith in Forest or something else, but I trust this man.

I *know* this man.

"What do we call you? Number Three is a mouthful." I need to work up to this.

He scared the shit out of me when he yanked me to him and spun me around. The knife to my throat paralyzed me and nearly triggered me. The only reason I didn't head into a full-blown panic attack is because of the breathing and centering exercises I've learned over the past two months.

"You can call Lover boy here whatever you like." Forest huffs a laugh. "The numbers are merely for convenience."

"I get *why* the numbers, but it's clunky." I turn my attention to Forest.

"Just call me Three." The man's head cocks to the side.

If I didn't know better, I'd say there was a self-satisfied smirk beneath that hood.

"I'd like to call you something else." I mumble and am surprised when he laughs.

"Looks like you haven't lost your humor." He gives a shake of his head.

"Z, give it a go." Forest places his massive hand on my shoulder. "If it's too much for you, just let me know. We'll never put you in a situation where you're not safe, but I will push you out of your comfort zone. Give Three a chance."

A quick glance around the courtyard shows everyone is involved in some kind of defensive move. I see hammer and heel palm strikes everywhere. My friends escape from bear hugs and headlocks. I'm the only one standing around like a fool. Well, me and Andrew. My failure to fight affects Andrew's training.

"Okay, fine." I stamp my feet and fist my hands. "I'll try."

I do it for Andrew.

Three reaches out, as if to shake my hand, and I know what he's going to do. I plan for it, prepare for it, and yet I still find myself spinning and getting slammed up against his broad chest.

Instead of a knife, he holds his hand around my throat.

"Okay, Z. Think. How are you going to escape?"

"Elbows?"

"Yes." The voice modulator removes any emotion, but I sense his patience.

"To be honest, it feels funny." I'm petrified. Somehow, if I can talk my way out of this, I'll call it a win.

"There's nothing funny about someone attacking you. This is why we practice. Come on, you can do it."

I make a half-hearted effort to jab with my elbow. I don't even move the massive bulk of Three.

"Andrew, what is she doing wrong?"

"She's not strong enough."

"Correct, but what can she *do*?"

"Z," Andrew stands right in front of me, "bend at the waist like I did. It opens you up so you can get a little momentum going." He demonstrates, jabbing his elbows up and behind him in quick succession. "You could stomp on his foot too."

"Good. Exactly." Three lightens up the grip on my throat, but he still controls me.

I remember what Andrew did and follow along in slow motion. I bend forward at the waist. I'm acutely aware of how my ass presses against Three's groin. It's hard, the thing I'm pressing against, like an erection, but it's round rather than long. I realize he's wearing a cup. I don't know why I find that so funny, but it makes me giggle.

"Ticklish?" Three digs his fingers into my ribs.

I squirm because I'm intensely ticklish there. Fortunately, he releases me.

"Andrew, let's show her how it's done." Three's mechanical voice pops a little, almost as if he's laughing.

Andrew stretches out to shake Three's hand. He gets yanked off his feet and spun around. Three's arm wraps around Andrew's chest and his hand goes for the choke hold.

But Andrew violently flexes at the waist. He twists and jabs his elbow back. One. Two. He clocks Three in the jaw. Three's grip loosens. Andrew spins around and jabs upward with the palm of his hand right into the bottom of Three's jaw.

Three's eyes widen in shock and he stumbles back. Andrew pushes him, using the entire weight of his body to force Three to stumble backward. Then Andrew spins around and gets away.

"Come on, Z, if I can do it, you can too." Andrew bounces on the balls of his feet.

I stare at Three as he works his jaw.

"Excellent job, Andrew. Great use of force and momentum to get free. Now, Z, are you willing to take a chance?"

"Are you really going to stalk us over the next week?" I need more information about what to expect.

"Stalk and abduct." He rolls his neck, limbering up to strangle me —again.

"When?"

"Whenever I want." The cockiness in his tone is mildly annoying, but also kind of sexy.

I'm more concerned that I find it insanely attractive. Fantasies of him abducting me and squirreling me off to some dark, private place, spin through my mind. Feminists would totally eat me alive for the not so politically correct fantasies I want him to fulfill. I'm a little embarrassed by how *sexual* they are, but then I remember what I'm supposed to be doing. Fantasies have no place in this, especially sexual ones.

"Why whenever? Can't we sleep in peace?"

Three's chin bumps up toward Forest.

"For the first few days, you won't be attacked in your sleep." Forest places his hand on my shoulder. "But it's a possibility."

"Do you really think any of us will be abducted twice in a lifetime?"

"I wish I could say that it never happens. But, that's not why we do this." Forest blows out a long breath. There's something about his voice that settles me.

"Then why?"

"Situational awareness." Three answers instead of Forest. The calm, hypnotic cadence he uses when he speaks sends shivers down my spine. "Think back to your abduction. If you had been more aware of your surroundings, would you have been taken?"

I bite my lower lip and stare at the ground. I'll never forgive myself for being such a dumbass, wandering around by myself. It's one of the things they teach us here.

Never go out alone.

Never get separated.

Stay with the crowds. The inside of a crowd is best. The edges are red zones where you can get picked off.

Does Three know about my abduction? He must know something. Everyone here carries a story.

"I don't know." I shrug my shoulders. The thing is, that's what I think. Everything about my abduction is my fault. I'm the one responsible.

"And since your kidnapping, do you have repeated thoughts about what you could've done better?"

"All the time," I say.

Andrew moves up beside me. "Me too, like *all* the time. All the things I could've done differently."

I throw my arm around Andrew. He rarely opens up during our group sessions, but I know he was brutally taken and raped.

"You did nothing wrong." I try building him up, using the same words others use on me. They're easy to say. Much harder to believe.

"That's why we train, *here*, where it's safe. Where you can learn from your mistakes." Three takes a step toward us, then stops. "By the time you leave here, those thoughts won't haunt you because you'll know you can defend yourself. You'll know that you'll have done everything possible for it not to happen again. There are no guarantees in life, but the doubt you feel about yourself, the anger you may have toward what you did or didn't do, this will help you move past it."

"And you believe that?" I rub my arms as goosebumps pepper my skin. Everything he says feels like the truth. My problem is I don't believe him.

"I do. So, let's do our best to make sure if it ever does happen again, you're prepared to fight and defend yourself."

"Okay."

Forest tells us there will be doubts, and to trust in the system. I'm going to take a huge leap of faith and try my best to do just that.

"Hey there, beautiful, it's nice to meet you." Three extends his hand. It's so natural, I almost forget this is pretend.

I brace against getting yanked. I plant my feet wide apart, and keep my body weight on the balls of my feet like we've been taught. It does nothing to stop him from pulling me right off my center of gravity.

I fall forward.

He spins me around.

That damn hand of his wraps around my windpipe.

He's too big to fight and panic sets in. I clutch at his fingers, trying to pry them off my throat, then remember what it is I'm supposed to do.

I bend forward as much as I can, as fast as I can. My ass presses against his groin again, but I get my elbow to jab upward where it connects with his chin.

It's not enough, but he releases me.

"Excellent." He takes two steps back and holds out his hand. "Again."

I take his hand and we go again.

And again.

We practice the same move for what feels like forever. Three alternates between me and Andrew. After about ten minutes, I can't catch my breath. I suck in air, laboring to breathe as my lungs burn and my vision swims with tiny black dots. I've never been this winded before, but Three isn't breathing hard at all.

"Come here, Z, let's do it again." A demanding taskmaster, Three doesn't let up.

"Can't we take a break?" I huff out each word, sucking in air to fuel my oxygen-deprived body.

"Will your abductor take a break? Will he go easy on you because you need to catch your breath?"

"No."

"Then… Again." His command snaps through the space separating us and I can't help but jerk.

He takes my hand and I fight for my life.

An hour later, he calls our first break. Andrew and I fall limp to the ground, breathing hard, sweat dripping off our brows. We stare up at the washed-out California sky and at the sun that's nearly overhead.

"Wow." It's all Andrew says.

"Yeah. Wow." But my *Wow* is for a different reason.

After an hour of close physical contact, something unexpected happens.

I'm crushing hard for Three. It makes no sense, but I love how he's patient with us, yet fiercely demanding as he extracts our best. Even when we're so tired that we're stumbling on our feet, he doesn't let up.

And let's face it, the enemy will never let up.

As I heave for breath, my thoughts turn to the man who remains an enigma. No face. No name. I barely see his eyes.

They're blazing blue.

He's stacked. Beneath that tactical vest and black clothing, it's all hard muscle. And he knows how to move. All fluid grace, he moves all that sinew and muscle with ease. It's the most physical contact I've had with a man in a very long time.

Not a college kid groping in the dark, but a real man who knows how to move.

While Andrew and I catch our breath, Three heads over to hang with the other men on his team. Moira comes over and plops down beside me.

"Holy fuck, that's intense," she says. "I've never been this tired. We're going to be sore tomorrow."

"No shit."

"Tell me it's wrong, but those men are F. I. N. E. *Fine!*" Moira lets out a breathy sigh. "And don't judge, but I'm developing a fetish for getting choked. Four is delicious and yummy. I want to strip him down and practice a little close body contact with him if you know what I mean."

"Moira!" I give her hand a little slap while Andrew gags beside me.

"That's so gross, Moira." Andrew pushes to a sitting position and stares out at the six men huddled together on the far side of the courtyard. I can't help but think they're talking about us.

"Sorry, Andy, but they're all smoking hot. Speaking of..." She rolls over on her side and props her cheek on her hand. "How's yours? Is he tall, dark, and dreamy too?"

"He's beating the shit out of me, but he does have dreamy blue eyes."

"Well, they're all beating the shit out of us." She giggles again. "But are you feeling anything—well, you know? Tingling down there when he holds you, because me and Four..." She sighs. "Definite chemistry going on."

"No, you perv." I knock her hand out from under her cheek and she flops over to her back, giggling. "They're our instructors. You're not supposed to think of them like that."

"Well, I wanna be the teacher's pet, and all I can say is, if Four tries to abduct me, say late at night, and wants to do unseemly things to me, I won't fight him."

Moira is sexually precocious. She grew up on the streets selling her body at twelve, then was abducted and sold to a monster who lent out her services at sixteen. She was a sex slave for five years before being rescued during a raid somewhere in the Philippines. I think she said it was Manila or something.

Right now, I'm thinking about everything she says, only I project myself and Three into those naughty scenarios. I must be twisted in the head to think there's anything sexy about a man trying to kidnap me.

"You guys thirsty?" Andrew climbs to his feet and stares down at us. His attention keeps flicking over to our instructors.

I wonder what he sees when he looks at them. Does he see the monsters who kidnapped him, or does he see the future man he might one day become? I've never seen an ounce of self-confidence in the kid, except when he smacked Three in the jaw. After that, he got quiet and fought as if his life depended on it. Give him another ten years, maybe more, and he could easily stand beside the men in black.

"Yeah, water sounds good. I could use a little *refreshing*." Moira pushes off the ground and joins Andrew. "You coming, Z?"

"Me? I'm so exhausted; I think I'll just take a little catnap." Somehow, I have a feeling our day has only just begun.

My eyes close against the bright California sunlight.

Most days, the clouds roll off the Pacific and I spend hours staring at them, forming shapes in my mind, but today there's not a cloud in the sky. No deep blue overhead. It's all pale and washed out; a ghost of what it could be. At least there's the ever-present ocean breeze. It keeps the air fresh and smells of possibility.

Instead of blackness behind my lids, the sun shines through my eyelids turning everything a glowing red. I take a deep breath and go over what we've learned.

It's one move. One move out of what seems like a million ways for lecherous men to attack poor defenseless girls. I can't wait until I'm old and ugly. No one kidnaps grandmas.

171

Will I ever have kids? Or has this experience ruined that perfect life? My mind drifts to that, wondering about the chances of finding love after tragedy. The one thing I have going for me is that I wasn't raped. Most of the other girls here were. I think all the boys were too. It haunts their faces when they think no one's looking.

I feel really bad thinking those thoughts, but it's true. I'm fortunate in many ways; not getting raped and not getting murdered.

A shadow passes over me. Maybe a stray cloud wandering in from the ocean. But then a breath huffs out beside me. A mechanically altered sound. I cover my eyes and peek up through my lashes. Sure enough, it's Three.

"I didn't see you get anything to drink. You need to stay hydrated." He holds out a paper cup filled with water.

"If I take that, are you going to put me in a choke hold?"

"Not this time." He laughs.

I sit up and spin around to face him. "Will I ever be able to relax around you?"

"Someday, I hope you will."

"Tell me, how does someone get this job? Beating up on a bunch of broken misfits?"

"Is that how you see yourself? Broken?"

I notice how he doesn't answer my question.

"Sometimes. Other times, I feel perfectly normal, like it never happened."

"That's good to hear. Hopefully, you'll have more and more of those moments." He lifts the water toward me. "You really need to drink. You have a long afternoon ahead of you."

A long afternoon of physical abuse disguised as tactical defense training. Moira's right about one thing. We're all going to be sore in the morning.

I reach for the cup, but draw back. "Promise you won't attack me."

His head cants to the side and he stares at me through his mask. "And if I don't?"

"Then I'll assume the water's laced with poison, or some date rape drug, and smack it out of your hand."

"Good answer." He laughs, but then he brings the cup to his lips and takes a sip. "No date rape drugs. No poison, and it's break time, so no attacks. It's perfectly safe and well-earned."

"Not sure about the well-earned part." Truthfully, I'm parched. The only reason I didn't go with Andrew and Moira is because I'm more exhausted than thirsty.

"You don't give yourself enough credit, Z. You worked really hard today. I'm proud of you, and you worked through at least one triggering event. That's something to be proud of."

"You noticed?"

"I did."

"I didn't think anyone noticed."

"I notice everything about you." He tips the bottom of the paper cup, encouraging me to drink. "You'll probably hate me by the time this week ends, but it's for the best, and good for your healing in the long run. Just remember, I'm on your side." He reaches out and brushes a strand of my hair off my face.

The moment he touches me, something shifts. I don't know what to call it, but I trust him.

"Best for me?" I shake my head and gulp down the rest of the water. "I don't know. To be honest, it's overwhelming. We've practiced an hour with just that one hold, but there are hundreds of ways someone could attack me. I'll never be able to learn it all."

"You don't have to learn it all. Trust in the program. Krav Maga can be intimidating at first, but there really are only eight major moves you need to learn. Those will help in nearly all situations, and it's not something you learn once and never work on again. To be effective, you need to make it a lifelong practice. It's great for the body, building muscles, increasing stamina, and building confidence."

"I suppose." I blow out a defeated breath. "Does it ever get easier?"

"With time."

"And what are my chances? Do I have a chance of escaping you?"

"If you're successful one time, you'll be farther along in your training than you think. Trust the..."

"I know, *trust the system*." It's the fucking mantra around this place.

"Is it working for you?" He crumples the paper cup he's holding.

"Is what working?"

"The program? It's been months, do you think it's worth it?"

"It's certainly better than being out there."

"Out there?"

"Outside the Facility. I feel safe in here."

"I understand that, but you won't be here forever."

"Forest says we can take as long as we need. And it's not like I'm not still living my life. I didn't have to drop out of my college classes. I guess that makes it worthwhile. I don't think I would've finished the year if I had to do it in person. Although, I'm thinking of taking a semester off in the fall. I'm not ready to go back and face all the questions."

"I would think that would be difficult."

"I just don't want to deal with it. I want to be normal, not the girl who was kidnapped."

"You're far beyond normal. You're quite an extraordinary woman with far more strength than you know."

"I wish I shared your optimism."

It feels good talking to Three instead of getting choked out by him. Not that I mind the physical activity, or the physical intimacy of it all.

Moira is right about one thing.

All six of the men decked out in black are hot as hell. My fantasies are kicked into overdrive. I like the physical struggle of it all.

Their sex appeal is in the confident way they carry themselves, that sense of sureness and the way they make no apologies for taking up space. It's in the ease of their movements, the fluid way they've mastered their bodies. The intensity it takes to maintain peak physical form testifies to the sharpness of their minds.

Moira may be all hot and bothered by the fighting, but I like a man with a brain. Someone I can talk to, like Three.

In many ways, he reminds me of Austin. My brother is driven to succeed both physically and mentally. His best friend is too. It's one of the reasons I fell in love with Axel.

"Can I give you a piece of advice?" Three leans in toward me, lowering his voice.

"Sure." I shrug. He can say whatever he wants as long as he talks to me.

"Don't bury your pain. It only gets harder the more you run from it. Don't pretend it didn't happen. It did. Don't ignore your fear. That too is real, and you need to own it. You need to accept the fear, the helplessness, and the worst thing of all—that you survived when

175

others did not. Acknowledge what happened. That's the first step in accepting it. You were abducted, held against your will. You were tortured and you survived. Embrace all of that and remember that you survived. Find strength in that and use that strength to work through the rest. You're worth loving."

Worth loving?

If only he knew how unworthy I really am.

EIGHTEEN

Axel

OUR FIRST DAY WITH THE RESIDENTS IS NOTHING SHORT OF TORTURE. I hold Zoe in my arms more in those few hours than in all the years that came before. Funny how she's been in my life for what seems like forever, but we rarely touched.

The more she's in my arms, the more confused I become. She's mine. I accept this, but it's not something I can act upon.

Something is definitely stirring between us. I'm just not sure what *it* is. I can tell she's attracted to me. Or, rather to the man she knows as Three. Honestly, that kind of pisses me off. Which, when I stop to think about it, should be fucking hilarious, except it's not.

How can I be jealous of myself?

Her entire demeanor loosens up as we practice. I spend an hour on that first technique. It's one of the fundamentals, and I won't move forward until they both master it.

But it's different when Andrew fights me than when Zoe does the same. When she's in my arms, the air crackles. A static charge buzzes between us, lifting the fine hairs on my arms, and on the back of my neck.

I've given up on my poor, trapped cock. It's confused as hell, and denied any release, it gives up and throws in the towel.

I gather Zoe and Andrew close. "We have a little less than an hour. I know you're tired, but you're doing an amazing job. I want to go over how to escape from a side headlock."

"We've practiced that one." Andrew bobs his head with enthusiasm.

"Really?" He's getting a bit too eager for my tastes. He's twelve, barely entering puberty. His voice doesn't even crack a little bit. It's time to take him down a notch. "Then show me."

When he comes to me, I hold my hand palm out.

"Z, grab him in a headlock. If he gets free, he gets to quit early."

"And if he doesn't?" Zoe perks up, looking at me with her amazing eyes. The setting sun reflects off her irises, stealing my breath. I find myself staring and shake my head to clear my thoughts.

"If he doesn't break your hold, you get to quit early."

"Now that's more like it." Zoe rubs her hands together and stares off at the setting sun. Her attention is starting to wander, which leaves me to decide what to do about it. The entire focus of this week is situational awareness and constant vigilance.

Forest wants these kids to not just prove they have the skills to take care of themselves, but to prove it to themselves. We'll see how that goes for Zoe.

Andrew frowns, but he's ready. The silly boy bounces back and forth on his feet. It'll be interesting to see which of them wins.

"Okay, Z, you're stalking Andrew. Lock your arm around his head, holding him tight to your side. Andrew, you don't move until I say."

Zoe approaches Andrew. "You ready to get beat by a girl?"

"I'm not afraid of you."

"I'm bigger than you."

"I'm just as strong as you." His retort nearly makes me snort. The kid is a scrappy little fucker.

"Z, put him in a headlock and stop his yapping."

She grins and does as I instruct. She wraps her arm around his head and locks him tight to her side. His nose is buried against her belly, just below her breasts.

Lucky fucker.

"And go!" I give the command with a shout and step back to watch the two of them go at it.

Zoe is a thing of beauty. She's awkward and unsure of her body, but she's determined to learn. I've never seen this side of her before today. Instead of an annoying little brat, I see a woman coming into her own.

Andrew flails a little. They're comical to watch. He struggles, twisting and pushing against her, but she's got her forearm pressed against his windpipe. That's the thing with a good choke hold. The victim's hands might be free, but cut off their air and all that strength fades pretty damn fast.

Andrew's face turns pink. Pink deepens to red. When it turns purple, I clap my hands.

"Release him, Z."

Zoe tightens her grip momentarily, then releases her hold on Andrew. He sputters and coughs as he falls to his knees.

"Choke holds are one of the deadliest things you'll encounter. To resist, to evade, you need to maintain as much strength as possible. Do you see how easily she overcame you? How your strength bled out?"

Andrew stays on his knees as he catches his breath.

"I didn't even have to hold him that hard." Zoe shows me how she held her wrist and locked into the hold. "It was really easy."

"Right. Easy for the attacker to choke you out. Now, to get out of a choke hold, the first thing you need to do is avoid getting choked."

"How do you do that?" Andrew's nearly caught his breath.

I'm surprised he asks, considering it's one of the basic moves they've supposedly been learning over the past month. Although, when I think about it, I wasn't that much different.

I trained in various forms of Martial Arts and considered myself an expert. I knew all the katas and had several black belts. When the time came to defend myself in unscripted combat, I forgot everything I learned.

This is why Forest brings in his Guardians once a month. The kids are taught all the moves. Many are quite proficient in them, but we force them out of the structured learning environment. They must take what they've learned, what their brains have learned, and take a step back to let the body do what it's been training for, to fight.

"Come here." Andrew steps close and I put him in a loose headlock. "You want to turn to your attacker's side. This puts your throat against their mid-section, which is broad, flat, and softer than the side of their arm. It will prevent them from choking off your air supply. Once you do that, take your hand and strike the groin with open-handed slaps. Those will get a reaction. Keep doing that until you have enough room to turn your head all the way out."

We go through it again. I take both of them through the move several times and am thankful for the cup protecting my groin with all the slapping they're doing down there. They do a passable job and the time comes to honor my promise and let Zoe out a few minutes early.

"Great job." Andrew works his way free of my choke hold. I glance up at the red tint in the sky as the sun begins to sink. I turn to Zoe, reluctant to see her go, but I'm a man of my word. "Z, you can stick around if you wish, but you won the right to a little free time."

Her head cocks to the side and her brows tug together. Her expressive eyes take me in as she bites her lower lip. Her hair is a tousled mess. Pink fills her cheeks from our exertion. Her body looks different to me. The curves are more defined. Her breasts fuller, rounder. Her hips flare outward, accentuating her trim waist. She has the kind of hips a man could really hold onto while he lost himself inside of her.

I want to be that man.

Does she know how fucking sexy she is? Because my heart sputters and just about stops. I could linger in this moment for the rest of my life if she would promise to never stop staring at me like that.

"I think... Um." Her eyes pinch as she sweeps her gaze from the top of my head all the way down to the tip of my boots. She returns slowly to my face and gives a little shake of her head. "Actually, I think I'll take off."

"Okay." I gesture to Andrew. "Looks like it's just you and me."

Zoe props a hand on her hip and stares at us. At me. Like I'm a puzzle she's trying to figure out. I'm just about to ask what she wants when she takes a step forward and asks a question of her own.

"Will you be testing us—stalking us—whatever it is tonight?"

"For the next week, my team will be here. It's time to learn how to keep an eye out for threats."

"Okay. I was just wondering."

"An essential part of your training is to think about the world differently. It's not about turning into a paranoid individual, looking for threats everywhere, but rather a way to show you how to live a normal life while maintaining your awareness of the world around you."

"I suppose that makes sense." Her shoulders hunch and she looks down at the ground. Something's upset her, but I don't have a clue what it is.

"Enjoy the rest of your day, Z."

"I will." She hugs herself and turns away.

I watch her go, admiring her trim figure as she picks her way through the courtyard, staying as far from the others as possible. Instead of heading back to the main campus, she turns left toward the cliffs overlooking the ocean.

Andrew clears his throat and my attention returns to my pupil.

"You ready for more?"

"Yeah, I thought it was going to be so easy, but this is nothing like practice."

"There's a reason for that." Andrew's a fighter. I received his file, along with Zoe's, although I didn't need to read hers to know what was inside. The little man in front of me has lived a complicated and brutal life. "Come on, let me show you a few moves they won't teach you."

His expression fills with a crooked grin, and I'm treated to a glimpse of the man he might someday become.

If he can work through his trauma, he'll be unstoppable. The kid is tenacious as shit, not afraid of hard work, and driven to master everything I have to teach him.

For the next half hour, I put him through his paces, until he's dripping in sweat and too tired to continue. Forest closes out the session and gives the kids another warning about what to expect in the coming days.

What they don't know is we won't be doing anything for the next three days. They're going to spend the rest of today looking over their shoulders, anticipating an attack. They'll do the same tomorrow and the day after that.

Forest wants their vigilance to fatigue. Then they'll learn their next vital lesson.

I gather with my team and we debrief Forest, giving him our assessment of his charges. My attention wanders more to Zoe than it should.

Where did she go? What is she thinking? How is she holding up? Is the Facility the right place for her to rebuild?

Trust the system.

If only it were that easy.

NINETEEN

Axel
___

IT'S HARD TO TRUST A SYSTEM TO REBUILD THE LIFE OF A LOVED ONE, but I have faith.

Zoe surprises me. She's incredibly beautiful. Odd how in the fifteen years I've known her I never appreciated that fact.

Not once did she tempt me when we were kids. I was never interested in her like that. Granted, I'm several years older than her. I was in sixth grade when she entered kindergarten. By the time she started sixth grade, I was a high school senior breaking the hearts of my classmates as my rampant sexuality came into full bloom. By the time she started high school, I'd already left home to enlist in the Navy. I never saw anything in her except the bratty little sister of my best friend who never left me alone.

But there's something about Zoe. On a deeper, primitive level, an instinctual directive calls out to me.

She's mine.

Inappropriate thoughts clutter my mind when I think about Zoe. My body reacts with its need to take and claim. My heart feels warm and light.

185

The worst part of my infatuation is that while quite a bit of it is sexual in nature, not all of it is.

Yes, she's attractive. Yes, she's matured into a beautiful young woman from the scrawny little kid and gangly preteen I knew. If this were just a physical craving, I'd figure a way to get her in my bed, work her out of my system, and move on. Only there's much more than simple physical attraction going on. It's more than lust.

I can't ignore the feelings stirring within me. They aren't purely physical, which would be preferable; they're turning into something more. A deep-seated need to claim her grows within me and with it comes a surety of faith that she not only belongs to me, but that I belong to her.

We're intrinsic halves of a whole, bound by more than the common history we share as kids who grew up together.

With these thoughts stirring in my mind and twisting at my gut, I go in search of Zoe.

Griff gives me a look when I break away from the team. He jogs up beside me.

"Yo, where you headed?"

"I need to walk."

"That's not what you've got scrawled on your face."

"And what is it you think is all over my face?" I pull to a stop and turn on Griff. He knows me far too well.

"That you're on a mission."

"Yeah, a mission to clear my head."

"Doesn't look like much head-clearing will be going on if you go after her."

"Who?"

"Oh, come on. Don't play that shit game with me. I don't have time for the bullshit that entails. You want her and you're heading out to stake your claim."

I'd respond with *'Am not'* but Griff knows me far too well. I can read him as well as he reads me. We make a pretty damn good team. Except right now, I want to punch him in the throat for standing between me and Zoe.

"What if I am?"

"Well, let's break that down. Instead of leading with your dick, think about what it'll do to her."

"What do you mean? I'm pretty damn sure it's going to go well."

Zoe wants me. She always has, and now that I see what she's been trying to tell me, there's not a single reason to waste any more time.

"Right. And maybe you forgot where you are? Where she might be in her head right now. This program is rough. She's got a lot of personal shit to deal with. Going after her is only going to twist her up inside."

He knows about last year when Zoe bared her heart and I promptly crushed it. I'm not happy about that, but at the time she needed to know there would never be an us. The best gift I could have given her was the push she needed to move on. I was practically a saint with how I let her down.

You were an ass about it.

Well, maybe I was, but I had zero interest in her then.

"I disagree." I turn to leave.

"Don't do it," Griff warns.

"You telling me what to do?"

"It's your funeral, buddy. I don't think you'll have the reception you think you'll have." He lifts his hands up and out, then slowly backs away. His expression is full of judgment.

"You're wrong."

"I hope so." He takes two steps back then spins around as he shakes his head.

I stomp away and head left out of the courtyard. I'm not sure what I'm thinking.

The Facility is huge, a couple hundred acres of prime real estate hugging the cliffs along the Pacific Coast Highway. Most of the land has been left in its natural state, with the main campus located at the north end of the land.

I leave those buildings behind thinking I'll run into Zoe and have a little chat with her. Instead, I wander the grounds, looking everywhere for her and come up empty-handed. She's disappeared.

The guys and I will be staying in guest housing for the next week. It's a practical concession considering our purpose. It's much easier to stalk the kids at all hours if we're close by, but I'm not ready to head back and face Griff's disapproval.

I know what I'm doing.

After an hour of looking around, I finally give up. The sun surrenders its reign on the day, slipping beyond the horizon. It lights the sky on fire in farewell. With nothing to do, I wander out toward the cliffs to watch Mother Nature show off.

The land is rugged, filled with low-lying grass and scrub oak. A steady wind blows off the ocean, bringing the light scent of the salt and brine to fill my nostrils. Seabirds soar overhead, looking for their next meal, and far out over the ocean, storm clouds build. They'll push toward land, and if we're lucky, there'll be rain tonight. Unfortunately, it's more likely the storm will blow itself out before reaching land.

I find a rocky precipice to watch the sunset and think about Griff's words. I don't get his hesitation and it bugs me. I walk all the way to the edge and peer down the thirty-meter drop. The rugged coastline of California is not for the faint of heart, not this far north. Down south, surfers carve up the waves, but here, long rollers pound against a rocky, unforgiving shoreline.

I gather a bunch of rocks and shuck them out into the air. I watch them fall to the beach below. Sunset is amazing and soon dusk sweeps in the night. I pull off my tactical vest and the helmet. The mask and voice modulator stays in place. We're not allowed to remove them while on assignment at the Facility. I tip my head back to watch the first stars make their appearance and think of Zoe.

The storm builds, flashing lightning in the clouds. As the night deepens, it approaches land and the light show becomes more impressive. The wind kicks up, but the storm's still some distance off. I lean back on my elbows and let my legs swing over the edge of my rocky outcropping.

The crunching of gravel sounds behind me. My body tenses, but I don't give any outward sign that I hear whomever it is. I wait, seeing if they'll announce themselves, but I already know who it is.

When she takes a step back, trying to be quiet and failing, I tip my head back.

"Got something you want to say? Or are you going to pretend I don't hear you?"

"I was trying to see if the Guardians were as situationally aware as you want us to be."

"Hun, I felt you the moment you arrived."

"I did too, and I just have one question."

Odd.

"What's your question?"

"When were you going to tell me?"

I draw my knees up, and spin around, placing the drop-off to my back.

Zoe stands twenty feet from me. The wind blows her blonde hair back off her face. The strands curl and dance in the wind. She changed clothes and wears a flowing knee-length dress, which is a problem because the wind blows it back around all her curves.

She's fucking breathtaking, but nervous. Her fingers twist together at her waist and she doesn't look me in the eye. It's dark enough for her features to be somewhat indistinct, but I feel her angry glare boring into me.

"Tell you what?"

"That it's you."

Well shit.

TWENTY

Zoe

___

After practice with the Guardians, I went for a long walk. I needed to clear my head and settle a few things. There's a weird dissonance within me, or rather with me and Three. It crystallizes, rather abruptly, during my shower.

I know why he seems so familiar, but I don't understand why Axel would play games with me.

That nagging sense of something familiar came in the way his body moved. My entire life, I watched Axel as he turned from a boy into a man. I know every nuance of his body because I'm obsessive like that.

From the way he breathes, to how he holds his head, I know him. The way he holds his body, how he shifts his weight, every flex of his muscles are things I've spent my life studying.

Obsessively.

The expressiveness of his face. It's memorized.

The way he breathes? Imprinted on my mind.

The moment he spun me during that first choke hold I knew, but it took a moment to put everything together because of the clash between what my mind thought versus what my body knew.

The disconnect between those two things kept me confused.

My body knew.

My mind took its damn sweet time figuring it out.

It was busy reacting to the knife at my throat and had to deal with a barrage of memories. Memories that brought blinding panic.

The breathing techniques we've learned are a godsend—no doubt about that. While Axel held the knife to my throat, I successfully aborted a crippling flashback.

It was a first.

Terror welled up inside of me. My throat tightened. My heart took off, running wildly out of control. It pumped fear throughout my body and I was swept along for the ride.

But I took a deep breath.

I focused on my anchor point. My racing heart slowed. The muscles in my throat eased. I fought the panic, and I won.

I stayed in control.

That's where the dissonance started.

My body knew who the man was, but my mind was too busy focusing on something else. When they, my mind and body, came back together, they were on separate pages. At least until I took the time to really think about my afternoon.

Three threw me, figuratively and literally. He tossed my ass on the ground more times than I want to admit. His voice, altered as it was, kept my mind and body confused. But I know now.

Axel is Three.

My body knew it. My mind needed to catch up. We're all on the same page now.

None of that explains why I curled into a ball in the shower and cried.

I haven't cried since my arrival when Skye and Forest told me their story.

Surrounded by their success, I understood what Skye meant when she said there is always light in darkness. For the first time, I believed I would be strong enough to find mine.

To believe I had a future brought me to tears.

I dried those tears and spent the following months working the program, having faith, if not always in myself, but in that I would make it through.

Then Axel appears decked out all in black, hiding his identity.

Am I that despicable he won't take the time to say *Hi*?

Which is why I need air.

It's why I'm out walking instead of sitting with my friends.

I need to think.

To be alone.

What I don't need is to run into him.

To make matters worse, he casually sits at my favorite meditation spot, like he doesn't have a care in the world. The tactical vest is off. The helmet too, but the mask still covers his face.

He doesn't react at first when I confront him, but his entire body stills. Slowly, he turns around and draws his knees to his chest.

"When did you figure it out?" The damn voice modulator distorts his voice and brings back the dissonance between my mind and body.

"Can you turn that thing off?"

"Answer my question."

"I'm not answering any of your questions until you turn that damn thing off."

"We're not allowed to remove the masks, or the voice modulators, while on Facility grounds."

"Like I care about that. You can't hide anymore. I know it's you." My fingers curl into tiny fists and my voice cracks as my anger builds. "Why didn't you say something?"

"And what would the purpose of that have been?"

"Other than the obvious?" I can't believe those words fall out of his mouth. "Am I that repugnant that you hoped I would never figure it out? Am I just another job again?"

My chest squeezes with pain. I guess crawling into bed with him and getting my ass kicked out of said bed is reason enough. Finding me stripped, beaten, and degraded in that building only adds to his disgust. I don't blame him.

I find myself disgusting most days as it is. I wasn't *good* enough to be sold as a sex slave. They had to dispose of me. I get what they did. Rather than kill me outright, why not make a quick buck and do it in front of an audience? At least then, my kidnapping would be worth the expense.

It's just, to see that reflected in Axel's eyes, is like killing me all over again. I'll never be anything more than an unwanted burden. Either as Austin's kid sister, or as a job for the Guardians, Axel has never once in his life chosen me.

I've always been thrust upon him.

My anger builds because I'm not a burden. And I don't need to deal with his shit on top of everything else.

I lash out. I lash out because I don't know how to be anything but angry and frustrated with him. All I ever wanted was for him to see me for—me.

Is that such a difficult thing to ask?

His silence irritates me. It pisses me off.

"The purpose?" I react to his question. "You're really asking that? It's not like we're strangers, and considering what we were doing…"

"What do you think we were doing, Zoe?"

"Don't call me that. My name is Z here."

"What do you think we *were* doing—Z?" He repeats back to me as my nails dig into the palms of my hands.

I'm so damn mad. The way he places an emphasis on what I thought we were doing pisses me off. We weren't doing anything other than working through defensive moves.

I bet he thought I was trying to get close to him. To touch him. Like I'd ever open myself up to rejection from him again.

"You know what I mean." I take a step back as he rises to his full height.

He moves toward me and damn but my mouth goes dry. The rest of my body heats from the inside out. I lick my lips. They're chapped from the wind. Or at least that's what I'm going with.

The thing is I like him. It's more than that. I crave him. I want so much from him, things he'll never willingly give.

No way am I thinking about the two of us out here, alone, in the dark, far away from any other people. I step back and shake out my fingers.

"I just don't understand why you didn't tell me who you were. Why would you let them assign you to me?"

"Maybe they didn't give me a choice? If you didn't figure it out, I'm Alpha Three, not Alpha One. I'm not the one in charge."

"No, but you could've said something."

"And what would I say?"

For every backward step I take, he takes two toward me, closing the gap between us. He's so close I can reach out and tap his chest—if I want to.

I very much want to.

My entire being itches to do just that. To feel the hard planes of muscle I know are under the soft cotton of his shirt. His massive biceps stretch the poor fabric tight. The cotton strains to contain his bulk. I've only ever seen him naked once. It's a night I'll never forget. The disdain and disgust are firmly imprinted on my mind.

"What would I say, Zoe?"

"That you don't want to be anywhere near me. That you hate me." *That I disgust you and am unworthy of your love.* Tears prick behind my eyes.

Lightning flashes over his shoulder. A storm rages offshore. The wind gusts and the surf far below roars with fury. It pounds the rocky shore beating it down.

Just like Axel does to me.

His eyes are black pits, swallowed up by the mask, and his body goes stock still.

"What did you say?" The modulation of his voice trips me up. It almost sounds as if he's surprised.

My mind hears the voice of Three, my instructor, while my body feels every inch of Axel's anger.

"Never mind." I swipe at my cheeks and erase the treacherous tears that leak weakness all down my face. "Tell them to assign me to someone else. I don't want to *inconvenience* you." I don't want to be an *assignment* he can't refuse.

"Zoe…" He sounds shocked. "Inconvenience me? Why would you say that?"

I didn't realize he might not have had a choice in who he's assigned to, but I'll fix that.

"Look, I don't want to be around you any more than you want to be around me. You've made that crystal clear. I'll fix it so you won't have to be bothered with me."

I thought I was coming to terms with what happened to me, but knowing Axel saw me at my weakest, that I'm nothing more than a job, is too much to handle.

It physically hurts. I press the heel of my hand against my chest. It hurts so damn much.

The next thing I know, Axel's in my face. He looms over me, so tall, so powerful, so incredibly male.

So fucking attractive and intoxicating and everything I've ever wanted in a man. I'm so damn screwed.

I try to take a step back, but he grabs at my arm and pulls me against his chest.

I can't breathe. Our physical proximity sets off all kinds of signals, signals that tangle and cross until I'm confused and desperate for him to touch me. I want him so badly it hurts.

But he can't stand to be with me.

My lungs suck in moist air. It smells like rain. The wind whips at my hair. For some reason, Axel gathers it in his fist. He leans toward me, hunches down. His calloused thumb sweeps gently across my cheek and a low, agonized groan escapes him.

"I don't hate you, and you're not an inconvenience." Another low rumble runs through his chest. "You're all I can think about. A

197

temptation I'm having a hard time resisting." He releases my hair and places both his hands on my cheeks. For a moment, it seems like he might kiss me.

A temptation?

Agonized tears leak from my eyes as he stares down at me from behind that mask.

We stand like that for a moment, breathing in each other's air, neither of us moving or backing down. The hood hides his expression.

I numbly stare back with fading hope about the kiss. It's simply too much to ask, but I hoped for it. My infatuation with Axel is beyond healthy. It's damaging, painful, and impossible.

I want to run.

There's something in his eyes. It's too dark to see, but some fundamental shift happens within him. I feel it. I just don't understand what it means.

"Ah, fuck it all to hell." He releases me and spins around. He cups his head in his hands and a string of expletives fall from his mouth. "Is that what you think?"

I try to remember what it is I just said. I've been too caught up in the fact he touched me—willingly touched me. And, of course, that imaginary kiss I dreamed up.

He turns back around as I tremble before him. My mind tells me to turn around. To run. *Dammit run!* My body refuses to move. My heart pounds. My head spins. Lightning flashes behind him followed by a peal of thunder, which makes me jump. The storm is almost on us.

"It's not what I think." My head dips. It hurts too much to look at him. "It's what I know. I never asked you to rescue me, and I certainly didn't ask for you to train me. I know how you feel about me." My gut twists knowing I repulse him.

I straighten my spine and firm my chin. My eyes drill into the holes of the mask where his eyes should be. I'm tired of being an unwanted burden.

Time to move on.

But I don't. I don't move, and I don't want to move on. I'll always love him.

Axel rips off the mask. Blazing blue eyes shine down on me. He tears at the fastenings of the voice modulator strapped over his larynx and tosses both the mask and voice box to the ground. An agonized expression crawls across his face as he digs his fingers into his hair. He takes a step toward me.

I firm my stance. He will not make me feel less than I am.

He looks at me, gaze skating across my face, skimming down my dress. Another low rumbly moan emanates from the back of his throat. It's needy, animalistic, and makes me shiver.

"You have no idea, do you?" He lowers his hands and grasps at the air.

"I don't think it matters what I think or don't think. Just… Please, put me out of my misery and go away. I can't deal with any more of your rejection on top of everything else." My heart seizes with the finality of what I'm saying. I'm tired and I'm done.

I turn to leave.

The entire world slows down as I pivot. Thunder cracks. The wind howls. The sky flickers with lightning. The wind kicks up and I shiver with the chilly air blowing off the ocean. The temperature is falling fast.

I take one step, but find myself spinning back around. Axel's hand wraps around my back and presses between my shoulder blades. His other hand wraps in my hair as his mouth crashes down on mine.

TWENTY-ONE

Zoe

MY HEART SEIZES AS AXEL'S TONGUE SPEARS INTO MY MOUTH, lashing out with angry strikes. Whatever higher brain functions I may have, disappear. My brain cells simply give up trying to make sense of whatever *this* is. I'm barely aware enough to catch the needy moan rumbling in his chest as he kisses me so thoroughly I forget to breathe.

Overwhelming.

Fantastic.

Toe-curling, panty-wetting, pussy-clenching; it's insane.

Better than any of my fantasies. I've kissed my share of boys, but this is the first time a real man took my breath away. I know what that means now.

It's so mind-blowingly fantastic that a whimper slips past the lock he has on my lips. He holds me tight against him, but my arms hang down by my sides.

I don't know what's happening. Which means, I'm too afraid to touch him. If I do, he'll realize who he's kissing and stop.

And I don't want this to ever stop.

The wind gusts and the first drops of rain hit my cheek. His tongue sweeps inside my mouth, lashing with fury as lightning rips across the sky. He takes, claims, and devours the tiny mewling sounds escaping my throat as thunder cracks all around us.

I make those sounds.

Then, just as fast as it started, his mouth is gone. I blink up at him, stunned beyond words, as the intensity of his beautiful eyes drill right down to my soul. He latches on and grabs a hold of me as shock ricochets through every fiber of my being.

"Does that feel like I'm repulsed by you?"

Axel kissed me. It's the best kiss of my life.

"Axel, what—what are you doing?" I want to ask '*Why*' and say something along the lines of '*But you do find me repulsive?*' but my mouth gapes.

His body tenses and that sound rumbles from the back of his throat: half growl, part grunt, fully male. It's intoxicating, feral, and sinfully sexy.

"Fuck." A string of expletive bursts out of him.

I flinch. Here comes the regret. I pull away, but his grip tightens.

"Don't."

"Don't what?" I'm surprised I'm able to piece two words together. My mind reels from the intensity of that kiss. It wasn't a run of the mill kind of kiss. He put his whole body into it.

That scares me to death.

My body, on the other hand, is revved up. Heat licks between my legs. My insides clench. My thong is soaked and my pussy aches to be filled fully by him.

By his dick.

I need a moment to absorb what happened. Instead, I'm thinking about his dick.

I saw it once, soft as it lay alongside his leg that night I crawled into his bed. I've imagined what it would look like hard and engorged. Now, I need to know how it'll feel once he's inside of me.

"Don't shut down on me." He presses his forehead against mine. "Whatever is going on inside that head of yours, that kiss isn't a mistake. It's not something I regret. Let me have this, Zoe. I need it." Another low moan escapes him as he tugs on my hair.

"But…"

Whatever I plan to say disappears beneath the press of his mouth and the fervent kiss that follows. I finally figure out what my hands are good for and wrap them around his biceps.

He plunders my mouth, taking, claiming, and driving me thoroughly insane. I rise on my toes to meet his intensity with a rising urgency and lifetime of unrequited love.

Why would I regret this when it's everything I've wanted?

He pulls me to him, pressing our bodies tight together. His hips grind against mine as he devours my mouth. His fingers twist in my hair. He tugs on the roots to angle my head the way he likes. He takes control of the whole thing.

He wants this as much or more than I do. I don't get it, but there's no way I'm stopping him.

I love his maddening control, or lack thereof. I'm certainly thankful he's in charge of whatever this is, because I have no idea what comes next. Do we walk away like it never happened? Or is this… Could this be the start of everything?

I sink into the kiss. My breathy sighs mingle with his low, guttural moans. The heat of his body envelopes me. The warmth of his mouth excites me. He drops a hand to my ass and squeezes.

Oh my God, he's touching my ass, like man-handling my ass.

My insides combust as he yanks my hips to him. We touch everywhere, from our mouths to our chests, our hips, and our groins press against each other. I want to climb him and cling to him. I loop my arms around his neck and simply hang on.

"Fuck… What you do to me isn't legal." He nips my bottom lip with a low, throaty growl. His hips jerk, thrusting his pelvis forward. His hands move over my ass, grabbing the fabric of my dress and pulling it up. As soon as he can, he palms my bare ass and gives another groan of desire. His fingers trace my bare skin, move to my hip, and hook under the tiny strap of my thong.

His lips brush mine, hot, fiery, passionate, and demanding. I cling to him savoring everything as he seduces my senses until I can no longer think straight.

"Zoe…" He whispers my name, prolonging each syllable as he savors them.

My heart flutters as his hand moves forward and his fingers stretch beneath the flimsy fabric of my barely-there thong. Never before has my name sounded so wonderful. The world falls away as his kiss turns slow and soft. His fingers stop their agonizing crawl right above my lightly shaved mound.

He pauses there as I tilt my pelvis, begging him not to stop, but to take this kiss and make it truly intimate. His thumb caresses my hip while the press of his fingers leaves me panting. Just a little further and he'll finally touch me in a way that can never be taken back.

Our breaths mingle as I run my fingers along the sweep of his shoulders, down the bulge of his biceps, and all the way to his wrists. I don't want him to stop. Our bodies press so hard against each other that the beating of his heart bangs against my chest. The slow, determined rhythm sends shivers down my spine.

The wind pelts us with rain as the skies overhead open up. At the threshold of hearing, a low booming sounds at the base of the cliff.

Waves, whipped into a frenzy by the storm pound the shoreline, thrusting furiously toward land.

When my fingers reach his wrist, he breaks off the kiss. I stare up at him as I take his hand and push it down until the pads of his fingers touch my most sensitive parts.

"Fuck..." His eyes widen.

I give a nod and bite my lower lip, letting him know, begging with my eyes, pleading for him not to stop.

He holds me against his chest. Head and shoulders above me, I bury into him and, for the first time in my life, my arms wrap around him in an embrace.

The steady beat of his heart is much slower than the frantic pounding of mine. But he tugs in each breath and props his chin over the top of my head.

As for his fingers, they slide down and touch right where I need him most.

His fingers skim over my clit and cause my insides to flutter, then shudder. A whole-body spasm overcomes me as I grip his arms and hang on.

"You want this?" His hand dives lower. Those fingers of his tease me with light flutters and longer, deeper strokes. Before I can answer, his long, thick finger slides between my folds. "Holy fuck, Zoe. You're dripping. Shit." He slides his finger out, stroking the lips of my pussy. "You're wet for me." He sounds almost like he's in awe, or that he's surprised. "That's fucking hot."

He wastes no time, and doesn't force me to form a coherent response to his question. I'm beyond words, trembling with each fluttering touch. His finger plunges inside of me as I cling to him and pant.

His finger makes me wonder how his dick will feel between my legs, sliding inside of me. Thinking about his dick, I imagine what the soft flaccid member I saw that one time will look like when it's angry, engorged, and hard. What is it going to feel like in my hand? Will he let me put it in my mouth?

A ripple of pleasure rolls through me. Damn, but thoughts of kneeling before him as he fills my mouth with his cock makes my insides go all tingly.

I'm no virgin, but my sexual experiences are nothing compared to his. He's six years older, slept his way through high school, and God only knows how many women he's taken to his bed since then. I am a relative novice with only two men to my name. Both in college. One on a dare and one in a half-drunken haze.

Neither of those experiences are what I consider real sex. None were mind-blowing, earth-shattering, full-body experiences. None are the kind of raw, passionate sex I crave. Neither of those boys really knew what they wanted, and, if they did, they were too afraid to take it.

With Axel's fingers sliding inside of me, my mind is barely rational. But I know one thing. This isn't something I control. I won't be calling the shots. He'll take and I'll give. And fuck if that's not what I want.

Another shudder rips through me as I imagine his body moving over mine.

"Axel..." My breathy moan barely rises above the howling of the wind.

"What, babe?" The pad of his thumb moves in a circle over my clit as his fingers pump in and out.

"I'm going to lose it." I feel what promises to be the best orgasm of my life barreling down on me. But I need him inside of me.

"What if I want you to lose it? I want to watch you come, sweetie."

I dig my nails into the skin of his biceps. "Please…" I lift up on my toes as another delicious shudder ripples through my body. "Fuuck…" I cry out, irrational with need.

"You sure about that, honey? You want to fuck?"

I bite my lower lip and give a shake of my head. I've never wanted anything more.

"Well, I'm sure we can make that happen, but there's something you need to know, babe."

It's the first time he's used endearments with me. I think he's trying them all out at once to see which one sticks. Hell, I'll take them all.

I rock my pelvis against his hand, mindless with the need rising within me.

The heat of his breath whispers against the soft hollow of my throat as he bends down.

"Ask me…" He slows down the maddening tempo of his fingers and I cry out with frustration as my orgasm ebbs. "Tell me you want to feel my cock filling you up. Tell me you want me to fuck you."

I nearly cry out with frustration. I was nearly there. I pant against his chest as a low chuckle rumbles out of him.

"Axel… Please!"

He teases me with a flick of his fingers and I nearly come unglued.

"Do you know what you've done, sweetie?"

I have no idea what the hell he's talking about and give a frustrated shake of my head as I wriggle against him.

"You've awakened the beast within me, and I love control. You sure you want to continue down this path?" He dips one finger inside of me and I cry out in frustration. I'm so fucking close.

"Yes, dammit." I'll say anything if it means he'll make me come. I rock forward and back, trying desperately to catch my orgasm before it fades away. He's maddening, keeping me on the cusp, cooling me off, and driving me wild again and again. I'm a needy ball of nerves.

Lightning flashes overhead and he pulls back his hand. "It's getting serious out here. We should probably head in."

I lean back and glare at him. "If you do that I'm never speaking to you again. I'll never let you fuck me. I'll never suck your monster cock, and you'll miss out on how good I can make you feel."

"Really?" His fingers tap over my clit and my eyes glaze over with a rush of pleasure. "Monster cock?"

I'd slap the smirk off his face except I'm delirious with the need to come. I'm out of my mind, and for the life of me, don't know why I say what I do.

"I'll do whatever you want if you just let me come."

"Really?" His grin widens as his fingers work their magic. "That's a *monster*-sized promise."

My entire body tightens, getting ready to detonate and explode, but he keeps me on the cusp, making me more frantic by the second.

"Will you come when I say, how I say, and as many times as I say? Whether it's on my fingers, my mouth, or my cock?" His fingers glide along my folds, teasing me as they pass over my entrance. "Will you do as I say? Is that what you're promising?"

I grit my teeth in frustration. "Yes, goddamn it. Yes!"

"Just remember, little brat, a promise is a promise." His long, thick finger plunges inside of me. My back arches and my breathing hitches. He wastes no time, expertly controlling my body, making me scream as he finds my sweet spot and exploits it.

Another finger slips inside of me and his thumb circles my clit. My hips jerk as his fingers spear inside of me with deliberate thrusts meant to drive me over the edge. He drags the pads of his fingers over my g-spot, places pressure on my clit.

"I want you inside of me, Axel." I need to feel him.

"I am inside of you." His fingers move with deliberate thrusts.

"I want your dick, asshole."

"You mean my monstrous cock?"

"I knew I would regret saying that and here we are."

"Yes, love. Here we are." My vision blurs as my orgasm barrels down on me. "Now, give me your mouth." He tilts my head and his lips hit mine, swallowing my scream.

It feels like nothing I've ever experienced. I pant through my orgasm as wave after wave of pleasure hit me. His fingers stroke me through it as his tongue ravages my mouth. My pussy spasms around his fingers with the best orgasm of my life.

"Fuuuck…" His low, throaty growl is possessive as hell. "You're fucking beautiful."

As soon as I figure out how to breathe, I realize where we are and the violence of Mother Nature surrounding us. Lightning rips across the sky as sheets of rain fall down on us.

My hand reaches down to cup his groin and come hard against the plastic shell of his athletic cup. I glance up at him and he smiles down at me as he sweeps wet hair off my face.

"You should see how fucking beautiful you are when you come." He slides his fingers out from between my legs and watches to make sure I see what he does. He sucks his fingers into his mouth and his eyes close. "You taste so fucking sweet."

I tug at his belt. "Let me taste you."

He wraps his arm around me and pulls me tight against his chest. "Damn straight, but we really are pushing it out here. I need to get you back to your room and out of the storm."

"But what about you?"

"Hun, this won't be the first time I've had to take care of business because of you."

"Me?"

"Yeah, did you miss the part where I said you're all I think about?"

I must have.

"It's at least a ten-minute walk back to the resident hall, and it's all open with no covering."

"Then we should probably run."

"Or…" I peek up at him and point over his shoulder. "There's a little cave just over there. We have to scramble down to it, but it'll cover us from the storm."

It's my favorite place to escape. It's about a ten-foot climb down the cliff, but the ledge is wide and safe. And the cave is deep. Even with the storm driving rain against the cliff, we'll be tucked back far enough to stay dry.

Or rather, we'll have a chance to dry off. My dress is soaked and his pants and shirt are too.

I grab his hand.

"Come on. It's not far." And I know how we can stay warm through the night.

The corner of his mouth tilts up. He reads my mind. Either that or we're both entirely on the same page for the first time ever.

"Hold up, brat. I need to grab my gear."

He seems to settle on *brat* for his endearment, and I don't mind that at all. I intend to be very bratty in the near future as I pay him back for teasing me. Two can play at that game.

TWENTY-TWO

Axel

ZOE'S ESSENCE COATS MY TONGUE. I CURSE MYSELF FOR BEING SUCH a dumb-fuck for so damn long. I denied myself this?

Why the hell did I do that?

Shit, she came apart on my hands, literally, and it was epic.

There's no going back now.

In many ways, she's always been mine, even if I'm an idiot too stupid to know what's been right in front of me all this time. All those years I wasted pushing her away when I could've had her in my bed—in my life!

All that wasted time.

I've staked my claim. Or at least I will when I finally get to slip inside of her and feel her wet warmth wrap around me.

I kept her out in the storm too long. Her long blonde hair is plastered to her face. Her dress is soaked through. The wet fabric molds indecently against the curves of her body. Her supple tits wait for a more in-depth exploration, and I can't wait to take her nipples between my teeth and really make her beg.

211

She's more open about sex than I thought. Don't know why, but I've always had the sense her experience is somewhat limited.

Which is great.

It means I get to introduce her to everything.

How far down the rabbit hole are you willing to travel, little brat?

I mean to take our first time slow, not bring out the fucking caveman, or the bossy tease. But shit, how can I resist when she's so damn exquisite?

She did mention a cave.

From the way she's looking at me, I sense our evening is barely beginning. However, if my little brat thinks to get the upper hand on me. She's going to be in for one helluva shock. Make no mistake, when it comes to sex, I'm definitely the one who leads.

"Come." She grabs my hand and turns her face up to the rain. Drops splatter across her cheeks and her eyes close.

It's getting colder by the second, but she doesn't seem to care.

"Let me get my gear first, brat. Then you can show me this cave of yours."

We should head back to the main buildings, but she's right about them being a bit of a hike. They're easily a ten-minute stroll away. Half that if we run, but I trust she knows what she's talking about.

I grab my tactical vest and strap it on. My helmet goes on my head. The mask and voice modulator, I hold in one hand while I reach for hers with the other.

"Lead on, brat."

She tilts her face down and stares out across the ocean. The storm is on us. Thick clouds blot out the moon. The stars are gone. Lightning skates across the sky, revealing clouds thick and heavy with moisture. It's hard to see the ocean through the blinding sheets of rain.

When she doesn't move, I give her hand a little tug.

"Need I remind you it's not wise to be out in the middle of a thunderstorm?"

"I know. But it's breathtaking." Her innocent eyes take in the fury Mother Nature unleashes, but I worry about the thunder and lightning. We've pushed our luck too far. "We don't get many storms here, so when we do, I always come out to watch them. There's something about their power that speaks to me." She taps her chest as if to make her point.

"Cave or a run back, brat? You pick, but we're moving out now."

She gives a petulant look but acquiesces with a nod. Turning away from where we came—separately—she trots to a little indentation in the cliff face.

Zoe releases my hand and walks fearlessly right up to the edge. My heart leaps into my throat when she gets too close to the drop. Turning toward me, she gives an impish grin and hops off the edge.

I rush to her, heart slamming in my throat, then stop when she drops less than two feet. She bursts out laughing.

"Oh, you should see the look on your face." She dares to point a finger at me, nearly doubling over in laughter.

I step to the edge and glance down at the ledge she stands on. It's a few feet wide. Invisible unless you're right at the edge and it slopes down alongside the cliff face.

"We're going to have a nice long talk about teasing me, little brat. I have a mind to toss you over my knee and smack some sense into that pert little ass of yours."

Her eyes widen and her jaw drops. Then she nibbles on her lower lip.

"Promises. Promises, Axel." She dares to prop her fists on her hips and stare back at me. It's an open challenge, but I don't think she understands what she's offering.

That kind of shit is fun, but it's a little too much, a little too fast, for our first time together. We'll explore mutual kink, and other fantasies, a little down the road.

"Hun, I never make a promise I don't keep. If I were you, I'd back those thoughts way the fuck up. Let's learn to walk before we run."

She nibbles on that damn lower lip and takes a strand of wet hair to twist in her fingers.

"What if I like to run?"

That's all it takes for the strain behind this goddamn athletic cup to pull another agonized groan from my lips. Erections in athletic cups are nothing short of pure torture. I can't wait to rip the thing off and free my poor, trapped cock.

As for what Zoe says, I know where I'm going to put it. If she keeps talking along those lines, we're never making it back to civilization again. I'll keep her in this cave of hers for the rest of our lives, showing her what a caveman does to the woman he claims as his own.

Unable to take my eyes off her, I hunger to slip inside of her, take her fully as mine, and feel the bliss of her sweet, wet heat enveloping and welcoming me home.

A powerful gust slams into her and pushes her forward onto her hands.

My gut twists thinking what would've happened if the gust came off the land instead from the sea.

Eyeing her path dubiously, I'm not convinced this is a good idea.

"How far down the cliff are we going? You think this is really a better idea than running back?"

"It's honestly just right there." She points down the side of the cliff, but I can't see what she means. "And it's perfectly safe."

I want to reach out and pull her off the edge. This seems crazy, but she's confident about her choice. For some reason, I have a sense it's really important that I trust her. It's not in anything she says, but rather in everything her body screams.

Her body has a language all its own, and I'm much more familiar with the nuances of it than I ever realized.

I guess I've spent a lifetime around her, absorbing everything on a subconscious level, while never really noticing how attached I became.

Or when.

"Okay, I trust you, but it's not too slick with the rain?"

She wipes the mud and sand off her palms and glances down the path. "It's really okay. Aren't you supposed to be fearless and able to scale tall buildings in a single bound or something like that?" She starts picking her way down the ledge. With a look over her shoulder, she checks to see that I follow.

I give a grin at the Superman reference. My ego's not against a little stroking. Come to think of it, neither is my cock.

She places her hand against the rocky side of the cliff, hugging the wall as she heads down. Wind buffets us. Rain drives into us. And the lightning gives enough light to show the way. From the confidence of her steps, she clearly does this a lot.

She edges around the rock, stoops down, then disappears inside a large cleft in the cliff face. I stoop to enter and crawl for a few feet.

The cavern widens and opens up. I no longer need to stoop. I stretch to my full height and look around.

Rain drives the first few feet inside, but the rest of the cave is bone dry. To my surprise, a stack of blankets sits toward the back of the cave. There's a tiny lantern and a gallon of what looks to be fuel. This place is special to her.

Zoe unfolds one of the blankets and shakes it out.

"What do you think?" She spins around in a circle. "Is this not the best place ever?"

"How did you ever find this?" I'm more than a little impressed.

"I was looking for a good place to jump."

Her answer takes a second to sink in. The way she puts it out there, floors me for a second, and it takes a moment to understand what it means.

"You what?" I reach out and steady myself against the cliff wall.

"The first month I was here." She speaks about attempting to take her life as if it means nothing.

"Zoe!" I rush to her and fold her into my arms. My hand goes to her head and I tuck her tight to my chest. My heart breaks thinking about what those few words mean. I know she went through hell. It's not something a man like me can imagine, but it never occurred to me she would attempt to end her life.

Why is she flippant about it? I think this scares me the most.

"It's okay." Her tiny hands grip my biceps, and she pulls back until she can look at me. "I'm still here."

"I wish I'd known. I would've—"

"You would've what?"

"I would've been there for you."

Her head cants to the side and it takes a moment before she responds. "When did things change?"

"What do you mean? When did what change?"

Anger simmers within me thinking about her facing her demons alone. An image of her standing on the side of the cliff fills my head. It makes me physically ill thinking she nearly took her life.

"When did things change for you?" She persists with her question.

"As far as?"

"Me." She pushes back and folds the blanket around her shoulders. Her body shivers.

"Come, we need to get dry. Then we'll talk."

"The only way to get dry, Axel, is to strip, and if we strip, there won't be much talking going on." She lets the blanket drop to the ground. She slowly draws up her skirt and sways seductively as she tests my resolve. "I want to make you feel as good as you made me feel."

In the flickering light of the storm, her toned legs draw my attention and my cock takes notice.

"Zoe..." I warn her to stop. "We need to talk before anything else happens between us."

Her skirt rises to the apex of her thighs, a bit more and the tiny patch of fabric covering her pussy comes into view.

I want to reach out and rip it off her, dive in and bury my face between her legs until she screams my name.

"Zoe..." I step toward her and grab her hands. "Talk first."

I want her with a raging hunger, but I refuse to take her without thought, without her knowing the full consequence of sleeping with me. She needs to understand she's different from all the others who came before. She's my one. Always has been. Always will be.

"I want you to finish what we started up there. I want you to *fuck* me."

217

The way she enunciates *fuck* pisses me off. It debases what's happening between us. This isn't about physical release. It's merging who we are. Of making her mine and spoiling her for all other men. Although, there will be no other men after me. Not while I'm alive.

"Talk first." I grab her hands and force her to release the fabric of her dress. It falls down, covering her, and I take a deep breath. My resolve is only so strong.

"Axel, I've waited too long..."

"I want to talk about what you said." I pick up the blanket and gently wrap it around her shoulders, I bring her close. "We have all night for the rest."

"What's there to know? I had a few bad days——"

"A few?" How many times did she come here thinking about ending her life?

"There's not much to say. It was hard after the hospital. I wondered why I should bother breathing and went to some really dark places."

"I wish I'd known. I wouldn't have left if I had."

"But you did leave and it hit me pretty hard."

Ouch.

"I had no choice, and every time we returned from a mission, I was right by your side."

"What do you mean?"

"In the hospital, when I wasn't out on a mission, I spent the night by your side."

"I didn't know that." Her brows draw together. "I wish I had. I wish I knew then what I know now. But this is the first time I've seen you in months."

"Visitors, with the exception of family, aren't allowed. But you can see how I jumped to be your instructor. You're mine, little brat, and

I'm going to teach you everything you need to know to make sure what happened to you never happens again." I bring her hands to my lips and kiss them softly. "What is it that you think you know?"

"That I'm not crazy. That you don't find me repulsive."

"I've never thought that. You're far from repulsive. Maddening perhaps. Frustrating for sure. Sexy as hell, and you've played the starring role in all my late-night fantasies for over a year. You've been giving my arm a workout, luv. You're all I think about."

"But that's new. You certainly didn't think that last year."

"Yeah, we really need to talk about that." I release her and grab a couple more blankets. "I take it you brought these here?"

"I spent a lot of nights here the first few weeks after I found this place."

"I'm surprised they let you stay out all night."

"I snuck out."

"Of course you did." I gesture for her to join me near the opening of the cave. We sit a couple feet back from where the rain reaches, staying mostly out of the wind. "I know why you like this place."

"You do?"

"It's a good spot to look out over the ocean and watch the storms."

I place a blanket on the ground, then gesture for her to join me. She sits beside me and I hook an arm over her shoulder.

"Tell me about those first few weeks."

I wish I could've visited, but Alpha team was out on assignment, chasing down empty leads. If those other girls are alive, they're spread out all over the world by now.

Not that the Guardians will ever stop. We'll do whatever it takes to bring those girls home.

"The nightmares started the first night." Zoe gives a little shiver and I adjust how we're sitting to provide her more warmth. We need to get out of our wet clothes, but she's right about one thing. The moment our clothes come off, there will be no more talking.

I squeeze her shoulders, lending her the strength she should have had back when she needed me the most.

"Go on."

"In the hospital, I didn't dream. I never really let myself think about what happened." She gulps a little, telling me she still needs to work through what happened. A trauma like that doesn't disappear over a matter of weeks. It can be lifelong. "There were people all around me when I was awake. Things got a little fuzzy when I got sick."

"Infection set in. You had sepsis and we nearly lost you."

"That's what I'm told." She twists and stares at me. Her gaze darts back and forth, bouncing from one of my eyes to the other. "Austin and Dad were there. I don't remember you being there."

"I came and went. We're working on finding the other girls."

She tenses beside me. "I take it they haven't been found."

"Not yet, but Bravo team is on it."

"I hope they're okay, but I try not to think about them too much. It brings back the nightmares."

"Tell me about the first time you came to the cliff." She mentioned multiple times. My heart breaks thinking about where her head must've been.

"It was the second day. The first day was a bit overwhelming. I got a tour of the whole place. Forest and Skye sat me down and told me their story. Forest explained the purpose of this place. How I would take what happened to me and turn it into a strength. I didn't believe him, even though I know he's the reason all of this exists. He said it would take time for my heart to catch up with my mind."

"Forest is a pretty incredible individual."

"Do you know his story?"

The muscles in my jaw clench. "I know it very well."

I'm not going to tell her about that operation in Manila where we lost Forest to a monster. How our overconfidence led us right into a trap. We freed several women that night. One of them is still here. She's assigned to Griff for training.

But Forest landed in the hands of a monster. John Snowden is dead. At least we got that right, but our failure to protect Forest never goes away.

"Well, he was right. My heart and mind weren't on the same page. The second day I was introduced to my group mates. They shared their stories with me."

"That must have been difficult."

"Only in how it made me feel. Their stories are similar to each other, but different from mine. About half were sexually abused by their parents or the foster families they were placed with. The other half were kidnapped and sold into slavery. I never really understood what it is you do. I mean, I knew you did things in the Navy as a SEAL, but I never really understood what it is you do for the Guardians. I have a better idea now."

Careful about pushing too hard, I can't stop myself from digging deeper. "How did listening to their stories turn into you coming here?"

"I wasn't like them. I felt guilty because I wasn't raped like them."

"You were kidnapped, Zoe. You were tortured." I leave off the nearly to death part. Technically, she was dead for a few minutes. I brought her back, but I'm not sharing that now, or ever. I don't want her to know how close she came to not walking out of that room.

"Yeah, but I wasn't *raped*." Her entire body goes still. "I wasn't good enough for that. And, this is going to sound really twisted, but after listening to all of their stories, I felt really bad. Like I wished I had been raped rather than what really happened. But it's worse than that. I didn't feel like I was good enough for them to want to rape me. That I repulsed them too."

Oh shit.

"Zoe…"

"No, you said you want to know, so please, let me finish."

"Okay. You're right." I kiss her temple and it's a struggle to end things there. She fits perfectly in my arms. "I'm listening."

"I sat around listening to all their stories. The things they endured are nothing like what happened to me. I knew I didn't belong here, or anywhere. All I could think about was that I wish they had killed me. Do you know I actually asked them to kill me? After they killed the second girl, I asked to be next."

"Shit, Zoe." I want to hold her in my arms forever, if only to keep the demons at bay. I never want her to experience anything but happiness in her life again. I vow to make that happen.

"I said I went to some dark places. Anyhow, the first nightmare hit me that night. All those girls died in front of me while I watched. I didn't deserve to live when they died. And then I came here and what everyone endured had been far, far worse. I was kidnapped for about a week. They were abused for years."

"You know that doesn't make what happened to you any less horrific. I was there. I know what they did."

"I know that *now*, but that night my mind traveled to some really dark places." She wipes at her cheeks and leans her head on my shoulder.

I like the way she feels. I love how her body fits against mine. I want her to find comfort in me.

"Will you tell me what happened?"

"Forest." She leaves it at that and the silence of the cave fills the space between us.

Outside, the wind howls and the rain sizzles as it falls. The booming of the waves below is loud. When it looks like she's not going to elaborate, I can't help but prod her to continue.

"What did he do?"

"I think he has a sixth sense about his rescues. That's what he calls us."

This I know. Forest is incredibly protective of the ones he saves.

"He followed me, although I didn't know it at the time. But when I decided to jump, he let me know he was there."

"And he pulled you back from the ledge?"

"Forest?" She laughs. "No. He left me right where I was."

"I don't get it." I'm going to murder Forest. I don't care that he's a fucking giant. I'm feeding the man his balls for leaving Zoe on the edge of a cliff.

"He said something… Something Skye said, but in a different way."

"What was that?"

"He told me when he was little, and the abuse was at its worst, he always looked up through a tiny window. In his darkest moments, he saw the summer sky. He said that light gave him hope, because he knew that while he was in darkness, there was hope. He just had to believe and have the strength to hold on. Then he told me to look up at the sky."

She sighs wistfully beside me. I keep as still as possible, worried she'll stop talking if I move.

"It was dark, well past midnight. The ocean was inky black. Eerily calm. There was no moon, no clouds, only stars. But he has this way with words. He told me to look up at the blackness and said, *'The stars can't shine if not for the darkness.'* He told me to find the stars around me. The only reason I could see them, the only reason they were there, was because of the darkness. Because of me. And he said one day, I would find my light. I wouldn't be left alone in the darkness."

It's a little abstract for me. Not what I would tell someone contemplating suicide.

"I'm glad he was there to talk to you." It feels fucking stupid saying that, but I've got nothing else.

"Well, that's what he said, and he left me there."

"Wait! He did what?" The fucker left a traumatized girl on the edge of a cliff? After I cut off his balls, I'm going to cut his dick off and feed it to him as well.

"He's a little quirky, but in a really chill kind of way. Honestly, if he had stayed, I probably would've done it. But those words. I don't know, they hit me and stuck with me. I spent the next two hours just standing there looking out over the ocean, staring at the sky, looking at the stars and the blackness between them. I felt something that night I'll never forget."

"And what's that?"

"That what happened to me wasn't my fault. There wasn't anything I could've done to save myself, or the other girls, but if I stayed here... If I worked his program, I'd learn how to make sure something like that never happened again. All I saw was the darkness. I never realized how important it was for the stars to have darkness around them if they were going to shine. I decided if I could use what happened to me and, I don't know, somehow make sure it never happens to someone else, then I matter. My existence means something if I can help other people shine."

"Damn, that's some pretty deep soul searching. You're a phenomenal person."

"I don't know about that…"

"You are, but if what he said meant so much to you, why did you come back and try again?"

"It's like riding a rollercoaster uphill. There are high highs followed by low lows. I came back here four times, each time I was done, ready to end it all. But every time, his words would ring in my head. The fifth time, I just glared at the darkness, the steep drop, the jagged rocks below, and I screamed my head off. I screamed and screamed and screamed." Her entire body tenses and I hold her tighter. "The next morning, I found a note under my pillow. It was a map to this cave, and I'm pretty sure Forest left it for me."

"Does everyone come here?"

"I don't think so. I think he knew I needed a place that was all my own. The first time I came here, I stayed until sundown and watched the sunset. The second time I came, there were blankets and that lantern. I spent my first night out here thinking about what happened, the other girls, and what it all means. I come here when I'm feeling overwhelmed and alone."

"You never have to feel alone again." I pull her into my lap and cradle her in my arms. "You have me now."

About ready to lean down and kiss her, I stop when she wrinkles her nose.

"What's wrong." I rub the pad of my thumb over the worry lines on her forehead.

"You never answered my question."

"Which one?" Although I know which question she means.

I don't want to answer, because I don't know. First off, it makes me feel like a jackass for the way I treated her. Second, I don't understand how or why things changed. Third, I think I've always selfishly known she belonged to me.

No matter how hard I tried to push her away, she always came back. I got used to that. Pushing her away is what I did because I'm a fucking asshole. In the back of my head, I always knew, no matter what I did, that she would always come back.

I hate that about myself. I hate how I used her to feed my stupid ego. I hate how much I hurt her.

"A year ago, you were pretty clear about what you wanted. Or rather, what you didn't want. You didn't want me. What changed?" And there it is. She asks the one question I don't want to answer.

I brace for her judgment and the pain I caused her.

"A year ago, I was an idiot, Zoe. And you surprised the shit out of me."

I had come back to visit Austin on a period of leave. Austin moved out of the main house a year prior into an apartment above his father's garage. He stayed there while going to law school. When I came to visit, I stayed in his old room.

Zoe was home on spring break. It was her freshman year. Their bedrooms were connected by a Jack-and-Jill bathroom. Me, being me, stripped down as I always do, to sleep in the nude. Sometime in the late night or early morning, Zoe snuck into my room and crawled under the covers thinking to seduce me. I guess she thought she could prove, through sex, that I couldn't resist her.

The three of us had a great day together, kicking back at the house, playing in the pool. I guess she got her wires crossed. I certainly never thought I led her on in any way. Especially not since I shared the explicit details of my sexual exploits with Austin.

She was always within earshot. Those stories alone should've told her to stay far away from me. I made it very clear I was a fuck 'em and leave 'em kind of guy.

She intended to prove me wrong. The resulting catastrophe ended in me kicking her out, and using the most damaging words I could think of to ensure she never did it again.

"You said I repulsed you. That you never liked me like that… But out there just now, you were all over me. What changed?"

I cut her off by pressing the tips of my fingers to her lips.

"I also never told you about how I ended that night."

"What do you mean?"

"I was mad. Furious even. I was pissed that you thought you could come in and seduce me. I was outraged because I didn't want to be attracted, or involved, with you in any way. I didn't want to risk losing my best friend. The things I said were cruel and I meant them to sting. I won't lie about what happened that night. I meant to hurt you so badly that you'd hate me. It's all I could think of, and I'm not proud of it, but that was also the first night I got hard thinking about you. The moment you left, I was hard. So fucking hard, and turned on, but still mad. I hated that you made me feel something for you."

"You got hard?"

"Yeah…" The corner of my lips tick up. "My first raging hard-on for my best friend's little sister. You were like family to me. It felt all kinds of wrong to think about you like that. It really messed with my head. And I'm really sorry I hurt you. I'll never be able to take that night back. But afterward, I thought about you every day. Most nights I went to bed with my dick in my hand thinking about you."

"You did?" She snickers at that.

"Yes, brat. I did." I give her a playful nudge. "You think it's funny?"

"Well—after the way you treated me, it's fair turnabout." She giggles again. "You masturbated thinking about me?"

I roll my eyes. This is not doing much to stroke my ego. A man doesn't admit this kind of shit to his woman. For some ungodly reason, I feel like she needs to know. Hell, I'm desperate for her to know how much I've fucking fantasized about her.

"Yes."

"What kinds of things did you think about?" She twists around to face me and settles on her knees. The eagerness in her eyes should be a warning but I'm too far gone for that. I'm also hard again. The slight reprieve my poor cock had these last few minutes is gone. My dick is about ready to drill its way free of the confining athletic cup.

"Zoe—I don't really think…"

"Oh, you're going to tell me." She pokes her finger at my chest and twists the fabric of my wet shirt. "And then, we're going to do every last one of them." Her eyes brighten and she nibbles on that lower lip of hers.

"You might want to know what they are before you go making statements like that." I shift uncomfortably, but there's no relief from my predicament. At least, not while my clothes are still on.

"I've waited for this my entire life. As payback for kicking me out of your bed, you're going to tell me all the filthy fantasies you've been having about me, and then you're going to show me."

"You have no idea what you're asking, little brat. Don't forget, I was in the Navy. I'm pretty good with knots."

"If we're done with the talking part, tell me what you I fantasized about after you kicked me out of your bed."

"So you can tease me?"

"Well, that's a given." She rocks back on her heels and gives me a solemn look. "But I mean it. I don't want you to treat me like Austin's little sister. I want you to do all the things you've ever dreamed of doing with me, to me, or for me. I've waited too long to hold back now."

I shift again, trying to find a comfortable position. It's hopeless. There's only one way I'm getting relief.

"If you must know, my fantasy involved you on your knees with my cock shoved down your throat, but how about we start things slow, and since I don't have any protection on me, we're going to be a little *limited* in what we can do tonight."

"Oh, I don't think there'll be any limits. I've been tested. I'm clean and I have years of protection that says I won't get pregnant. I guess it just depends on you."

I'm clean. I get tested regularly. Damn, if the mention of the IUD they forced on her doesn't put a damper on the whole thing. It's almost enough to steal my erection.

Almost.

While I sit here and stare, Zoe reaches for my belt.

TWENTY-THREE

Zoe

_____

IT'S LIKE A DREAM. OR A FANTASY COMING TRUE.

All my life, I've waited for this moment. He wants me. I see the need brimming in his eyes, the desire lighting him up from within. I feel it dripping off his tongue with every lusty groan and ravenous rumble vibrating in the back of his throat.

My fingers skim his heated skin. Feather-light, I'm not in a hurry to rush through this. Not after waiting forever to be right here, doing this—undressing him.

I get his belt undone, flick open the button of his fly and slowly lower the zipper of his pants. The slight rasp makes my heart skip and my breaths deepen.

This really is happening. To me. With him.

Suddenly, he grabs my face and pulls me toward him. Our lips lock. Our hands explore exposed flesh. Unlike our previous kiss, this one is soft, reserved, nearly reverent.

I slip my hand inside his pants and come against the hard, plastic molding of an athletic cup. I give a little snicker and pull away from his kiss.

"There seems to be something in the way."

"You have no idea, but let's not rush this." He kisses the tip of my shoulder, which brings about a whole-body shudder. "I need to see your skin, brat." He tugs at my dress, drawing it up my legs.

I lift a little on my knees and let him draw it over my hips, up my waist, and over the curve of my breasts. I'm small enough I can get away without wearing a bra and I'm not wearing one now. I nibble my lower lip a little.

Is he going to be disappointed?

A lusty sigh escapes him as he drags the dress over my head and helps extricate my arms from the wet fabric.

"God, you're fucking beautiful."

I sit back on my heels, nervous and unsure. My previous confidence evaporates now that I'm bared to him. It's dark in the cave, but there's enough light flickering from the lightning flashing across the sky to make out his features.

He places the palm of his hand against the small of my back and pulls me to him. A kiss at the hollow of my throat catches my breath. The roughness of his tongue, as he swirls it against my skin, accelerates my heart.

I arch against the sensation and sink into the moment. He kisses down my breast bone, fluttering kisses between my breasts while I stare down at him. He moves to my left breast. When his mouth covers my nipple, a jolt of pure pleasure runs through my body, heating my core and bringing a gasp to my lips. His tongue darts out, teasing flicks that draw my nipple into a tight, needy little bud. Then he moves to my other breast. My entire body comes alive.

"Axel..." I claw at his wet shirt, pulling it up to his shoulders. To get it off, he breaks contact with my breast and stares up at me. Our gazes lock and I give a little nod. We're not going to stop and that terrifies me as much as it excites me.

My entire body shivers as his gaze sweeps across my naked flesh.

Well, I'm not entirely naked. My thong stands in the way as do the rest of his clothes.

"Tell me you want this, Zoe, because if we go any further, I won't be able to stop."

"Please don't stop."

"Then you need to get up. These pants aren't coming off without removing my boots."

I reluctantly push off his lap and take a step back. He unties his boots and pulls them off while I admire the hard planes of muscle flexing and bunching as his body moves. Once his boots are off, he stands and gives a cocky grin as he hooks his fingers on his pants and yanks them off.

He stands before me in nothing but boxers. I've seen him in swim trunks. I've devoured the perfection of his body before, but this is the first time I get to do so openly. My mouth drops as his fingers hook under the waistband of his briefs.

"You like what you see, brat?"

"Very much."

"So do I. Fuck, but you're amazing." His gaze travels my body and stops at my midsection. Self-consciously, I cover the long scar running from the bottom of my ribs on the left all the way across to the top of my hip on the right. There are other scars, a plethora of little reminders that will stay with me for life.

In my eagerness, I forgot all about them. With his eyes roaming my body, they're all I can think about now.

My body cools off as self-doubt replaces the heat from before. I'm an ugly mess of ruined flesh beneath my clothes. It's got to be revolting.

"Stop that." His words rumble in the cave.

"Huh?"

"Whatever just went thought your head, stop it."

I clutch at my midsection, unable to hide all the ugliness from the penetrating intensity of his gaze. The thing is, I can't stop these thoughts. They run through me without a care for the destruction they leave in their wake. The self-loathing they uncover is tough to resist. The memories that surface are impossible to push aside.

A low, plaintiff cry escapes me.

He rushes to me and takes both my hands. I resist, unwilling to show him the marks that I'll carry with me for the rest of my life.

"Stop that." His tone cuts and commands. "Don't ever think you're less than you are because of those." He pulls my arms apart, revealing the expanse of my skin to his scrutiny. "You're beautiful. You're a survivor. Remember that."

"But they're ugly." *I'm ugly.*

He traces the long gash with the pad of his fingers. "They tell the story of your strength. These scars speak to where you've been. They say nothing about who you are, or where you're headed." He looks at me, really looks at me.

I flinch as he takes in my skinny frame. My breasts, which I've always wished were bigger. He stares into my face, traveling all around it, eyes wide and loving.

"You steal my breath when I look at you. You make my heart thunder and my skin shiver. To know you're willing to give yourself to me; it's an indescribable feeling. You're beautiful and strong, perfect in every way. I'm lucky to have you. I'm lucky you saw in me what I refused to acknowledge for far too long."

"It's just the scars remind me of... Plus, they're gross and ugly."

"They're exquisite reminders of your strength. What happened to you doesn't define you." He squeezes my hands as he lowers to his knees. His face is eye level with the scars. The slow tilt of his face brings the simmering heat of his eyes back to mine. His fingertips trace the puckered flesh with reverence instead of revulsion.

The heat of his mouth presses over the ugliest scar. His lips caress me. Oh, how I want to kiss that mouth and drown in the taste of him. I love the way he focuses on me, my needs, and ignores his own needs for mine.

I stand in awe as he kisses each and every scar, from the largest and ugliest to the smallest hairline imperfection marring my skin. He erases what those men did to me and replaces the pain with unfettered adoration.

If possible, I fall deeper in love with him because of it. From one hip bone to the other, he covers me in kisses, returning back to center. There he pauses and hooks a finger under the string of my thong.

"I need to be inside of you. I can't stand it any longer." He slowly removes the tiny excuse of clothing, revealing me fully to him. He takes in a slow, deep inhale and a lusty moan escapes him. "You have no idea what you do to me."

I have a fairly good idea, and after the tender kisses, my blood heats again. Especially with his mouth so close to my core. I nibble on my lower lip, wanting—needing him to make me fly again.

Another swirl of his tongue, this one right around my belly button curls my toes. My fingers spear into his hair as desire sweeps through me.

"Axel..."

"Yes, luv?" He stares up at me with a full-bodied smirk curving the corners of his lips.

"You're wearing far too many clothes."

"Oh, we'll get to that." He buries his nose between my legs and forces my feet apart. The sinful press of his tongue sends me into oblivion.

My entire body shakes as an orgasm rips through me. He keeps me on my feet, supporting me with his hands. When I can see straight again, I collapse down on the blanket and lie on my back. It's dark, but I can make out the contours of the cave roof.

Axel gathers the rest of the blankets. He shakes them out, then lays them down on top of each other. He reaches for his briefs, and in one fluid movement, shucks them, and the athletic cup, down to his ankles. With his eyes on me, he kicks his clothes to join the rest of our things on the ground.

"Come here, little minx. It's time."

My arms and legs feel like wet noodles after that orgasm, but I somehow manage to move. I can't help myself. Axel stands before me, gloriously nude, and I can barely see any of it. The storm is moving swiftly, which means the lightning comes less often. There's more darkness in the cave than I'd like.

His silhouette shifts. His arm crosses the centerline of his body and I know what he's doing. He holds his cock, stroking it by the low rumble coming from his chest.

I've never seen a man touch himself. I've never been with a man with the confidence in his body that Axel has in his. Although, if I'm being honest, Axel's body is chiseled perfection, a weapon honed to perform at its peak.

And he's going to share it with me.

"Do you know how beautiful you are?" His arm moves and his hips give a little thrust. "I'm afraid I might embarrass myself. I want you so bad it hurts."

"Do you?" I can't help my insecurities. They're rooted in a lifetime of rejection by the man who stands in front of me. He professes his love. Or rather, his need. It still feels like a dream.

"Do I want you?" He sounds shocked.

"Yeah."

"More than I can say." He steps toward me and grabs my hand.

Before I blink, he places it on his cock, molding my fingers around his impressive girth. I suck in a breath, surprised by the thickness of his erection and how hard he is for me. How did all of this fit behind that athletic cup? He had to have been in physical distress.

For me.

The corner of my mouth tilts up. There's no doubt he's hard for me.

"Feel what you do to me." He covers my hand with his and pushes my hand to the root of his cock. With a twist and a pull, he moves my hand back up to the tip where a drop of wetness spreads across my hand. "So fucking hard for you. I haven't decided how I'm going to take you."

"You haven't?" I don't know why, but butterflies dance in my belly. I assume he'll take me like all the other boys I've known. Me on my back.

"No." His low rumbly moan does funny things to my insides. My sex throbs, heating up and growing slick for him.

"I want to fuck you against the wall. Drive into you on the ground. Take you on your knees and that mouth of yours is figuring prominently in my fantasies right now."

237

I've never talked about sex with a man before. We didn't use words, just stripped and had sex. There may, or may not, have been a little cuddling afterward.

But this is blatant, in your face, raw sexuality. He doesn't shy away from saying what's on his mind. I feel him weighing each of his options, deciding how he'll take me our first time together. Meanwhile, he shows me how to stroke him, moving our hands together up and down his impressive length.

I'm more than a little worried if he'll fit inside of me. My body gives a little shiver. As if he's in tune with my thoughts, his dick jumps in my hand.

"If you have a preference darling, you've got two seconds to voice it. Otherwise…"

"I don't want to choose." I place my hand against his cheek. "I've dreamt of this moment my entire life." I'm not really sure what I'm saying, or what it even means, but something tells me this isn't something I want to control. "Just put me out of my misery and fuck me—however you want." I press my legs together, trying to soothe an ache only he can relieve.

He cups my face, and we stand there for a moment, gazing into each other's eyes. I take a moment to let everything sink in.

"I'll never walk away from you again, luv. You're mine and you need to know what that means. I've never staked a claim on a woman before, not like this." He takes my hand and places it over his heart. "You're mine, for now, and always."

His words slam into me as his lips slam against mine in a soul-shattering kiss. Rough and raw, whatever restraint he had crumbles. My heart slams against my chest, beating erratically as his kiss overtakes and consumes me.

There's nothing gentle or soft left in him. He takes with brutal aggression, demanding my surrender. I willing give him everything as his body collides with mine. The long, turgid, length of his erection jabs against my stomach as he pushes me back, driving me further into the cave.

The rough rock slams against my back as he grabs me by the ass. Before I realize what's happening, he lifts me into the air. I give a little squeak as he positions me over the flare of his cock.

"I can't do slow and gentle for our first time. I need to be inside of you now." His demand flips some kind of animalistic switch inside my head. I loop my arms around his neck and wrap my legs around his hips.

"Yes, please." Anything to put me out of my misery.

I breathe as he shifts my weight where he wants it. Slowly, he lowers me down. The tip of his cock pushes in and breaches my entrance. A gasp escapes me. Either I'm super tight, or he's fucking huge. Every muscle in my body burns as he inextricably lowers me down, sheathing himself inside of me. He said he couldn't do gentle, but this is tortuously slow. Every nerve in my body fires off at the same second, overcome by the moment. He's inside of me and we're fucking. It's a thousand times better than my most erotic fantasies. So fucking good. So hot. I'm overcome with emotion as sizzling jolts of electricity fire throughout my body. He hasn't moved, yet I'm ready to come. "How're you doing?" His words are terse, clipped, and strained with need. "Okay?"

I bury my head against his shoulder and a tiny sob escapes me.

"Zoe?" He starts to lift me off his cock, but I tighten my legs around his hips.

"I'm good. I'm just overwhelmed." I never thought there would be a day when he wanted me as much as I wanted him.

"Overwhelmed in a good way considering my dick is inside of you?" He huffs a soft laugh. "You feel fucking amazing. Hot, tight, wet— mine." He says the last with a growl.

"Yes, yours in the best possible way." This is when I want to tell him I love him, but I won't be the first to say those all-important words. I can't. They need to come from him first, and not while we're fucking each other's brains out. Or rather, not while he's fucking my brains out.

Alpha male all the way, Axel is a take-charge kind of man. When it comes to sex, there's no doubt in my mind he'll dominate and control every aspect of it. I'm perfectly, one hundred percent, A-okay with that. I can't imagine him any other way.

"Let me know if I hurt you." He shifts his grip, getting a better grip on my ass. Pressing me against the wall of the cave, he widens his stance. I simply hang on for whatever comes next. The burning sting of the initial stretch lessens as my body accommodates to his size.

"I need you to move." My toes curl as my body comes alive. I rock a little against him, letting him know I need more.

My ragged breaths fill the room as his abs clench and his hips flex. He pulls nearly all the way out, then jabs forward spearing me with his cock.

"Fuuuck!" He growls and does it again. "Feels so fucking good."

He moves—a slow glide out, followed by a vigorous thrust in.

My teeth clamp together with each powerful thrust. His low, guttural moans fill the cavern as deep, dark desire sweeps us away.

I move with him, as much as he allows. His hips thrust, increasing as his urgency overtakes him. Each of my breathy moans is punctuated by a low growl from him. He slams into me and pants with exertion as he drives home again and again.

My pussy clenches around his cock, taking him in as deep as I can. My eyes close and I grip his powerful shoulders. My legs lock around his hips as every part of me tunes into him, hyperaware of every delicious lick of heat, every agonizing slide, each punishing thrust.

"Mouth." He demands. It's more a grunt than a word, voiced in desperation and command. "I want your mouth when I come."

"Anything you want." I respond immediately and right my head so he can take my mouth.

"God, you don't want to be making that kind of promise. Not if you knew everything I want to do to you."

"Then do it." Our eyes lock for a split second as something fundamental shifts between us. "Anything you want…"

"Fuuuck." He grabs one of my wrists, then takes the other one. One hand supports my ass. The other takes my hands and presses them over my head, shackling me against the stone wall of the cave.

My pussy pulses around his cock as he thrusts harder. My back scrapes against the wall, but I'm oblivious to the mild discomfort. My entire world narrows down to the man fucking me and the promise in his eyes. He's doing more than fucking me. Axel is staking his claim.

I moan beneath the press of his lips, and struggle to release my hands so I can touch him. He gives a sharp shake of his head and pins my arms overhead. His bruising kiss punctuates each punishing thrust. He pounds harder, faster, more frantic, but still powerfully in control.

Inside my head, my emotions spin. My body demands something powerful and raw, a taking and claiming, but my soul craves something far different.

It needs his promise and the affirmation I can't live without.

His tongue spears and lashes, nearly in time with the pounding of his cock. My insides clench and tighten as a blistering heat sweeps inside of me.

The sounds he makes, the grunts and groans, are feral and wild. His gasps for air are so fucking sexy they drive me insane. I plead with him for more. To take me harder, faster, and he does.

We race together toward completion but I reach that pinnacle first. My pussy tightens as a rush of exquisite pleasure swallows me whole. His climax hits a moment later as he slams home, seating himself deep within me as my pussy milks him dry.

My head tips forward and I turn to gently kiss the sheen of perspiration on his neck. The press of my lips is tender, sweet, and I hope he understands what I'm trying to say.

He takes a step back. My hands are released and he supports me fully. "Did I hurt you?"

My back is sore, and there may be a few new bruises, but I don't care.

I nuzzle against him. "Only in the most delicious way."

His spent cock softens and begins to slip out. I clench my legs around his hips, not ready to be separated so soon. Our connection, now that it's made, is real and deep and awe-inspiring.

TWENTY-FOUR

Axel

WE MAKE LOVE THROUGH THE NIGHT, CURLING TOGETHER EVERY now and then to fitfully doze. I love how Zoe fits against my body. Her soft curves drive my lusty fantasies.

The moment I think I'm spent, my dick says otherwise.

I take her on the floor, moving over her until her back arches and her pussy milks my cock. I turn her to her knees and pound into her from behind. I thought we were done then, so I held her in my arms as the surf lulled us to sleep. Only she woke me with her hand on my cock and treated me to the wonders of her mouth. My little brat continues to surprise me.

I sit in the predawn twilight and stare out on a calm ocean. All the fury from last night's storm is gone, but not forgotten. As the night gives up its reign of the heavens, a light glow fills the sky.

We need to be getting back before the rest of the Facility wakes, but I'm reluctant to wake Zoe. She's a vision of beauty with her golden curls spilled in wanton disarray all over the covers. She sleeps peacefully, her features relaxed and happy.

At least I hope she's happy.

After last night, a fundamental shifting of our relationship means everything is different. She's no longer my best friend's sister, but rather belongs to me. I'm a little worried how Austin will take the news.

Two days ago, I would've thought our friendship worth far more than any fling with his sister. Now, it's different. I can't imagine my life without Zoe in it.

If Austin doesn't approve, we'll cross that bridge when we need to, but he needs to know his sister is mine.

A soft moan sounds behind me. I turn around to admire the sleepy form of my girl as she stretches her arms overhead. The blanket covering her slips down her body to reveal the soft curve of her breast.

"Good morning." She rubs the sleep from her eyes and blinks against the light. "What time is it?"

I dressed while she slept, knowing if I didn't, we'd never leave the privacy of her little cave. I could stay here forever, forgetting the existence of the outside world, but that is not an option for either of us.

While she stretches and runs her fingers through her hair, I fetch her dress. It's nearly dry from the storm last night, but needs a good wash. Like my clothes, dirt and sand cover it.

"Time to get dressed and return to the land of the living." I bring her dress over and squat beside her. My gaze latches onto her breast and the nipple begging to be kissed. With a groan, I settle back on my ass. If I touch her, we're never getting out of here.

"Do we have to?"

"I think if we don't, they'll send out a search party."

A low groan escapes her as she rolls to her back and pulls the blanket up to her chin. I don't know whether to be upset her perky little breast is no longer on display, or sigh in relief that the temptation is temporarily removed.

"I can't believe we…" She pulls the blanket up to her nose and peeks out at me.

"You can't believe we did what?" I stare down at her, loving this shy side of her. There was no shyness last night. Not once did she back down from any of my demands, allowing me to lead us as I pleased.

Zoe's sexual experiences are far fewer than mine, but she's very willing to please.

"You know." The tiniest blush fills her cheeks.

"I do." I bend and hover over her face. "But I want to hear you say it."

This is probably a mistake, but fuck if I care. My dick doesn't think it's a mistake. Hard and eager, it wants another taste of her before we leave. I'm of a mind to indulge myself.

"I can't believe we had sex. It feels like a dream."

"It didn't feel like a dream when you were coming on my cock, or all over my face, and let's not forget my fingers." And I'll never forget her sucking my cock. Damn, that was a powerful orgasm.

She pulls the covers over her head, then lowers it again.

"Like I said, I can't believe it." She glances toward the opening of the cave. "I suppose it's time to head back to reality?"

I don't like the sound of that. I yank the blanket off her body, treating my eyes to the deliciousness of her body.

"Axel!" She grabs at the blankets, and looks like she wants to say something else. When she sees me yanking down my pants, her eyes widen.

"There's no heading *back* to reality. What happened last night, and what's about to happen now, is very real." I shove my pants down to my ankles and spread her legs. I'd take my pants off, but my dick leads this show. It's eager for one more taste of her before we leave this place behind.

Zoe's eyes widen as I take her. It's a fast and furious fuck. Her body responds and it doesn't take long before her orgasm crashes into her. I follow right behind her as pleasure courses through me.

"Fuck..." She presses a hand to her forehead as I pull out. "What was that?"

"A little reminder." I tap her forehead. "This is real—and you're mine."

She rolls to her side and props her head on her hand. "You really mean that, don't you?"

"More than you realize."

"But what about..." She glances outside.

"I won't lie to you. I'm not going to hide what happened between us, but I'm not going to advertise it either. I don't kiss and tell. It's not respectful."

"I guess I just assumed..." While I put myself back together, she sits and props her elbows on her knees.

"I hope whatever it was you were going to say isn't that this was a one night stand. When I said you're mine, I meant it. However, out there, we need to be careful. If you want everyone to know what we did, that's up to you. But I won't be sharing any of our intimate details with anyone."

"What about practice?"

"What about it?"

"Won't it be hard to—you know, after we..." Her lower lip curls inward. She's so fucking cute when she does that.

"Your training is a part of the process. I won't hold back, if that's what you're referring to. You need to understand that."

"It's just… Won't it be weird?" She takes her dress and slowly slips it over her head.

"Only if we make it weird, but if you want one of the other guys to work with you, we can make that happen."

"Won't they ask questions?"

"I'm not going to lie, they're pretty damn perceptive. There's only one reason to switch, especially since I told all of them in no uncertain terms that you were mine."

"You said that?"

"I told you that you've been on my mind."

"Wow."

"It sinking in yet, brat?"

"I think so. I've just… I've never had someone as intense as you."

"That's because you've never had a man claim you before. I'm not some college kid looking for a fuck-buddy. This thing between us, it's real. You're mine, and I protect what's mine. If that's too much for you, then we need to stop this before we go any further."

"I think I'm beginning to see that."

"And?"

"And what?" She turns innocent eyes on me.

"Do you understand what it means when I say you're mine?"

"Honestly, I don't know." She tucks her knees to her chest. "I'm still trying to process all of this." She gestures between us.

I squat down before her and take her hands in mine. "Well, the way I see it, you can look at it two ways."

"Huh?"

"Either, we fucked to get each other out of our systems." Her entire body tenses and I rush to continue. "Or—I finally got my head out of my ass and realized you've always been mine. One day, you'll forgive me for being such a jerk, but what happened last night, and this morning, and hopefully many more nights and mornings to come…" I take a deep breath realizing what it is I'm saying. "What happened is me realizing how much I fucking love you."

Her eyes widen and her lower lip trembles.

"Axel, you shouldn't say that, not unless you're sure."

"Oh, I'm pretty damn sure, which is why the moment we leave this little love cave of ours, you need to understand two things."

"What?"

"First off, I love you. I always have." Her eyes turn misty. "Second, it's because I love you that I'll be as harsh as possible when it comes to your training. I do you no favors in taking things easy on you because I'm afraid to hurt your feelings. Do you understand?"

"I'm sorry, I'm still reeling from the first thing."

I scoop her into my arms and bury her beneath a hungry kiss, which leaves her breathless. She looks up at me, eyes shimmering with tears, and an expression of the most devout love filling her face.

"I love you too." She fiddles with the hair over my ear, reminding me I need to get a haircut.

I no longer keep my hair military regulation short, but I try not to let it get too long.

"Then, when I throw you on your ass, don't look to me for mercy. I won't give it to you because we're sleeping together. If anything, I'll be much harsher than I am with Andrew. If you think it's going to be a problem, I'll swap with my teammate. Out there, I'm in charge. This doesn't change any of that."

"You won't train me?"

"Not if this—" I make the same gesture she made, pointing to myself then to her, "if this compromises your training, I won't allow it."

"What happens after this week?"

"You mean when we complete this training?"

"Yes."

"Most likely, Alpha team will head out again."

"Meaning I won't see you."

"Not while I'm out. I'm a Guardian. I always will be and that means the mission comes first."

"I know." She presses her lips together and gives it a think. "And your missions rescue people like me."

"Most of the time. Rarely, we're tagged for personal protection, but yes, we're not called hostage rescue specialists for nothing."

She tilts her head and stares out of the cave entrance toward the placid waters of the Pacific.

"Then I need to be as competent and capable as possible when you're not around, don't I?"

"Yes." There is no other answer.

"Then I guess I'm willing."

"For what?" I've almost forgotten what we're talking about.

"Teach me everything you can, and don't go soft on me because we're sleeping together. I do assume we'll still be…"

"Will be what?"

"Doing more of this." She spins in a slow circle.

"You can count on that." Fuck, I'm hard again. Shit. Fuck. Fuck. We don't have time for another round. "We really need to be heading back. I don't know about your schedule, but I need to meet the guys for breakfast and go over notes from last night."

"And plan my attempted abduction?" Her eyes curve with mischief.

"It won't be an attempt, little brat. You will fail."

"Then I suppose there will be consequences for failing?" She nibbles on her lip again, drawing a groan from me. "Maybe some —reprimanding?"

Shit, I seriously don't need her going down that lane.

Not yet.

Soon, but not yet.

TWENTY-FIVE

Zoe

THE DAYS BLEND INTO ONE ANOTHER WITH TWO CONSTANTS UNITING them. First, Axel is an uncompromising taskmaster. Alpha to the core, he demands, if not perfection, then at least a determined effort to come close.

I constantly fall short.

Skye keeps telling us size doesn't matter. If we practice, we can put a man like Forest down. I don't know what she's smoking, injecting, or otherwise snorting, but I've yet to budge Forest. I can shift Axel's center of gravity. I did that once. But Forest?

Never going to happen.

I think he lets her push him around. I mean, mentally, I get it. The concepts are ones I grasp. It's just that putting them together with the limitations of my body is where I fall short.

Speaking of... My body is a mass of bruises from all the training. My ego is similarly bruised.

They said they'd be *abducting* us, testing our readiness. For what, I'm not sure. The outside world is tough, but we don't need to be combat-ready when we do go out and face it.

I've done the math. The chances for any of us being abducted twice in one lifetime is astronomical. Also, there's the age thing. We're all getting older. Like Moira, she's twenty-two—kind of past the age of a nubile kidnapping victim.

Andrew is still young. At twelve, I can kind of see it, and not to be too gross about it, but he's hot.

For a twelve-year-old.

I see why he's a commodity. But me? As far as the slave trade goes, I'm pushing forty, maybe sixty. I don't have Moira's stunning looks. I don't have Andrew's angelic qualities. I'm plain Jane ordinary, and over the hill.

I get Forest and his wish to help us take control of our lives. Personal defense makes sense for any woman in this world. I just don't think I'll need it.

I'm wiser now. More sensitive to the world around me. I'll never go to Cancun again, and if I do, I'll never walk around alone. It's a bit overkill in my estimation.

I work the program because I trust Skye, but I really don't believe in it. As for the defensive training, how can it hurt?

Speaking of defensive training, I'm tired of looking over my shoulder in anticipation of an attack.

The only *attack* that comes from Axel are his nightly visits to my bed. I'm pretty sure it's against all the rules, but he sleeps with me every night.

My muscles are sore from sparring with him during the day. My body is drained from the fucking we do all night.

He's a machine and fucking insatiable. It's like he can't get enough of me. I find it overwhelming like I need to pinch myself to make sure this is really happening. I guess there's a small corner of my mind that is still a skeptic when it comes to Axel.

As for me, I'm taking a breather with Moira and Andrew. We just finished another afternoon of ass-kicking. It's what I call our sessions with the Guardians. Most days, it's me against Axel, but they've been switching things up.

Today, Axel and his buddy Four teamed up on me, Andrew, Moira, and Stacy, the other girl assigned to Four.

"Fucker." Moira crumples the paper cup in her hand as Number Four saunters past. He flashes her a dismissive wave while she sneers at him.

"What's up between the two of you?" I shove her playfully on the shoulder.

Four made it a point to put Moira on her back over and over again.

"He's an ass," she says.

"Um, as opposed to not being an ass?" I take a sip of my water and watch the Guardians at their table. "They're not here to take things easy on us."

Axel's made that point entirely too clear. Not that I expect him to take it easy on me, but I'd be lying if a little piece of me *assumed* he would. We are fucking after all.

Like—a lot.

"Word." Andrew stretches out his shoulder. Axel held him in a brutal shoulder lock during practice. Andrew tapped out and I learned a lesson.

There is no mercy when a Guardian is involved.

"You okay there?" I subconsciously rub at my shoulder. Today's lesson on no mercy was brutal. So far, Andrew and I are flunking in a spectacular way.

The Guardians are massive men. Put six of them around one of our tables and they look like giants. Too much brawn all in one place. I shouldn't stare at them, but it's hard not to. They simply draw the eye.

Honestly, it's intimidating.

"Yeah." Andrew's eyes pinch. "I think they're plotting our downfall."

"Probably." I agree with Andrew, especially given the looks Axel and Four keep shooting our way. "Keep your eyes peeled. Has anyone been abducted by them yet?" My attention swivels to the other tables where our classmates gather with slumped shoulders and defeated expressions.

We're all struggling.

Forest pushes us too hard. We need more practice with the basics before subjecting us to the Guardians. Those men don't coddle. They have no sympathy. They're cold-hearted brutes, at least on the outside.

I know what Axel thinks about the training. He's uncompromising when it comes to helping me learn how to defend myself. Their indifference comes from honest compassion.

They're heroes to us all.

Which means, they demand nothing but our best.

Axel and his team are the ones who rescued me. I'm pretty sure they're also responsible for the rescue of several of my friends as well.

They just don't let on that they care.

"Molly said she saw hers lurking around her room." Andrew works out the kinks in his shoulder. The kid, for all his quirks, is highly informed about all things happening around the Facility.

If I have a question, he knows the answer.

"What happened?" Moira perks up. She, too, is aware of Andrew's uncanny knack for knowing the ins and outs of the gossip chain.

"Nothing." He honestly looks disappointed. "She slipped into Corrine's room and they called a monitor to walk them to breakfast."

"We can do that?" My brows pinch. "I didn't think we could ask for help."

"Evidently, we are supposed to do just that." Andrew slumps over the table. "I haven't heard of anyone else getting snatched." He looks disappointed.

"You want to be abducted?"

"No, but I want to know if I can handle myself if it happens. Or at least learn how I can do better."

Yeah, Andrew suffers from extreme hero worship. He wants to be a Guardian, but his twelve-year-old body limits that aspiration. He needs time to mature and develop. His head is already in the game. Dangerously so, if anyone asks me. Although, last I looked, nobody cares what I think.

Axel looks up from his table and turns his astute gaze on us.

Andrew's spine straightens and I swear he puffs out his scrawny chest. He's caught between a boy and a man, too big to be a boy, but too small to be a man. All he wants in life is to be found worthy in the eyes of the Guardians.

Sadly, they treat him like any of the rest of us. Puberty is rough and he's right in the thick of it.

255

Moira gives a little flick of her fingers. "I may, or may not, have been abducted." She sneaks a peek at me.

"You?" I can't hide my surprise. "When? And why are you just now telling us?"

"Because…" She's grumpy.

"No *because*. What happened?"

"I fucked up."

"You what? How did that happen?"

Andrew snickers, then stops when Moira punches him in the arm. The same arm Axel nearly dislocated earlier.

"Hey, that hurts!" Andrew grabs his arm and shifts away from Moira.

"Wasn't supposed to tickle." Moira says with a grump.

"Come on. What happened?" I need the deets, like now.

Axel hasn't come after me yet, but like everyone else, I expect it any moment. Honestly, I'm tired of looking over my shoulder.

It's *exhausting*!

If Moira can tell me what to look out for, maybe I can avoid getting snagged. Honestly, I'll fail. Axel basically said I would, and from the way he worked me over on the mat, I've got zero chance of fighting him off.

Moira's mouth gives a little twitch. I know her well enough to know she's holding out. I slug her arm.

"No way. You *have* to tell. No secrets. Remember?"

She gives me a squint. "If we're playing the no secret game, you have something to fess up to."

Oh hell no.

I'm not doing that, especially in front of Andrew. Not that Axel's been taking it easy on me, but I don't want Andrew knowing there's something going on between me and Axel.

"If you're talking about Z and Three, don't bother." Andrew glances over at me and gives an exaggerated wink.

"What? There's nothing—"

"Oh please!" Andrew smacks his thigh. "I'm not blind. I know what it looks like when two people are fucking."

Well, shit.

"You're *fucking* Three?" Moira's eyes widen as she shoves her knuckles into her mouth. "Damn, girl. He's fine. Maybe not as fine as Four, but go you." She makes a fist and wants to give me a fist bump.

I look at her as if she's grown a second head, all the while trying not to shit my pants. If Andrew knows, and Moira knows... A quick glance across the dining room and I shrivel beneath Forest's glacial stare.

Does he know?

He can't. We've been careful. Obsessively so. Except, Andrew knows. Now Moira does too.

Shit!

I always forget Andrew's past. He's seen more than any twelve-year-old should. I see him as a boy, but he's not innocent. He was abducted into sexual slavery, forced to serve, and survived. He survived using his wits and by playing one master off the other.

The things he shares in Group make my skin crawl. In many ways, I'm getting an education into all things dealing with sex and the depravity of man. That my education comes in the form of a twelve-year-old is something I'll deal with later.

"How do you know?" I pinch his arm and demand an answer.

"You look at him when you think he's not looking at you. He does the same. When you're supposed to be looking at him, you don't, like you don't want to *look* like you're looking at him. It's a classic crush on the teacher."

My gut says to reply with '*Is not!*' but I press my lips together and give him a dirty look instead.

"What's this?" Moira's eyes widen and her mouth gapes. "You've been holding out on me."

"It's nothing."

Except I can barely walk with all the fucking we're doing.

"Liar." Moira dissolves in a fit of giggles.

"Stop that." I pinch her. "Everyone's looking at us."

"Isn't that what you want? Three looking at you?" She pinches me back.

We're attracting attention, but not from Axel. His teammate unfolds himself from the chair, which barely contains his bulk. My mouth goes slack-jawed watching Four prowl toward us.

That's what he looks like, an animal on the hunt. I slink back in my chair as he closes the distance. When I glance over at Moira, her eyes are glued to Four's powerful form.

He towers over us and gives a little jerk of his chin, directed at Andrew. "Up bud. Three wants a word with you."

"He does?" Andrew slides out of his seat and gulps. "Yeah." He practically runs to Axel.

Four takes Andrew's seat, placing him next to Moira.

"So, what are the two of you talking about?"

"Nothing." Moira shifts a little closer to me. When she does, Four grabs her and slides her back until she's practically sitting in his lap. She's not, but it's close.

Like, *close* close.

"Didn't look like nothing, and considering the stares the two of you are giving me and my buddies, I'm wondering if it has to do with last night?" The vocal modulator makes his voice menacing.

It certainly sends shivers racing down my spine. A shudder ripples through Moira's body. I tune in to the way she's most definitely *not* looking at Four.

"Moira, what happened last night?"

Four gives a low chuckle and tilts his head, waiting for Moira to answer. When she doesn't, he pokes her in the arm.

"What did we say about not telling the truth?"

"Not speaking isn't lying." Her eyes narrow to thin slits.

"It's also not speaking the truth. Now, do we need a repeat of last night? I'm surprised you're sitting considering how I reddened that ass of yours."

"Um…" I sit back a second. I'm a little slow when it comes to sex, but even I pick up on this vibe. "I'm just going to…"

"You are going to join Three. He told me to send you to him. As for Moira, we're going to discuss the ramifications of trying to seduce the teacher."

Holy fucking shit!

Four doesn't hold his punches. I'm pretty sure I know what happened last night.

Precocious and Moira go hand in hand. I can totally see her trying to seduce Four. I also see Four not falling for that shit. He reminds me of Axel, a man who's used to being in charge.

I stand and abandon Moira to whatever fate Four has planned and cross the distance to the table the Guardians claim as theirs.

259

Andrew talks animatedly with the men, discussing grappling holds and takedown moves. He's eager, overly so.

Three, aka Axel, moves to the side, giving me a place to sit. I lower myself into the spot he indicates, careful to make sure no part of my body touches his.

Andrew grows more animated, asking about the team's exploits.

I know these men only by their designations. They're strangers to me, and yet they are all intimately familiar with my story. This is the team who rescued me. Men who saw me at my worst, the lowest of the low, helpless, defenseless, and if what Forest says is true—dead.

I have yet to confront Axel about that. Part of me doesn't want to. My mind isn't ready to grapple with that small detail of my rescue. I suppose, at some time, Axel will tell me what he did for me. Until then, I leave it on the side as something to deal with later.

The men laugh as Andrew becomes more animated. He's interested in the guns they use. The tactics they train with. Every Guardian comes from a branch of the military special ops community. Axel is a former Navy SEAL. Andrew wants to follow in their footsteps.

Axel hates when I say 'a former Navy SEAL.' To him, once a SEAL, always a SEAL. I should respect that, and I do, but I can't stop thinking it.

Axel nudges my hip with his finger. It's discreet and beneath the table. No one can see it. The pad of his thumb traces a line of fire across my back. He hooks it right under the waistband of my exercise shorts.

I squirm and he chuckles. Bastard knows what he's doing.

"What about you, Z?" Number One catches my attention, but I'm not sure what we're supposed to be talking about. My entire body is attuned to Axel and what he's doing with that damn thumb of his.

"Huh?" I pinch my eyes together. "I'm sorry, what?"

260

"Hand check." One glances at Axel.

Axel lifts his hands innocently. "I was asking Andrew if he was excited about the trip to Santa Monica. Did you sign up?"

Oh, right. The trip outside.

"Um, no. I think I'll take a pass this time around." This is actually the first time I've been allowed to go on an excursion beyond the protective walls of the Facility. Not that I'm a prisoner here. I can leave anytime I choose. It's just, I'm afraid.

I'm terrified of what might happen out there. Not that we won't be supervised. Our monitors will be with us every step of the way. I'm just not ready.

My demons aren't defeated yet.

"It's okay, Z." Axel whispers behind me. "You'll have plenty of opportunities to head out beyond the gates."

I try to compose myself. Andrew's eyes are on me. One seems particularly interested in Andrew. His eyes keep cutting between me, Axel, and Andrew. I pray to God he sees nothing more than a Guardian and his two pupils. I don't want to get Axel in trouble for sleeping with me.

"Well, I'm going." Andrew jumps out of his seat. "Noodles says he'll show me how to surf."

Noodles? I wrack my brain trying to figure out who that is; then it hits me. Forest happens, amongst all his projects, to manage the mega rock band Angel Fire. They have an estate a few miles south of the Facility. I remember something about one of them being into surfing. It figures Forest would connect Andrew to a rock legend. What a way to brighten a kid's life?

As for me, I couldn't care less about rock music and all that comes with it. I need simple. Safe. Something that I understand.

"You signed up?" I turn my attention to Andrew.

"You bet." He gives me a cheeky grin. "You should come." His nose wrinkles as he gives me a once over. "You're pale, like a ghost, and we can't really swim here. The beaches in Santa Monica are awesome."

The beaches here are pretty cool too. I head down to the rocky shore as often as I can. Andrew's right. They're not safe for swimming, but I can spend hours down there at low tide scouring the tide pools for all manner of cool and interesting sea creatures.

"Well, we'll see." I have *zero* interest in spending the day on a beach in public.

The overhead bell rings. I give a groan. Andrew bounces on his feet. Axel taps my hip. It's time for more sparring practice.

"You ready?" Axel practically breathes down my neck.

"Do I have a choice?"

"No, but how about we make it interesting?"

I glance around. When his voice hits those vocal registers, I know where his mind is at.

"What do you have in mind?" I'm not against playing games. They tend to work in my favor after bed check.

·

TWENTY-SIX

Axel

FOUR DAYS INTO OUR TIME AT THE FACILITY WITH THE RESCUES AND I'm fidgety. I'm not a fan of that word, rescues. Makes it sound like the people here are strays we took off the street instead of incredibly resilient people fighting to reclaim their lives.

Human trafficking disgusts me, and since it doesn't appear to be going away any time soon, I'll be employed until I hang up my boots. I'm itching to get back out in the field. We all are. Six girls are still out there, lost and alone. Months have passed since Zoe's rescue. God only knows what's happening to those girls, if they're even alive.

I'm torn. All I get is this one week with Zoe, then it's back out in the field, chasing down leads. Or maybe we'll get assigned to a new case. Honestly, it doesn't matter. We're all itching to get back out there.

We're warriors, men who went into the military with one goal in mind: protect and serve. Out of the military, that inner drive doesn't go away. If anything, it's stronger now.

One thing's for certain; our missions provide immediate gratification. Back when I was kicking doors, the objective may have been clear, but how it translated into a coherent plan to combat terrorism, and fight our enemies, often became a thing of faith.

"What's got you down?" Zoe drapes a blanket around my shoulders.

We're back at the cave, watching another beautiful sunset. Unlike last time, no storm rages outside. The ocean is calm and peaceful. Maybe that's why I'm in a brooding mood.

"Sorry, brat, my mind was wandering." I tug her down to sit beside me. "It's beautiful out there."

"This is my favorite time of day." She snuggles into my embrace.

"Really? Why's that?"

"It's another day I get to put behind me."

I stiffen a bit. It's far too easy for me to forget she's still navigating the aftereffects of her abduction.

"I like sunrises best. There's something about the dawning of a new day that speaks to me. But we don't get to see sunrises here."

"No, they kind of just creep up on us, but I'd rather see a sunset than a sunrise any day." She takes my hand in hers and interlaces our fingers.

These tiny touches fill my heart with love. I wrap my arm around her, trying to pull her tighter against me. Turning her hand over, I trace out the lines on her palm.

"We'll agree to disagree, little brat, but I'm happy to have some time alone with you."

I sneak into her bed every night, but that's fiery passion and sex. This quiet moment is where our souls connect, sitting and enjoying something as simple as a sunset and holding hands.

Not that we didn't fuck the moment we got here. I can't keep my hands off her hot little body, and she seems to have a similar problem keeping her hands off me. Neither of us are complaining.

"Have you thought about Santa Monica?" The day after we leave, a group of her classmates are planning an excursion into town. "It's the height of summer and the perfect time to hit the beach."

She shivers a little. Her reluctance bothers me. Since her rescue, she's been surrounded by others. First, the doctors and nurses at the hospital. Second, by the devoted staff here at the Facility.

"I don't think that's my speed."

Says the girl who flew to Cancun for spring break with her college friends. Zoe is, or used to be, adventurous.

"I worry about you." I bring her hand to my mouth and gently kiss the back of her knuckles.

"You don't have to."

"But I do." And after tonight she's going to need to blow off a little steam.

I worked a deal out with Griff after I realized there would be no way I could abduct Zoe. If her triggers activate, I don't want them to transfer to me. My desire is to be the one she turns to for solace, not the one pretending to kidnap her.

She's feisty on the mat, but like most of the kids here, all that training goes out the window when faced with a real-life experience.

Griff will step in for me and he won't be easy on her. I would, and that does her no good. I glance at my watch and give a sigh.

"What's wrong?"

"Sorry, it's just I have to get back for a briefing."

"About us?" She means the other kids, but my mind heads to *us*, like the two of us. It took less than a day for my team to figure it out.

Max chewed me out, but he didn't remove me as her instructor. Honestly, I think the fuckers had a betting pool in place.

"Not us, but our next assignment."

"Oh." She's fucking adorable when she pouts. "I guess that means you'll be heading out soon."

"Most likely." Mitzy called the meeting, which makes me worry. Bravo should be on task. If she's calling a meeting, it sends red warning flags all over the place.

"Well, I guess we can say goodbye to the sun and walk back."

"No." I grip her hand and give it a little shake. She needs to walk back alone. I'll trail behind and watch.

"No?"

"I know how much you enjoy it here. You should stay and finish watching the sunset." The sun is about ten minutes from kissing the horizon. "The best part of the show hasn't started yet. I don't want you to miss it."

"I don't mind walking back with you." Her soft smile melts my heart. I'd love to walk back with her, hand in hand, like two lovers. Turns out, I have a soft, gooey, romantic side to me.

Focus!

Right, I force myself back on task and blurt out the first thing that comes to mind.

"You can come if you want, but I'm running back." I have to be careful or she'll suspect something's up. "I didn't get my run in earlier and have a few miles to get in. If I leave now, I'll have just enough time to get it in before the briefing. If that's okay with you, then by all means, join me."

I leave it to her, fully aware that she hates to run. I also know she won't ask me to walk with her instead of jog back. Zoe knows I work hard to keep myself in top physical shape.

"Ugh, you're always working out." She flops back and stares up at me. Propping her arm over her face, she peeks up at me. "But I'm totally not complaining. I like the results."

"You mean you like when I fuck you up against the wall." I admit it takes a degree of strength to pull it off.

"Definitely." She licks her lips. My girl is insatiable, not that I'm complaining.

"Stop that."

"Stop what?"

"Looking at me like you want to swallow my dick."

"Well, I don't know about swallow, but a little licking."

I adjust my growing erection and give a curse. "You are a fucking tease, and now I have to run with a woody."

"Or, you can stay and we can see about that whole dick-swallowing thing."

Fuck me, but she's irresistible. I'd stay if I didn't know Griff was getting into position. I need a little time to find a place where I can watch the whole thing unfold.

"I'm leaving before I can't walk at all." I gently tap her leg and shake my head. "When I see you tonight, you will pay for this."

"Promises, promises." She leans up on her elbows and shakes her head. "Someday, I expect you to make good on your promises."

One day I most definitely will, but not until I'm one hundred percent certain doing so won't activate her triggers. I'm all for some rough sex, but she's talking mixing a bit of kink into things. I'm smart enough to know she's far from ready for any of that.

"I will see you later tonight."

She bites her lower lip. "Then, I will see you then. Now go run." She dismisses me with the flick of her fingers. I don't hesitate and escape while I still have the capacity to think. Give me another minute or two and I'd be buried balls deep in my girl and fuck the consequences.

I run back toward the main campus, but take a slight detour on the way there. Griff and I discussed the best way to take her out. There's a slight bend in the path where the scrub brush thickens. I've walked back from the cave often enough to know Zoe pays far too much attention to the ocean.

It's literally the last place an attack can come from, which makes this the perfect lesson in situational awareness. I don't care if she wants to stare out at the ocean, but she needs to develop the habit of scanning her surroundings. All the kids need to learn that vital skill.

They need to hardwire it in their brains.

I find Griff hidden behind a hollow in a hill. Dressed all in black, he'll be nearly invisible once darkness falls.

"She decided to stay, huh?" Griff and I took bets on whether she'd come back with me. He didn't think I could convince her to stay. "Thought I'd see the two of you skipping back holding hands."

"Fuck you."

"Sorry, bro, not into you that way."

I punch him and we trade a few before rolling to our backs and laughing.

"Guess this is yours." He fishes into his pocket and pulls out a raggedy button. We don't bet with money. It's a thing Max has about gambling. Instead, we swap buttons. It's stupid but is kind of becoming a tradition.

I palm the button and glance around. There's not a lot of time to get hidden, and no way to know how long we'll need to wait.

"Over there." Griff points to a grouping of small boulders. "Saw a baby rattler over there earlier. If you're real nice, he'll let you cuddle while we wait."

"Ha ha, not funny." I make my way over to the clustering of rocks. With Griff, I don't know if he's joking about seeing the snake or not. I give a solid kick to the rocks and listen for the telltale sound of a rattle going off. Only after I listen for a good bit, and kick the rocks a few more times, do I hunker down to wait.

My job is to watch. There's always one Guardian who observes a takedown. It's the best way to provide effective feedback after the fact. Our job, although it may not look like it, isn't to scare them shitless. It's to train and advise.

We wait longer than I expect. I know Zoe likes her sunsets, but it's past twilight and getting dark. I'm almost of a mind to head back to the cave to check on her when movement out of the corner of my eyes gets my attention.

It's Zoe, walking like she's on a stroll without a care in the world. As I expect, she casts her gaze out toward the ocean rather than on the path. Griff won't have to work hard to take her down.

She comes around the corner. Head turned seaward, oblivious to her surroundings. She passes Griff's position without a care. He practically oozes up out of the ground. A deadly shadow taking the form of a man.

His skills at interrogation, aka torture, are the best I've ever seen, but that doesn't hold a candle to watching the man stalk a person. Fucker has fun with it too. He steps right behind Zoe. Follows her a few steps. When she shows no sign she's aware of him, he attacks.

Griff grabs Zoe from behind, trapping her arms to her side. This is where she should attempt to free herself. Instead, panic sets in. Griff lifts her off her feet as she kicks and screams. Only there's no one here to help.

Even knowing what comes next, I can't help but feel a little bile rising in the back of my throat. We decided on an attempted rape for her lesson tonight instead of an abduction. I decided it would be less traumatizing considering her history, but I regret that decision now.

He walks her off the path. She futilely kicks against him. He slams her to the ground and pounces on top of her.

Zoe gives it a good go, but she's forgotten everything we taught her. Her first panicked scream changes once she realizes this is her test. At least she's thinking. That's actually a good sign. Half the kids we've test never get beyond their initial panic.

Griff gets her hands and pins them over her head. He shoves her legs apart. I can almost see the gears in her head spinning as she tries to figure out what to do.

When he lowers his bulk on top of her, I've had enough.

"That's enough, Four, she gets the point."

Zoe screams in frustration. He releases her hands and she slaps his shoulders, trying to push Four off her body.

"You're not going to move me like that." His modulated voice, makes her go still. "I'm on top of you, getting ready to rape you. What can you do?"

This is the second part of the test. We never leave them feeling defeated. We'll spend the next hour breaking down each and every step until she's satisfied.

Seeing Four on my girl makes acid burn in my throat. I want to give him a swift kick in the nuts, but this is an essential part of the program. We've sworn an oath to trust in Forest's odd rules.

Damn, if I don't hate every bit of this.

TWENTY-SEVEN

Zoe
___

FOUR'S BODY PRESSES DOWN ON ME. I'VE ROYALLY FUCKED THIS UP. I'm pissed at myself, and a few slaps help release my anger.

"Come on, Z, what can you do?" Axel steps into my line of sight.

"Were you watching the whole time?" My anger switches to him. "You set me up." I squirm beneath Four, pissed as all fuck.

"You knew something like this would be coming." He gives a jerk of his chin toward the menacing presence of Four. I understand even more, after this, why they wear all black and disguise their voices. They're more than intimidating. Four's fucking frightful.

Axel doesn't have his face mask and vocal modulator on. At least I don't have to deal with that.

What to do?

I struggle beneath Four. He released my hands, but I don't have the strength to move him. His hips wedge indecently between my legs. The weight of his body presses down on my chest. There's no kneeing him in the groin. I give up in defeat.

"I don't know." I don't like the whiny sound in my voice, but what really worries me is the fear laced underneath it. Have I learned nothing in the months since I've been here?

Four grabbed me just like that man in Cancun. He lifted me off my feet exactly the same way. The only difference was that man loaded me into a waiting van with three other men. They're the ones who subdued me. Four merely threw himself on me.

Four pushes off the ground and stands. He offers me his hand. I look up at him dubiously, but take it and shake off the dirt from my clothes.

I'm glad it's dark out. Neither of them can see the embarrassment heating my cheeks.

"What did you do wrong, Z?" When Axel reverts to calling me Z, I know we're in instruction mode.

I give a frustrated huff and shrug. "I don't know."

"Come on, Z, you know better than that. Think." Four takes a step back and glances back the way I came.

"Just tell me." Another angry huff pushes past my lips.

"Telling you does nothing to help you." Axel moves close, but he maintains his distance. This would be the perfect time for the man who's professed his love to—I don't know—hug me? I could use a little reassurance right now, not the grilling they're giving me.

"I can't win against someone as big as you." They're huge men, well over six-feet and nearly double my weight. "I've lost before I start."

"No, you lost because you weren't paying attention to your surroundings." Axel's words cut to the truth. "You knew, at some point, you would be tested. Your goal isn't to grapple with us, but to avoid having to do so in the first place. The best fighter is the one who avoids the fight in the first place."

"But I *was* paying attention."

"You only think you were." Four places his hands behind his back. "When did you first know I was there?"

"When you grabbed me." I hang my head because I never saw him.

"Come." He unhooks his hands and gestures for me to follow. I glance at Axel, still needing that reassuring hug, but he only gives a jerk of his head toward Four.

I follow along like an obedient puppy to where he grabbed me.

"You first knew I was here when I grabbed you?" Four points at a spot on the trail.

"Yeah."

"What were you doing?" He pushes, but I scrunch my nose trying to remember.

"I don't know." I glance over my shoulder. In all honesty, I was thinking about Axel fucking me against the cave wall and wondering what he would do when he visited me later tonight.

I fantasize about him a lot. Okay, all the damn time. There's no way in hell I'm saying that to Four.

Four cants his head to the side. "We can't help if you don't help yourself. How are you going to know what to change if you're not willing to do the work to find out what you did wrong?"

Well shit. He makes a good point.

"I don't know. I was daydreaming." I glance over at Axel and watch as a huge smirk fills his face. Bastard knows what I was thinking about.

"Okay." His attention shifts to Axel. "What, or who, you were daydreaming about is irrelevant. Point is, when you daydream, that part of your brain isn't engaged in monitoring your surroundings. Our goal is to get you to constantly be in control of yourself. That means, actively paying attention to what's going on around you. It's a skill you learn only with practice."

273

Four delivers his lecture sternly. Slowly, I release the anger and embarrassment I feel in being so easily overtaken.

"How do I do that?"

"Like Four says, with a lot of practice. Since we know this is a deficiency of yours, we'll spend tomorrow testing you."

"Testing me?" I gulp. I don't know if I can endure an entire day of what Four just did to me. These guys are good, and they're more than intimidating. There was real fear when Four picked me up off the ground.

For a moment, I thought I was back in Cancun.

"Well, shit…" My mouth kind of drops with the realization of what happened.

Axel's brows tug together in confusion.

"I aborted a trigger and didn't even realize it until now."

"What trigger?" Four's modulated voice deepens with concern.

"A man grabbed me from behind, just like you did. And he lifted me off my feet, just like you did." Four and Axel exchange glances. "I started to shut down, but I stopped that. I knew where I was, and I knew this was a test, which I failed, but I didn't shut down. Don't I get credit for that?"

Axel finally closes the distance between us. He wraps his arms around me and kisses the top of my head. "We didn't know how you were abducted, Zoe. If we had, we would've never incorporated that into the scenario."

I'm crying. No idea when the tears started, or why they're falling. I'm not sad or unhappy. I'm thrilled. I totally flunked at what they're trying to do, but I had a personal victory. I'll take whatever success I can.

Axel releases me and wipes away my tears with the pad of his thumb. Four stands stoically behind him. I'm about ten thousand percent sure that personal relationships between Guardians and their charges are major no-go territory, but Four doesn't appear to be surprised one bit. I guess everyone knows.

"I'm sorry about that." Four dips his head. "We tailor each lesson to minimize activation of known triggers. My apologies, but let's talk about what you can do better next time."

Next time.

Well, there's a promise if I ever heard one. He definitely gets right to the point. Where's my 'attaboy' pep talk?

Four walks me through what happened step by step. Axel coaches me through various tactics I could've used. I know this stuff. We've practiced it. I can't believe I forgot everything.

An hour later, all my joints, tendons, muscles, and ligaments scream in pain. My entire body trembles with exhaustion. I should be upset about the attack, but I'm kind of excited and giddy about it instead. I practically bounce on the balls of my feet as Axel walks me back to my room.

And I keep my head on a swivel.

One thing they promise is I will be tested again soon. If I see the attack coming, they'll abort it. If not, then I get another chance to prove I'm not some flighty blonde with no head on her shoulders.

"You look a lot more excited than I'd expect." Axel strolls along beside me. He gave up holding hands once we drew close to the buildings. He saunters beside me, hands firmly clasped behind his back and gives me the side-eyes.

"I am excited." I'm bursting with enthusiasm. I'm not good at the whole self-defense thing, but I feel myself learning. I don't expect to become an expert in Krav Maga in the short few months I've been practicing, but I'm getting it.

I'm also stronger. It's great conditioning for the body.

"And this newfound enthusiasm is from what?" He's been mostly quiet on the walk home. After the extra instruction by him and Four, he's kind of clammed up on me.

"It's because I'm getting better, slowly, but better than when I knew nothing."

"And?"

"And, it helps me to feel more in control."

"That's good. That's the whole purpose behind it."

A shadow moves at the edge of a building and I draw up short. Not sure when my testing is to begin, I'm suspicious of everything.

"Who's there." My voice rings out with far more confidence than I expect. That's my catchphrase. If I challenge someone, then I pass the test.

A huge man separates from the edge of the building and walks toward us.

"Zoe." Forest inclines his head toward me, then his icy gaze slants to Axel. "Aren't you missing something, Loverboy?" He covers his face with his hand, mimicking the mask Axel is supposed to wear at all times.

"Yeah, kind of not necessary, don't you think? Especially since—"

"Don't care what the two of you are *especially* doing. When you're in public places, you wear your gear." Forest's glacial glare softens when he turns his attention back to me. "If you will excuse us, Z, I need Loverboy here for a quick minute."

Axel's eyes squint, but he turns to me and takes both my hands in his. He gives them a little squeeze. "I'll see you later."

Not giving one fuck about Forest watching us, I lift on tiptoe and kiss Axel on the lips.

"I'll catch you later."

"Come on, I don't have all day." With that, Forest spins on his heels and walks away. Axel hesitates. He's torn between escorting me back to my room and going after his boss. Or rather, his boss's boss? There might be one more layer in there. I'm not really up on all things Guardian.

But I do find myself standing alone in the dark. There's a lot of empty space between me and the residence hall. In that space, shadows lurk. Any one of them could be a Guardian waiting to ambush me.

After what happened with Four, there's no way I'm letting down my guard. Nevertheless, I practically sprint to my room. Once inside, I firmly shut it behind me, taking care to turn the lock. I check the windows, making sure their locks are engaged. Then I lean against the wall and tremble as adrenaline spikes through my body.

I guess it's only now hitting me what happened. Not only that, but how incredibly vulnerable I am. Not sure if I'll ever feel safe again, I decide to leave that to ponder in the morning. After spending the first part of the night with Axel in the cave, and the second part on the dirt beneath Four, I'm overdue for a shower.

One more quick check of the locks and I feel reasonably certain no Guardian will be able to sneak in on me. Axel, however, knows the combination to the keypad on the outside. After a long, hot shower, I try waiting up for Axel by reading a book, but when I can no longer keep my eyes open, I call it a night.

I'm surprised when I wake up to an empty bed. Where is Axel?

Funny how in a matter of days, he's already claimed his place beside me in my bed. Our relationship feels both incredibly reckless, yet ponderously slow. After all, I've been after him nearly my entire life. I do feel like we've gone from zero to sixty in the blink of an eye. Hopefully, I'll run into him at breakfast.

With that thought on my mind, I rush through getting ready. I nearly forget to pay attention to my surroundings, too eager to see him, but I force myself to slow down. I want to show Axel I can do this. I also need to prove it to myself. I'm my own worst enemy when pressured to focus on something else. Those are his words. Distraction is my enemy.

I force myself to slow down and scan my surroundings, making sure to check my peripheral vision as well as natural blind spots.

Head on a swivel! Four's words rattle around in my head.

And boy, do I swivel.

When I get to the dining room, the Guardian table is uncharacteristically empty. They don't socialize with us. Something about it interfering with the dynamics of training, but they are always around.

"Hey, Z!" Moira calls me over. She sits with a gaggle of our friends.

"Hey." I slip into a seat next to her. "Howzit going?"

"I have something to tell you. Oh, but you probably already know." She gives a little jab to my ribs. "I bet Three told you already."

"No. I haven't seen him since last night."

I debate recounting my run-in with Four, but decide against it. I don't think she'd take it very well knowing Four pinned me to the ground. Something's definitely going on with the two of them. They're not sleeping together. Four seems too straight-laced to be breaking the rules. Unlike Axel. Although our situation is a bit more complicated, considering our history.

"Well…" Her eyes brighten. "You'll never guess what happened."

"I'm all ears." I cut into my eggs and get ready for another one of her colorful stories.

"For one thing, they've moved up the outing." Moira gives a little clap. "We're headed to the beach, and we get to stay an extra two days." She gives a girlish squeak. "I'm so ready to see something outside these walls and work off a little excessive energy if you know what I mean. Those Guardians might be fucking hot, but when they're not fucking you, it's just a waste of some good Grade-A Prime beef, if you know what I mean."

I say nothing. How am I supposed to respond to that comment considering I'm doing that? I focus instead on what she says about the beach.

"Why two extra days?"

"Because the Guardians got called out last night." Moira pokes my shoulder. "I thought Three would've told you?"

"No." I try not to let that hurt my feelings. "Forest pulled him aside last night when we were walking back. I went back to my room, but Three never showed afterward. How did you know?"

"Um, because our Viking Lord stomped into dinner and said, '*Yo dudes, pack your gear, you're rolling out!*' Then he asked where Three and Four were." Moira looks at me with suspicion.

I cave and tell everyone about getting attacked by Four. Evidently, I'm the only one who's been subjected to that particular pleasure. I have the bruises to prove it.

"Well, shit. We've all been looking over our shoulders waiting to get jumped and you have two of the sex gods jump you in one night. Then they yank away our play toys." She pouts a little, but her pout slips into a grin and then a fit of giggles. "Fucking lucky girl."

"They didn't both jump me."

"You mean Four just watched you and Three go at it." Her eyes narrow and she shoves me. "Z's a kinky girl, y'all."

"It wasn't like that." But now I have an audience. They don't let me ask my question without grilling me all about my takedown. Once I've answered them, I puff out my breath. "Now, what happened with the Guardians?"

"Don't know. Forest shooed them all out of here and then went in search of Three and Four. They told us just before you got here that classes are suspended for the rest of the week. But the good news is the outing is moved up to tomorrow." She grabs my knee and squeezes. "I know you didn't want to go, but you have to now. I need a wingwoman in the bars. You watch my back, and I watch yours. We're going to kill this situational awareness thing."

I'm still reeling from the fact all of Alpha team got pulled out. I dare not hope, but there's only one reason I can think of that would get them yanked. As much as I try not to think about the other girls, I pray that's why Alpha team left.

I close my eyes and say a silent prayer. Hope, Grace, Lily, Joy, Katie, and Iris are lost to me, but there's a chance the others will be found.

If Axel's out on a mission, the last thing I want is to hang out at the Facility alone while everyone heads to the beach.

"I'll go."

"Yay!" Moira claps her hands. "I knew I could count on you."

I just hope it's not a huge mistake.

TWENTY-EIGHT

Axel

GATHERED AROUND A STRATEGY TABLE, WE'RE SILENT AS MITZY briefs us on our mission. My knee bounces as I shed the excess energy zinging around my body.

"And you're sure this is the same group?" I challenge Max and CJ rather than Mitzy.

I'm smarter than that. As expected, Mitzy gives an exaggerated eye roll and flips me off.

"The intel is solid, Alpha Three." She says it with a sneer, as if using my team designation makes me less of a person and easier to degrade.

"What's wrong, Axel?" CJ taps the table and scans the reports.

"Doesn't it seem too convenient?"

"Convenient?" Mitzy shouts and lifts her arms. "You want to know how fucking convenient it's been tracking all this shit down? Do you know how many rabbit holes I've gone down?"

"Not criticizing the work, just going with my gut. As for rabbit holes, we're the ones jumping down them." Sometimes, I feel a need to remind her our safety depends on the quality of her intelligence. If she's wrong, we risk walking into a shit show.

"Why is your gut twisted over this?" Max calls me out.

Griff gives a sharp shake of his head. Bastard can read my mind. I'm not ready to leave Zoe, but my hesitation has nothing to do with leaving her behind. Something about this mission feels off.

It's not something I can verbalize. It's more of a tingling, a sense of wrongness stroking me the wrong way.

"All I'm saying is we've been jumping down your rabbit holes for months with nothing to show for it. Now you say you've got a new lead? Sounds pretty damn convenient."

"Tell that to Bravo team." Mitzy props her hands on her hips. "They fought through hell to get this."

"And what is—*this?*"

"It's everything. It's confirmation they know we're tracking them. That gives us an opportunity."

"Which is?"

"They don't know we know." She crosses her arms as if making some brilliant observation.

"Come on. That means shit. Am I the only one who thinks this feels off?" I glance around the table. "'*They don't know we know.*' How many times have we played this game?"

The room is packed. Alpha team sits around one end of the table. Mitzy and her tech team perch at the other end with all their tablets and computers lighting up their faces with a blue glow. Forest sits in the center with Sam, the head of Guardian HRS, opposite him. This is one high-level meeting with Forest and Sam in attendance.

Sam turns his attention to CJ. "And what do you think about this?"

"I trust my team's instincts." CJ's gaze sweeps around the table. "What do the rest of you think?"

Max presses his lips together and glances over at me. I spread my hands out wide. "Can't say what it is, Max. It's just a feeling."

"You and your fucking feelings." Griff leans back, folding his arms across his chest. He turns his attention to Max. "You know where I stand."

Griff is a suspicious fuck when it comes to my hunches. I'm not, but my sixth sense has saved our asses more than I'd like to admit.

"Our intel is solid," Mitzy says in a huff. "They think we're incapacitated, therefore, won't be expecting another attempt so soon. And if you don't go, those girls…"

"We'll go." Max makes the decision for the team. "Now, about Bravo team. What happened?"

I lean back and keep my thoughts to myself. I won't go against Max. He's Alpha-One, not me. Honestly, I don't know if my feelings toward Zoe are clouding my judgment. It's been a matter of days since things started between us. My gut could very well be wrong, guided more by my desire to stay with Zoe rather than head out into the field. Those feelings are a liability. Until I can get to the bottom of them, I can't let them hinder my operational readiness.

Max looks to me, waiting for acknowledgment that I'm on board. I give him a terse nod.

Bottom line, twelve lives are at risk if we don't go. I'm not willing to risk that.

"As you know—" Mitzy begins, telling us shit we already know. "Bravo team's been digging around in Cancun…"

Alpha team focused on the other end of the human-trafficking ring, Colombia. Our primary objective was to find what happened to those other six girls. Bravo's been working the front end, trying to uncover the players in the operation. Do that and we take the whole thing down.

That's the ultimate objective.

One of the kidnapping capitals of the world, Cancun is a favored vacation spot for many Americans. People don't understand how incredibly dangerous it can be for Americans who venture away from the resorts. Hell, look what happened to Zoe? She was taken right off the streets near a popular tourist beach.

I listen to Mitzy breakdown Bravo team's unfortunate mission. "We got a lead on a scheduled shipment of twelve girls. Bravo team was to infil at the docks and rescue the girls under cover of darkness before the container loaded onto the cargo ship. Only the girls weren't in the container like we thought. Fortunately, Bravo spotted the explosives before breaching the container. That raised a red flag and they backed away until we could regroup. That's the only reason we didn't lose the entire team. Unfortunately, someone detonated the bomb."

"Which means—" Sam speaks up, "—someone was watching them."

"Exactly."

"As it is, two of Bravo team sustained injuries severe enough to render Bravo non-functional."

"How did they know Bravo would be there?" Knox, who rarely speaks, surprises me. "Do we have a leak in our operation?"

We're all thinking the same thing.

"No leak." Mitzy presses her lips together. "More like we were set up."

"Explain." Max isn't happy. His best friend, Brady leads Bravo. I'm surprised Max is as calm as he is right now. I'd be flipping my lid if I knew my best friend's team had been sent into a setup.

"The tablet you recovered on HR-23A opened a lot of doors, but drew unwanted attention." Mitzy turns around to the large screen behind her. She brings up a mind map of her team's work so far. "The operation went to ground and shut down after your team's rescue of Zoe. We knew this would likely happen, and as expected, they're back at it. Shutting down was costing them millions in revenue. We followed their communications traffic and discovered they were prepping a new shipment. Twelve more girls gathered over the span of a week to be shipped to Colombia. Bravo was tagged to intercept that shipment."

HR-23A is the designation for the mission where we rescued Zoe. Guardian HRS is still working on finding the six girls who weren't recovered.

"You said we were set up? How?" Max leans forward to scan his team. His piercing gaze lands on me last.

We've worked together long enough, most of our communication occurs without words. He wants to know what my gut says about this. I give a shake of my head. Something feels off, but I can't place it. My feelings are more in turmoil over leaving Zoe without saying a goodbye than really focused on this conversation.

"It's my belief they are testing their communications channels." Mitzy continues. "Seeing if they had a breach in their operation that led to Zoe's rescue. That's where we made a mistake."

I get what happened.

"They sent out false info, then waited to see who would bite?"

"Correct."

"And Bravo paid for that mistake. They were lead right into a trap."

"Yes." Mitzy bends her head. She's not happy about what happened. Intelligence is her game. It's where she excels. To be bested by anyone is a huge blow to her ego. I understand that, but my sympathies only go so far.

"So why are we here? Are we being sent out with corrupted data?"

"Yes and no." Mitzy's attention shifts to Forest. He gives a nod and she continues. "They moved the girls to a different shipment. The information we intercepted came across channels they used to set up our team. Which we walked right into. Alternate info was sent along different channels."

"So now we have nothing." My gut twists thinking about the loss of those girls.

"Not exactly nothing." Mitzy perks up. "I've been tracking their activity for months. With a little cross-referencing, there's one contact who fell off the communications chain."

"So, you're tracking those emails?" My brows tug together, trying to figure everything out.

"Not emails ."

"Then what?"

"Games." Mitzy points to the large screen and an online RPG game pops up. "The fuckers moved their conversations to Steam."

"Ah, brilliant. How'd you figure that out?"

"Digging. Lots and lots of digging." Mitzy's expression is difficult to read. She's pissed to have been so easily fooled, but excited to have figured it out. "I know where the girls are."

"And?" I hate how she leaves us in suspense.

"They're en route to Columbia. The bastards moved them to a different shipping container. It was loaded earlier in the day, before Bravo team ever got to the port. That ship left dock before the explosion shut the whole port down. I'm monitoring their game for updates."

"Their game?" Griff coughs. "They're really running their op through a game?"

"Yes, it's slick too."

"And you're what? Playing this game with them? I can't believe they'd let some strange player in their private chats."

"Well…" Mitzy rolls her shoulders back. "I'm kind of well-known in the gaming world."

"She's a fucking legend," Forest says with a low, rumbling chuckle.

She gives him a side-eyes look and shakes her head. "Not sure if I'd say *legend,* and it's not like I just wandered into their private chat. They're playing a very popular game, one I helped to write. I think they believe they've hidden themselves well. Once I connected the dots, I opened a back door to their chat. I know everything they're saying."

"How the fuck did you do that?" Griff shakes his head.

I'm right there with him. How did Mitzy get from tapping phones, following text and email chains, to spying on them through an online gaming platform?

Mad doesn't begin to describe Mitzy's mind.

"After Bravo's mission went to shit, I realized they separated their lines of communication. I backtracked and noticed a spike in activity on their Steam accounts. I dug around a little and now we know what ship the girls are on. Best part is, they have no idea I'm watching. I have to guess on some of the code they're using, but twelve golden eggs is hard to miss. They're in 'Titon's basket' getting ready for delivery. Titon happens to be the name of a cargo container ship, the same one that departed before the fiasco with Bravo team. I'm still working out some of what they're saying, like the Golden Goose laying the twelve golden eggs. I get the eggs, still working on the goose part."

CJ turns to our side of the table. His astute gaze measures our response and willingness to go on this mission.

"Well, Alpha?" His question is meant for us all, but it's directed to Max.

"Alpha's in." Max doesn't hesitate.

Not that any of us would ever refuse. We will, however, express our concerns. This is how the Guardians work. Our tech team presents a plan. We poke holes in it. Everything gets patched back together by the entire team, operatives and technical alike. Only then do we move.

"Correct." Forest speaks for the first time. "It's a four-day transit from Cancun to Colombia. We have less than forty-eight hours to get to those girls before our window of opportunity closes. Once that ship docks, we won't follow the girls."

I pick up on what he's not saying. It's not that we *can't* follow, but that we won't. He's not willing to risk the edge Mitzy has by showing our hand too soon.

"Bravo team is non-functional with two of their teammates in medical. Which is why Alpha is going. We're wheels up in an hour. That's enough time to grab your gear and get to the airport. We'll talk infil on the way."

"How do we know this isn't a setup too?" CJ presses, needing more reassurance he's not sending his team in with our asses swinging in the wind. It's what makes him a great battle commander.

"We assume it is." Sam answers instead of Forest. "Their business is taking a beating by closing down for this long. Not to mention, their clientele is getting antsy without a fresh supply of slaves. We don't want their clients going elsewhere any more than they do. Mitzy's team is working that angle as well. They set up Bravo. They know the team's nonfunctional. What they don't know is we have alternate teams. I'm counting on them getting careless. You'll be working with Charlie on this. They usually send four men with the girls. Just enough to feed and water them during the transit. We expect there'll be a larger force protecting this shipment. Your job is to get the girls. Charlie will deal with hostiles."

Zoe endured that voyage. Fire burns in my belly thinking how she, and the other girls, were treated. They treated them like dogs; worse than dogs.

"If Charlie team is coming, why aren't they at this briefing?" Max asks the question we're all thinking.

"Charlie is prepping your insertion equipment."

"And what is our insertion plan?"

"We're dropping you in ahead of the cargo ship. You board, take out the hostiles, get the girls, and exfil. We'll go over the details during the flight."

"Well shit, if that's all there is to it." Griff slugs me in the arm. "Like a fucking walk in the park."

"Right." I don't like anything about this damn mission. "And how do we get twelve hostages off the ship?"

It's no coincidence twelve Guardians are going in for twelve girls.

"We're working on that." Forest gets to his feet. We all stand when he does.

This briefing is over.

With an hour to head to Guardian HRS headquarters, there's no way to say goodbye to Zoe. I hate leaving her, but this is important.

That odd tickling sensation is back, it prickles along my nerves. I can't shake the feeling something feels off.

TWENTY-NINE

Zoe

MOIRA POUNDS ON THE DOORS TO ALL OUR ROOMS. SHE BARRELS down to the very last door. Mine.

Pound. Pound. Pound.

"You better not be backing out. Get up! Get up!" Her energetic voice pulls a groan out of me. I roll over and cover my head with the pillow. Why did I agree to this?

"I'm up!"

I'm totally not up. I haven't packed. And I'm desperately trying to come up with an excuse as to why I can't go on this beach adventure.

I haven't been *out in the world* since my abduction during spring break. It's now June, the height of the summer season. The really sad thing about this is, before my kidnapping, I would've been the one banging on everyone's doors.

I used to be the life of the party. Now? I just want to crawl under a rock and exist. That's it.

Exist.

I'm a mess. I feel like crawling out of my skin. My nerves are misfiring, sending out distress signals, warning me to stay in bed.

Why is this so hard?

"Z!" Moira pounds on the door again. "You better not leave me to spend all day with these kids alone."

Moira is twenty-two. I'm nineteen. The next eldest is Julie at seventeen. "I got you an ID." She drops her voice to a whisper. "You promised."

"I'm coming." Shit, I can't leave her alone. I'm supposed to be her wingman, keeping an eye out for her while we hit up the bars.

With zero grace, I roll out of bed.

"The bus is leaving in twenty minutes. We're not waiting, and you'd better have your ass on board."

"I will." Except I need to pack.

Okay, what do I need for a few days at the beach? I grab a small bag and shove a string bikini and one-piece swimsuit into it. I toss a couple dresses in my bag plus add some shorts and tank tops. Then I go in search of toiletries. Whatever else I need will be bought on the spot. Slinging my bag over my shoulder, I grab a sunhat and head out.

A limousine bus waits for our little gaggle of misfits. Not everyone is going. Andrew and the one other boy, Peter, are on board. But little Zara is staying behind. We have a handful of minders with us, employees who are our constant companions and trained in dealing with any unforeseen meltdowns from our triggers getting activated.

"Z, I saved you a seat." Moira waves me all the way to the back.

As I'm the last to arrive, the doors close behind me and the engine rumbles to life.

"We're traveling in style." I glance around at the plush seats, inlaid wood sidings, and check out the cup holders and the video screens on the back of each seat.

Okay, maybe I'm a little excited.

I work my way to the back as the bus lurches forward. I grab the seat beside me to keep from tumbling forward. Andrew looks up, eyes bright with excitement.

"Glad you decided to come, Z. It's really going to be a ton of fun."

Peter sits across the aisle from him. Not much of a talker, he flashes a goofy grin.

We all spread out, each of us taking an entire row for ourselves— hell two rows—if we want.

"Here." Moira slips me a fake ID.

"How did you get this?" I turn it over in my hand. "It looks so real."

"Wouldn't be any good if it wasn't."

In front of us, the boys talk animatedly about meeting up with Noodles. Evidently, he's the keyboarder for the mega rock band Angel Fire and is taking time off to hang with the boys and teach them how to surf.

I plan on spending my time sunbathing on the beach. Several awesome romance novels wait for me to devour them as I soak up the rays. Moira keeps talking about hitting the bars and dancing all night long. If Axel were here, I'd be excited to do just that. Although, I don't know if he'd approve of the fake ID. I know Austin's thoughts on the matter.

"You certainly pack light." Moira eyes my backpack.

"Best way to travel." I stow my backpack in the overhead bin. "Besides, we can buy whatever we need there." The thought of a little retail therapy sounds wonderful.

"Did you call Austin? Is Mr. Lickable going to meet us?"

"You have to stop calling him that."

"Why?"

Her smile is bright, but I sense mischief is afoot and remind myself to insert myself between the two of them. Moira likes men. I'd think she'd want to steer clear of them after everything she's been through, but she doesn't. Frankly, I don't get it.

"Because it's gross, and yes. My brother is meeting us Saturday night. He knows the best restaurants, but you can only come if you're on your absolute best behavior. And don't tell him I have a fake ID. He'd flip."

My brother's overprotectiveness only gets worse with age. The six-year age gap means he's more paternalistic than I'd like. Why didn't I get the cool brother who gave me fake IDs instead of the rule follower? Although, I'm pretty happy to have Moira. Our sisterly bond grows daily.

Moira and I settle in and take out our phones to plan our invasion of Santa Monica. I get a little time to start one of my books, but spend most of the drive staring out the window.

I can't stop thinking about Axel and hope his mission is going well. Not a fan of clingy girls, my thoughts wander to him more than I'm willing to admit. I need to stop that. If we're going to be together, I need to accept the things that are important to him. Being a Guardian is his calling, which means I'll spend a lot of time alone while he's out doing what he loves.

It takes a few hours to drive down the coast, but we soon pull up outside a beachfront mansion. Rather than pay for individual hotel rooms, the Facility rented out a jaw-dropping gorgeous, beach house. We all scream when we realize what's happening. It's a surprise from Forest.

Picking rooms occurs after drawing lots. Moira and I will share a room, and with first pick, we take a room overlooking the beach with a private balcony. It also has a set of stairs leading directly from the balcony to the sand. That's going to make slipping out, and back in, that much easier when we head out at night.

"Come on. Let's hit the beach." Moira strips before I can shut the door.

Andrew and Peter, have the room across from us. They rubberneck our view before I slam the door in their faces. The saddest thing about them is Moira's naked body draws no reaction. They've seen far too much in their short lives.

"I didn't pack beach gear. Did you see any beach towels?" I hurry to change.

Moira flings open the patio doors. The sound of waves crashing against the shore pours into our room. The heavenly scent of salt and sea floods my nostrils, and I can't help but take a moment to breathe it all in. Off in the distance, seabirds call out to one another as they hunt for their next meal. The sun is a bright, fiery ball shining down on everything and puffy, white clouds dot the sky. All in all, it's perfect.

"Did you pack sunscreen?" My complexion might be darker than Austin's, but I still burn if I'm not careful, not to mention I'm not a fan of freckles.

"Got it." Moira's a blonde, like me, and she flashes a tube of sunscreen. "Hurry!"

"Slow down. The beach is going nowhere."

"Oh, I know, but doesn't it feel good to be free?"

"Moira?" I give her a long, hard look. "Is this your first time out of the Facility?"

She's been there for several months, maybe a year.

"It is." She gives me a sheepish look.

"How can that be? How often do they do this?"

"This?"

"Field trips to the *outside* world." I use air quotes for emphasis. We're all safely ensconced behind the protective walls of the Facility. While we deal with our unique tragedies, that separation allows us to heal.

I feel like a kid again. Like we're on a school-sponsored field trip. Only the Facility is no school and we're not on any field trip.

"It depends really."

"On what?"

"The group. The individual. Honestly, this is the first time I don't feel terrified being back out with the masses. I've had a few chances to go, but each time nightmares and flashbacks kept me from going. I'm only here because you are."

"I'm only here because you are." I'd be happy sitting at the Facility spending my time combing the tide pools on our beach.

"Triggers are a bitch." She blows out her cheeks with frustration. "We have to push through them, right? What else can we do? Hide out from the world forever?" She gives a shrug like it means nothing. "I don't want my triggers to rule my life. So, I figure why not come on this trip."

I know how powerful those triggers can be.

"I understand feeling uncomfortable." I glance out at the beach with more than a little trepidation and shiver. My chest tightens and my breathing accelerates.

"That's right, you were taken near a beach." Moira places a hand on my shoulder and gives a reassuring squeeze. "You're going to be okay, Z, and I'll be right by your side."

That's our pact. We've promised to stick together, glued at the hip.

"One street away actually. We didn't have enough money to book a hotel on the beach. But it was spring break. There were tons of people around. It was early and I thought nothing about walking by myself."

"I'm sorry, Z. We don't have to go out if you don't want to. I shouldn't have pushed you." She stares longingly out at the beach.

"But what about you?" I don't want to be the reason she stays in. That's not right.

"I can hang on this porch with you, or I can go out with the others. I don't really think anyone but us will be wandering around."

She's right about that, and I make a decision.

"Moira, I don't want to hide out in our room for four days. Forest always tells us to face our fears and conquer them. This is me facing my fear, just promise to be there, if I need a little reassuring."

I refuse to let what happened influence how I lead my life, but I'm terrified. That itchy, scratchy sensation pricks at my skin—a trigger just waiting to be activated.

"You sure?" Her eyes brighten and I can see she needs this as much as me. I've been at the Facility for a handful of months. It's been nearly a year for her.

"If you promise to stay by my side."

"It's a deal, and we'll stand together, side by side, fighting demons and slaying dragons." She spreads sunscreen over her face, chest, arms, and legs. "Here, lather up. We've got a few hours before the sun sets to get into all kinds of trouble."

"Let me get your back. Then you can get mine." I take the sunscreen from her and rub a palmful onto her back.

"Do you know why this is so perfect?" Her excitement simmers down, but only by a bit.

"No." I don't. It's easy to say you're going to beat back your fear and slay a trigger. It's something else to actually do it.

"Think about it. Nobody knows us. We can shed our pasts and just be Moira and Z. No one will be looking at us like we're fragile, broken things. You know, watching to see if we suddenly trigger on something random. Also—" she comes over and takes my hands in hers, "—no Guardians are here attacking us when we least expect it. We let our hair down and just breathe. We can make up funny backstories to tell all the guys we run into. Maybe we tell them we're sisters traveling up and down the coast? That would be fun, wouldn't it?"

"Maybe we're on summer break, driving cross country? Wouldn't that be fun?"

"That would be great. A fifty-State tour. Oh, we'd have tons of fun with the men we find."

"Yeah, that would be fun." I don't think I'll ever be brave enough to do something like that.

I love her outlook. Her determination to take back her life is often the anchor I use when mine is spinning out of control. Someday, I want to be more like her, strong and determined. I want to put all the ugliness away.

"I know you miss Three, but you get what I mean, right?"

"I do." Axel not being here bums me out a little, but I shrug it off. Part of recovery is learning to love ourselves and not becoming reliant on another person. As much as I wish Axel were here, this is a great opportunity to put a little bit of what I'm learning to the test.

Never before did I look at hanging out at a beach with such trepidation. That's something I need to change if I'm ever going to regain my confidence. So, I will focus on the positive and only the positive.

It's gorgeous outside. The temperature is perfect. Warm, not too hot, a bit humid, but in a good way. And I'm with my best friend. Those are all wonderfully positive things.

"Is this really your first time off Facility grounds?" I still can't believe she hasn't left the Facility in all that time.

"Yes." She gives a little screech of excitement. "So, you can understand why I'm excited. And you're here. I didn't have anyone close to my age to hang out with before. I get sick of teenagers."

"Technically, I'm still a teenager, and Julie is seventeen."

"Julie is a child. At her age, I…" Her voice drops off.

Julie isn't like us. She was never abducted. She wasn't forced into sexual slavery like Moira. She wasn't nearly killed like me. Julie had a beautiful life until a freak accident took both her parents. The foster family she was placed with is another story, however.

Her foster father took her virginity and stole her innocence. The Facility is helping her heal and in a few months, she'll become a legal adult. That would terrify me. One of the reasons I'm doing as well as I am is because of the support my family gives. I couldn't imagine having to do this alone, and Julie is all alone.

I take Moira's hands in mine. "At her age, you were surviving the best you could, and that's saying something."

"Yeah, funny how it always manages to sneak up on you." She pauses, then giggles and jabs me in the ribs. "You know what else sneaks up on you?"

"What?"

"Not really a *what* but *who*. You've got a real man warming your bed."

"A real man who's not here." I can't help it, I miss him.

"You're right. He's not here. He's out saving lives. He saved mine." Moira places the back of her hand over her forehead and sighs dramatically.

"Wait, he what?"

She gives a little flip of her hand. "There aren't that many Guardian teams. There's Alpha, Bravo, and Charlie. I don't think there's a Delta, although I could be wrong. Two of those teams were

299

with Forest in Manila. Chances are pretty good he's one of the men who saved me."

"What?" I'm trying to process what she's saying. "Forest? The op that went to shit?"

"Yeah, well for him it went to shit, but for me it meant freedom. Let's just say the Guardians are everyday heroes. How much *more* perfect can Three be? And Four." She gives a little giggle. "Now, if I can just get Four to stop acting like I'm some broken doll, maybe I can start having fun with him like you are with Three."

"He's pretty damn amazing." And I miss him. I press the heel of my hand against my breastbone. My heart aches. It's a physical pain I can't shed.

"They're all fucking hot. I mean, they could look like anything beneath the masks, but they're stacked with muscle, and let's face it, men like that tend to be well endowed. I should know." An uncomfortable silence settles over us. Moira isn't wrong. She's been with hundreds of men, maybe thousands. It's one of those delicate questions I don't ask. "Anyway, they're all like nuclear-thermal, panty-melting hot."

That one comment speaks volumes about what she's endured in her short life, nearly half of which was spent servicing the desires of men, either willingly or unwillingly. Although, I don't think any twelve-year-old decides to sell her body on the street because she wants to. That's the thing with my new friends. We're all misfits with one tragic tale after another.

"You know, I'm not sure about this wingman thing. Three won't be thrilled knowing I'm hanging out at bars picking up men." I'm still really confused *why* she wants to pick up a guy at all. Wouldn't she shy away from sex? Not run right to it? Although, it might be her way of coping. Who the hell am I to judge?

"All you have to do is flirt a little. Stand with me at the bar so I don't look desperate. I'm not asking you to sleep with anyone. Three can't get upset if you're there as *my* chaperone."

300

"First off, you don't need any help picking up men." Moira is a blonde bombshell.

"I've never had a man approach me without reaching into his wallet. I just want a couple of fun nights, laughing, drinking, and dancing. Something a normal girl might do."

"Yeah, but how am I supposed to *watch over you* if you're banging some hot guy?" No way am I letting her out of my sight.

"Girl, sex is sex. It doesn't have to always be in a bed."

Didn't I know that? I press my hand to my back, where tiny bruises lay alongside my spine. My bed is well broken in, but the best sex is when we're in the cave. There's something animalistic about it, a switch that flips in Axel's head. More primal. More hungry. More of that alpha shit Moira keeps going on and on about.

Moira hooks her arm over my shoulder and we gaze out over the beach. "And for the record, I'm not looking for sex."

"Then why are we hitting up a bar?"

"Because it's something I've never done, at least not for fun. I want one night to experience what normal is supposed to feel like."

"Then we should probably wait for Austin and have a little muscle to back us up." Austin is a big man, well built, works out in the gym, and used to spar with Axel when they were growing up. He's been in a fair number of fistfights and can hold his own. He only looks small when standing beside Axel.

"I thought he wouldn't like his baby sister flashing her shiny new fake ID."

"He won't, but I'll talk to him. If he understands *why* we want to go, I bet he turns belly up. Austin is a by-the-books kind of man, but he understands. I think he'll get it."

"You're playing the victim card, aren't you?"

"You bet." I wrap my arm around her waist and we stare out at the beach. "Unless you want to just hang out here and watch the sunset? We can hit up a liquor store, test out my ID, and grab something to drink."

"Like I'm bringing any kind of alcohol into this house, filled with these kids. I'm not adding to their corruption."

"I get it. You have a soul."

"Not a very shiny one, but it gets better every day."

"We certainly have lived complicated lives." It's hard to remember she survived by hooking on the streets since age twelve.

"Ain't that the truth." Her expression darkens for a moment, but it's there and gone like a flash. We're taught to live life looking forward and not to dwell in the past.

"Ain't ain't a word, missy." I mess her hair with my hands, teasing as I try to lighten the mood.

"Who made you the grammar police?" She gives me a playful shove. "And to answer your question, how about we grab a drink and watch the sunset on the beach? Maybe we'll find some hot guys and, I don't know, play volleyball in the sand? Sit around a bonfire while some guy sings to us? Normal stuff."

"Sounds wonderful."

To my surprise, the beach house comes fully equipped with beach chairs, umbrellas, towels, and coolers. We pack water, soda, and a few snacks we loot from the kitchen and head out. Andrew and Peter come with us. They're not meeting Noodles until the morning and are overly excited about hanging out with a rock star. We ditch them as fast as humanly possible.

Two hours later, we're sitting on the beach with a bunch of college kids hanging out after the end of the semester. I look at them with longing. That's what I should be doing, hanging with my friends without a care in the world.

Instead, I sit beside Moira while she flirts with some nameless guy. They're in the light touching phase of their courtship.

I wonder how difficult it must be for Moira. She's never taken things slow with a man. As soon as he handed over cash, she was all business until he finished. Get in and get out. Make another buck and stay alive. She told me that was her motto when hooking it on the streets.

As for our day, it's dreamy.

We walked along the shore until we came across this group of college kids playing beach volleyball. After a little small talk, they asked if we wanted to play. There was no way we were going to refuse.

I suck at volleyball and ate a ton of sand in my attempts to hit the ball. Once the sun went down, we built a bonfire, or rather watched the guys light it. One of the girls unpacked a guitar. It's like the universe responded to our wish.

One normal night.

Our first night out can't be more perfect than this.

My phone buzzes with an incoming text. I glance at it and check in. We have minders, people helping us navigate a world that is more complicated than it should be. They're not guards. It's not like they tell us what we can and cannot do, at least for me and Moira.

For the younger kids, it's a bit different. The Facility obtains guardianship of the charges under their protection. The younger kids will eventually transition to foster homes vetted by the Facility. Kids like Julie, who are older, will slowly obtain their freedom, like Moira and me, as restrictions and parental oversight are lifted at age eighteen.

I check in with our minder, sending a quick text saying we're fine and make sure to use our code. Many of us, as previous abductees, know the value in that.

Moira and I discussed our code words for this weekend. They're really more like phrases. In person, or over the phone, if Moira compliments me on my hair, it means she feels safe. If she mentions my eye makeup, that's a sign of danger. For a text, I simply send a purple heart. Red, which is the first heart to appear on the keypad, is our danger signal.

I send our minder a purple heart to let them know we're okay. Our phones have trackers, which help our minders know where we are. They also gave us necklaces to wear with tiny GPS trackers inside.

Moira and I can turn our trackers off. The kids cannot.

Moira giggles and passes on another beer, asking for water instead. We agreed on this as well. No more than three drinks for the night and no more than two in one hour. We're obsessively paranoid, but this is our new way of life.

The guy she sits beside drapes his arm over her shoulders. They laugh at some joke and snuggle tighter. I talk to two girls about clothes and the latest fashions. It's a safe topic, a brainless topic.

A couple of guys sitting opposite me pound liquid courage before making their moves on the girls they've picked out. I made it clear I have a boyfriend, which cools off any potential advances toward me. I'm more than happy to talk fashion and makeup.

And I'm really having a great night.

The girl across the way tunes her guitar, and soon we're all laughing, drinking, singing, and having the best night of our lives.

For the first time, in a very long time, I feel normal.

The beer relaxes me. Moira and her guy get more handsy. The fire dies down. One by one, our new friends get up and leave until there are only six of us left. Moira's lips lock with her new beau while I stare into the dying embers of the fire and ignore the groping going on behind us.

A shiver worms its way down my spine.

It's not cold out. In fact, it's a balmy night, but something feels off.

It's also late.

I get up. "Come on, Moira. We need to be getting back." My lips feel funny. Tingly. The beer is hitting me harder than I thought. I'm ready to head back and crash. "Your makeup is smudged, girl."

"Oh, spoilsport." Moira extricates herself from the guy she's been kissing and we make our goodbyes.

We're not in any danger, but it's the only thing I can think of to get Moira to give it up and head home with me.

It's a short hike back to the rented house. We take our time and walk along the waterline. The waves roll in and splash against our shins. It feels wonderful. Perfect.

"What an amazing day." I twirl in the moonlight and stare up at the stars. The spinning makes me dizzy and I nearly trip and fall in the water.

Moira laughs at me, then does nearly the same thing.

My eyes pinch as I look at her staggering on the sand. "I thought you switched to water?"

"I did." She spins again and stumbles. "I feel so light and free."

She looks intoxicated.

We hold each other's hands and twirl until we're dizzy. We're drunk on life.

Maybe, a bit too drunk.

That tingling sensation returns. I smack my lips together. They feel weird.

"Moira?"

"Yeah?"

"Are you drunk?"

"Yeah." She spreads her arms out wide and spins in a circle, head tipped back to stare at the stars. "They're spinning."

"No, you are."

Moira runs into me and practically hangs off me as I smack my lips together.

The beach is deserted. Well, nearly deserted. Two men walk toward us, but they're some distance away. When I spin around, there are three more about a hundred yards back the other direction.

"We need to get home." A sense of apprehension washes over me.

"Or…" Moira's words slur. "We sleep on the beach."

"We can't do that." My tongue trips over itself as I push the words out.

Blinking hard, I peer down the dark, desolate beach. The prickling intensifies.

I grab her hand and pull her down the beach.

I haven't had a drink since Cancun, but still, two beers and I'm practically falling down drunk? And I know Moira's been nursing the same bottle of water for the last hour. There's no reason for her to be acting this way. She's barely able to stand.

The men in front of us draw closer. They'll run into us if they don't veer off. I pull Moira away from the water's edge and scan our surroundings. The three men behind us are closer than before. Much closer.

"What are you doing?" Moira's speech becomes more difficult to understand.

I blink, trying to focus.

A glance over my shoulder shows the men, all of them, angling away from the water. They're headed right at us.

"Red heart. Red heart." I can't remember whatever danger phrase we came up with, but I have enough sense to pull out my phone and text a red heart to our minders.

I pull Moira into a jog. The men behind us sprint.

Moira looks over her shoulder and screams as one of the men grabs her from behind. The other shoves a black hood over her head. I'm pinned from behind. I kick and scream, then remember my training.

I shift my hips to the side. Palm open, I strike my attacker's groin with open-handed slaps. The man grunts out a curse. I raise the opposite elbow while turning around. My arms stay tight to my chest. Now, I can knee him in the groin, which I do—aggressively.

I've practiced this with Axel. I've escaped against Axel.

"Shit," one of them says. "I thought the bitches were going to be drugged."

"She is. They both are." The one holding me grunts as my knee repeatedly knocks against his groin. His grip loosens.

"Does this look drugged?"

"Fuck!" The one holding me releases me after a vicious knee to his groin.

I push against him and run. Or try.

Another man grabs me. Holds me tight. I can't breathe.

Blackness covers my vision as a hood is yanked down over my head.

I don't stop. I kick and scream. There's a prick of pain in my arm. It burns, but then everything gets fuzzy. My struggling stills. My body doesn't respond.

"Ditch their phones." It's the last thing I hear before the world goes black.

307

THIRTY

Axel

"T-MINUS TEN. CHECK YOUR GEAR." CJ WALKS DOWN THE LINE shouting over the deafening turbulence. The back-loading ramp of the modified C-130 is down, open to the black sky. Our reference point is a lonely tanker far below us. Wind buffets us as we stand beside Charlie team and get ready to jump.

Three inflatable six-man Zodiacs occupy the cargo area, one in front of the other. Normally, it's one rib, one team, but we're twelve men going in to rescue twelve women. We need the third Zodiac to evacuate and meet the trawler at exfil.

As for infil? We're getting ready to jump out of a plane and into the cold, black waters of the Gulf of Mexico. This is the best damn job in the world.

Knox stands directly in front of me. Max is at the lead as Alpha-One. Knox keeps repeating the same movements. He holds out his arms, a little above his head, palms out, then quickly lowers and draws his right hand to his hip where the rip cord to his parachute sits. He mimics pulling it, then reaches for the secondary at his shoulder.

309

Over and over, he goes through the motions. Knox is our best jumper, but also our most superstitious. He'll do that twelve more times by my count before he's satisfied.

"T-minus five!" CJ continues the countdown. Max lifts his right hand and spreads his fingers wide. Knox follows. I do the same, relaying the countdown to those behind us who can't hear CJ over the thundering turbulence and roar of the four jet engines as their turboprops cut through the air.

Feeling like I should be doing something, I reach back to my right hip. Yup, handle is right where it should be. All my gear is strapped tight. Altimeter check. Fins check. Helmet strapped in.

Beside me, Charlie-Three, gives a huge grin. "Never gets old, does it?" Walt stands right beside me and still shouts to be heard over the deafening noise swirling at the back of the fuselage.

"Pays to be a winner!" We tap fists.

"So that others may live!" He replies back with the Air Force PJ motto. Certified paramedics, parajumpers are the Air Force's special ops equivalent to the SEALs, with the same brutal training I underwent in BUDS.

"The only easy day was yesterday!" I shout back the Navy SEAL motto.

"Damn straight. *De Oppresso Liber!*" Charlie-Two, who goes by Hank, twists to join our conversation. It means *'To free the oppressed.'* Hank's a former Green Beret. The Guardians are well represented by all branches of the military special ops community.

The Green Beret creed is probably best aligned with what Guardians stand for. We're a fighting force for those who cannot fight for themselves. Our mission, the calling that gets us out of bed every day, is to free the oppressed, liberating them so they may live in freedom.

"Two-minutes." CJ does a quick walk between our ranks. As our battle captain, he's in charge of Alpha, Bravo, Charlie, and Delta teams. The foundation of our success rests on his shoulders.

We're geared up for infil with parachutes strapped to our backs and fins to our boots. Black neoprene wetsuits cloak our bodies. We're ready for a swim after a little free fall. If that isn't enough, we carry our weapons, comm-gear, masks, helmets, and snorkels.

CJ checks out the three Zodiacs behind us. Unlike the teams, he wears black fatigues and a harness with a thirty-foot lead anchored to the floor. Everyone not wearing a parachute gets anchored to the plane with a tether when the back, cargo bay ramp is open. CJ gets a thumbs-up from the loadmaster. The ribs are good to go.

Since we have two teams and three inflatables, Alpha and Charlie divide into three groups. Griff and I are with Max and Knox. Tex, Hank, Walt, and Gabe are with the second rib. Liam and Wolfe buddy up with Jeb and Blake from Charlie.

We'll each follow our respective Zodiacs out of the plane and meet up in the murky waters of the Gulf below. And we're going in dark. No need to alert the cargo ship about our little surprise. The inflatables are equipped with radar beacons, but no lights. That's how we find them once we land in the water. My goal is to land close to the Zodiac and avoid an arduous swim.

"One-minute!" CJ shouts.

Max passes the time down the line. We each raise our right hand and lift our forefinger, passing the message to those behind us. First to go, my team does a final check of our gear, making sure stupid stuff like chin straps are secure. Altimeters are tight to our left wrists. Fins are locked tight to our boots. That kind of shit.

"Thirty seconds!" CJ makes a pinching gesture.

This is when my adrenaline spikes. I love jumping out of planes, but there's always that little gut check that whispers this is not what a sane man does. Hurtling out of a perfectly good airplane is for idiots, but damn if I'm not one of them.

CJ lifts his arm over his head and swiftly chops down. The loadmaster cuts the last tether holding our Zodiac in place. It slides down the rails toward the open, loading bay ramp. As it falls out, the draw cord deploys the parachute. The small boat falls into the blackness of the night sky.

CJ turns to us, waving us forward. We high step it down the ramp, lifting our feet high so we don't trip on our fins. Max jumps out of the plane, arms out, legs back and disappears. Knox follows. Then it's my turn.

It's noisy as shit. Windy as hell. I leap into the blackness and grin like a goddamn fool. *Best fucking job in the world.* I locate Max and Knox's canopies and pull the rip cord on my parachute. The buffeting turbulence from the plane and free fall disappears. Into that silence, I drift toward the dark waters below.

I track the path of our rib, pulling on the guide wires of my chute to steer my descent. Thankfully, it's a calm night. No storms, but that doesn't mean this shit is easy. We're slipping into Gulf waters with six-to-eight-foot swells. It's going to be a tough swim, especially with all the shit I carry.

The water races up to meet me and I brace for impact. A few feet before my feet hit the water, I release my canopy. Don't want it collapsing over my head.

The shock of the chilly waters isn't something I can brace for. It steals my breath and jolts my system. But this is what I train for. Most of what comes next is pure muscle memory.

I inflate my BCD and pop to the surface where I complete a quick check of my gear, making sure nothing came loose during the descent and plunge into the chilly waters. Then I locate the rib, using its beacon locator. With strong, swift kicks, I cut through the water and head toward the waiting rib.

Max and Knox are ahead of me, already on board. Griff splashes down behind me. Max and Knox lean over the rubber sidewalls of the Zodiac and hoist me aboard. We do the same for Griff when he catches up to us a few moments later.

While Knox sets up the outboard engine, Max, Griff, and I watch for the other two teams. Knox gets the engine going and we meet up with the second rib, and then the third. Rigid inflatables, our transportation is tough. After an equipment check, we head out for a rendezvous with our objective.

The cargo ship is a quarter of a mile ahead of us. The easiest way to approach is from the stern. The wake a boat that size puts out smooths out the water, but it's also the most visible part of the ocean for the crew on board. As a result, we come in at a forty-five degree angle to the port side of the ship, bouncing over the ship's wake and gritting our teeth. It's a rough, pounding ride. Spray hits our goggles and streams off, making everything a little blurry.

While everyone stares at the wake behind a ship, hardly anyone bothers looking over the side. As for getting on the ship? That requires a bit of muscle.

We attach our boats to the hull with magnetic locks. Then with a bit of rope, lots of skill, and intense physical conditioning, we haul ourselves up hand over hand.

Once topside, our teams split. Alpha team will locate the girls and move them back for extraction. Charlie is on the lookout for the extra guards with orders to shoot on sight.

We work in absolute silence. All communication made through hand signals. The girls will be locked inside a container on the bottom two rows of containers, which stack high above our heads. From what we know, and Zoe's descriptions of her transit, they feed and water the girls once a day at night. Zoe remembers seeing their heads and shoulders, which means the girls are probably stacked in the second tier of containers.

All we have to do is find out which container is the one we want out of the thousands on board. This is a smaller cargo ship, but there are still well over ten thousand containers to search. Which might sound challenging.

Fortunately, we have Mitzy and half a dozen drones with infrared sensors to assist us. Once Alpha team moves from the side to a secure location, we reach into our packs and pull out the drones. Charlie is doing the same, giving us a dozen drones to search the ship.

Far overhead, a much larger drone watches over us. That drone will report the positions of the crew and guards to Charlie and guide them in for the kill. Our goal is to slip in and slip out without being seen or raising an alarm. My earpiece crackles with static as Mitzy initiates a communications check.

Overlord: Comm check.

Max: Alpha-one check.

Tex: Charlie-one check.

Max keeps his voice low. His mic attaches over his larynx, which allows him to whisper and still be heard by Mitzy's team.

Overlord: Go for dragons.

Mitzy wanted to call her little drones dragonflies. Max got her to agree to shorten that to dragon. It's totally foolish, but we don't often win arguments with the fiery technical guru.

Max: Alpha dragons ready.

Tex: Charlie dragons ready.

Overlord: Copy that.

We do nothing other than fold out the mechanical arms that hold the tiny drone rotors. Everything else is automated or controlled by Mitzy's technical team.

The drone in my hand shudders. The rotors spin up. I keep my palm flat and wait for it to take flight. My actions are repeated by my team around me.

Overlord: Dragons go.

Six drones lift into the air. They will search the containers, looking for the heat signatures of twelve girls. Meanwhile, we huddle in the darkness and wait.

The size of a cargo container never ceases to amaze me. The thousands of containers on board transport the equivalent of the volume of the Empire State building. That's this one ship. Mind-blowing.

And we have twelve drones to search all of it.

Fortunately, we're only searching the containers that a man can reach. This cuts those numbers way down. As for Charlie team, Mitzy calls out the positions of the men walking the deck.

Despite their immense size, there are less than thirty crew on board a ship like this. Half of those are officers. The other half, deckhands. Of those, at least a third are asleep. And then there are the guards for the precious cargo.

Alpha team squats in-between the towering stacks waiting for the drones to do their jobs. Meanwhile, Mitzy directs Charlie to the crewmen. Deckhands will receive a sedative dart to their necks. They'll take a nice long snooze. The guards will get something a little more final: one bullet to the head and one to the chest. We listen in to Charlie's progress until Mitzy's voice squawks in our ears.

Overlord: Target acquired.

She rattles off the location of the container with the girls while we move.

Max: Copy. Moving out.

On the move, Mitzy takes us on a path to avoid those deckhands still walking around. Charlie team takes out the security detail and converges on our location.

With my night vision goggles on, the entire deck shines in an eerie green glow. We move silently, slipping between the rows. Max comes across one of the crew taking a smoke break and takes him out with a dart. We move forward until we're only a few yards from the container holding the girls.

Four men stand guard, but they're sloppy and bored. Instead of watching for threats, their weapons are on the deck and they huddle around a game of cards.

Charlie team approaches from the other side. Tex and Max talk out who will take down the guards. The kill shots will occur simultaneously.

"Only four?" I tap Knox's shoulder in front of me, keeping my voice low. A tingling sensation sweeps down my spine. We expect twice that number.

Knox relays my concern to Max, not that he needs to. He and Tex are already discussing it.

Mitzy sends the drones on a search mission for any other guards. We're only guessing on the security surrounding the kidnapping victims. And after what happened with Bravo team, we're overly cautious. There's really no way to tell, except we have Mitzy and her dragons to help in the search.

That tingling sensation down my spine intensifies. Seconds later, Mitzy calls out the location of four other men. Max signals for Liam and Wolfe to separate and circle around. Tex does the same, sending Charlie-Five and Six to take out those men.

We huddle in the darkness until Liam calls out that they're in position. A few seconds later, Jeb does the same.

We're ready.

Max gives the signal. Eight shots fire. Eight men go down.

Smooth as fucking silk.

Griff and I move in on the container. As expected, there's a goddamn lock on the exterior. A quick search of the fallen men reveals a key. They would've done better with a combination lock, although this is good for us. We won't have to shoot the lock to break it, which would draw unnecessary attention.

Griff works the lock and pops open the container seals. When we open the doors, twelve young women huddle against the back wall. While I stand guard, Max tells the girls what's going on. He spares no time and gets them to come out.

Hesitant and unsure, they slowly file out. Griff takes the first girl. I grab the second. We pair off like that until the last girl is out of the container. They're barefoot and stripped down to bras and panties. The next little bit is going to be hell for them.

Just short of the side railing, I turn to the girl with me. "We have to go over the edge." Her eyes widen and she shakes her head. A tiny mewl escapes her. "You must not make any noise. No screaming. You get me?"

She gives a tentative nod, but fear rims her eyes. I explain the harness as I secure her in it, telling her what will happen next.

So far, Mitzy reports our activity is undetected. Twelve men place twelve girls into climbing harnesses. We tie them to our backs and head to the rail where three ropes snake down to the inflatable ribs bouncing alongside the hull.

Going down will be much easier than the hand over hand climb up the ropes.

"Close your eyes. Whatever you do, don't scream. I've got you. Do you trust me?" I've yet to get her to say a word, but she gives a tight nod. When I strap her to my back and stand, her arms snake around my neck, choking me. I replace her hands on the straps of my shoulder harness. "Grab here. Close your eyes. Not a sound."

317

Now that she's on my back, I can't see her, but she grips the straps of my shoulder harness. Griff gives me the signal to go. I hook my carabiner onto the line and I haul myself, and my burden, over the side of the ship.

She gives a little squeak, but then goes silent. I lean back until my legs fully brace against the side of the ship. Then I let the rope run out as I push back and drop.

I'm surprised she doesn't scream. Or maybe she does and I don't hear her over the rushing of water along the hull. The ship's engines drone and the props chop through the water near the stern. To my left, Liam carries his burden to the back boat and one of the men from Charlie team carries his to the one in the middle.

We all hit our respective boat at the same time. It's rough as shit. The Zodiacs bounce in the water, getting tossed around. I go to my knees and run the rest of the rope through my carabiner. With a wave over my head, I signal I'm off the rope. Moving forward, I get out of the way as Griff makes his way down the side of the ship. Only then do I unhook my burden from my back.

"Sit there." I point to the front of the rib. "Grab here."

The girl does as instructed, and I turn to help Griff.

One by one, our team rappels down the lines until all the boats are full. Mitzy's dragons join us. While Griff and I take care of the four girls in our boat, Max corrals Mitzy's little drones while Knox engages the engine and cuts us free of the cargo container ship.

We slip back out into the night with yet another successful mission behind our backs.

We couldn't ask for a more perfect execution of our mission. A mile to the stern, we meet up with a trawler. The girls are cold, shivering from the transport, but they're free. We hand them off to Skye's medical team and head for a debrief. Not an hour later, I settle into my bunk.

All I can think about is Zoe. My girl was locked inside a container, similar to the one we rescued these girls from, for days. She endured horrific conditions, degradations, and I'm not going to think about what they intended. I don't understand how she keeps herself together as well as she does.

Those men were selling her murder for pleasure.

A deep rumble vibrates within me. I wish I'd taken more time to kill those men.

I can't wait to hold my girl in my arms. With dreams of Zoe drifting through my mind, I let exhaustion drag me into a sleep. I plan on spending the rest of my life with Zoe and can't wait to let her know.

Sometime later, I'm being roughly shaken awake.

"Axel! Get up."

I open sleep encrusted eyes and stare up at Griff. A quick glance at the time and I shove him away.

"What the fuck?" And why the hell is he up?

"You need to get up." The tone in his voice tells me something's gone horribly wrong. "Now."

We completed a flawless mission. Slipped in and out without raising the alarm. Saved twelve girls from the horror of human trafficking. It was textbook perfect.

"Get up." He shoves me again.

"Why?"

"Forest is on the phone." The set of Griff's expression turns my stomach. Something horrible has happened. "He's sending a chopper."

"Why? What's wrong?"

"It's Zoe."

319

THIRTY-ONE

Zoe

"Tie the bitches up." Cruel words stir me from the darkness. "Fucking cunts were supposed to be drugged."

"They were." Another voice answers.

"You tell that to my fucking balls." A man swallows a groan. "Fucking cunt bitch-slapped my balls."

He's the one who grabbed me. I should be happy about his poor balls. I tried. I tried really hard to fight. Axel is going to be upset I didn't get free.

"I paid those kids good money to spike their drinks."

What? Our perfect night was perfectly fucked up.

Fear runs through me, hijacking my senses, sharpening everything I feel. The hard floor beneath me presses against my back. The heavy weight of my limbs confirms I'm drugged. The ragged pulse of my breathing is my fear spiking. The hard pit in my stomach is nothing short of pure terror.

I gulp against a scratchy throat. Work moisture into a dry mouth. Pant and heave as panic sweeps me away.

Forest would tell me to focus. Axel would tell me to stop, think first, react only after I assessed the situation.

Well, I've assessed this situation and we're fucked. Drugged? Those kids seemed so nice. So normal. This is so fucked up.

Wherever I am, we're in motion. Not the sickening slow rolling of a boat. This is more jarring, like the back of a van or truck. We surge forward. Stop. Then I roll back as the driver steps on the gas. I rock to the left with a turn. Where are they taking us?

I give a little moan. The toe of a boot slams into my belly. My moan morphs into a shriek. Another kick to my ribs cuts off the shriek. Something cracks inside of me. A rib caving beneath the boot strike? I don't know, except it hurts.

My hands go to my head. My knees draw up. I curl into a fetal position to protect what I can.

Rough hands grip my wrists. Yank them down. Separate them. Someone pushes down on my knees. They force my legs straight. Then, they roll me to my belly. First one hand, and then the other, is manhandled behind my back.

Scratchy rope binds my wrists together. The rope goes around my ankles. Sharp pain rips through me—bone grating on bone—as they bend my legs back and tie them to my wrists. Everything hurts. My ribs are definitely broken.

Hog-tied, I can't move. Each breath rips through me, pure agony, as my injured ribs grate against each other.

Moira.

Where's Moira?

Rough fabric scratches against my face. I remember the hood. I remember the men. Five men sent to abduct two women.

Why?

This can't be happening again. I squeeze my eyes shut and scream with frustration. *This can't be happening again.*

A moan sounds somewhere to my left.

Moira!

She's alive.

"Make sure they don't have anything on them that can be tracked."

"We ditched the phones."

"Check!" The voice is sharp, cutting, and filled with hate. He's the one in charge. "Strip them."

No. No. No. No!

Not that. Please not that.

It's the one thing I hold on to. I won't survive rape. I'm not like the others. I'm not strong enough.

Something cold touches between my shoulder blades. It yanks upward, slicing through my top. Then it's at the crack of my ass. A sharp tug up and my shorts are cut free. I stop struggling, afraid the knife will slice my skin as they strip me. From the sounds beside me, they're doing the same to Moira.

"Satisfied?" The owner of that voice kneels beside me. He grabs my ass. "We could have a little fun…"

I tense.

"Do that and lose your dick," the leader says with a snort.

"Come on. They're fucking cunts. Whores. Why can't we have a taste?"

"Because…" The gruff voice snaps back. "You don't have a million to bid for them. The bidders expect their merchandise to be untouched by us."

"Fucking stupid rule. How will they know?"

"Because I'll tell them. Keep your fucking dick in your pants."

"What about their mouths?"

"You want to risk it, go right ahead."

Please, not that. Anything but that.

Moira cries out.

"Bite me and it's the last thing you do." The second man's voice is like sandpaper against my nerves.

I rock violently to the side as the van takes a hard-left turn. The necklace around my neck clanks against my teeth.

My necklace.

I try to get the round disc in my mouth. Beside me, Moira gags and heaves. I don't want to know what's happening, but how can I not? With effort, I get the tracking disc between my teeth. It's a pressure-activated disc. I bite down as hard as I can.

If my text with the red heart made it through, this will let our minders know where we are. All we have to do is hold on.

A scream erupts from the man beside me. A soul-scorching howl.

"Cunt bit my dick!"

The leader gives a low, guttural laugh. "Fucking putz."

"She bit my dick off." He hops backward, trips over me, and howls with fury.

Then he's up. A solid *thunk* sounds. Moira gasps. Another *thunk*. And another. Over and over again, he kicks her as she cries out.

"Fucking putz!" The leader shouts. "Don't you dare damage the merchandise."

"Fucking bitch! Cunt! Whore!" Each word is punctuated by a solid kick, a thwacking against flesh. Moira's cries weaken.

324

They stop.

A gun goes off and my breathing stops as a body falls on top of me. My arms draw back, pulling dangerously on my sockets. Then someone shoves the dead weight off me.

"What the fuck is going on back there?"

"Jack's dead," the leader says.

"Dead?"

"Yeah."

"How?"

"I shot him."

"Why?"

"He just cost the boss a million bucks." He toes my hip with the tip of his boot. "This one should bring much more. Second time's the charm, sweetie. We're going to love hearing you scream."

A low mewl escapes me.

I know what he means. Fear slithers inside of me and curls around my belly. I'm going to die—again.

THIRTY-TWO

Axel

In less than five minutes, Alpha and Charlie team gather in the mess hall of the trawler. CJ paces back and forth. He holds a finger to the earpiece in his left ear. Max comes to me the moment I enter.

"What's going on?" My nerves are shot, and by the expression on Max's face, he has nothing but bad news for me.

"Zoe and Moira never made it back to the house. Zoe sent a distress signal on her phone, which alerted the team in Santa Monica. They found her phone, Moira's too, but not the girls. An hour ago, Zoe activated her tracker."

"Moira?" Griff stiffens beside me.

"Yes. They're both missing." Max's gaze lingers on Griff, which makes me wonder if there's not more going on between Griff and Moira than I thought. Not that I thought anything was going on at all. Griff's the consummate professional. He doesn't mix business with pleasure. If there is something between him and Moira, how did I miss it?

"Fuck." I run a hand through my hair and tug on the roots. California suddenly feels very far away. We're stuck in the Gulf of Mexico, heading toward Galveston on a slow-as-shit trawler. We're not in a good place to launch a mission. Yet, that's what it looks like we're about to do. Why is that?

Griff shifts restlessly beside me. His worry over Moira is clear as day, not that he'll admit it.

"Take a seat." Max gestures to the small table.

We settle in, shoulder to shoulder, and look to CJ for our orders. The rest of Alpha team shuffles in. Half of Charlie team's already present. We're all tired as fuck after rescuing the girls from the cargo container.

"This is what we've got so far." CJ gives a clap of his hands, then rubs his palms, like he's getting ready to go to bat. Which he kind of is as our battle commander. "It's a first pass. If you have suggestions, pipe in. Charlie team stays on the trawler and escorts the twelve girls to Galveston. They'll off-load and transfer to one of Guardian HRS's private jets. Then it's a quick flight to California for processing by Facility personnel."

Processing means families will be notified. Girls will be reunited with terrified mothers, fathers, and other family members. If they have no family, the Facility will become their home until the girls decide what they want.

A pinprick of awareness skitters along my nerves. It makes my teeth buzz. My fingers tingle. I don't like this one bit. Beside me, Griff's knee bounces like a jackhammer.

"Stop that." I grab Griff's knee and whisper. "You're making me anxious."

"Why the fuck are *you* not crawling out of your skin?" He gives me a murderous stare. The man wants blood.

"Because I can't do anything."

I get what he's saying. Those same emotions swirl inside of me, but there's no target to direct them at, yet. Until then, I focus on what I can do. Right now, that means sitting through a strategy session. My hands shake as my mind spins. A thousand variants of *what the fuck happened* flit through my mind.

"Go over it again." I need to hear it again.

"Sometime after midnight, Pacific time, Zoe sent an alert text. Their phones were found on the beach." Mitzy speaks to the group through a secure line. "Guardian HRS is mobilizing assets like crazy."

"Sign of struggle?" I ask.

"Significant," Mitzy replies.

"And?"

"It's a beach. It's not like there was a clear path to follow." Mitzy doesn't like wasting breath on unnecessary words. Her frustration is clear. I get it. I feel it.

"How long until her tracker was activated?"

"Ten minutes after she sent the text," Mitzy says.

"Moira's?"

"Nothing so far. We're working to activate it remotely."

"Why isn't that built in? You should always be tracking those things."

"It's called privacy, and it's not like they were supposed to be in danger. It's a public beach in a crowded part of town, and they're both adults. We don't spy on our charges, but you know that."

"Obviously, the assumption they weren't in danger is wrong. Not to mention this occurred after midnight. No crowds. Perfect place for an abduction."

"We're not going down that path." Mitzy's reply is curt and final. I get it. Pointing fingers and placing blame is a waste of time. "However, there is one more thing. Her tracker's on the move."

"What's that mean?"

"From the rate of speed we're tracking, they're on a plane headed to—"

"A plane?" I push to my feet, pissed to hell.

"Yes. It's headed—"

Before she can complete her sentence, I finish it. "To Colombia." My gut sinks like a lead weight. "She's the Golden Goose."

"Yes. How did you know?" It's rare to impress Mitzy, but she's a bit shocked.

Evidently, Max and CJ are as well. Charlie team crowds into the small room with us and hold up the walls. Their mission is spelled out, babysitters to our new group of rescues, but we need all the brains we can get. So far, none of them join in the conversation.

"How confident are you about the flight path?"

"Very."

It's an unnecessary question. Mitzy doesn't put out information she isn't one hundred percent certain is reliable.

"This is the same operation that grabbed Zoe the first time. Which means this is personal."

"That's our conclusion." CJ taps the table. "Which is why we're spinning up to intercept."

Originally, we thought Zoe was a target of convenience, picked off the street because she was pretty, alone, and oblivious. For them to come after her a second time, in what is obviously a coordinated attack, sends up all kinds of red flags.

There's no need to say any of this. We all think it. We all feel it.

330

"The good news—" Mitzy continues, "—is they don't know we're tracking them. We pulled all flight plans for planes leaving the local area within a one hour drive from when she sent the alert text. We matched her movement, speed and direction, and found the plane. Colombia is the destination. There's no sign they're deviating from it."

"How far ahead are they?" Max crosses his arms and blows out a breath. I'm right there with him doing the mental math.

"Two hours."

"We need to discuss infil." Max is multi-tasking, listening, and contributing, to our conversation while peering at a computer screen. His job is to run the op, but dammit, it's my girl with her life on the line. "A helicopter is en route to pick us up. We take that to Colombia. Transportation will meet us on the ground."

It never ceases to amaze me how Guardian HRS acquires assets. We have people all over the globe ready to supply our teams with whatever we need at a moment's notice. Like the ground transportation. The helicopter. This trawler.

No need to worry about weapons. We carry our own and are well stocked for anything short of a minor war.

"The only thing we don't know is where they'll take the girls after they land." CJ holds a hand over his mouth as he yawns. Pretty soon, everyone in the room yawns. I grit my teeth.

"I'm spinning up Overlord. We should have eyes on the ground by the time that plane lands. Regardless, we'll follow the tracker. It's still in play. If they discover it, Overlord is the backup." Overlord's high tech spy gear will follow Zoe while we're still en route.

"Something doesn't make sense." I can't help coming back to this. Zoe's in the hands of monsters for the second time in her life,

"Your spider-senses buzzing?" Griff, who sits beside me, turns his astute gaze to me.

331

"Like a motherfucker." My sixth sense is loud as fuck. "It's a set up."

"We agree." Max pushes back from the table.

My gut sinks as I piece together what's happening.

"Griff…"

"Yeah?"

"Work this with me, will ya?"

"Sure." He knows how my brain works. Sometimes, I think better out loud.

"Do we know what the price was on Zoe's auction?" The bad feeling in my gut intensifies.

"Mizty?" CJ turns the question over to Mitzy.

"One second." She sounds stressed. "I'm trying to get Overlord airborne."

Once again, the assets we have distributed across the globe astounds me.

"Let's assume high dollar." I can only imagine an operation of this scale caters to an exclusive clientele. Exclusive live-stream snuff means money—lots of money. Disposable wealth on that scale implies a complicated funneling operation through various channels. Their clients don't want a transaction like this pointing back to them. "They either sold multiple tickets to her murder or sold it as an exclusive to one client. No way to know for sure, but let's assume the former."

"Six events were logged. One million apiece." Mitzy comes back to the conversation. "That makes sense."

Shit. Six million to watch a girl die. But does it make sense? This is what worries me.

"How were those transactions processed?"

"Bitcoin transfers, which means they're untraceable, and to answer your next question, there's no way to refund that money. The money trail is dirty as shit. Their clients wouldn't want that returned to them."

"That's what I'm thinking. Let's assume the money is still in play. That means they stiffed six customers. They didn't provide their *service* and can't refund the money."

"Which means, they need to deliver." Liam speaks up for the first time, but his words are more growl than anything else.

This is personal to me because of my relationship with Zoe, but it's personal for my team as well. One of our rescues is back in the hands of her tormentors. Alpha team won't stand for that kind of shit.

"Correct," Max says. "But why Zoe?"

"I'm surprised they didn't snag another girl in Cancun. That seems to be how these guys operate." Griff is restless beside me.

I get what Griff's saying. Why not grab another random girl? Zoe's kidnapping is the opposite of random.

"That's what I'm wondering," I say. "Which makes me think this may not be six customers, but rather one irate customer demanding they fulfill their promise with the girl that got away—Zoe."

"Fucker." Griff tilts his head and stares at the flickering fluorescent light overhead.

"Yeah, ultimate privilege. I'm thinking some entitled bastard is pulling their strings. There's no reason to put all that effort into kidnapping Zoe unless the client specifically requested her. Not to mention, that's not how their operation is set up. They prey on tourists, people who are easy to pick off, and whose disappearances are often not reported for days. I can't imagine six men would care, let alone bother, about their live-stream snuff being the same girl. We're definitely dealing with one over-privileged fucker with millions to throw away."

"I'm surprised he doesn't fly in special to watch in person," Wolfe grumbles beside me.

"Too risky, I suppose. This asshole likes to get his rocks off, but not by putting himself at risk. The money transfer is crazy secure." Mitzy blows out a frustrated breath.

"What about the live feed?" Knox, who's been silent, pipes up. "If we could intercept that transmission isn't there a way to track it to its source? We nail this client and find out who he hired for this shit."

A chill washes over me. The only way to follow that transmission is if it's streaming. If that's the case, it means bad things for Zoe.

"I don't know about that," Mitzy replies. "Depending how it's routed, maybe not."

I keep talking it out. It helps me keep my head in the game rather than spiral out of control on a murderous rampage.

"They grabbed Moira and Zoe on the beach. We assume Zoe is the target. Moira's collateral."

"Agreed." CJ sounds pissed. More than pissed, he's furious.

"The location is a message." Knox curses. "They're out for revenge."

"Payback." Max agrees.

"So, we're agreed? We're walking into a trap?" I state the obvious. "This is well planned, which means..."

"They're flushing out our organization." Max finishes the sentence.

"Yes." CJ's response is short and to the point.

"But we're still going in?" Trap or no trap, I'll do whatever it takes to free Zoe, even if that means taking my last breath.

"The only easy day was yesterday." Griff grins as he recites the Navy SEAL motto.

"Ain't that the truth." I run a hand through my hair. "No wonder my nerves are shot. It's just the six of us up against how many?"

"Mitzy, we need Overlord in position ASAP. Full thermals." It's Max's turn to curse. "This is going to be a shit show."

"Outmanned. Outgunned. Outmaneuvered. It's just another day. A fucking walk in the park." Griff gives me a fist bump.

"Damn straight."

"Infiltration is going to be difficult. They'll land two hours before we can get there. As of now, we don't know where they'll take the girls. Either the tracker, or Overlord, will answer that question by the time we have boots on the ground." Max circles us back to mission execution planning. "Since they're expecting us, we have to assume they'll be watching the airfields. They know we're coming. What they don't know is how we'll approach. I'm open to suggestions." He stares at each of us in turn.

Knox throws out a suggestion. We chew on that a bit before rejecting it. It feels like we're wasting time. I force myself to slow down. The time we take now will save us from making lethal mistakes later on.

"We assume they'll take them to another building. This isn't something they'd do in the open. We won't know where, or the building schematics until we're there, and we must assume they'll have all entrances guarded and all routes monitored." Max tugs at his chin.

"The perfect ambush. They see us coming and wait." Knox gives a nod.

"We sure that's the only way?" Wolfe taps his forehead.

"Pretty damn sure," I say.

"Then, we make our own way." Wolfe glances at me. "Regain the surprise factor."

"And how the fuck are we going to do that?"

"They're thinking two-dimensionally. We'll approach by car or foot and breach the doors, but what if we come in through the roof?"

"And how are we going to get on the roof?" Liam gives a snort. "Fucking fly?"

"Climb up or rappel down?" Knox is thinking it through, but he gives a shake of his head. "We can't fly a helicopter without making a shit ton of noise. That doesn't work."

"No." Wolfe's persistent, but he's a crafty fucker, kind of like Alpha's own MacGyver. "But we can still land on it."

"How?" Like the rest of the team, I don't get where he's going with this.

"Pull up a map of the area." He points to the computer. "Here's our assumptions. We assume they're setting us up, which we don't really know. They could simply be fulfilling their client's demands and know nothing about us. I think that's more likely, but I'm not willing to risk my neck on that. If we go with the assumption they know we're coming, then we must assume they know we have some way of tracking the girls. Which means we're being played."

"Hmm." CJ paces down the length of the cramped mess area. "That makes sense."

"Can't go in by ground. They expect that. Can't come up through the ground. That's impossible. Which means we come in by air. If they're aware we took those twelve girls from them, they know we're somewhere in the Gulf. Which means they also know our only way off this ship is by air, which is a helicopter. They'll be watching for that. I say that's where we fuck them up."

"Come again?" Max's eyes pinch.

"We don't go to Colombia. We use the helicopter to get off this ship. Fly to..." He scans the map and points. "Here."

"And do what?" Max's still trying to figure out where Wolfe is going with this. I'm beginning to see what he's thinking.

"Rent a plane. Take our chutes. And..."

"We land on the roof." I nod vigorously seeing his plan. "Wolfe's right. Wherever they go, they'll be watching for us and I think we should give them what they're looking for."

"Come again?" CJ likes this plan. I see it in the gleam of his eyes, but my last statement threw him.

"After we land, we send the helicopter to Colombia. Make it look like we're doing exactly what they think. We use Charlie for that."

"We're good for that. So, you want us to do what? Be bait?" Tex, who's been leaning against the wall and silently observing our team work the mission, steps forward.

"Exactly. Take your time. Be slow, methodical. Maybe take a wrong turn or two? Anything to slow you down. We're assuming they'll be watching you, and if they are, no one will see us coming." I tap Wolfe on the arm. "Fucking brilliant idea."

"Meh, I try." He gives a little shrug, but the bastard's pleased with himself. He's also a certified genius. He's got the Mensa shirt to prove it.

"If we're taking Charlie, I want to get the girls off this ship as fast as possible." CJ rubs his neck. "How does that look for transport, Mitzy? Got an extra helicopter hanging around?"

"You're kidding, right?" Mitzy gives a snort. "This is the Gulf of Mexico with tens of thousands of oil rigs peppered everywhere and helicopters are their main mode of travel. I'll get the team on it. We'll send three."

"Three?"

"If you want to delay Charlie, I suggest Alpha team takes the chopper already inbound. We can get... Hang on..." Indistinct chatter comes over the speakers as we all wait on Mitzy. The comm channel pops with static when she returns. "Great news. We've got two helicopters on the way. One will arrive twenty minutes before ours. I suggest Alpha take that. Our chopper will arrive next, it has room for twenty. I'd put your new rescuees on that. It has the range to get them to Galveston. The third is a smaller chopper, but it only seats six. Five if you exclude the pilot."

Tex gives a nod. "We'll send Jeb and Blake to escort the girls. If we're just the diversion, the rest of Charlie will take the third helicopter to Colombia. I'm sure we can figure out how to look like fucking idiots with our thumbs up our butts and delay. Wouldn't be the first time we were used as bait." The way he says that, with his thick Texan drawl, is funny as shit.

I can't help but smirk, and I'm not the only one.

"Alright, we have a plan." CJ claps his hands. "Let's run through it again."

We run through it several times. When CJ gets word the chopper is ten minutes out, he calls an end to our planning session.

"You guys feel up to landing on the roof of a building you've never seen?" CJ does a gut check. If it doesn't feel right, we'll say no.

"As long as Overlord guides us in..." I look to my team, but I already know what I'll see. Five thumbs up.

Hell yeah, we're up to it.

THIRTY-THREE

Zoe

Instead of days, it takes hours to make the trek to a place I know all too well. Trussed up with my arms and legs tied behind my back, excruciating pain pulses through my body. My legs cramp. My shoulder sockets burn. My back arches painfully.

When they finally free me from the hog-tie, heat rushes through my arms and legs, followed by agonizing pinpricks as circulation returns to my extremities.

Panic rises within me as they drag me into the building and past the room with the showers.

There's not a single technique I learned at the Facility that pushes back the blinding terror. I'm back in the room where terrible things happened and girls I knew for only days died.

I try to breathe out, long and slow like they taught me, but my breaths chug like a runaway freight train. My shoulders scream in pain from being trussed up in the plane. My legs feel like jelly. My fingers and toes burn as blood rushes in. My lips tingle and black spots dance in my vision. I'm living my worst nightmare.

"She must be something special." A man, with midnight-black hair and a jagged scar that runs from his eye to the corner of his mouth, paces in a wide circle around me. He stares at my naked body with disinterest and points at the restraints I wear.

A metal collar wraps around my neck. A long, black rod hangs down from it. My wrists are handcuffed at the end by my waist, and the whole thing is secured to my body by a leather belt. I can't lift my hands. My feet are shackled. The heavy chains make it hard to walk, let alone kick.

At least I got in a few good hits before they restrained me. But my strength fades. I don't know how much longer I can hold out. Not when I know what's in store for me.

I want to hurl obscenities at these men, but they took away my voice with a filthy gag. Like the last time I was here, a photographer takes pictures. A burst of light follows each snap as he documents the last minutes of my life.

In however many hours we were on the plane, I've said my goodbyes. I did this the last time, saying farewell to my brother and father. Instead of my college friends, I say goodbye to my new family, to the kids at the Facility who shared their trauma and showed me how to be strong. To Alpha team who saved me. And finally, to Axel, the man I love.

"You've caused quite a bit of trouble." The man with the dark hair steps up to me. He reeks of foul body odor and stale beer. His smell is pungent enough to make my eyes water. "But all is good now."

He takes a step back and takes in my nakedness. I've been naked since they cut off my clothing in the van.

Don't look.

My gaze skitters over to a lump in the corner. Moira's blonde hair spills over her shoulders. Her body sprawls on the ground, limp and unmoving. I haven't heard a sound from her since the van. They kicked her viscously, and I don't know if she's alive or dead.

340

He gives a derisive snort when he catches the direction of my gaze. "Oh, don't worry about your friend. We have plenty planned to keep her occupied." He snaps his fingers and men jump into action. "Tie her up."

I squirm, but it's not much. They've immobilized me. Instead of letting me shuffle to the center of the room, they drag me.

"He wants her arms up and out. Spreader between her feet, like it was the first time." My tormentor shouts instructions.

I scream as they free my wrists only to tie them out to the side. Or I try to scream. All that comes out is a muffled sound behind the gag. They unshackle my feet, attach cuffs around my ankles, then kick my legs out to put a metal bar between my feet. Securing the cuffs to the bar, my legs are spread wide.

I feel helpless, lost, and very alone. I don't know if my message got through. There's no way to know if the necklace around my neck is working, but I pray.

There are ten men: one with the scar, the three stringing me up, the photographer, his assistant, and four burly guards manning the only exit.

The photographer moves all around me, snapping pictures of my pain. Tears spill from my eyes and the bastard takes a close up of those.

I hate these men. I hate them all. Flashbacks from when I was here previously slam into me. Joy's cries cut off with a gurgling noise as they sliced open her neck. Katie as they suffocated her with a plastic bag. Lily as they drown her while she hangs upside down and fights for her life. Hope beaten and stoned. Iris fighting for her life. Grace's soft goodbye as she accepted her fate.

And now these men will finish what they started. My entire body trembles, my heart slams against my ribs, my breaths quicken. Despite all of that, an eerie calmness sweeps over me as the man with the black hair uncoils a bullwhip.

He comes to me and pulls the gag from my mouth. "Don't want to muffle your delicious screams now, do we?"

The men tying me up tug on the ropes. My arms lift up and out to the side. A hot light shines down from above. Not because they need it to see, but because the photographer needs the light for his pictures. There are other cameras. Video cameras recording my death.

Somewhere, on the other side of that screen, an evil man has paid to watch me die.

"Shall we begin?" The man holding the whip raises his hand over his head then snaps his arm forward.

The harsh *crack* sounds like a bullet going off. The tip of the whip bites into my hip and searing pain rips through me.

Tears fall. I cry for Austin, for my dad, for my friends back home. But I mourn Axel and the life I'll never share with him the most. At least we had a few stolen moments and I can die knowing he loves me.

I shift my focus to one of the cameras. My eyes pinch. I speak my last words with vehemence to the monster who paid for this.

"You will be hunted. They will find you and they will kill you. Enjoy what time you have left you miserable piece of shit."

The man with the whip rushes forward and backhands me across the face. My teeth slice the inside of my cheek as my head whips violently to the side. Blood fills my mouth and I spit it out.

"Shut your mouth, you little cunt." To emphasize his displeasure, he slams his fist into my gut.

The pain overwhelms me and I'm caught huffing and struggling to breathe. But I do breathe. Blood wells in the back of my throat, making me gag. This time, I spit the blood in his face.

"Or what? You'll kill me?" A crazy laugh rushes out of me as the last of my sanity flees. I'm going to die, and I don't fucking care.

Axel and his team will find whoever is behind all of this. He will bring them to justice.

Guardian justice.

I tip my head back and stare at the bright fluorescent lights overhead. The ceiling is twenty feet over my head and peppered with skylights, which in the daytime would fill the interior with natural lighting. Now, they're nothing more than voids of the deepest black.

I don't want this man's ugly face to be the last thing I see. I pretend I'm looking at the stars.

Something shifts overhead: a shadow separating from the blackness. Not a shadow. It's a man cloaked in black. He drops through, not a skylight, but a hole in the roof. Another body follows, and then two more.

Four men rappel silently out of a hole while two more aim the noses of their weapons inside. None of my captors notice. They all look hungrily at me.

My breath stops. I'm too scared to move and draw attention overhead. A tightness fills my chest as I hold my breath. I don't dare to hope, but I know. I know he's here.

Axel is here to save me again.

A whole-body shiver ripples through me. The men watching laugh. They think it's terror rushing through me, but they couldn't be more wrong.

The power cuts out. I'm plunged into darkness. The men cry out and shout to one another. Flashes of light punctuate the darkness. Tiny blips of sound. Axel's team is using silencers. One by one they take the men out.

A thud sounds behind me. There's another to my left. Another one behind me. I keep count as bodies fall.

It takes a moment. My heart stops and a hollowness fills my chest. But then it's off racing again.

Men shout as gunfire pops all around me.

Someone comes up behind me. I tense, expecting the worst. A presence crouches. There's a tugging at my ankles. A tugging at my wrists. One of my arms drops. I'm too weak to move it. The other one follows. My left foot is freed. Then my right. I sway on my feet.

"Zoe?" Axel's hot breath brushes past my ear.

I'm too shocked to respond. I give a nod, not that he can see. It's pitch black inside the building.

"Can you walk?" Axel grabs me by my neck and presses his forehead against mine. "We need to move. Can. You. Walk?"

I stare into the darkness. I may have blinked. I'm not sure. "Ten. There are ten men." The words rush out all at once.

"We know."

"Moira?" That's a voice I don't recognize. "Where's Moira?"

I try to speak, but no sound comes out. I clear my throat and point in the general direction where I remember them depositing her body. I say nothing. I can't. I'm to overwhelmed.

A third voice speaks. "We need to move."

"I've got Zoe." Something clinks beside me. "I'm going to put you in a harness. Steady yourself on my shoulders."

Tears stream down my face as deep sobs rip out of my chest. I can't see shit, but he seems to have no problem with his vision. He places my hands on his shoulders so I can steady myself, then crouches. He gives a little tug to my left ankle. I lift my foot and he slides something over it. He does the same with my other leg.

Something slides up my legs, but it's not shorts or pants. I reach down and feel a thick canvas strap of a harness. Axel wraps something around my waist. More straps. A buckle. He secures everything together, pulling and tugging as the harness wraps around me. I sway unsteadily on my feet.

"I have you." His hand goes in mine, and I stumble forward.

How can he see when it's pitch black?

There's movement. Indistinct sounds I can't make out. I sense two other men moving around us.

Axel grabs my hand. He pulls it over his shoulder and loops my other one around his neck.

"I'm going to strap you to my back. Grab your wrists and hold on."

Hold on?

The world shifts, tilting violently, as I'm lifted off my feet. Somehow, I hang off Axel's back.

"It might be easier if you close your eyes, luv."

Close them? I can't see anything.

He grabs my legs and wraps them around his hips. Then we're moving. More sounds reach my ears, like a latch opening and closing.

Axel's body weight shifts, then he steps up. I dangle off his back and grab at his shoulders as a tiny shriek escapes me. His left arm moves up. Something rasps in front of him. His breathing deepens with exertion.

We shift to the right, then to the left. I swing wide with each movement. My stomach lurches with the sensation of falling, but I trust him not to let me fall.

His arms move methodically up then down. Up then down. Almost as if he's climbing a ladder, but all I saw were four black ropes

345

before the lights went out.

Hands reach down through a rectangle that's less black than my surroundings. They grab Axel at the shoulders and haul us up.

I squeeze my eyes shut. Wind blows across my face. My eyes open, and I find myself staring at a man wearing a pair of night-vision goggles. One of Axel's teammates, although I don't know who.

We're on the roof, and while still dark, I can see better than in the pitch-black inside.

Axel frees himself from the line, unhooking something from around his hands. One of the men stoops down and removes something similar from around each of Axel's boots.

"Griff?" a deep voice asks.

"On his way up. Max and Knox are grabbing the gear. Our ride?" Axel moves away from the open skylight and squats into a crouch.

"On its way."

"How're you doing, Zoe?" Axel asks.

Words fail me. I tighten my grip around his neck and sob.

"I've got you." He grabs my hand and gives a squeeze. I need him to wrap me in his arms. Instead, I dangle awkwardly on his back. He shows no sign of letting me off his back.

"Axel—Axel…" I whisper his name over and over again.

The two men on the roof peer down into the open hole. The rope rolls side to side. Soon, a man's head appears and I understand how Axel climbed up the rope. The man gives a yank of his wrist and reaches up. A cylindrical tube of metal glides up the line. He pulls sharply down and the tube cinches tight around the rope. He jerks first one foot, and then the other, and rises out of the hole.

The two men on the roof grab his shoulders and haul him up over the edge.

"Where's Moira?" one of them asks.

"Gone." Griff's voice is cold and lacking all emotion. "Max and Knox are coming up."

I glance around and see two of the four ropes shifting side to side as the men below climb.

"Two minutes." One of the men holds up two fingers. "Keep down, but get ready."

Axel hefts his weapon and crawls to a corner of the roof. He stays below the low wall. Griff follows and takes a knee.

"She wasn't there?" Axel asks.

"No." His blunt reply is like a stab to my heart.

"She was in the corner. I saw them put her there."

"They must've moved her. She wasn't there."

I cry. I can't help it. Moira's gone.

Silence descends between us.

It's brighter out here, but it's still hard to see the men who are dressed all in black. Shadows shift and creep toward us.

"Ready?"

"Alpha-Two, check."

"Alpha-Three, check." Axel's response is more of a rumble.

"Alpha-Four, check," Griff says.

"Alpha-Five, check."

"Alpha-Six, check."

Somewhere overhead, a helicopter chops through the air. It's loud and sounds really low.

"Get ready. Weapons up. Heads on a swivel." I don't know who's speaking, except it's not Axel. I think it's the first man.

Axel tenses. Knuckles to the ground, he shifts. One knee down. The other in front. The helicopter closes in on us and I crane my neck looking for it.

Then it's there, coming in fast, not more than twenty feet over our heads. The sound is deafening. Wind beats down on us. Axel is up on his feet and jogs forward as the free end of a rope dangling down from the helicopter slithers across the edge of the roof.

Shots fire from the ground.

Axel clips something to the rope and continues trotting forward. Griff does the same behind us. I tense as the other side of the roof approaches. Axel shows no sign of slowing down.

Right when I think he's about ready to jump off the roof, the rope lifts him into the air. I squeeze my eyes shut and swing loosely behind him. I swallow my scream as gunfire erupts from the ground aimed for us.

Axel returns fire as we're lifted higher. Griff is a few feet below us on the line. Like Axel, he shoots at the ground. Flashes of light flicker below us.

We're dangerously exposed, but for every twenty of their shots, Axel and Griff fire back with a single shot. Slowly, the gunfire from below slows.

I glance down and see the last man from Axel's team lifted off the building. We swing from the line as the helicopter rises and angles away from the building.

The world beneath us falls away as the deafening noise of the helicopter gets louder and louder.

I glance up and see a man sticking his head out of the open bay of the helicopter. He's getting closer. Then I realize we're being reeled in.

Axel clips his weapon to the front of his vest and reaches out a hand as we get close. We're hauled inside.

Axel frees himself from the line and moves to the far side of the helicopter. He turns his back to the low bench, takes a knee, then releases the clips and straps holding me to his back.

Before I'm able to settle into the seat, Axel spins around and pulls me into his arms.

"I've got you."

Filled with overwhelming joy, I grab at him as he covers my mouth with his.

Griff is pulled into the helicopter and collapses on the floor. Axel releases me and goes to his friend.

"Griff?"

"Fucker got me in the leg." Griff clutches his leg.

I leap to my feet and kneel beside Griff. A dark, glistening stain saturates his pants. It's spreading fast.

The man at the winch glances over his shoulder, but he's got four men to pull up the line. Griff grunts in pain. He's losing a lot of blood.

Axel yanks his belt free, and wraps it around Griff's leg, high above the wound. He slides the webbing through the buckle and pulls it tight while Griff holds pressure on the wound.

"Zoe, check for a pulse," Axel calls out. "The artery needs to be fully compressed." The bleeding slows down. Axel tightens the tourniquet until it stops." He slides his finger down Griff's boot to feel for a pulse. "How you doing, Griff?"

"Not dead yet." Griff leans back. "Fucking bad day in the office."

The rest of Axel's team comes up the line. One of them squats beside me. "What happened?"

I point to the tourniquet and the bleeding. It's too loud to keep shouting, and my voice is pretty much done.

Whether it's a residual of my fear, or the elation I feel from being rescued, I sway back and forth. I'm giddy because I'm free, but terrified because Moira isn't. What did they do to her?

"I'm calling it in. Skye's team is waiting at the airfield. Time?"

"Zero two-hundred hours." The man at the winch calls out.

"Sorry, brother." Axel dips his finger in Griff's blood and draws a zero, a two, and a horizontal line on Griff's forehead.

Griff looks up at him and shakes his head.

"What's that for?" I don't understand why he did that.

"It's the time the tourniquet went on," Griff speaks without emotion and stares at his leg. "I've got two hours to get it fixed. After six, I lose the leg."

"Don't worry, Skye's team is alerted." Axel leans back and takes a deep breath. "We're only thirty-minutes out. You're not losing your leg today."

"Thanks." Griff huffs out an agonized breath. "Hurts like a motherfucker." He turns his attention to me. "Swift thinking there, buttercup."

"It's the least I could do after you saved my life, not once but twice."

"Ah, it's all in a day's work, luv." His brows draw tight with pain and he stares out the open bay of the helicopter.

I move back to the farthest corner inside the helicopter. All of the men of Alpha team are finally off the rope and on board. The nose of the helicopter tips forward and we pick up speed.

I stare at the six amazing and beautiful men who sacrifice their lives to save people like me. 'Thank you' feels incredibly inadequate.

While I can't hear over the noise, I see their grim smiles, the way they all try to ease Griff's pain. I watch Axel hover over his friend as he tries to assess the extent of his injury. These men share a tight bond—closer than family—they're more than brothers.

I tug my knees to my chest and blow out a breath. I remember asking what the chances were of being kidnapped twice in one lifetime. When I get back to the Facility, I plan on doubling down on my training.

I'll never be what these men are, but I vow to never be a burden again. I'm a survivor, and it's time I step up my game.

Axel glances over at me. Love simmers in his eyes. I know he wants to come to me, but he won't leave his patient. I say a silent prayer for Moira and hope she survives. I don't really know what happens next.

After my prayer, I keep my eyes closed and slowly rock back and forth. Before I can be that survivor, I allow myself this one moment to completely fall apart. Tears stream down my face. The deafening noise of the helicopter smothers my sobs. But I cry, and I sob. I let it all out.

And I know I'm finally free. I'm no longer caught in a nightmare.

Someone sits beside me and I crack open an eye. Axel wraps his arm around my shoulder and pulls me tight against his side.

"We'll find her." He makes it a promise. Somehow, I believe him. Then he lowers his lips to mine. "I love you."

"I love you, too."

I curl into him and let my tears fall. He runs his fingers through my hair, combing out the tangles while pressing his warm lips against my temple.

And he holds me.

THIRTY-FOUR

Axel

ZOE'S SAFE. HER WOUNDS ATTENDED TO. I LEAVE HER WITH THE other girls and my teammates who will watch over her, to look in on Griff.

Griff's alive. The tourniquet saved his life. Skye's medical team salvaged his leg by some modern medical magic, and they did it in the back of a plane. To them, it's just another day. To me, and I'm sure Griff, it's nothing short of miraculous.

He won't be losing a leg.

We're back at headquarters. He's in surgery, hooked up to their machines, knocked out with hefty doses of morphine while they repair the rest of the damage. Skye promises he'll heal up just fine. I told him not to worry because chicks dig scars. When they wheel him out of the operating room, I rush Skye.

"How's Griff?" I look to her for answers.

Tia and Ryker are with him. They work to transfer his breathing circuit to the bedside ventilator.

"The leg will heal, but it's going to take some time." Skye pulls off her surgical mask and scrub hat. "You should get some rest."

I run a hand through my hair and stare at my wounded teammate. Max, Knox, Liam, and Wolfe are gone. Liam and Wolfe went to look after the girls we rescued from the cargo container. Max and Knox are with CJ, Sam, and more than likely, Forest. They're trying to decide what to do next. We saved Zoe, but Moira's still lost.

"I'm not leaving his side." I look for a chair, or stool, something to sit on. I'm surviving on fumes, too tired to think, but I won't leave Griff until I know he's okay.

"He's going to be sedated all night." Skye takes my hand. "I promise to call you as soon as he wakes. You need to take care of yourself. Go, get some rest."

When I give her a look, she releases my hand and gives me the stare of death.

"Axel…" She grips my chin and forces me to look into eyes far too wise for her age.

I'm easily a foot taller than the doc, yet it's as if she's looking down at me.

"Go. To. Bed. Doctor's orders. You won't be any use to your team asleep on your feet." She gives me a shove toward the door. "Seriously, go. If you don't, I'll have Forest drag you to bed."

If I had any energy, I would fight her, but I can barely stand upright. I wander back to my quarters, worried about Griff, but the closer I get to my bed, the more my thoughts turn to Zoe.

I hate leaving her alone, but I needed to check on my team.

There are also the girls we rescued. I won't be able to sleep until I see them tucked safely into bed with Guardian's watching over them. I try not to think about Moira.

Opening the door to the common room, Liam places a finger over his lips. He stands closest to the door. Wolfe is on the opposite side of the room. They need sleep as much, or more, than me. Instead, they'll stand guard over the girls until morning.

Liam walks over as I scan the beds. Twelve young women lay in the cots set out for them. It's the best we can do until Forest's team can process them. They'll receive the same offer given to Zoe, a chance to find their way in the world again.

I'm so fucking proud of my girl. The way she handled herself is beyond amazing. The way she kept it together is fucking awe-inspiring.

"Where's Zoe?" I keep my voice to a whisper as I shift closer to Liam.

"Your girl went to your quarters looking for you." Instead of a smirk, something I expect from Liam, a genuine smile fills his face. "She's something special."

"She sure is."

"You better not keep her waiting."

"I won't."

I palm my face and drag it down to my chin. Damn, I'm tired. The pungent smell of gunpowder, sweat, and blood fills my nostrils. No way am I getting any sleep smelling like this, and I'm not slipping into bed with Zoe with any of her kidnappers' blood on me.

We didn't get a chance to talk after everything happened. Things moved too fast during our crazy exfil. But I need to feel her tonight. There are things that need to be said.

When I enter my room, she's nowhere to be found, which leaves me scratching my head. Zoe wouldn't wander. She's learned that lesson. The stink from my fatigues assaults my nostrils. I need a shower. Chances are pretty damn good I'll find her there.

I grab a towel and head to the communal showers. The door slams behind me as I enter the bathroom. Pine-scented cleaner assaults my senses along with the acrid smell of the liberal bleach used to keep the bathroom sparkling white.

Water runs in one of the shower stalls and steam billows out from the top. A low moan fills the room. A sob of anguish followed by a low whimper.

I know that tortured sound. I've heard it before, a low, keening wail of anguish. It tunnels inside my body, spearing straight for my heart where it settles in and burns.

It's the sound of my girl in pain.

"Zoe?" There's no need to ask. I know it's her, but the last thing I want is to spook her. I've been told I'm a light-foot, capable of sneaking up on anything and anyone.

"Axel?" I hear sounds that make me think she's huddled on the floor and is quickly standing. I can even picture her wiping the tears from her cheeks. She hates when she cries; sees it as a sign of weakness. I see it as a sign of truth.

Strength.

Resilience.

Bravery.

"Yeah, brat, it's me." I rip at the buttons of my fatigues. I pull at the laces of my boots. Without really caring where my things wind up, I kick off my boots, slip out of my trousers, and divest myself of my clothes. I yank the shower door open, and sure enough, she's in the corner wiping at her cheeks. "Ah, babe, come here."

The moment I open my arms, she dives into my embrace. Her arms wrap around my waist and she snuggles against my chest.

"What about Moira?" Her words are muffled, considering how she's got her head buried against my chest.

I don't answer. As far as this goes, it's not over, but I won't burden her with that. We intend to ferret out the men behind her abduction. We will find Moira. The Guardians have declared war on that organization, and we'll dismantle it piece by piece.

My body shakes with its need to comfort Zoe, to console her, and tell her it's all over. I can't believe a year ago I kicked her out of my bed and broke her heart. What the hell had I been thinking when she's everything I've ever wanted?

I need her like I need air to breathe. With her in my arms, another burning, pressing need, makes itself known. My dick weeps because the last thing she needs now is sex, but there's no hiding what's happening between my legs.

She nuzzles against me. Her breasts slide over my chest, and I suppress a low groan of desire as her nipples graze against my skin. Her belly presses against mine, and I bite my lower lip as desire sweeps through me.

I close my eyes and inhale the light fragrance of her shampoo. I'm stoically trying to ignore the way her breasts keep sliding across my chest. Her nipples prick into tiny buds, which draw delicious moans from me as they drag against my chest. My fingers curl in her wet mane, and I close my eyes beneath the assault of holding heaven in my arms.

"Damn, but this feels right." I grip the soft curves of her hips and hold her tight to me.

Moments pass as we do nothing other than hold each other. Slowly, she relaxes in my arms. Damn, but the way this woman makes me feel. I come undone in her arms.

"You were crying," I say.

"Yeah."

"Why?"

"Because I almost lost you."

"Me? You're the one who…" I can't finish what I was going to say.

"I survived because of you."

She leans back and gazes up at me. Her palms slide around my waist and roam toward my chest. Feather-light, there's nothing timid in her touch. Her fingertips wake every nerve in my body. Whatever exhaustion I felt earlier flees in the wake of the intense, deep hunger rising within me.

"Zoe…" I'm cautious. I never want to take advantage of her. After everything we've been through, we both need rest.

"Don't." She places her finger over my lips. "Don't tell me you don't need this." Her soft voice is barely audible above the spray of the water.

Steam wraps around us as she looks up at me and smiles. She bends forward and places her lips on my chest. Her kiss is reverent, soft, absolutely sure.

"Aren't you tired? I don't want to…"

"Honestly, if you don't fuck me now, I *will* kill you." She grins at me with an impish smile on her face. "But you're filthy and kind of reek. You need to get clean." She reaches for the soap and tilts her head at me. "What will it be? Sleep or sex."

"Sex, then sleep, sounds pretty fucking wonderful." I reach for the soap, but she yanks it out of my reach.

"No. Let me." This time, her touch is sure and determined as her hands roam my body. She begins at my chest, washes my neck, and tells me to spin around while she cleans the blood, sweat, and gunpowder residue from my body.

Fuck if I'm not aching and hard for her—always for her. I lift on tiptoe when she reaches around and grabs my dick. Slick with soap, her breasts slide against my back while her hand glides up and down my cock.

"My dick's not that dirty, little brat." I grab her hand, remove it, and spin around. "If you keep touching me like that, I'm not going to last."

"Maybe that's what I want?"

"I've only got one round in me, and I'm not wasting that on your hands."

She gives a little twist of her wrist as she slides her hand down my cock. My eyes close and a groan escapes my mouth. My balls draw up as heat coils at the base of my spine.

"I'm serious. You're not getting out of here until I'm buried deep inside of you." I need this, more than I'm willing to admit. I need the connection that only comes from being buried deep within her body.

"No talking. More fucking." Her finger goes to my lips. While my eyes widen, she rinses off the soap and places her lips on my chest. "I thought I was going to die. I said my goodbyes, and I wasn't sad."

"You what?"

"I accepted I would die, and I was happy."

"Happy?"

"Yeah, happy because I had you. I knew you loved me. I wasn't afraid to die because I knew I had you."

"I wasted too fucking long to figure it out. Forgive me for being a self-absorbed asshole. To think I ever broke your heart fills me with so much regret." My arms wrap around her waist. "I do love you. I always have, I just didn't know how much until you were taken from me. I'm sorry it took so long to realize what you knew all along. I'm desperately in love with you." The truth spills from my lips.

Her body shivers, which, in turn, makes my dick jump. Our bodies are in tune with one another.

"Fuuuck." I grit my teeth and try to get a hold of my body. I almost come right there, but I'm not missing out on sliding inside of her hot body.

"Works for me." She dips her head and her mouth finds my nipple. The swirl of her tongue has me biting my lower lip. My hips drive forward. They know what they want.

My control slips and the only hope I have for fucking her is to do it now. One more kiss, lick, or the sound of her delicious moans, and I'll be coming all over her belly. I don't want that.

I grab her by the arms and push her away. Every inch of her naked body is visible to my greedy gaze. I take in my fill of her luscious tits. My gaze follows the scars she'll carry for life. Faint bruises mar her body, but I look at her toned, lean muscles, her tits, which fit perfectly in my hands, her narrow waist and the flare of her hips. Those hips were made for one purpose, and that's for my hands to grip when she's on her knees before me.

"You're absolutely, stunningly perfect. Beautiful."

She's a piece of beauty, an artist's representation of perfection. And she's all mine.

"Axel, if you don't hurry up and fuck me, I'm seriously going to go insane." Her eyes flash. Her nipples respond, drawing tight and tempting as her chest heaves.

"I'm simply taking all of you in. You're fucking amazing, do you know how perfect you are?"

She sees the scars scattered across her body as imperfections. There's a new one, an angry line of purple and red wrapping around her belly and hip. I see her scars as evidence of her strength and the roadmap to our future.

That's when it hits me, sweeping all doubt aside. I'm more than in love with her. I'm desperately and forever hers.

Water cascades down her body, down her face. She blinks the water away and stares up at me. Her face shines with love and echoes my desires. She's naked, fully exposed to me, and hides none of her scars. She trusts me to accept all of her.

She's a survivor. Never a victim. And she's hot as hell.

"I want you." She places a hand on my bicep. "Please, stop making me wait."

My heart slams against my ribs. My dick begs to stop fucking around and start fucking her. My mouth crashes down on hers and her body collides against mine, pushing me until my back hits the shower wall. Her hand wraps around my cock as my fingers dig into her thick mane, owning this kiss.

I inhale as best I can. Her taste coats my mouth, driving me insane. Every muscle in my body burns. Every cell fights against me as I attempt to keep myself in check. I want to savor this, not rush through it, and I definitely won't come until after she's screaming my name. But my need may make that impossible.

All I want is to dominate her, take from her, but I reel that shit in as her kisses take over. Her tongue becomes more assertive. Her hand strokes me toward oblivion. I sense she needs to control this.

"I'm yours, Zoe. Whatever you need from me, take it."

"I want all of you." Her hand tightens around my cock, but she pulls back from her kiss. Her soft eyes brim with fiery passion and uncertainty. "But I don't know how... I don't know what to do."

"Tell me how you want me."

Her lips curl between her teeth and her eyes pinch together. "I want you to make the noise stop, to push back the memories of what those men did. I need to feel and not think."

I know what my girl needs. My hands move down her back and I cup the soft swell of her ass. I hoist her up and wrap her legs around my hips. She buries her face in the hollow of my neck as I walk her backward until she's against the wall. This is how I took her the very first time.

I hold her in place with one hand while my other hand glides around her ass to slip between her folds. She wet and that has nothing to do with the water cascading all around us. I tease her opening until her breathing turns ragged. My dick responds to her choppy pants, enlarging with each beat of her breaths.

My heart fills nearly to bursting. She's mine. Fully and completely mine. I dip my finger into her wet heat and close my eyes with her low moan. My finger glides in and out, joined quickly by a second finger, as I stroke her toward climax. Once I get inside of her, I won't take long. So, I make sure to please her first.

My control hangs by a thread. The timbre of her low moans changes as the first waves of her orgasm slam into her, sweeping her away as she clings to me.

Deep, dark desire wells up inside of me, sweeping away any restraint I may have. With desperation and an urgency I've never felt before, I line up my cock and slam deep inside of her with one thrust. Her pussy pulses around my cock, and I know that I've found heaven in her arms.

Her head arches back. Her eyes close. A scream rips out of her throat as her second orgasm rushes through her. She grips my neck and holds on as I become hyperaware of every delicious feeling.

"Give me your mouth."

Her eyes open and she takes my mouth. With our lips locked together, I slam deep into her hot, wet depths. My hips move I as drive home, pounding without tenderness but rather the ferocity she craves. My body needs to take her like this, and goddamn if she doesn't love it.

My soul craves something different, however, which is why I take her mouth. My hips drive relentlessly forward, pounding my dick inside her pussy, while my lips take her with reverence, nice and slow.

I take what she offers, claiming her body for my own, and I give her my devotion, my love, my heart, and everything else in exchange.

She grips my nape as another strangled scream erupts from her mouth. Her entire body clenches as the pleasure from my body sweeps through hers—again.

Heat coils in my gut and gathers low in my balls. With that blistering heat driving me, I fuck her harder, driving deeper, chasing my release as the sounds she makes drive me forward. So fucking sexy, I can't take much more. I race toward completion, needing to join her pleasure. Her pussy clenches and pulsates around my cock. Her hips match my punishing rhythm as her throaty groans plead for more.

My climax hits with the force of an explosion, exquisite pain melded perfectly with delicious pleasure. The force of my orgasm makes me weak in the knees and I have to stop for a moment. If I don't, I'll drop Zoe.

My head falls forward and I kiss along her neck. I'll never tire of this feeling, this sense of completion when I hold her in my arms. The scent of soap and sex fills the air. Her soft skin brushing against my lips is the feeling of coming home.

Her hands twist the hair at my nape. Her ragged breathing settles. One of her hands rests on my shoulder. Her thighs clench tight around my hips. I'm not ready to let her go and it seems as if she feels the same.

"Tell me you belong to me," I demand.

"I belong to you." Her reply comes with no hesitation.

"Tell me you're mine."

"I'm yours." She gives a soft laugh. "I like the way you fuck."

"I like the way you feel when I fuck you."

Our connection is real, more real than I ever could've known. She grabs my neck and releases her grip on my hips. I'm reluctant to release her, but sudden fatigue sweeps through my body.

"We should probably get to bed." She peeks up at me with an impish grin.

"I doubt I'll sleep a wink. Not with you in my arms." The corner of my lips twist in a smile as I remember my doctor's orders.

Go to bed.

Oh, I'm going to bed, all right, but I'm not nearly done fucking the woman I love.

I know what love feels like. I know what it feels like to nearly lose everything. And I know one way to tie Zoe to me forever. There will never be another Zoe Lancaster.

This woman is all mine.

"Zoe…" We walk to bed holding hands.

"Yeah?"

"You need to say yes."

"Why?"

"Because I'm putting a ring on your finger." I don't ask and I'm not waiting for her answer. It's simply the way it's meant to be. Her eyes brim with tears as I take her into my arms. "You're mine now, forever and always."

"Forever and always."

THIRTY-FIVE

Zoe

Once upon a time, there was a girl
Trapped in a nightmare

A Guardian saved her
Now, she's living a fairy tale
With him.

That girl is me

THIRTY-SIX

Moira

HARD. COLD. UNFORGIVING.

A concrete floor, damp air, and a bone-chilling cold define my existence. The pounding in my skull is unbearable. Gently, I explore the damage to my head. No surprise, dried blood greets my probing fingers. There are lumps. Too many to count.

Those don't worry me. Those are survivable. What I don't feel are depressions, evidence of skull fracture which point toward irreversible damage to my brain.

I'm alive, but I'm not surprised.

I excel at surviving. It's the one thing I wish I could fail at, but I don't.

Moira Stone is a goddamn, fucking survivor.

The low drone of male voices rumbles somewhere to my left, and the stench of sweat, urine, and blood fills my nostrils. I'm not sure how much of that is contributed by me, and I don't care. Frankly, I don't care about much right now.

This isn't my first shit show. Been here before. Have the scars to prove it.

I'm no innocent. For years, I peddled my flesh on the streets. I knew how to play the innocent little girl and get depraved men to feed me the cash I needed to survive for one more night. Hooked on coke, heroine, and basically anything I could ingest, inject, or inhale, my life consisted of one high followed by another desperate low.

At least until I fell into the wrong pair of hands. I'd been sixteen, a veritable old-timer on the streets. I should've known better, but that's what happens when one moment of weakness hits.

It steals your breath and destroys your life.

The fear, the confusion, the overwhelming hopelessness, and that useless sense of hope, those emotions rip through me, suffocating me, drowning me, and devouring my will to live.

Notice how I said live; not survive.

I've been here before, but I won't survive this again. I don't want to.

If I could end it all now, I would, but the grace of death is not mine. That kind of power lies in the hands of the monsters arguing over their cards.

The universe is one sick prick.

I will live, and I'll endure the vileness to come. I'll do it because I'm too much of a coward to do what must be done.

"Hey, she's up." The cackling voice turns my blood to ice.

I pray for death, or some kind of reprieve. I won't get it. This is my fate; to hope where there is nothing to hope for, nothing left to live for. I exist only to feel pain.

"Doesn't look like she's up to me." The second of three men shifts his attention my direction.

Under that glare, my body grows still. I dig deep, tunneling into the darkness, only this time, my tricks don't work. The rank stench of blood, sweat, and fear fills my nostrils, irritating the sensitive passages to make me gag and cough.

The third man of the trio rises from his seat. As he does, gas rips past his anus and rumbles through the room. The noxious odor of his fart rolls toward me, but not before reaching his fellows first.

"Holy shit, Shelly, what the fuck did you eat?"

"Don't call me Shelly."

"I'll call you whatever the fuck I want." The first man, the one I identify as the leader waves his hand in front of his nose. "That's the last fucking time you get to pick dinner."

"You like Joe's burritos." Shelly defends himself.

"Yeah, I love Joe's burritos, but not your goddamn farts. Take that shit outside."

"Whatever." The weight of Shelly's gaze settles on me. "What are we going to do about her?" He comes over to me and taps my hip with the steel tip of his boot. "Have they called yet?"

"No."

"What about…"

"I'll deal with that."

Two options present themselves to me. I could play dead, pretend I'm not in fact awake. I might convince them to leave me alone. More likely, he'll only kick harder until pulling a groan from me. Option number two is much more distasteful to me.

The fucking survivor in me goes for option two.

I curl into myself, protecting my vulnerable midsection and hack as if I'm going to vomit. Men aren't too keen to shove their dicks in a woman spewing her guts.

I cup my head and mumble like I don't know what's going on.

Except I do.

I remember every goddamn thing until I blacked out. From the abduction on the beach to getting dragged into the back of the van. I remember fighting. That foolish belief the Facility actually taught me how to survive gave me courage I couldn't afford.

That decision resulted in a blow to the head and no memory of what happened next. Not that it matters. I know exactly what's happening now. If these men sense weakness they'll take what isn't freely offered. If I do that, my chances of survival drop to zero. These are not the men I need to fight. Fighting will come later.

Survival is now. I did when I was twelve, and I'll do it again. As for the fight to come?

I'm not looking forward to it.

"Please don't hurt me." I cower like a weakling. My hands move from the caked blood on my scalp to my stomach and I play up the retching noises.

Shelly presses the toe of his boot to my head. It's meant as a show of strength, demonstrating what he could do, if he so chose.

This is what I need to know. How much leeway do these men have? Can they do what they want to me? Or is there another force pulling their strings? Either option terrifies me, but I hope for the latter. Not because it saves me anything, but because it buys me time.

I allow myself to cry, to whimper, and to curl into a tighter ball. My knees draw up and I rock on the hard concrete floor.

"Please don't hurt me..." I mumble those words over and over again.

The men laugh at my desperation. Shelly kicks me in the gut with that steel tipped boot of his.

I'll kill him first.

Keep reading to find out what happens to Moira.
Will Griff rescue her?
==> Rescuing Moira,
The Guardians: Hostage Rescue Specialists, book 3.
elliemasters.com/RescuingMoira.

Ellie Masters The EDGE

If you are interested in joining Ellie's Facebook reader group, THE
EDGE, we'd love to have you.

The Edge Facebook Reader Group
elliemasters.com/TheEdge

Join Ellie's ELLZ BELLZ.
Sign up for Ellie's Newsletter.
Elliemasters.com/newslettersignup

Please consider leaving a review

I HOPE YOU ENJOYED THIS BOOK AS MUCH AS I ENJOYED WRITING IT. If you like this book, please leave a review. I love reviews. I love reading your reviews, and they help other readers decide if this book is worth their time and money. I hope you think it is and decide to share this story with others. A sentence is all it takes. Thank you in advance!

CLICK ON THE LINK BELOW TO LEAVE YOUR REVIEW

AMAZON

Books by Ellie Masters

The LIGHTER SIDE

Ellie Masters is the lighter side of the Jet & Ellie Masters writing duo! You will find Contemporary Romance, Military Romance, Romantic Suspense, Billionaire Romance, and Rock Star Romance in Ellie's Works.

YOU CAN FIND ELLIE'S BOOKS HERE:

ELLIEMASTERS.COM/BOOKS

Military Romance

Guardian Hostage Rescue

Rescuing Melissa

(Get a FREE copy when you join Ellie's Newsletter)

Rescuing Zoe

Rescuing Moira

The One I Want Series

(Small Town, Military Heroes)

By Jet & Ellie Masters

Rockstar Romance

The Angel Fire Rock Romance Series

Contemporary Romance

The LaRouge Triplets

Billionaire Romance

Billionaire Boys Club

Hawke: Billionaire in Paradise

Nondisclosure: Billionaire Prince

Contemporary Romance

Cocky Captain

(VI KEELAND & PENELOPE WARD'S COCKY HERO WORLD)

Sweet Contemporary Romance

Finding Peace

Romantic Suspense

EACH BOOK IS A STANDALONE NOVEL.

The Starling

Redemption

~AND~

Science Fiction

Ellie Masters writing as L.A. Warren

Vendel Rising: a Science Fiction Serialized Novel

About the Author

ELLIE MASTERS is a multi-genre and best-selling author, writing the stories she loves to read. Dip into the eclectic mind of Ellie Masters, spend time exploring the sensual realm where she breathes life into her characters and brings them from her mind to the page and into the heart of her readers every day.

When not writing, Ellie can be found outside, where her passion for all things outdoor reigns supreme: off-roading, riding ATVs, scuba diving, hiking, and breathing fresh air are top on her list.

Ellie's favorite way to spend an evening is curled up on a couch, laptop in place, watching a fire, drinking a good wine, and bringing forth all the characters from her mind to the page and hopefully into the hearts of her readers.

FOR MORE INFORMATION
elliemasters.com

f facebook.com/elliemastersromance
🐦 twitter.com/Ellie__Masters
📷 instagram.com/ellie_masters
BB bookbub.com/authors/ellie-masters
g goodreads.com/Ellie_Masters

Connect with Ellie Masters

Website:
elliemasters.com
Amazon Author Page:
elliemasters.com/amazon
Facebook:
elliemasters.com/Facebook
Goodreads:
elliemasters.com/Goodreads
Instagram:
elliemasters.com/Instagram

Final Thoughts

I hope you enjoyed this book as much as I enjoyed writing it. If you enjoyed reading this story, please consider leaving a review on Amazon and Goodreads, and please let other people know. A sentence is all it takes. Friend recommendations are the strongest catalyst for readers' purchase decisions! And I'd love to be able to continue bringing the characters and stories from My-Mind-to-the-Page.

Second, call or e-mail a friend and tell them about this book. If you really want them to read it, gift it to them. If you prefer digital friends, please use the "Recommend" feature of Goodreads to spread the word.

Or visit my blog https://elliemasters.com, where you can find out more about my writing process and personal life.

Come visit The EDGE: Dark Discussions where we'll have a chance to talk about my works, their creation, and maybe what the future has in store for my writing.

Facebook Reader Group: The EDGE

Final Thoughts

Thank you so much for your support!

Love,

Ellie

Dedication

This book is dedicated to you, my reader. Thank you for spending a few hours of your time with me. I wouldn't be able to write without you to cheer me on. Your wonderful words, your support, and your willingness to join me on this journey is a gift beyond measure.

Whether this is the first book of mine you've read, or if you've been with me since the very beginning, thank you for believing in me as I bring these characters 'from my mind to the page and into your hearts.'

Love,

Ellie

Books by Jet Masters

If you enjoyed this book by Ellie Masters, the LIGHTER SIDE of the Jet & Ellie writing duo, and aren't afraid of edgier writing, you might enjoy reading BDSM themed books written by Jet, the DARKER SIDE of the Masters' Writing Team.

The DARKER SIDE
Jet Masters is the darker side of the Jet & Ellie writing duo!

Romantic Suspense
Changing Roles Series:
THIS SERIES MUST BE READ IN ORDER.
Book 1: Command Me
Book 2: Control Me
Book 3: Collar Me
Book 4: Embracing FATE

HOT READS
A STANDALONE NOVEL.
Down the Rabbit Hole

Light BDSM Romance
The Ties that Bind

EACH BOOK IN THIS SERIES CAN BE READ AS A STANDALONE AND IS ABOUT A DIFFERENT COUPLE WITH AN HEA.

Alexa
Penny
Michelle
Ivy

HOT READS
Becoming His Series

THIS SERIES MUST BE READ IN ORDER.

Book 1: The Ballet
Book 2: Learning to Breathe
Book 3: Becoming His

Dark Captive Romance

A STANDALONE NOVEL.

She's MINE

THE END